Acclaim for PHILIP ROTH's
I Married a Communist

"Senator Joseph McCarthy's power in the fifties . . . the subject is great and manifold, and Roth is the man to mine it. . . . [Roth is] a master chronicler of the American twentieth century."   —*Commonweal*

"This book draws strength from that terrible time . . . when we first learned, as a people, to give way to brutality, innuendo and deceit. Roth explores our expedients and tragedies with a masterly, often unnerving, blend of tenderness, harshness, insight and wit."
                    —*The New York Times Book Review*

"*I Married a Communist* pushes the cultural time-line back to the days of Joseph McCarthy. . . . [Roth gives] a literary spin to love and betrayal, blacklists, and naming names."
                    —*The Philadelphia Inquirer*

"The blacklistings and betrayals of the McCarthy era cast their long, disturbing shadows in this darkly brilliant new novel. . . . Energized by Roth's eloquent, highly charged language [*I Married a Communist*] reveals itself as a cross between insightful political fiction and a Greek tragedy whose hero's life is altered by fate, his own failings, by the forces of history and by the large and small treacheries of the public and private life around him."   —*People*

"[*I Married a Communist*] demonstrates how paranoid, debased politics can land-mine a United States capable, then as now, of seeming hopeful and wide open. . . . Roth balances his portrait of America as a country where every man is free to define himself with his realization that the capricious Fates—and politicos, stoolies and media clowns—actually determine the entries in the vast dictionary of humanity."   —*San Francisco Chronicle*

"Roth is able to capture, with pitch-perfect artistry, the powerful allure of the [American Communist] movement's cultural idealogy, from a smiling Paul Robeson to the soaring Soviet Army Chorus and Band."
                                        —*The Plain Dealer*

PHILIP ROTH
I Married a Communist

Philip Roth received the 1960 National Book Award in fiction for *Goodbye, Columbus*. He has twice received the National Book Critics Circle Award—in 1987 for the novel *The Counterlife* and in 1992 for *Patrimony*. *Operation Shylock* won the PEN/Faulkner Award for Fiction and was chosen by *Time* magazine as the best American novel of 1993. In 1995, Roth's *Sabbath's Theater* received the National Book Award in fiction. In 1998, he received the Pulitzer Prize for *American Pastoral* and was a White House recipient of the National Medal of Arts. His other books include the trilogy and epilogue *Zuckerman Bound*; the novels *Letting Go, My Life as a Man,* and *The Professor of Desire*; and the political satire *Our Gang*. *I Married a Communist* is his twenty-third book.

INTERNATIONAL

Books by PHILIP ROTH

I Married a Communist
American Pastoral
Sabbath's Theater
Operation Shylock
Patrimony
Deception
The Facts
The Counterlife
Zuckerman Bound
The Prague Orgy
The Anatomy Lesson
Zuckerman Unbound
The Ghost Writer
The Professor of Desire
Reading Myself and Others
My Life as a Man
The Great American Novel
The Breast
Our Gang
Portnoy's Complaint
When She Was Good
Letting Go
Goodbye, Columbus

PHILIP ROTH

I Married
a Communist

VINTAGE INTERNATIONAL

Vintage Books

A Division of Random House, Inc.

New York

FIRST VINTAGE INTERNATIONAL EDITION, NOVEMBER 1999

The author wishes to thank the Newark Public Library and its director, Alex
Boyd, for use of its archival resources; to recognize particularly the generosity of
the library's city historian, Charles Cummings; to thank New Jersey historian
John Cunningham for his guidance; and to acknowledge, as a primary source,
Newark's Little Italy: The Vanished First Ward, by Michael Immerso (Rutgers
University Press, 1997). The name Katrina Van Tassel is taken from "The Legend
of Sleepy Hollow" by Washington Irving.

Lines from *On a Note of Triumph* by Norman Corwin are reprinted by permission of the author. "With thee, in the Desert" (Poem 209) by Emily Dickinson is
reprinted by permission of the publishers and the Trustees of Amherst College.
From *The Poems of Emily Dickinson*, Thomas H. Johnson, ed. Cambridge, Mass.:
The Belknap Press of Harvard University Press, copyright © 1951, 1955, 1979,
1983 by the President and Fellows of Harvard College.

Library of Congress Cataloging-in-Publication Data
Roth, Philip.
I married a communist / Philip Roth.
p. cm.
ISBN 0-375-70721-2
I. Title.
[PS3568.O855I18 1999]
813'.54—dc21 99-18314
CIP

www.vintagebooks.com

Printed in the United States of America
10 9 8 7 6 5 4 3

To my friend and editor

Many songs have I heard in my native land—
Songs of joy and sorrow.
But one of them was deeply engraved in my memory:
It's the song of the common worker.
  Ekh, lift up the cudgel,
  Heave-ho!
  Pull harder together,
  Heave-ho!

> — "Dubinushka," a Russian folksong.
> *In the 1940s performed and recorded,
> in Russian, by the Soviet Army Chorus
> and Band.*

I Married
a Communist

1

IRA RINGOLD'S older brother, Murray, was my first high school English teacher, and it was through him that I hooked up with Ira. In 1946 Murray was just back from the army, where he'd served with the 17th Airborne Division at the Battle of the Bulge; in March 1945, he'd made the famous jump across the Rhine that signaled the beginning of the end of the European war. He was, in those days, a crusty, brash, baldheaded guy, not as tall as Ira but rangy and athletic, who hovered over our heads in a perpetual state of awareness. He was altogether natural in his manner and posture while in his speech verbally copious and intellectually almost menacing. His passion was to explain, to clarify, to make us understand, with the result that every last subject we talked about he broke down into its principal elements no less meticulously than he diagrammed sentences on the blackboard. His special talent was for dramatizing inquiry, for casting a strong narrative spell even when he was being strictly analytic and scrutinizing aloud, in his clear-cut way, what we read and wrote.

Along with the brawn and the conspicuous braininess, Mr. Ringold brought with him into the classroom a charge of visceral spontaneity that was a revelation to tamed, respectablized kids who were yet to comprehend that obeying a teacher's rules of decorum had nothing to do with mental development. There was more importance than perhaps even he imagined in his winning predilection for heaving a blackboard eraser in your direction when the answer you gave didn't hit the mark. Or maybe there wasn't. Maybe Mr. Ringold knew very well that what boys like me needed to learn was not only how to express themselves with precision and acquire a more discerning response to words, but how to be rambunctious without being stupid, how not to be too well concealed or too well behaved, how to begin to release the masculine intensities from the institutional rectitude that intimidated the bright kids the most.

You felt, in the sexual sense, the power of a male high school teacher like Murray Ringold—masculine authority uncorrected by piety—and you felt, in the priestly sense, the vocation of a male high school teacher like Murray Ringold, who wasn't lost in the amorphous American aspiration to make it big, who—unlike the school's women teachers—could have chosen to be almost anything else and chose instead, for his life's work, to be ours. All he wanted all day long was to deal with young people he could influence, and his biggest kick in life he got from their response.

Not that the impression his bold classroom style left on my sense of freedom was apparent at the time; no kid thought that way about school or teachers or himself. An incipient craving for social independence, however, had to have been nourished somewhat by Murray's example, and I told him this when, in July 1997, for the first time since I graduated from high school in 1950, I ran into Murray, now ninety years old but in every discernible way still the teacher whose task is realistically, without self-parody or inflating dramatics, to personify for his students the maverick dictum "I don't give a good goddamn," to teach them that you don't have to be Al Capone to transgress—you just have to *think*. "In human society," Mr. Ringold taught us, "thinking's the greatest transgression of all." "Cri-ti-cal think-ing," Mr. Ringold said, using his knuckles to rap out each of the syllables on his desktop, "—there is the ultimate subversion." I told Murray that hearing this early on from a manly guy like him—seeing it *demonstrated* by him—provided the most valuable clue to growing up that I had clutched at, albeit half comprehendingly, as a provincial, protected, high-minded high school kid yearning to be rational and of consequence and free.

Murray, in turn, told me everything that, as a youngster, I didn't know and couldn't have known about his brother's private life, a grave misfortune replete with farce over which Murray would sometimes find himself brooding even though Ira was dead now more than thirty years. "Thousands and thousands of Americans destroyed in those years, political casualties, historical casualties, because of their beliefs," Murray said. "But I don't remember anybody else being brought down quite the way that Ira was. It wasn't on the great American battlefield he would himself have chosen for his destruction. Maybe, despite ideology, politics, and history, a genuine catastrophe is always personal bathos at the core. Life can't be impugned for any failure to trivialize people. You have to take your hat off to life for the techniques at its disposal to strip a man of his significance and empty him totally of his pride."

Murray also told me, when I asked, how he had been stripped of *his* significance. I knew the general story but little of the details because I began my own army stint—and wasn't around Newark again for years—after I graduated college in 1954, and Murray's political ordeal didn't get under way until May 1955. We started with Murray's story, and it was only at the end of the afternoon, when I asked if he'd like to stay for dinner, that he seemed to feel, in unison with me, that our relations had shifted to a more intimate plane and that it wouldn't be incorrect if he went on to speak openly about his brother's.

Out near where I live in western New England, a small college called Athena runs a series of weeklong summer programs for elderly people, and Murray was enrolled as a student, at ninety, for the course grandly entitled "Shakespeare at the Millennium." That's how I'd run into him in town on the Sunday he arrived—having failed to recognize him, I was fortunate that he recognized me—and how we came to spend our six evenings together. That's how the past turned up this time, in the shape of a very old man whose talent was to give his troubles not one second more thought than they warranted and who still couldn't waste his time talking other than to a serious point. A palpable obstinacy lent his personality its flinty fullness, and this despite time's radical pruning of his old athletic physique. Looking at Murray while he spoke in that familiarly unhidden, scrupulous way of his, I thought, There it is—human life. There is endurance.

In '55, almost four years after Ira was blacklisted from radio for being a Communist, Murray had been dismissed from his teaching job by the Board of Education for refusing to cooperate with the House Un-American Activities Committee when it had come through Newark for four days of hearings. He was reinstated, but only after a six-year legal struggle that ended in a 5–4 decision by the state supreme court, reinstated with back pay, minus the amount of money he had earned supporting his family those six years as a vacuum salesman.

"When you don't know what else to do," Murray said with a smile, "you sell vacuum cleaners. Door to door. Kirby vacuum cleaners. You spill a full ashtray onto the carpet and then you vacuum it up for them. You vacuum the house for them. That's how you sell the thing. Vacuumed half the houses in New Jersey in my day. Look, I had a lot of well-wishers, Nathan. I had a wife whose medical expenses were constant, and we had a child, but I was getting a pretty good amount of business and I sold a lot of people vacuum cleaners. And despite her scoliosis problems, Doris went back to work. She went back to the lab at the hospital. Did the blood work. Eventually ran the lab. In those days there was no separation between the technical stuff and the medical arts, and Doris did it all: drew the blood, stained the slides. Very patient, very thorough with a microscope. Well trained. Observant. Accurate. Knowledgeable. She used to come home from the Beth Israel, just across the street from us, and cook dinner in her lab coat. Ours was the only family I ever knew of whose salad dressing was served in laboratory flasks. The Erlenmeyer flask. We stirred our coffee with pipettes. All our glassware was from the lab. When we were on our uppers, Doris made ends meet. Together we were able to tackle it."

"And they came after you because you were Ira's brother?" I asked. "That's what I always assumed."

"I can't say for sure. Ira thought so. Maybe they came after me because I never behaved the way a teacher was supposed to behave. Maybe they would have come after me even without Ira. I started out as a firebrand, Nathan. I burned with zeal to establish the dignity of my profession. That may be what rankled them more than anything else. The personal indignity that you had to undergo as a teacher when I first started teaching—you wouldn't believe it. Being treated like children. Whatever the superiors told you, that was law. Unquestioned. You will get here at this time, you will sign the time book on time. You will spend so many hours in school. And you will be called on for afternoon and evening assignments, even though that wasn't part of your contract. All kinds of chickenshit stuff. You felt denigrated.

"I threw myself into organizing our union. I moved quickly into committee leadership, executive board positions. I was outspoken—at times, I admit, pretty glib. I thought I knew all the answers. But I was interested in teachers' getting respect—respect, and proper emoluments for their labors, and so forth. Teachers had problems with pay, working conditions, benefits . . .

"The superintendent of schools was no friend of mine. I had been prominent in the move to deny him promotion to the superintendency. I supported another man, and he lost. So because I made no bones about my opposition to this son of a bitch, he hated my guts, and in '55 the ax fell and I was called downtown to the Federal Building, to a meeting of the House Un-American Activities Committee. To testify. Chairman was a Representative Walter. Two more members of the committee came with him. Three of them up from Washington, with their lawyer. They were investigating Communist influence in everything in the city of Newark but primarily investigating what they called 'the infiltration of the party' into labor and education. There had been a sweep of these hearings throughout the country—Detroit, Chicago. We knew it was coming. It was inevitable. They knocked us teachers off in one day, the last day, a Thursday in May.

"I testified for five minutes. 'Have you now or have you ever been . . . ?' I refused to answer. Well, why won't you? they said. You got nothing to hide. Why don't you come clean? We just want information. That's all we're here for. We write legislation. We're not a punitive body. And so forth. But as I understood the Bill of Rights, my political beliefs were none of their business, and that's what I told them—'It's none of your business.'

"Earlier in the week they'd gone after the United Electrical Workers, Ira's old union back in Chicago. On Monday evening, a thousand UE members came over on chartered buses from New York to picket the Robert Treat Hotel, where the committee staff members were staying. The *Star-Ledger* described the picketers' appearance as 'an invasion of forces hostile to the congressional inquiry.' Not a legal demonstration as guaranteed by rights laid down in the Constitution but an *invasion*, like Hitler's of Poland and Czechoslovakia. One of the committee congressmen pointed out to the press—and without a trace of embarrassment at the un-Americanness lurking in his observation—that a lot of the demonstrators were chanting in Spanish, evidence to him that they didn't know the meaning of the signs they were carrying, that they were ignorant 'dupes' of the Communist Party. He took heart from the fact that they had been kept under surveillance by the 'subversives squad' of the Newark police. After the bus caravan passed through Hudson County on the way back to New York, some big cop there was quoted as saying, 'If I knew they were Reds, I'd of locked all thousand of them up.' That was the local atmosphere, and that was what had been appearing in the press, by the time I got to be questioned, the first to be called up on Thursday.

"Near the end of my five minutes, in the face of my refusal to cooperate, the chairman said that he was disappointed that a man of my education and understanding should be unwilling to help the security of this country by telling the committee what it wanted to know. I took that silently. The only hostile remark I made was when one of those bastards closed off by telling me, 'Sir, I question your loyalty.' I told him, 'And I question yours.' And the chairman told me that if I continued to 'slur' any member of the committee, he would have me ejected. 'We don't have to sit here,' he told me, 'and take your bunk and listen to your slurs.' 'Neither do I,' I said, 'have to sit here and listen to *your* slurs, Mr. Chairman.' That was as bad as it got. My lawyer whispered to me to cut it out, and that was the end of my appearance. I was excused.

"But as I got up to leave my chair, one of the congressmen called after me, I suppose to provoke me into contempt—'How can you be paid by the taxpayers' money when you are obligated by your damnable Communist oath to teach the Soviet line? How in God's name can you be a free agent and teach what the Communists dictate? Why don't you get out of the party and reverse your tracks? I plead with you—return to the American way of life!'

"But I didn't take the bait, didn't tell him that what I taught had nothing to do with the dictates of anything other than composition and literature, though, in the end, it didn't seem to matter what I said or didn't say: that evening, in the Sports Final edition, there was my kisser on the front page of the *Newark News,* over the caption 'Red Probe Witness Balky' and the line '"Won't take your bunk," HUAC tells Newark teacher.'

"Now, one of the committee members was a congressman from New York State, Bryden Grant. You remember the Grants, Bryden and Katrina. Americans everywhere remember the Grants. Well, the Ringolds were the Rosenbergs to the Grants. This society pretty boy, this vicious nothing, all but destroyed our family. And did you ever know why? Because one night Grant and his wife were at a party that Ira and Eve were giving on West Eleventh Street and Ira went after Grant the way only Ira could go after somebody. Grant was a pal of Wernher von Braun's, or Ira thought so, and Ira laid into him but good. Grant was—to the naked eye, that is—an effete upper-class guy of the sort who set Ira's teeth on edge. The wife wrote those popular romances that the ladies devoured and Grant was then still a columnist for the *Journal-American*. To Ira, Grant was the incarnation of pampered privilege. He couldn't stand him. Grant's every gesture made him sick and his politics he abhorred.

"Well, there was a big, loud scene, Ira shouting and calling Grant names, and for the rest of his life Ira maintained that a Grant vendetta against us began that night. Ira had a way of presenting himself without camouflage. Comes just as he is, holding nothing back, without a single plea. That was his magnetism for you, but it's also what made him repellent to his enemies. And Grant was one of his enemies. The whole squabble took three minutes, but according to Ira, three minutes that sealed his fate and mine. He'd humiliated a descendant of Ulysses S. Grant and a graduate of Harvard and an employee of William Randolph Hearst's, not to mention the husband of the author of *Eloise and Abelard,* the biggest bestseller of 1938, and *The Passion of Galileo,* the biggest bestseller of 1942—and that was it for us. We were finished: by publicly insulting Bryden Grant, Ira had challenged not only the husband's impeccable credentials but the wife's inextinguishable need to be right.

"Now, I'm not sure that explains everything—though not because Grant was any less reckless in the use of power than the rest of Nixon's gang. Before he went to Congress, he wrote that column for the *Journal-American,* a gossip column three times a week about Broadway and Hollywood, with a dollop of Eleanor Roosevelt–defiling thrown in. That's how Grant's public service career began. That's what qualified him so highly for a seat on the Un-American Activities Committee. He was a gossip columnist before it became the big business it is today. He was in there at the start, in the heyday of the great pioneers. There was Cholly Knickerbocker and Winchell and Ed Sullivan and Earl Wilson. There was Damon Runyon, there was Bob Considine, there was Hedda Hopper—and Bryden Grant was the *snob* of the mob, not the street fighter, not the lowlife, not the fast-talking insider who hung out at Sardi's or the Brown Derby or Stillman's Gym, but the blueblood to the rabble who hung out at the Racquet Club.

"Grant began with a column called 'Grant's Grapevine,' and, if you remember, he nearly ended as Nixon's White House chief of staff. Congressman Grant was a great favorite of Nixon's. Sat as Nixon did on the Un-American Activities Committee. Did a lot of President Nixon's arm-twisting in the House. I remember when the new Nixon administration floated Grant's name back in '68 for chief of staff. Too bad they let it drop. The worst decision Nixon ever made. If only Nixon had found the political advantage in appointing, instead of Haldeman, this Brahmin hack to head the Watergate cover-up operation, Grant's career might have ended behind bars. Bryden Grant in jail, in a cell between Mitchell's and Ehrlichman's. Grant's Tomb. But it was never to be.

"You can hear Nixon singing Grant's praises on the White House tapes. It's there in the transcripts. 'Bryden's heart is in the right place,' the president tells Haldeman. 'And he's tough. He'll do anything. I mean anything.' He tells Haldeman Grant's motto for how to handle the administration's enemies: 'Destroy them in the press.' And then, admiringly—an epicurean of the perfect smear, of the vilification that burns with a hard, gemlike flame—the president adds: 'Bryden's got the killer instinct. Nobody does a more beautiful job.'

"Congressman Grant died in his sleep, a rich and powerful old statesman, still greatly esteemed in Staatsburg, New York, where they named the high school football field after him.

"During the hearing I watched Bryden Grant, trying to believe that there was more to him than a politician with a personal vendetta finding in the national obsession the means to settle a score. In the name of reason, you search for some higher motive, you look for some deeper meaning—it was still my wont in those days to try to be reasonable about the unreasonable and to look for complexity in simple things. I would make demands upon my intelligence where none were really necessary. I would think, He *cannot* be as petty and vapid as he seems. That can't be more than one-tenth of the story. There must be more to him than that.

"But why? Pettiness and vapidity can come on the grand scale too. What could be more *unwavering* than pettiness and vapidity?

Do pettiness and vapidity get in the way of being cunning and tough? Do pettiness and vapidity vitiate the aim of being an important personage? You don't need a developed view of life to be fond of power. You don't need a developed view of life to *rise* to power. A developed view of life may, in fact, be the worst impediment, while *not* having a developed view the most splendid advantage. You didn't have to summon up misfortunes from his patrician childhood to make sense of Congressman Grant. This is the guy, after all, who took over the congressional seat of Hamilton Fish, the original Roosevelt hater. A Hudson River aristocrat like FDR. Fish went to Harvard just after FDR. Envied him, hated him, and, because Fish's district included Hyde Park, wound up FDR's congressman. A terrific isolationist and stupid as they come. Fish, back in the thirties, was the first upper-crust ignoramus to serve as chairman of the precursor of that pernicious committee. The prototypical self-righteous, flag-waving, narrow-minded patrician son of a bitch— that was Hamilton Fish. And when they redistricted the old fool's district in '52, Bryden Grant was his boy.

"After the hearing, Grant left the dais where the three committee members and their lawyer were seated and made a beeline for my chair. He was the one who'd said to me, 'I question your loyalty.' But now he smiled graciously—as only Bryden Grant could, as though he had invented the gracious smile—and he put out his hand and so, loathsome as it was to me, I shook it. The hand of unreason, and reasonably, civilly, the way fighters touch gloves before a fight, I shook it, and my daughter, Lorraine, was appalled with me for days afterward.

"Grant said, 'Mr. Ringold, I traveled up here today to help you clear your name. I wish you could have been more cooperative. You don't make it easy, even for those of us who are sympathetic. I want you to know that I wasn't scheduled to represent the committee in Newark. But I knew you were to be a witness and so I asked to come because I didn't think it would be much help to you if my friend and colleague Donald Jackson were to show up instead.'

"Jackson was the guy who had taken Nixon's seat on the committee. Donald L. Jackson of California. A dazzling thinker, given to public statements like, 'It seems to me that the time has come to be an American or not an American.' It was Jackson and Velde who led the manhunt to root out Communist subversives in the Protestant clergy. That was a pressing national issue for these guys. After Nixon's departure from the committee, Grant was considered the committee's intellectual spearhead who drew their profound conclusions for them—and, sad to say, more than likely he was.

"He said to me, 'I thought that perhaps I could help you more than the honorable gentleman from California. Despite your performance here today, I still think I can. I want you to know that if, after a good night's sleep, you decide you want to clear your name—'

"That was when Lorraine erupted. She was all of fourteen. She and Doris had been sitting behind me, and throughout the session Lorraine had been fuming even more audibly than her mother. Fuming and squirming, barely able to contain the agitation in her fourteen-year-old frame. 'Clear his name of *what?*' Lorraine said to Congressman Grant. 'What did my father *do?*' Grant smiled at her benignly. He was very good-looking, with all that silver hair, and he was fit, and his suits were the most expensive Tripler's made, and his manners couldn't have affronted anyone's mother. He had that nicely blended voice, respectful, at once soft and manly, and he said to Lorraine, 'You're a loyal daughter.' But Lorraine wouldn't quit. And neither Doris nor I tried to stop her right off. 'Clear his name? *He* doesn't have to clear his name—it's not dirty,' she told Grant. 'You're the one who's dirtying his name.' 'Miss Ringold, you are off the issue. Your father has a history,' Grant said. 'History?' Lorraine said. 'What history? What's his history?' Again he smiled. 'Miss Ringold,' he said, 'you're a very nice young lady—' 'Whether I'm nice has nothing to do with it. What is his history? What did he do? What is it that he has to clear? Tell me what my father did.' 'Your father will have to tell us what he did.' 'My father has already spoken,' she said, 'and you are twisting everything he says into a pack of lies just to make him look bad. His name *is* clean. He can go to bed at night. I don't know how you can, sir. My father served his country as well as the rest of them. He knows about loyalty and fighting and what's American. This is how you treat people who've served their country? Is that what he fought for— so you could sit here and try to blacken his name? Try to sling mud all over him? That's what America is? That's what you call loyalty? What have *you* done for America? Gossip columns? That's so American? My father has principles, and they're decent American principles, and you have no business trying to destroy him. He goes to school, he teaches children, he works as hard as he can. You should have a *million* teachers like him. Is that the problem? He's too good? Is that why you have to tell lies about him? *Leave my father alone!*

"When Grant still wouldn't reply, Lorraine cried, 'What's the matter? You had so much to say when you were up there on the stand—and now you're Mr. Dumbmouth? Your little lips sealed shut—' Right there I put my hand on hers and I said, 'That's enough.' And then she got angry with me. 'No, it's *not* enough. It's not going to be enough until they stop treating you like this. Aren't you going to say *anything*, Mr. Grant? Is this what America is—nobody says anything in front of fourteen-year-olds? Just because I don't vote—is that the problem? Well, I'd certainly never vote for you or any of your lousy friends!' And she burst into tears, and that was when Grant said to me, 'You know where to reach me,' and he smiled at the three of us and left for Washington.

"That's the way it goes. They fuck you and then they tell you, 'You were lucky you got fucked by me and not by the honorable gentleman from California.'

"I never did get in touch with him. The fact was that my political beliefs were pretty localized. They were never inflated like Ira's. I was never interested like he was in the fate of the world. I was more interested, from a professional point of view, in the fate of the community. My concern was not even so much political as economic and I would say sociological, in terms of working conditions, in terms of the status of teachers in the city of Newark. The next day the mayor, Mayor Carlin, told the press that people like me should not be teaching our children, and the Board of Education put me on trial for conduct unbecoming a teacher. The superintendent saw this was his warrant for getting rid of me. I didn't answer the questions of a responsible government agency, so ipso facto I was unfit. I told the Board of Education that my political beliefs were not relevant to my being an English teacher in the Newark school system. There were only three grounds for dismissal: insubordination, incompetence, and moral turpitude. I argued that none of these applied. Former students came down to the board hearing to testify that I had never tried to indoctrinate anybody, in class or anywhere else. Nobody in the school system had ever heard me attempt to indoctrinate anyone into anything other than respect for the English language—none of the parents, none of the students, none of my colleagues. My former army captain, he testified for me. Came up from Fort Bragg. That was impressive.

"I enjoyed selling vacuum cleaners. There were people who crossed the street when they saw me coming, even people who may have felt ashamed doing it but who didn't want to be contaminated, but that didn't bother me. I had a lot of support within the teachers' union and a lot of support outside. Contributions came in, we had Doris's salary, and I sold my vacuum cleaners. I met people in all lines of work and I made contact with the real world beyond teaching. You know, I was a professional, a schoolteacher, reading books, teaching Shakespeare, making you kids diagram sentences and memorize poetry and appreciate literature, and I thought no other kind of life was worth living. But I went out selling vacuum cleaners and I acquired a great deal of admiration for a lot of people I met, and I am still grateful for it. I think I have a better outlook on life because of it."

"Suppose you hadn't been reinstated by the court. Would you still have a better outlook?"

"If I had lost? I think I would have made a fair living. I think I would have survived intact. I might have had some regrets. But I don't think I would have been affected temperamentally. In an open society, as bad as it can get, there's an escape. To lose your job and have the newspapers calling you a traitor—these are very unpleasant things. But it's still not the situation that is total, which is totalitarianism. I wasn't put in jail and I wasn't tortured. My child wasn't denied anything. My livelihood was taken away from me and some people stopped talking to me, but other people admired me. My wife admired me. My daughter admired me. Many of my ex-students admired me. Openly said so. And I could put up a legal fight. I had free movement, I could give interviews, raise money, hire a lawyer, make courtroom challenges. Which I did. Of course you can become so depressed and miserable that you give yourself a heart attack. But you can find alternatives, which I also did.

"Now, if the *union* had failed, that would have affected me. But we didn't. We fought and eventually we won. We equalized the pay of men and women. We equalized the pay of secondary and elementary school teachers. We made sure that all after-school activities were, first, voluntary and, then, paid for. We fought to get more sick leave. We argued for five days off for any purpose whatsoever that the individual chose. We achieved promotion by examination—as opposed to favoritism—which meant that all minorities had a fair chance. We attracted blacks to the union, and as they increased in numbers, they moved into leadership positions. But that was years ago. Now the union is a big disappointment to me. Just become a money-grubbing organization. Pay, that's all. What to do to educate the kids is the last thing on anybody's mind. Big disappointment."

"How awful was it for those six years?" I asked him. "What did it take out of you?"

"I don't think it took anything out of me. I really don't think so. You do a helluva lot of not sleeping at night, of course. Many nights I had a hard time sleeping. You're thinking of all kinds of things— how do you do this, and what are you going to do next, whom do you call on, and so forth. I was always redoing what had happened and projecting what would happen. But then the morning comes, and you get up and you do what you have to do."

"And how did Ira take this happening to you?"

"Oh, it distressed him. I'd go as far as to say it ruined him had he not already been ruined by everything else. I was confident all along that I was going to win, and I told this to him. They had no legal reasons for firing me. He kept saying, 'You're kiddin' yourself. They don't need legal reasons.' He knew of too many guys who had been fired, period. Eventually I won, but he felt responsible for what I went through. He carried it around with him for the rest of his life. About you, too, you know. About what happened to you."

"Me?" I said. "Nothing happened to me. I was a kid."

"Oh, something happened to you."

Of course it should not be too surprising to find out that your life story has included an event, something important, that you have known nothing about—your life story is in and of itself something that you know very little about.

"If you remember," Murray said, "when you graduated from college you didn't get a Fulbright. That was because of my brother."

In 1953–54, my last year at Chicago, I'd applied for a Fulbright to do graduate work in literature at Oxford and been turned down. I had been near the top of my class, had enthusiastic recommendations, and, as I now remembered it—for the first time, probably, since it happened—was shocked not only at being turned down but because a Fulbright to study literature in England went to a fellow student who was well below me in class standing.

"This true, Murray? I just thought it was screwy, unfair. The fickleness of fate. I didn't know what to think. I wuz robbed, I thought—and then I got drafted. How do you know this is so?"

"The agent told Ira. The FBI. He was on Ira for years. Stopping around to visit him. Coming around to try to get him to name names. Told him that's how he could clear himself. They had you down for Ira's nephew."

"His nephew? How come his nephew?"

"Don't ask me. The FBI didn't always get everything right. Maybe they didn't always want to get everything right. The guy told Ira,

'You know your nephew who applied for a Fulbright? The kid in Chicago? He didn't get it because of your being a Communist.'"

"You think that was true."

"No doubt about it."

All the while I was listening to Murray—and looking at the needle of a man he'd become and thinking of this physique as the materialization of all that coherence of his, as the consequence of a lifelong indifference to everything other than liberty in its most austere sense . . . thinking that Murray was an essentialist, that his character wasn't contingent, that wherever he'd found himself, even selling vacuum cleaners, he'd managed to find his dignity . . . thinking that Murray (whom I didn't love or have to; with whom there was just the contract, teacher and student) was Ira (whom I did love) in a more mental, sensible, matter-of-fact version, Ira with a practical, clear, well-defined social goal, Ira without the heroically exaggerated ambitions, without that passionate, overheated relationship to everything, Ira unblurred by impulse and the argument with everything—I had a picture in my mind of Murray's unclothed upper torso, still blessed (when he was already forty-one) with all the signs of youth and strength. The picture I had was of Murray Ringold as I had seen him late one Tuesday afternoon in the fall of 1948, leaning out the window and removing the screens from the second-floor apartment where he lived with his wife and daughter on Lehigh Avenue.

Taking down the screens, putting up the screens, clearing the snow, salting the ice, sweeping the sidewalk, clipping the hedge, washing the car, collecting and burning the leaves, twice daily from October through March descending to the cellar and tending the furnace that heated your flat—stoking the fire, banking the fire, shoveling the ashes, lugging ashes up the stairs in buckets and out to the garbage: a tenant, a renter, had to be fit to get all his chores done before and after going to work, vigilant and diligent and fit, just as the wives had to be fit to lean from their open back windows while rooted to the floor of the apartment and, whatever the temperature—up there like seamen at work in the rigging—to hang the wet clothes out on the clothesline, to peg them with the clothespins an item at a time, feeding the line out until all the waterlogged family wash was hung and the line was full and flapping in the air of industrial Newark, and then to haul the line in again to remove the laundry item by item, remove it all and fold it into the laundry basket to carry into the kitchen when the clothes were dry and ready to be ironed. To keep a family going, there was primarily money to be made and food to be prepared and discipline to be imposed, but there were also these heavy, awkward, sailorlike activities, the climbing, the hoisting, the hauling, the dragging, the cranking in, the reeling out—all the stuff that would tick by me as, on my bicycle, I traversed the two miles from my house to the library: tick, tock, tick, the metronome of daily neighborhood life, the old American-city chain of being.

Across the street from Mr. Ringold's Lehigh Avenue house was the Beth Israel Hospital, where I knew Mrs. Ringold had worked as a lab assistant before their daughter was born, and around the corner was the Osborne Terrace branch library, where I used to bicycle for a weekly supply of books. The hospital, the library, and, as represented by my teacher, the school: the neighborhood's institutional nexus was all reassuringly present for me in virtually that one square block. Yes, the everyday workability of neighborhood life was in full swing on that afternoon in 1948 when I saw Mr. Ringold hanging out over the sill undoing a screen from the front window.

As I braked to descend the steep Lehigh Avenue hill, I watched him thread a rope through one of the screen's corner hooks and then, after calling down "Here she comes," lower it along the face of the two-and-a-half-story building to a man in the garden, who undid the rope and set the screen onto a pile stacked against the brick stoop. I was struck by the way Mr. Ringold performed an act that was both athletic and practical. To perform that act as gracefully as he did, you had to be very strong.

When I got to the house I saw that the man in the garden was a giant wearing glasses. It was Ira. It was the brother who had come to our high school, to "Auditorium," to portray Abe Lincoln. He'd appeared on the stage in costume and, standing all alone, delivered Lincoln's Gettysburg Address and then the Second Inaugural, concluding with what Mr. Ringold, the orator's brother, later told us was as noble and beautiful a sentence as any American president, as any American *writer,* had ever written (a long, chugging locomotive of a sentence, its tail end a string of weighty cabooses, that he then made us diagram and analyze and discuss for an entire class period): "With malice toward none, with charity for all, with firmness in the right as God gives us to see the right, let us strive on to finish the work we are in, to bind up the nation's wounds, to care for him who shall have borne the battle and for his widow and his orphan, to do all which may achieve and cherish a just and lasting peace among ourselves and with all nations." For the rest of the program, Abraham Lincoln removed his stovepipe hat and debated the pro-slavery senator Stephen A. Douglas, whose lines (the most insidiously anti-Negro of which a group of students—we members of an extracurricular discussion group called the Contemporary Club—loudly booed) were read by Murray Ringold, who had arranged for Iron Rinn to visit the school.

As if it weren't disorienting enough to see Mr. Ringold out in public without a shirt and tie—without even an undershirt—Iron Rinn wasn't wearing any more than a prizefighter. Shorts, sneakers, that was it—all but naked, not only the biggest man I'd ever seen up close but the most famous. Iron Rinn was heard on network radio every Thursday night on *The Free and the Brave*—a popular weekly dramatization of inspiring episodes out of American history—impersonating people like Nathan Hale and Orville Wright and Wild Bill Hickok and Jack London. In real life, he was married to Eve Frame, the leading lady of the weekly repertory playhouse for "serious" drama called *The American Radio Theater.* My mother knew everything about Iron Rinn and Eve Frame through the magazines she read at the beauty parlor. She would never have bought any of these magazines—she disapproved of them, as did my father, who wished his family to be exemplary—but she read them under the dryer, and then she saw all the fashion magazines when she went off on Saturday afternoons to help her friend Mrs. Svirsky, who, with her husband, had a dress shop on Bergen Street right next door to Mrs. Unterberg's millinery shop, where my mother also occasionally helped out on Saturdays and during the pre-Easter rush.

One night after we had listened to *The American Radio Theater*, which we'd done since I could remember, my mother told us about Eve Frame's wedding to Iron Rinn and all the stage and radio personalities who were guests. Eve Frame had worn a two-piece wool suit of dusty pink, sleeves trimmed with double rings of matching fox fur, and, on her head, the sort of hat that no one in the world wore more charmingly than she did. My mother called it "a veiled come-hither hat," a style that Eve Frame had apparently made famous opposite the silent-film matinee idol Carlton Pennington in *My Darling, Come Hither*, where she played to perfection a spoiled young socialite. It was a veiled come-hither hat that she was well known for wearing when she stood before the microphone, script in hand, performing on *The American Radio Theater*, though she had also been photographed before a radio microphone in slouch-brimmed felts, in pillboxes, in Panama straw hats, and once, when she was a guest on *The Bob Hope Show*, my mother remembered, in a black straw saucer seductively veiled with gossamer silk thread. My mother told us that Eve Frame was six years older than Iron Rinn, that her hair grew an inch a month and she lightened its color for the Broadway stage, that her daughter, Sylphid, was a harpist, a Juilliard graduate, and the offspring of Eve Frame's marriage to Carlton Pennington.

"Who cares?" my father said. "Nathan does," my mother replied defensively. "Iron Rinn is Mr. Ringold's brother. Mr. Ringold is his *idol*."

My parents had seen Eve Frame in silent movies when she was a beautiful girl. And she was still beautiful; I knew because, four years earlier, for my eleventh birthday, I had been taken to see my first

Broadway play—*The Late George Apley* by John P. Marquand—and Eve Frame was in it, and afterward my father, whose memories of Eve Frame as a young silent-film actress were still apparently amorously tinged, had said, "That woman speaks the King's English like nobody's business," and my mother, who may or may not have grasped what was fueling his praise, had said, "Yes, but she's let herself go. She speaks beautifully, and she did the part beautifully, and she looked adorable in that short pageboy, but the extra pounds are not becoming on a little thing like Eve Frame, certainly not in a fitted white piqué summer dress, full skirt or no full skirt."

A discussion as to whether or not Eve Frame was Jewish invariably occurred among the women in my mother's mahjong club when it was my mother's turn to have them for their weekly game, and particularly after the evening a few months later when I had been a guest of Ira's at Eve Frame's dinner table. The starstruck world round the starstruck boy couldn't stop talking about the fact that people said her real name was Fromkin. Chava Fromkin. There were Fromkins in Brooklyn who were supposed to be the family she had disowned when she went to Hollywood and changed her name.

"Who cares?" my serious-minded father would say whenever the subject came up and he happened to be passing through the living room, where the mahjong game was in progress. "They all change their names in Hollywood. That woman opens her mouth and it's an elocution lesson. She gets up on that stage and portrays a lady, you *know* it's a lady."

"They say she's from Flatbush," Mrs. Unterberg, who owned the millinery shop, would routinely put in. "They say that her father is a kosher butcher."

"They say Cary Grant is Jewish," my father reminded the ladies. "The fascists used to say that *Roosevelt* was Jewish. People say everything. That's not what I'm concerned with. I'm concerned with her *acting,* which in my book is superlative."

"Well," said Mrs. Svirsky, who with her husband owned the dress shop, "Ruth Tunick's brother-in-law is married to a Fromkin, a

Newark Fromkin. And she has relatives in Brooklyn, and they swear their cousin is Eve Frame."

"What does Nathan say?" asked Mrs. Kaufman, a housewife and a girlhood friend of my mother's.

"He doesn't," my mother replied. I had trained her to say that I didn't. How? Easy. When she had asked, on behalf of the ladies, if I knew whether Eve Frame of *The American Radio Theater* was, in actuality, Chava Fromkin of Brooklyn, I had told her, "Religion is the opiate of the people! Those things don't matter—I don't care. I don't know and I don't care!"

"What is it like there? What did she wear?" Mrs. Unterberg asked my mother.

"What did she serve?" Mrs. Kaufman asked.

"How was her hair done?" Mrs. Unterberg asked.

"Is he really six six? What does Nathan say? Does he wear a size sixteen shoe? Some people say that's just publicity."

"And his skin is as pockmarked as it looks in the pictures?"

"What does Nathan say about the daughter? What kind of name is Sylphid?" asked Mrs. Schessel, whose husband was a chiropodist, like my father.

"That's her real name?" asked Mrs. Svirsky.

"It's not Jewish," said Mrs. Kaufman. "'Sylvia' is Jewish. I think it's French."

"But the father wasn't French," said Mrs. Schessel. "The father is Carlton Pennington. She acted with him in all those films. She eloped with him in that movie. Where he was the older baron."

"Is that the one where she wore the hat?"

"Nobody in the world," said Mrs. Unterberg, "looks like that woman in a hat. Put Eve Frame in a snug little beret, in a small floral dinner hat, in a crocheted straw baby doll, in a veiled big black cartwheel—put her in *anything,* put her in a Tyrolean brown felt with a feather, put her in a white jersey turban, put her in a fur-lined parka *hood,* and the woman is gorgeous, regardless."

"In one picture she wore—I'll never forget it," said Mrs. Svirsky, "—a gold-embroidered white evening suit with a white ermine muff. I never saw such elegance in my life. There was a play—which was it? We went to see it together, girls. She wore a burgundy wool dress, full at the bodice and the skirt, and the most enchanting scrollwork embroidery—"

"Yes! And that matching veiled hat. Tall burgundy felt," said Mrs. Unterberg, "with a crushed veil."

"Remember her in ruffles in whatever that other play was?" said Mrs. Svirsky. "No one wears ruffles the way she does. White *double* ruffles on a black cocktail dress!"

"But the name *Sylphid*," asked Mrs. Schessel yet again. "Sylphid comes from *what?*"

"Nathan knows. Ask Nathan," Mrs. Svirsky said. "Is Nathan here?"

"He's doing his homework," my mother said.

"Ask him. What kind of name is Sylphid?"

"I'll ask him later," said my mother.

But she knew enough not to—even though secretly, ever since I had entered the enchanted circle, I was bursting to talk about all of it to everyone. What do they wear? What do they eat? What do they say *while* they eat? What is it *like* there? It is spectacular.

The Tuesday that I first met Ira, out in front of Mr. Ringold's house, was Tuesday, October 12, 1948. Had the World Series not just ended on Monday, I might, timorously, out of deference to my teacher's privacy, have speeded on by the house where he was taking down the screens with his brother and, without even waving or shouting hello, turned left at the corner onto Osborne Terrace. As it happened, however, the day before I had listened to the Indians beat the old Boston Braves in the final game of the Series from the floor of Mr. Ringold's office. He had brought a radio with him that morning, and after school those whose families didn't yet own a television set—the vast majority of us—were invited to spill directly out of his eighth-period English class and down the hall to crowd into the English department chairman's little office to hear the game, which was already under way at Braves Field.

Courtesy, then, necessitated that I slow way, way down and call out to him, "Mr. Ringold—thanks for yesterday." Courtesy necessitated that I nod and smile at the giant in his yard. And—with a dry mouth, stiffly—stop and introduce myself. And respond a little daffily when he startled me by saying, "How ya' doin', buddy," by replying that on the afternoon he'd appeared at Auditorium, I'd been one of the boys who had booed Stephen A. Douglas when he announced into Lincoln's face, "I am opposed to negro citizenship in any and every form. [Boo.] I believe this government was made on a white basis. [Boo.] I believe it was made for white men [Boo], for the benefit of white men [Boo], and their posterity for ever. [Boo.] I am in favor of confining citizenship to white men . . . instead of conferring it upon Negroes, Indians, and other inferior races. [Boo. Boo. Boo.]"

Something rooted deeper than mere courtesy (ambition, the ambition to be admired for my moral conviction) prompted me to break through the shyness and tell him, tell the trinity of Iras, all three of him—the patriot martyr of the podium Abraham Lincoln, the natural, hardy American of the airwaves Iron Rinn, and the redeemed roughneck from Newark's First Ward Ira Ringold—that it was I who had instigated the booing.

Mr. Ringold came down the stairs from the second-floor flat, sweating heavily, wearing just khaki trousers and a pair of moccasins. Right behind him came Mrs. Ringold, who, before retreating back upstairs, set out a tray with a pitcher of ice water and three glasses. And so it was—four-thirty P.M., October 12, 1948, a blazing hot autumn day and the most astonishing afternoon of my young life—that I tipped my bike onto its side and sat on the steps of my English teacher's stoop with Eve Frame's husband, Iron Rinn of *The Free and the Brave*, discussing a World Series in which Bob Feller had lost two games—unbelievable—and Larry Doby, the pioneering black player in the American League, whom we all admired, but not the way we admired Jackie Robinson, had gone seven for twenty-two.

Then we were talking about boxing: Louis knocking out Jersey

Joe Walcott when Walcott was way ahead on points; Tony Zale regaining the middleweight title from Rocky Graziano right in Newark, at Ruppert Stadium in June, crushing him with a left in the third round, and then losing it to a Frenchman, Marcel Cerdan, over in Jersey City a couple of weeks back, in September . . . And then from talking to me about Tony Zale one minute, Iron Rinn was talking to me about Winston Churchill the next, about a speech that Churchill had made a few days earlier that had him boiling, a speech advising the United States not to destroy its atomic bomb reserve because the atomic bomb was all that prevented the Communists from dominating the world. He talked about Winston Churchill the way he talked about Leo Durocher and Marcel Cerdan. He called Churchill a reactionary bastard and a warmonger with no more hesitation than he called Durocher a loudmouth and Cerdan a bum. He talked about Churchill as though Churchill ran the gas station out on Lyons Avenue. It wasn't how we talked about Winston Churchill in my house. It was closer to how we talked about Hitler. In his conversation, as in his brother's, there was no invisible line of propriety observed and there were no conventional taboos. You could stir together anything and everything: sports, politics, history, literature, reckless opinionating, polemical quotation, idealistic sentiment, moral rectitude . . . There was something marvelously bracing about it, a different and dangerous world, demanding, straightforward, aggressive, freed from the need to please. And freed from school. Iron Rinn wasn't just a radio star. He was somebody outside the classroom who was not afraid to say anything.

I had just finished reading about somebody else who wasn't afraid to say anything—Thomas Paine—and the book I'd read, a historical novel by Howard Fast called *Citizen Tom Paine,* was one of the collection in my bicycle basket that I was returning to the library. While Ira was denouncing Churchill to me, Mr. Ringold had stepped over to where the books had tumbled from the basket onto the pavement at the foot of the stoop and was looking at their spines to see what I was reading. Half the books were about baseball and were by John R. Tunis, and the other half were about American history and were by Howard Fast. My idealism (and my idea of a man) was being constructed along parallel lines, one fed by novels about baseball champions who won their games the hard way, suffering adversity and humiliation and many defeats as they struggled toward victory, and the other by novels about heroic Americans who fought against tyranny and injustice, champions of liberty for America and for all mankind. Heroic suffering. That was my specialty.

Citizen Tom Paine was not so much a novel plotted in the familiar manner as a sustained linking of highly charged rhetorical flourishes tracing the contradictions of an unsavory man with a smoldering intellect and the purest social ideals, a writer *and* a revolutionary. "He was the most hated—and perhaps by a few the most loved—man in all the world." "A mind that burned itself as few minds in all human history." "To feel on his own soul the whip laid on the back of millions." "His thoughts and ideas were closer to those of the average working man than Jefferson's could ever be." That was Paine as Fast portrayed him, savagely single-minded and unsociable, an epic, folkloric belligerent—unkempt, dirty, wearing a beggar's clothes, bearing a musket in the unruly streets of wartime Philadelphia, a bitter, caustic man, often drunk, frequenting brothels, hunted by assassins, and friendless. He did it all alone: "My only friend is the revolution." By the time I had finished the book, there seemed to me no way other than Paine's for a man to live and die if he was intent on demanding, in behalf of human freedom—demanding both from remote rulers and from the coarse mob—the transformation of society.

He did it all alone. There was nothing about Paine that could have been more appealing, however unsentimentally Fast depicted an isolation born of defiant independence and personal misery. For Paine had ended his days alone as well, old, sick, wretched, and alone, ostracized, betrayed—despised beyond everything for having written in his last testament, *The Age of Reason*, "I do not believe in the creed professed by the Jewish church, by the Roman church, by the Greek church, by the Turkish church, by the Protestant church, nor by any church that I know of. My own mind is my own church." Reading about him had made me feel bold and angry and, above all, free to fight for what I believed in.

Citizen Tom Paine was the very book that Mr. Ringold had picked out of my bicycle basket to bring back to where we were sitting.

"You know this one?" he asked his brother.

Iron Rinn took my library book in Abe Lincoln's enormous hands and began flipping through the opening pages. "Nope. Never read Fast," he said. "I should. Wonderful man. Guts. He was with Wallace from day one. I catch his column whenever I see the *Worker*, but I don't have the time for novels anymore. In Iran I did, in the service read Steinbeck, Upton Sinclair, Jack London, Caldwell . . ."

"If you're going to read him, this is Fast at his best," Mr. Ringold said. "Am I right, Nathan?"

"This book is great," I answered.

"You ever read *Common Sense*?" Iron Rinn asked me. "Ever read Paine's writings?"

"No," I said.

"Read 'em," Iron Rinn told me while still leafing through my book.

"There's a lot of Paine's writing quoted by Howard Fast," I said.

Looking up, Iron Rinn said, "'The strength of the many is revolution, but curiously enough mankind has gone through several thousand years of slavery without realizing that fact.'"

"That's in the book," I said.

"I should hope so."

"You know what the genius of Paine was?" Mr. Ringold asked me. "It was the genius of all those men. Jefferson. Madison. Know what it was?"

"No," I said.

"You do know what it was," he said.

"To defy the English."

"A lot of people did that. No. It was to articulate the cause *in* English. The revolution was totally improvised, totally disorganized. Isn't that the sense you get from this book, Nathan? Well, these guys had to find a language for their revolution. To find the words for a great purpose."

"Paine said," I told Mr. Ringold, "'I wrote a little book because I wanted men to see what they were shooting at.'"

"And that he did," Mr. Ringold said.

"Here," said Iron Rinn, pointing to some lines in the book. "On George III. Listen. 'I should suffer the misery of devils, were I to make a whore of my soul by swearing allegiance to one whose character is that of a sottish, stupid, stubborn, worthless, brutish man.'"

Both quotations from Paine that Iron Rinn had recited—employing his *The Free and the Brave* people-bound, in-the-rough voice—were among the dozen or so that I had myself written down and memorized.

"You like that line," Mr. Ringold said to me.

"Yes. I like 'a whore of my soul.'"

"Why?" he asked me.

I was beginning to perspire profusely from the sun on my face, from the excitement of meeting Iron Rinn, and now from being on the spot, having to answer Mr. Ringold as though I were in class while I was sitting between two shirtless brothers well over six feet tall, two big, natural men exuding the sort of forceful, intelligent manliness to which I aspired. Men who could talk about baseball and boxing talking about books. And talking about books as though something were at stake in a book. Not opening up a book to worship it or to be elevated by it or to lose yourself to the world around you. No, *boxing* with the book.

"Because," I said, "you don't ordinarily think of your soul as a whore."

"What's he *mean*, 'a whore of my soul'?"

"Selling it," I replied. "Selling his soul."

"Right. Do you see how much stronger it is to write 'I should suffer the misery of devils, were I to make a *whore* of my soul' rather than 'were I to *sell* my soul'?"

"Yes, I do."

"Why is that stronger?"

"Because in 'whore' he personifies it."

"Yeah—what else?"

"Well, the word 'whore' . . . it's not a conventional word, you don't hear it in public. People don't go around writing 'whore' or, in public, saying 'whore.'"

"Why don't they?"

"Shame. Embarrassment. Propriety."

"Propriety. Good. Right. So this is audacious, then."

"Yes."

"And *that's* what you like about Paine, isn't it? His audacity?"

"I think so. Yes."

"And now you know *why* you like what you like. You're way ahead of the game, Nathan. And you know it because you looked at one word he used, just one word, and you thought about that word he used, and you asked yourself some questions about that word he used, until you saw right through that word, saw through it as through a magnifying glass, to one of the sources of this great writer's power. He is audacious. Thomas Paine is audacious. But is that enough? That is only a part of the formula. Audacity must have a purpose, otherwise it's cheap and facile and vulgar. Why is Thomas Paine audacious?"

"In behalf," I said, "of his convictions."

"Hey, that's my boy," Iron Rinn suddenly announced. "That's my boy who booed Mr. Douglas!"

So it was that I wound up five nights later as Iron Rinn's backstage guest at a rally held in downtown Newark, at the Mosque, the city's biggest theater, for Henry Wallace, the presidential candidate of the newly formed Progressive Party. Wallace had been in Roosevelt's cabinet as secretary of agriculture for seven years before becoming his vice president during Roosevelt's third term. In '44 he'd been dropped from the ticket and replaced by Truman, in whose cabinet he served briefly as secretary of commerce. In '46, the president fired Wallace for sounding off in favor of cooperation with Stalin and friendship with the Soviet Union at just the point when the Soviet Union had begun to be perceived by Truman and the Democrats not only as an ideological enemy but as a serious threat to peace whose expansion into Europe and elsewhere had to be contained by the West.

This division within the Democratic Party—between the anti-Soviet majority led by the president and the "progressive" Soviet sympathizers led by Wallace and opposed to the Truman Doctrine and the Marshall Plan—was reflected in the split within my own household between father and son. My father, who had admired Wallace when he was FDR's protégé, was against the Wallace candidacy for the reason Americans traditionally choose not to support third-party candidates—in this case, because it would draw the votes of the left wing of the Democratic Party away from Truman and make all but certain the election of Governor Thomas E. Dewey of New York, the Republican candidate. The Wallace people were talking about their party polling some six or seven million votes, a percentage of the popular vote vastly greater than had ever gone to any American third party.

"Your man is only going to deny the Democrats the White House," my father told me. "And if we get the Republicans, that will mean the suffering in this country that it has always meant. You weren't around for Hoover and Harding and Coolidge. You don't know firsthand about the heartlessness of the Republican Party. You despise big business, Nathan? You despise what you and Henry Wallace call 'the Big Boys from Wall Street'? Well, you don't know what it is when the party of big business has its foot in the face of ordinary people. I do. I know poverty and I know hardship in ways you and your brother have been spared, thank God."

My father had been born in the Newark slums and become a chiropodist only by going to school at night while working by day on a bakery truck; and all his life, even after he had made a few bucks and we had moved into a house of our own, he continued to identify with the interests of what he called ordinary people and what I had taken to calling—along with Henry Wallace—"the common man." I was terrifically disappointed to hear my father flatly refuse to vote for the candidate who, as I tried to convince him, supported his own New Deal principles. Wallace wanted a national health program, protection for unions, benefits for workers; he was opposed to Taft-Hartley and the persecution of labor; he was opposed to the Mundt-Nixon bill and the persecution of political radicals. The Mundt-Nixon bill, if passed, would require the registration with the government of all Communists and "Communist-front" organizations. Wallace had said that Mundt-Nixon was the first step to a police state, an effort to frighten the American people into silence; he called it "the most subversive" bill ever introduced in Congress. The Progressive Party supported the freedom of ideas to compete in what Wallace called "the marketplace of thoughts." Most impressive to me was that, campaigning in the South, Wallace had refused to address any audience that was segregated—the first presidential candidate ever to have that degree of courage and integrity.

"The Democrats," I told my father, "will never do anything to end segregation. They will never outlaw lynching and the poll tax and Jim Crow. They never have and they never will."

"I do not agree with you, Nathan," he told me. "You watch Harry Truman. Harry Truman has got a civil rights plank in his platform, and you watch and see what he does now that he's rid of those southern bigots."

Not only had Wallace bolted from the Democratic Party that year, but so had the "bigots" my father spoke of, the southern Democrats, who had formed their own party, the States Rights Party—the "Dixiecrats." They were running for president Governor Strom Thurmond of South Carolina, a rabid segregationist. The Dixiecrats were also going to draw away votes, southern votes, that routinely went to the Democratic Party, which was another reason Dewey was favored to defeat Truman in a landslide.

Every night over dinner in the kitchen, I did everything I could to persuade my father to vote for Henry Wallace and the restoration of the New Deal, and every night he tried to get me to understand the necessity for compromise in an election like this one. But as I had taken as my hero Thomas Paine, the most uncompromising patriot in American history, at the mere sound of the first *syllable* of the word "compromise," I jumped up from my chair and told him and my mother and my ten-year-old brother (who, whenever I got going, liked to repeat to me, in an exaggeratedly exasperated voice, "A vote for Wallace is a vote for *Dewey*") that I could never again eat at that table if my father was present.

One night at dinner my father tried another tack—to educate me further about the Republicans' contempt for every value of economic equality and political justice that I held dear—but I would have none of it: the two major political parties were equally without conscience when it came to the Negro's rights, equally indifferent to the injustices inherent to the capitalist system, equally blind to the catastrophic consequences for all of mankind of our country's deliberate provocation of the peace-loving Russian people. Close to tears, and meaning every word, I told my father, "I'm really surprised at you," as though it were he who was the uncompromising son.

But a greater surprise was coming. Late on Saturday afternoon he told me that he would rather I didn't go down to the Mosque that evening to attend the Wallace rally. If I still wanted to after we had spoken, he wouldn't try to stop me, but he at least wanted me to hear him out before I made my decision final. When I'd come home on Tuesday from the library and triumphantly announced at dinner that I had been invited to be a guest of Iron Rinn, the radio actor, at the Wallace rally downtown, I was obviously so thrilled at meeting Rinn, so beside myself with the personal interest he'd shown in me, that my mother had simply forbidden my father from raising his reservations about the rally. But now he wanted me to listen to what he felt he had a duty, as a parent, to discuss, and without my flying off the handle.

My father was taking me as seriously as the Ringolds were, but not with Ira's political fearlessness, with Murray's literary ingenuity, above all, with their seeming absence of concern for my decorum, for whether I would or would not be a good boy. The Ringolds were the one-two punch promising to initiate me into the big show, into my beginning to understand what it takes to be a man on the larger scale. The Ringolds compelled me to respond at a level of rigor that felt appropriate to who I now was. Be a good boy wasn't the issue with them. The sole issue was my convictions. But then, their responsibility wasn't a father's, which is to steer his son away from the pitfalls. The father has to worry about the pitfalls in a way the teacher doesn't. He has to worry about his son's conduct, he has to worry about socializing his little Tom Paine. But once little Tom Paine has been let into the company of men and the father is still educating him as a boy, the father is finished. Sure, he's worrying about the pitfalls—if he wasn't, it would be wrong. But he's finished anyway. Little Tom Paine has no choice but to write him off, to betray the father and go boldly forth to step straight into life's very first pit. And then, all on his own—providing real unity to his existence—to step from pit to pit for the rest of his days, until the grave, which, if it has nothing else to recommend it, is at least the last pit into which one can fall.

"Hear me out," my father said, "and then you make up your own mind. I respect your independence, son. You want to wear a Wallace button to school? Wear it. It's a free country. But you have to have all the facts. You can't make an informed decision without facts."

Why had Mrs. Roosevelt, the great president's revered widow, withheld her endorsement and turned against Henry Wallace? Why had Harold Ickes, Roosevelt's trusted and loyal secretary of interior, a great man in his own right, withheld his endorsement and turned against Henry Wallace? Why had the CIO, as ambitious a labor organization as this country had ever known, withdrawn its money and its support from Henry Wallace? Because of the Communist infiltration into the Wallace campaign. My father didn't want me to go to the rally because of the Communists who had all but taken over the Progressive Party. He told me that Henry Wallace was either too naive to know it or—what was, unfortunately, probably closer to the truth—too dishonest to admit it, but Communists, particularly from among Communist-dominated unions already expelled from the CIO—

"Red-baiter!" I shouted, and I left the house. I took the 14 bus and went to the rally. I met Paul Robeson. He reached out to shake my hand after Ira introduced me as the kid at the high school he'd told him about. "Here he is, Paul, the boy who led the booing of Stephen A. Douglas." Paul Robeson, the Negro actor and singer, cochairman of the Wallace for President Committee, who only a few months earlier at a Washington demonstration against the Mundt-Nixon bill had sung "Ol' Man River" to a crowd of five thousand protesters at the foot of the Washington Monument, who'd been fearless before the Senate Judiciary Committee, telling them (when asked at their hearings on Mundt-Nixon if he would comply with the bill if it was passed), "I would violate the law," then answering no less forthrightly (when asked what the Communist Party stood for), "For complete equality of the Negro people"—Paul Robeson took my hand in his and said, "Don't lose your courage, young man."

Standing backstage with the performers and speakers at the Mosque—enveloped simultaneously in two exotic new worlds, the leftist milieu and the world of "the wings"—was as thrilling as it would have been to sit down in the dugout with the players at a major league game. From the wings I heard Ira do Abraham Lincoln again, this time tearing into not Stephen A. Douglas but the warmongers in both political parties: "Supporting reactionary regimes all over the world, arming Western Europe against Russia, militarizing America . . ." I saw Henry Wallace himself, stood no more than twenty feet away from him before he went onto the stage to address the crowd, and then stood almost at his side when Ira went up to whisper something to him at the gala reception after the rally. I stared at the presidential candidate, a Republican farmer's son from Iowa as American-looking and American-sounding as any American I had ever seen, a politician against high prices, against big business, against segregation and discrimination, against appeasing dictators like Francisco Franco and Chiang Kai-shek, and I remembered what Fast had written of Paine: "His thoughts and ideas were closer to those of the average working man than Jefferson's could ever be." And in 1954—six years after that night at the Mosque when the candidate of the common man, the candidate of the people and the people's party, raised gooseflesh all over me by clenching his fist and crying out from the lectern, "We are in the midst of a fierce attack upon our freedom"—I got turned down for a Fulbright scholarship.

I did not and could not have made a scrap of difference, and yet the zealotry to defeat Communism reached even me.

Iron Rinn had been born in Newark two decades before me, in 1913, a poor boy from a hard neighborhood—and from a cruel family—who briefly attended Barringer High, where he failed every subject but gym. He had bad eyesight and useless glasses and could barely read what was in the lesson books, let alone what the teacher wrote on the blackboard. He couldn't see and he couldn't learn and one day, as he explained it, "I just didn't wake up to go to school."

Murray and Ira's father was someone Ira refused even to discuss. In the months after the Wallace rally, the most Ira ever told me was this: "My father I couldn't talk to. He never paid the slightest bit of attention to his two sons. He didn't do this on purpose. It was the nature of the beast." Ira's mother, a beloved woman in his memory, died when he was seven, and her replacement he described as "the stepmother you hear about in the fairy tales. A real bitch." He quit high school after a year and a half and, a few weeks later, left the house forever at fifteen and found a job digging ditches in Newark. Till the war broke out, while the country was in the Depression, he drifted round and round, first in New Jersey and then all over America, taking whatever work he could get, mostly jobs requiring a strong back. Immediately after Pearl Harbor, he enlisted in the army. He couldn't see the eye chart, but a long line of guys were waiting for the examination, and so Ira went around up close to the chart, memorized as much of it as he could, then got back in line, and that was how he passed the physical. When Ira came out of the army in 1945, he spent a year in Calumet City, Illinois, where he shared a room with the closest buddy he'd made in the service, a Communist steelworker, Johnny O'Day. They'd been soldier stevedores together on the docks in Iran, unloading lend-lease equipment that was shipped by rail through Teheran to the Soviet Union; because of Ira's strength on the job, O'Day had nicknamed his friend "Iron Man Ira." In the evenings, O'Day had taught the Iron Man how to read a book and how to write a letter and gave him an education in Marxism.

O'Day was a gray-haired guy some ten years older than Ira—"How he ever got into the service at his age," Ira said, "I still don't know." A six-footer skinny as a telephone pole, but the toughest son of a bitch he'd ever met. O'Day carried in his gear a light punching bag that he used for his timing; so quick and strong was he that, "if forced to," he could lick two or three guys together. And O'Day was brilliant. "I knew nothing about politics. I knew nothing about political action," Ira said. "I didn't know one political philosophy or one social philosophy from another. But this guy talked a lot to me," he said. "He talked about the workingman. About things in general in the United States. The harm our government was doing to the workers. And he backed up what he said with facts. And a nonconformist? O'Day was so nonconformist that everything he did he did not do by the book. Yeah, O'Day did a lot for me, I know that."

Like Ira, O'Day was unmarried. "Entangling alliances," he told Ira, "is something I don't want any part of at no time. I regard kids as hostages to the malevolent." Though he had but a year's education more than Ira, on his own O'Day had "skilled himself," as he put it, "in verbal and written polemics" by slavishly copying passage after passage out of all sorts of books and, with the aid of a grade school grammar, analyzing the structure of the sentences. It was O'Day who gave Ira the pocket dictionary that Ira claimed remade his life. "I had a dictionary I read at night," Ira told me, "the way you would read a novel. I had somebody send me a *Roget's Thesaurus.* After unloading ships all day, I would work every night to improve my vocabulary."

He discovered reading. "One day—it must have been one of the worst mistakes the army ever made—they sent us a complete library. What an error," he said, laughing. "I probably read every book they had in that library eventually. They built a Quonset hut to house the books, and they made shelves, and they told the guys, 'You want a book, you come in here and get one.'" It was O'Day who told him—who still told him—which books to get.

Early on, Ira showed me three sheets of paper titled "Some Concrete Suggestions for Ringold's Utilization" that O'Day had prepared when they were in Iran together. "One: Always keep a dictionary at hand—a good one with plenty of antonyms and synonyms—even when you write a note to the milkman. And use it. Don't make wild passes at spelling and exact shades of meaning as you have been accustomed to doing. Two: Double-space everything you write in order to permit interpolation of afterthoughts and corrections. I don't give a damn if it does violate good usage insofar as personal correspondence is involved; it makes for accurate expression. Three: Don't run your thoughts together in a solid page of typing. Every time you treat a new thought or elaborate what you're already talking about, indent for a new paragraph. It may add up to jerkiness, but it will be much more readable. Four: Avoid clichés. Even if you have to drag it in by the tail, express something you've read or heard quoted in other than the original words. One of your sentences from the other night at the library session in point of demonstration: 'I stated briefly some of the ills of the present regime . . .' You've read that, Iron Man, and it isn't yours; it's somebody else's. It sounds as if it came out of a can. Suppose you expressed the same idea something like this: 'I build my argument about the effect of landed proprietorship and the dominance of foreign capital on what I have witnessed here in Iran.'"

There were twenty points in all, and the reason Ira showed them to me was to assist with *my* writing—not with my high school radio plays but with my journal, intended to be "political" where I was beginning to put down my "thoughts" when I remembered to. I'd begun keeping my journal in imitation of Ira, who'd begun keeping his in imitation of Johnny O'Day. The three of us used the same brand of notebook: a dime pad from Woolworth's, fifty-two lined pages about four inches by three inches, stitched at the top and bound between mottled brown cardboard covers.

When an O'Day letter mentioned a book, any book, Ira got a copy and so did I; I'd go right to the library and take it out. "I've been reading Bower's *Young Jefferson* recently," O'Day wrote, "along with other treatments of early American history, and the Committees of Correspondence in that period were the principal agency by which the revolutionary-minded colonists developed their understanding and coordinated their plans." That's how I came to read *Young Jefferson* while in high school. O'Day wrote, "A couple of weeks ago I bought the twelfth edition of *Bartlett's Quotations,* allegedly for my reference library, actually for the enjoyment I get from browsing," and so I went downtown to the main library, to sit among the reference books browsing in *Bartlett* the way I imagined O'Day did, my journal beside me, skimming each page for the wisdom that would expedite my maturing and make me somebody to reckon with. "I buy the *Cominform* (official organ published in Bucharest) regularly," O'Day wrote, but the *Cominform*—abbreviated name of the Communist Information Bureau—I knew I wouldn't find in any local library, and prudence cautioned me not to go looking.

My radio plays were in dialogue and susceptible less to O'Day's Concrete Suggestions than to conversations Ira had with O'Day that he repeated to me, or, rather, acted out word for word, as though he and O'Day were together there before my eyes. The radio plays were colored, too, by the workingman's argot that continued to crop up in Ira's speech long after he'd come to New York and become a radio actor, and their convictions were strongly influenced by those long letters O'Day was writing to Ira, which Ira often read aloud at my request.

My subject was the lot of the common man, the ordinary Joe—the man that the radio writer Norman Corwin had lauded as "the little guy" in *On a Note of Triumph*, a sixty-minute play that was transmitted over CBS radio the evening the war ended in Europe (and then again, at popular request, eight days later) and that buoyantly entangled me in those salvationist literary aspirations that endeavor to redress the world's wrongs through writing. I wouldn't care to judge today if something I loved as much as I loved *On a Note of Triumph* was or was not art; it provided me with my first sense of the conjuring *power* of art and helped strengthen my first ideas as to what I wanted and expected a literary artist's language to do: enshrine the struggles of the embattled. (And taught me, contrary to what my teachers insisted, that I could begin a sentence with "And.")

The form of the Corwin play was loose, plotless—"experimental," I informed my chiropodist father and homemaking mother. It was written in the high colloquial, alliterative style that may have derived in part from Clifford Odets and in part from Maxwell Anderson, from the effort by American playwrights of the twenties and thirties to forge a recognizable native idiom for the stage, naturalistic yet with lyrical coloration and serious undertones, a poeticized vernacular that, in Norman Corwin's case, combined the rhythms of ordinary speech with a faint literary stiltedness to make for a tone that struck me, at twelve, as democratic in spirit and heroic in scope, the verbal counterpart of a WPA mural. Whitman claimed America for the roughs, Norman Corwin claimed it for the little man—who turned out to be nothing less than the Americans who had fought the patriotic war and were coming back to an adoring nation. The little man was nothing less than Americans themselves! Corwin's "little guy" was American for "proletariat," and, as I now understand it, the revolution fought and won by America's working class was, in fact, World War II, the something large that we were all, however small, a part of, the revolution that confirmed the reality of the myth of a national character to be partaken of by all.

Including me. I was a Jewish child, no two ways about that, but I didn't care to partake of the Jewish character. I didn't even know, clearly, what it was. I didn't much want to. I wanted to partake of the national character. Nothing had seemed to come more naturally to my American-born parents, nothing came more naturally to me, and no method could have seemed to me any more profound than participating through the tongue that Norman Corwin spoke, a linguistic distillation of the excited feelings of community that the war had aroused, the high demotic poetry that was the liturgy of World War II.

History had been scaled down and personalized, America had been scaled down and personalized: for me, that was the enchantment not only of Norman Corwin but of the times. You flood into history and history floods into you. You flood into America and America floods into you. And all by virtue of being alive in New Jersey and twelve years old and sitting by the radio in 1945. Back when popular culture was sufficiently connected to the last century to be susceptible still to a little language, there was a swooning side to all of it for me.

> It can at last be said without jinxing the campaign:
> Somehow the decadent democracies, the bungling bolsheviks, the saps and softies,
> Were tougher in the end than the brownshirt bullyboys, and smarter too:
> For without whipping a priest, burning a book or slugging a Jew, without corraling a girl in a brothel, or bleeding a child for plasma,
> Far-flung ordinary men, unspectacular but free, rousing out of their habits and their homes, got up early one morning, flexed their muscles, learned (as amateurs) the manual of arms, and set out across perilous plains and oceans to whop the bejesus out of the professionals.
> This they did.

> For confirmation, see the last communiqué, bearing
>> the mark of the Allied High Command.
> Clip it out of the morning paper and hand it over to
>> your children for safe keeping.

When *On a Note of Triumph* appeared in book form, I bought a copy immediately (making it the first hardcover I'd ever owned outright rather than borrowed on my library card), and over several weeks I memorized the sixty-five pages of free-verse-like paragraphs in which the text was arranged, relishing particularly the lines that took playful liberties with everyday street-corner English ("There's a hot time in the old town of Dnepropetrovsky tonight") or that joined unlikely proper nouns so as to produce what seemed to me to be surprising and stirring ironies ("the mighty warrior lays down his Samurai sword before a grocery clerk from Baltimore"). At the conclusion of a great war effort that had provided a splendid stimulus for fundamental feelings of patriotism to grow strong in someone my age—almost nine when the war began and halfway to thirteen when it came to a close—the mere citing, on the radio, of American cities and states ("through the nippy night air of New Hampshire," "from Egypt to the Oklahoma prairie town," "And the reasons for mourning in Denmark are the same as they are in Ohio") had every ounce of the intended apotheosizing effect.

> So they've given up.
> They're finally done in, and the rat is dead in an alley
>> back of the Wilhelmstrasse.
> Take a bow, G.I.,
> Take a bow, little guy.
> The superman of tomorrow lies at the feet of you com-
>> mon men of this afternoon.

This was the panegyric with which the play opened. (On the radio there'd been an unflinching voice not unlike Iron Rinn's assertively identifying our hero for the praise due him. It was the determined, compassionately gruff, slightly hectoring halftime voice of the high school coach—the coach who also teaches English—the voice of the common man's collective conscience.) And this was Corwin's coda, a prayer whose grounding in the present made it seem to me—already an affirmed atheist—wholly secular and unchurchy while at the same time mightier and more daring than any prayer I had ever heard recited in school at the beginning of the day or had read, translated in the prayer book at the synagogue, when I was alongside my father at High Holiday services.

> Lord God of trajectory and blast . . .
> Lord God of fresh bread and tranquil mornings . . .
> Lord God of the topcoat and the living wage . . .
> Measure out new liberties . . .
> Post proofs that brotherhood . . .
> Sit at the treaty table and convoy the hopes of little
>   peoples through expected straits . . .

Tens of millions of American families had sat beside their radios and, complex as this stuff was compared to what they were used to hearing, listened to what had aroused in me, and, I innocently assumed, in them, a stream of transforming, self-abandoning emotion such as I, for one, had never before experienced as a consequence of anything coming out of a radio. The power of that broadcast! There, amazingly, was *soul* coming out of a radio. The Spirit of the Common Man had inspired an immense mélange of populist adoration, an effusion of words bubbling straight up from the American heart into the American mouth, an hour-long homage to the paradoxical superiority of what Corwin insisted on identifying as absolutely ordinary American mankind: "far-flung ordinary men, unspectacular but free."

Corwin modernized Tom Paine for me by democratizing the risk, making it a question not of one just wild man but a collective of all the little just men pulling together. Worthiness and the people were one. *Greatness* and the people were one. A thrilling idea. And how Corwin labored to force it, at least imaginatively, to come true.

*

After the war, for the first time, Ira consciously entered the class struggle. He'd been up to his neck in it his entire life, he told me, without any idea what was going on. Out in Chicago, he worked for forty-five dollars a week in a record factory that the United Electrical Workers had organized under a contract so solid they even had union hiring. O'Day meanwhile returned to his job on a rigging gang at Inland Steel in Indiana Harbor. Time and again O'Day dreamed about quitting and, at night in their room, would pour his frustration out to Ira. "If I could have full time for six months and no handcuffs, the party could really be built here in the harbor. There's plenty of good people, but what's needed is a guy who can spend *all* his time at organizing. I ain't that good at organizing, that is true. You have to be something of a hand holder with timid Bolsheviks, and I lean more to bopping their heads. And what's the difference anyway? The party here is too broke to support a full-timer. Every dime that can be scraped up is going for defense of our leadership, and for the press, and a dozen other things that won't wait. I was broke after my last check, but I got by on jawbone for a while. But taxes, the damn car, one thing and another . . . Iron Man, I can't handle it—I *have* to go to work."

I loved when Ira repeated the lingo that rough union guys used among themselves, even guys like Johnny O'Day, whose sentence structure wasn't quite so simple as the average workingman's but who knew the power of their diction and who, despite the potentially corrupting influence of the thesaurus, wielded it effectively all his life. "I have to take it on the slow bell for a while . . . All this with management poising the ax . . . As soon as we pull the pin . . . As soon as the boys hit the bricks . . . If they move to force the acceptance of their yellow-dog contract, it looks like blood on the bricks. . . ."

I loved when Ira explained the workings of his own union, the UE, and described the people at the record factory where he'd worked. "It was a solid union, progressively led, controlled by the rank and file." *Rank and file*—three little words that thrilled me, as did the idea of hard work, tenacious courage, and a just cause to fuse the two. "Of the hundred and fifty members on each shift, a hundred or so attended the biweekly shop meetings. Although most of the work is hourly paid," Ira told me, "there's no whip swinging at that factory. Y'understand? If a boss has something to tell you, he's courteous about it. Even for serious offenses, the offender's called into the office together with his steward. That makes a big difference."

Ira would tell me all that transpired at an ordinary union meeting—"routine business like proposals for a new contract, the problem of absenteeism, a parking-lot beef, discussion of the looming war" (he meant war between the Soviet Union and the United States), "racism, the wages-causes-prices myth"—going on and on not just because I was, at fifteen and sixteen, eager to learn all that a workingman did, how he talked and acted and thought, but because even after he cleared out of Calumet City to go to New York to work in radio and was solidly established as Iron Rinn on *The Free and the Brave,* Ira continued to speak of the record plant and the union meetings in the charismatic tongue of his fellow workers, talked as though he still went off to work there every morning. Every night, rather, for after a short while he had got himself put on the night shift so that he could have his days for "missionary work," by which, I eventually learned, he meant proselytizing for the Communist Party.

O'Day had recruited Ira into the party when they were on the docks in Iran. Just as I, anything but orphaned, was the perfect target for Ira's tutorials, the orphaned Ira was the perfect target for O'Day's.

It was for his union's Washington-Lincoln birthday fund-raiser his first February out in Chicago that somebody got the idea to turn Ira, a wiry man, knobbily jointed, with dark, coarse Indian-like hair and a floppy, big-footed gait, into Abe Lincoln: put whiskers on him, decked him out in a stovepipe hat, high button shoes, and an old-fashioned, ill-fitting black suit, and sent him up to the lectern to read from the Lincoln-Douglas debates one of Lincoln's most telling condemnations of slavery. He got such a big hand for giving to the word "slavery" a strong working-class, political slant—and enjoyed himself so much doing it—that he continued right on with the only thing he remembered by heart from his nine and a half years of schooling, the Gettysburg Address. He brought the house down with the finale, that sentence as gloriously resolute as any sounded in heaven or uttered on earth since the world began. Raising and wiggling one of those huge hairy-knuckled, superflexible hands of his, plunging the longest of his inordinately long fingers right into the eyeball of his union audience each of the three times, he dramatically dropped his voice and rasped "the people."

"Everybody thought I got carried away by emotion," Ira told me. "That that's what fired me up. But it wasn't emotions. It was the first time I ever felt carried away by *intellect*. I understood for the first time in my life what the hell I was talking about. I understood what this country is all about."

After that night, on his weekends, on holidays, he traveled the Chicago area for the CIO, as far as Galesburg and Springfield, out to authentic Lincoln country, portraying Abraham Lincoln for CIO conventions, cultural programs, parades, and picnics. He went on the UE radio show, where, even if nobody could see him standing two inches taller even than Lincoln, he did a bang-up job bringing Lincoln to the masses by speaking every word so that it made good plain sense. People began to take their kids along when Ira Ringold was to appear on the platform, and afterward, when whole families came up to shake his hand, the kids would ask to sit on his knee and tell him what they wanted for Christmas. Not so strangely, the unions he performed for were by and large locals that either broke with the CIO or were expelled when CIO president Philip Murray began in 1947 to rid member unions of Communist leadership and Communist membership.

But by '48 Ira was a rising radio star in New York, newly married to one of the country's most revered radio actresses and, for the moment, safely protected from the crusade that would annihilate forever, and not only from the labor movement, a pro-Soviet, pro-Stalin political presence in America.

How did he get from the record factory to a network drama show? Why did he leave Chicago and O'Day in the first place? It could never have occurred to me at that time that it had anything to do with the Communist Party, mainly because I never knew back then that he was a member of the Communist Party.

What I understood was that the radio writer Arthur Sokolow, visiting Chicago, happened to catch Ira's Lincoln act in a union hall on the West Side one night. Ira had already met Sokolow in the army. He'd come to Iran, as a GI, with the *This Is the Army* show. A lot of left-wing guys were touring with the show, and late one evening Ira had gone off with a few of them for a bull session during which, as Ira remembered it, they'd discussed "all the political stuff in the world." Among the group was Sokolow, whom Ira came quickly to admire as someone who was always battling for a cause. Because Sokolow had begun life, in Detroit, as a Jewish street kid fighting off the Poles, he was also completely recognizable, and Ira felt at once a kinship he'd never wholly had with the rootless Irishman O'Day.

By the time Sokolow, now a civilian writing *The Free and the Brave*, happened to turn up in Chicago, Ira was onstage for a full hour as Lincoln, not only reciting or reading from speeches and documents but responding to audience questions about current political controversies in the guise of Abraham Lincoln, with Lincoln's high-pitched country twang and his awkward giant's gestures and his droll, plainspoken way. Lincoln supporting price controls. Lincoln condemning the Smith Act. Lincoln defending workers' rights. Lincoln vilifying Mississippi's Senator Bilbo. The union membership loved their stalwart autodidact's irresistible ventriloquism, his mishmash of Ringoldisms, O'Dayisms, Marxisms, and Lincolnisms ("Pour it on!" they shouted at bearded, black-haired Ira. "Give 'em hell, Abe!"), and so did Sokolow, who brought Ira to the attention of another Jewish ex-GI, a New York soap opera producer with left-leaning sympathies. It was the introduction to the producer that led to the audition that landed Ira the part of the scrappy super of a Brooklyn tenement on one of daytime radio's soap operas.

The salary was fifty-five dollars a week. Not much, even in 1948, but steady work and more money than he made at the record plant. And, almost immediately, he began doing other jobs as well, getting jobs everywhere, jumping into waiting taxis and rushing from studio to studio, from one daytime show to another, as many as six different shows a day, always playing characters with working-class roots, tough-talking guys truncated from their politics, as he explained it to me, in order to make their anger permissible: "the proletariat Americanized for the radio by cutting off their balls and their brains." It was all this work that propelled him, within months, onto Sokolow's prestigious weekly hour-long show, *The Free and the Brave*, as a leading player.

Out in the Midwest, there had begun to be physical difficulties for Ira to cope with, and these, too, furnished a motive for him to try his luck back east in a new line of work. He was plagued by muscle pain, soreness so bad that several times a week—when he didn't have to just endure the pain and go off to play Lincoln or do his missionary work—he'd head right home, soak for half an hour in a tub of steaming water down the hall from his room, and then get into bed with a book, his dictionary, his notepad, and whatever was around to eat. A couple of bad beatings he'd taken in the army seemed to him the cause of this problem. From the worst of the beatings—he'd been pounced on by a gang from the port who had him down for a "nigger lover"—he'd wound up in the hospital for three days.

They'd begun baiting him when he started to pal around with a couple of Negro soldiers from the segregated unit stationed at the riverfront three miles away. O'Day was by then running a group that met at the Quonset hut library and under his tutelage discussed politics and books. Barely anybody on the base paid attention to the library or to the nine or ten GIs who drifted over there after chow a couple of nights a week to talk about *Looking Back-*

ward by Bellamy or *The Republic* by Plato or *The Prince* by Machiavelli, until the two Negroes from the segregated unit joined the group.

At first Ira tried to reason with the men in his outfit who called him nigger lover. "Why do you make derogatory remarks about colored people? All I hear from you guys about the Negro is derogatory remarks. And you aren't only anti-Negro. You're anti-labor, you're anti-liberal, and you're anti-brains. You're anti every goddamn thing that's in your interest. How can people give their three or four years to the army, see friends die, get wounded, have their lives disrupted, and yet not know why it happened and what it's all about? All you know is that Hitler started something. All you know is that the draft board got you. You know what I say? You guys would duplicate the very actions of the Germans if you were in their place. It might take a little longer because of the democratic element in our society, but eventually we would be completely fascist, dictator and all, because of people spouting the shit you guys spout. The discrimination of the top officers who run this port is bad enough, but *you* people, from poor families, guys without two nickels to rub together, guys who are nothing but fodder for the assembly line, for the sweatshop, for the coal mines, who the system *pisses* on—low wages, high prices, astronomical profits—and you turn out to be a bunch of vociferous, bigoted Red-baiting bastards who don't know . . ." Then he'd tell them all they didn't know.

Heated discussions that changed nothing, that, because of his temper, Ira admitted, made things only worse. "I would lose a good deal of what I wanted to impress them with because in the beginning I was too emotional. Later I learned how to cool down with these kind of people, and I believe that I impressed a few of them with some facts. But it is very difficult to talk to such men because of the deeply ingrained ideas they have. To explain to them the psychological reasons for segregation, the economic reasons for segregation, the psychological reasons for the use of their beloved word 'nigger'—they are beyond grasping such things. They say nigger because a nigger *is* a nigger—I'd explain and explain to them, and that's what they'd answer me. I pounded home about education of children and our personal responsibility, and still, for all my goddamn explaining, they beat the shit out of me so bad I thought I was going to die."

His reputation as a nigger lover turned truly dangerous for Ira when he wrote a letter to *Stars and Stripes* complaining about the segregated units in the army and demanding integration. "That's when I used my dictionary and *Roget's Thesaurus.* I would devour those two books and try to put 'em to practical use by writing. Writing a letter for me was like building a scaffold. Probably I would have been criticized by somebody who knew the English language. My grammar was God knows what. But I wrote it anyway because this is what I felt I should do. I was so goddamn angry, see? Y'understand? I wanted to tell people that this was *wrong.*"

After the letter was published, he was working one day up in the loading basket, above the hold of the ship, when the guys operating the basket threatened to drop him into the hold unless he shut up worrying about niggers. Repeatedly they dropped him ten, fifteen, twenty feet, promising next time to let go and break every bone in his body, but, scared as he was, he wouldn't say what they wanted to hear, and in the end they let him out. Then the following morning someone in the mess hall called him a Jew bastard. A nigger-loving Jew bastard. "A southern hillbilly with a big mouth," Ira told me. "Always made remarks in the mess hall about Jews, about Negroes. This one morning I'm sitting there near the end of the meal—there weren't that many guys left in the place—and he started to yap off about niggers and Jews. I'm still boiling from the incident the day before on the ship, and so I couldn't take it anymore, and I took off my glasses and I gave 'em to a guy I was sitting with, the only guy who'd still sit with me. By then I'd walk in the mess hall, two hundred guys sitting there, and because of my politics I'd be totally ostracized. Anyway, I went at that son of a bitch. He was a private and I was a sergeant. From one end of that mess hall to the other I kicked the shit out of him. Then the first sergeant comes up to me and says, 'You want to press charges against this guy? A private attacking a noncommissioned officer?' I quickly said to myself, I'll probably be damned if I do and damned if I don't. Right? But from that moment on, nobody ever made an anti-Semitic remark when I was in the vicinity. That didn't mean they'd ever let up about niggers. Niggers this and niggers that, a hundred times a day. This hillbilly tried again with me that same night. We were washing off our mess kits. You know the stinking little knives they have there? He came at me with that knife. Again I had him, I put him away, but I didn't do anything more about it."

Hours later Ira got ambushed in the dark and wound up in the hospital. As best he could diagnose the pains that began to develop while he was working at the record factory, they were from the damage caused by that savage beating. Now he was always pulling a muscle or spraining a joint—his ankle, his wrist, his knee, his neck—and as often as not from doing virtually nothing, no more than stepping off the bus coming home or reaching across the counter for the sugar bowl in the diner where he went to eat.

And this is why, however unlikely it seemed that anything would materialize from it, when something was said about a radio audition, Ira leaped at the chance.

Maybe there were more machinations than I knew of behind Ira's move to New York and his overnight radio triumph, but I didn't think so back then. I didn't have to. Here was the guy to take my education beyond Norman Corwin, to tell me, for one thing, about the GIs that Corwin didn't talk about, GIs not so nice or, for that matter, so antifascist as the heroes of *On a Note of Triumph*, the GIs who went overseas thinking about niggers and kikes and who came home thinking about niggers and kikes. Here was an impassioned man, someone rough and scarred by experience, bringing with him firsthand evidence of all the brutish American stuff that Corwin left out. It didn't require Communist connections to explain Ira's overnight radio triumph to me. I just thought, This guy is wonderful. He *is* an iron man.

2

THAT NIGHT in '48 at the Henry Wallace rally in Newark, I'd also met Eve Frame. She was with Ira and with her daughter, Sylphid, the harpist. I saw nothing of what Sylphid felt for her mother, didn't know about their struggle until Murray began to tell me of all that had passed me by as a kid, everything about Ira's marriage that I didn't or couldn't understand or that Ira had kept from me during those two years when I got to see him every couple of months, either when he came to visit Murray or when I visited him at the cabin—which Ira called his "shack"—in the hamlet of Zinc Town, in northwest New Jersey.

Ira retreated to Zinc Town to live not so much close to nature as close to the bone, to live life in the raw, swimming in the mud pond right into November, tramping the woods on snowshoes in coldest winter, or, on rainy days, meandering around in his Jersey car—a used '39 Chevy coupe—talking to the local dairy farmers and the old zinc miners, whom he tried to get to understand how they were being screwed by the system. He had a fireplace out there where he liked to cook his hot dogs and beans over the coals, even to brew his coffee, all so as to remind himself, after he'd become Iron Rinn and a bit enlarded with money and fame, that he was still nothing more than a "working stiff," a simple man with simple tastes and expectations who during the thirties had ridden the rails and who had got incredibly lucky. About owning the Zinc Town shack, he used to say, "Keeps me in practice being poor. Just in case."

The shack furnished an antidote to West Eleventh Street and an asylum from West Eleventh Street, the place where you go to sweat out the bad vapors. It was also a link to the earliest vagabond days, when he was surviving among strangers for the first time and every day was hard and uncertain and, as it would always be for Ira, a battle. After leaving home at fifteen and digging ditches for a year in Newark, Ira had taken jobs in the northwesternmost corner of Jersey, sweeping up in various factories, working sometimes as a farmhand, as a watchman, as a handyman, and then, for two and a half years, until he was nearly nineteen and headed west, sucking air in shafts twelve hundred feet down in the Sussex zinc mines. After the blasting, with the place still smoky and reeking sickeningly of dynamite powder and gas, Ira worked with a pick and a shovel alongside the Mexicans as the lowest of the low, as what they called a mucker.

In those years, the Sussex mines were unorganized and as profitable for the New Jersey Zinc Company, and as unpleasant for New Jersey Zinc's workers, as zinc mines anywhere in the world. The ore got smelted into metallic zinc down on Passaic Avenue in Newark and also processed into zinc oxide for paint, and though by the time Ira bought his shack in the late forties Jersey zinc was losing ground to foreign competition and the mines were already headed for extinction, it was still that first big immersion in brute life— eight hours underground loading the shattered rock and ore into rail cars, eight hours of enduring the awful headaches and swallowing the red and brown dust and shitting in the pails of sawdust . . . and all for forty-two cents an hour—that lured him back to the remote Sussex hills. The Zinc Town shack was the radio actor's openly sentimental expression of solidarity with the dispensable, coarse nobody he'd once been—as he described himself, "a brainless human tool if ever there was one." Another person, having achieved success, might have wanted to abolish those gruesome memories for good, but without the history of his unimportance made somehow tangible, Ira would have felt himself unreal and badly deprived.

I hadn't even known that when he came over to Newark—when, after I got out of my last class, we took our hikes through Weequahic Park, circling the lake and ending up at our neighborhood's dining simulacrum to Coney Island's Nathan's, a place called Millman's, for a hot dog with "the works"—he wasn't visiting Lehigh Avenue solely to see his brother. On those after-school afternoons, when Ira told me about his years as a soldier and what he'd learned in Iran, about O'Day and what O'Day taught him, about his own recent former life as a factory worker and a union man, and his experiences as a kid shoveling muck in the mines, he was seeking refuge from a household where, from the day he arrived, he'd found himself unwelcome and unwanted by Sylphid and more and more at odds with Eve Frame because of her unforeseen contempt for Jews.

Not all Jews, Murray explained—not the accomplished Jews at the top whom she'd met in Hollywood and on Broadway and in the radio business, not, by and large, the directors and the actors and the writers and the musicians she'd worked with, many of whom were regularly to be seen at the salon she'd made of her West Eleventh Street house. Her contempt was for the garden-variety, the standard-issue Jew she saw shopping in the department stores, for run-of-the-mill people with New York accents who worked behind counters or who tended their own little shops in Manhattan, for the Jews who drove taxis, for the Jewish families she saw talking and walking together in Central Park. What drove her to distraction on the streets were the Jewish ladies who loved her, who recognized her, who came up to her and asked for her autograph. These women were her old Broadway audience, and she despised them. Elderly Jewish women particularly she could not pass without a groan of disgust. "Look at those faces!" she'd say with a shudder. "Look at those hideous faces!"

"It was a sickness," Murray said, "that aversion she had for the Jew who was insufficiently disguised. She could go along parallel to life for a long time. Not *in* life—parallel to life. She could be quite convincing in that ultracivilized, ladylike role she'd chosen. The soft voice. The precise locution. Back in the twenties, English Genteel was a style that a lot of American girls worked up for themselves when they wanted to become actresses. And with Eve Frame, who was herself starting out in Hollywood then, it took, it hardened. English Genteel hardened into a form like layers of wax—only burning right in the middle was the wick, this flaming wick that wasn't very genteel at all. She knew all the moves, the benign smile, the dramatic reserve, all the delicate gestures. But then she'd veer off that parallel course of hers, the thing that looked so much like life, and there'd be an episode that could leave you spinning."

"And I never saw any of this," I said. "She was always kind and considerate to me, sympathetic, trying to make me feel comfortable—which wasn't easy. I was an excitable kid and she had a lot of the movie star clinging to her, even in those radio days."

I was thinking again, as I spoke, of that night at the Mosque. She'd said to me—who was finding it impossible to know what to say to her—that she didn't know what to say to Paul Robeson, that in his presence she was tongue-tied. "Are you as in awe of him as I am?" she whispered, as though *both* of us were fifteen years old. "He is the most beautiful man I have ever seen. It's shameful—I cannot stop looking at him."

I knew how she felt because I hadn't been able to stop looking at *her,* looking as though if I looked long enough, a *meaning* might emerge. Looking not only because of the delicacy of her gestures and the dignity of her bearing and the indeterminate elegance of *her* beauty—a beauty hovering between the darkly exotic and the softly demure and shifting continuously in its proportions, a type of beauty that must have been spellbinding at its height—but because of something visibly aquiver in her despite all the restraint, a volatility that at the time I associated with the sheer exaltation that must come of being Eve Frame.

"Do you remember the day I met Ira?" I asked him. "You two were working together, taking the screens down on Lehigh Avenue. What was he doing at your place? It was in October '48, a few weeks before the election."

"Oh, that was a bad day. That day I remember very well. He was in a bad way, and he came to Newark that morning to stay with Doris and me. He slept on the couch for two nights. It was the first time that happened. Nathan, that marriage was a mismatch from the start. He'd already pulled something like it before, except at the other end of the social spectrum. You couldn't miss it. The enormous difference in temperament and interests. Anybody could see it."

"Ira couldn't?"

"See? Ira? Well, to be generous about it, for one thing, he was in love with her. They met and he fell for her, and the first thing he did, he went out and bought her a fancy Easter parade hat that she would never have worn because her taste in clothes was all Dior. But he didn't know what Dior was, and he bought her this big ridiculous expensive hat and had it delivered to her house after their first date. Lovestruck and starstruck. He was dazzled by her. She *was* dazzling—and dazzlement has a logic all its own.

"What did she see in him, the big rube who hits New York and lands a job in a soap opera? Well, it's not a great riddle. After a short apprenticeship, he is not a simple rube, he is a star on *The Free and the Brave,* so there's that. Ira took on those heroes that he played. *I* never bought it, but the average listener believed in him as their embodiment. He had an aura of heroic purity. He believed in himself, and so he steps into the room, and bingo. He shows up at some party, and there she is. There is this lonely actress in her forties, three times divorced, and there's this new face, this new guy, this *tree,* and she's needy, and she's famous, and she surrenders to him. Isn't that what happens? Every woman has her temptations, and surrendering is Eve's. Outwardly, a pure, gangling giant with huge hands who'd been a factory worker, who'd been a stevedore, who was now an actor. Pretty appealing, those guys. It's hard to believe something that raw can be tender too. Tender rawness, the goodness of a big rough guy—all that stuff. Irresistible to her. How could a giant be anything *else* to her? There's something exotic to her about the amount of harsh life he's exposed himself to. She felt that he'd really lived and, after he heard her story, he felt that *she'd* really lived.

"When they meet, Sylphid's away in France for the summer with her father, and Ira doesn't get to see that stuff firsthand. And so these strong, if *sui generis,* maternal urges of hers Ira gets instead, and they have this idyll together all summer long. The guy never had a mother after the age of seven, and he's starved for the attentive, refined care that she lavishes on him, and they're living alone in the house, without the daughter, and ever since he came to New York he's been living, like a good member of the proletariat, in some dump on the Lower East Side. He hangs out in cheap places and eats in cheap restaurants, and suddenly these two are isolated together on West Eleventh Street, and it's summer in Manhattan and it's great, it's life as paradise. Sylphid's picture is all around the house, Sylphid as a little girl in her pinafore, and he finds it wonderful that Eve's so devoted. She tells the story of her horrible experiences with marriage and men, she tells him about Hollywood and the tyrannical directors and the philistine producers, the terrible, terrible tawdriness, and it's Othello in reverse: ' 'twas strange, 'twas passing strange; 'twas pitiful, 'twas wondrous pitiful'—he loved her for the dangers *she* had passed. Ira's mystified, enchanted, and he's *needed.* He's big and he's physical, and so he rushes in. A woman with pathos. A beautiful woman with pathos and a story to tell. A spiritual woman with décolletage. Who better to activate his protective mechanism?

"He even takes her to Newark to meet us. We have a drink at our house, and then we all go down to Elizabeth Avenue to the Tavern, and she behaves well. Nothing inexplicable. It seemed so surprisingly easy to know what to make of her. That evening he first brought Eve to our place and we went out for dinner, I didn't see anything wrong myself. It's only fair to say that it's not Ira alone who couldn't figure this out. He doesn't know who she is because, to be honest, *nobody* would have right off. Nobody could have. In society, Eve was invisible behind the disguise of all that civility. And so, though others might proceed slowly, because of his nature, Ira, as I said, rushes right in.

"What registered on me right off weren't her inadequacies but his. She struck me as too smart for him, too polished for him, certainly too cultivated. I thought, Here is a movie star with a mind. Turned out she'd been reading conscientiously since she was a kid. I don't think there was a novel on my shelves that she couldn't talk about with familiarity. It even sounded that night as though her inmost pleasure in life were reading books. She remembered the complicated plots of nineteenth-century novels—I would teach the books and I still couldn't remember them.

"Sure, she was showing her best side. Sure, like everyone else on first meeting, like all of us, she was keeping a prudent watch over her worst side. But a best side was there, she *had* one. It looked real and it was unostentatious, and in someone so renowned, that made it very winning. Sure, I saw—I couldn't help but see—that this was by no means a necessary union of souls. The two of them were more than likely without any affinity at all. But I was dazzled myself that first night by what I took to be her quiet substance on top of the looks.

"Don't forget the effect of fame. Doris and I had grown up on those silent films of hers. She was always cast with older men, tall men, often white-haired men, and she was a girlish, daughterly-looking thing—*granddaughterly*-looking thing—and the men were always wanting to kiss her and she was always saying no. Took no more than that in those days to heat things up in a movie house. A movie of hers, maybe her first, was called *Cigarette Girl.* Eve's the cigarette girl, working in a nightclub, and at the end of the movie, as I remember, there's a charity event to which she's taken by the nightclub's owner. It's held at the Fifth Avenue mansion of a rich, stuffy dowager, and the cigarette girl is dressed up in a nurse's uniform and the men are asked to bid to kiss her—money that will go to the Red Cross. Each time one man tops another's bid, Eve covers her mouth and giggles behind her hand like a geisha. The bidding goes higher and higher, and the stout society ladies looking on are aghast. But when a distinguished banker with a black mustache—Carlton Pennington—bids the astronomical sum of one thousand dollars and steps up to plant the kiss we've all been waiting to see, the ladies surge madly forward to watch. At the finale, instead of the kiss at the heart of the screen, there are their big corseted society behinds obscuring everything.

"Quite something that was in 1924. Quite something *Eve* was. The radiant smile, the hopeless shrug, the acting they did in those days with their eyes—she'd mastered it all as just a kid. She could do defeated, she could display temper, she could do crying with her hand to her forehead; she could do the funny pratfalls too. When Eve Frame was happy, she would do a run with a little skip in it. Skipping with happiness. Very charming. She played either the poor cigarette girl or the poor laundress who meets the swell, or she played the spoiled rich girl who is swept off her feet by the trolley conductor. Movies about crossing class barriers. Street scenes of the immigrant poor with all their crude energy and then dinner scenes of the privileged American rich with all their strictures and taboos. Baby Dreiser. You couldn't watch those things today. You could barely watch them then, if not for her.

"Doris and Eve and I were the same age. She'd started out in Hollywood when she was seventeen, and then, still back before the war, she was on Broadway. Doris and I had seen her from up in the balcony in some of those plays, and she was good, you know. The plays weren't so wonderful, but as a stage actress she had a direct way about her, unlike what had made her popular as the girlish silent-film star. On the stage she had a talent for making things that weren't very intelligent seem intelligent, and things that weren't serious seem somewhat serious. Strange, her perfect equilibrium on the stage. As a human being she wound up exaggerating everything, and yet as a stage actress she was all moderation and tact, nothing exaggerated. And then, after the war, we'd hear her on the radio because Lorraine liked to listen, and even on those *American Radio Theater* shows, she brought an air of tastefulness to some pretty awful stuff. To have her in our living room looking through my bookshelves, to talk to her about Meredith and Dickens and Thackeray—well, what is a woman with her experience and her interests doing with my brother?

"That night I never figured on their getting married. Though his vanity was clearly flattered and he was excited and proud as hell of her over lobster thermidor at the Tavern. The toniest restaurant Jews ate at in Newark, and there, escorting Eve Frame, the epitome of theatrical class, is the onetime roughneck from Newark's Factory Street, and not an ounce of uncertainty in him. Did you know that Ira was once a busboy at the Tavern? One of his menial jobs after he quit school. Lasted about a month. Too big to be rushing with those loaded trays through the kitchen door. They fired him after he broke his thousandth dish, and that's when he headed up to Sussex County to the zinc mines. So—nearly twenty years pass and he's back at the Tavern, a radio star himself and showing off that night for his brother and sister-in-law. The master of life exulting in his own existence.

"The owner of the Tavern, Teiger, Sam Teiger, spots Eve and comes over to the table with a bottle of champagne, and Ira invites him to have a drink with us and regales him with the story of his thirty days as a Tavern busboy in 1929, and, now that his life hasn't come to nothing, everybody enjoys the comedy of his mishaps and the irony that Ira should ever have got back here. We all enjoy his sporting spirit about his old wounds. Teiger goes to his office and returns with a camera and he takes a picture of the four of us eating our dinner, and afterward it hangs in the Tavern foyer, along with the photographs of all the other notables who've ever dined there. No reason that picture wouldn't have hung there till the Tavern closed for business after the '67 riots had Ira not been blacklisted sixteen years earlier. I understand they took it down then overnight, as though his life *had* come to nothing.

"To go back to when their idyll first began—he heads home at night to this room he rented, but gradually enough he doesn't, and then he's at her place, and they're not kids, and the woman hasn't been up to much lately, and it's passionate and wonderful, locked up alone in that West Eleventh Street house like a pair of sex criminals tethered to the bed. All the spontaneous intrigue of that at the onset of middle age. Letting go and falling into the affair. It's Eve's release, her liberation, her emancipation. Her *salvation*. Ira's given her a new script, if she wants it. At forty-one, she thought it was all over and instead she's been saved. 'Well,' she says to him, 'so much for the patiently nurtured desire to keep things in perspective.'

"She says things to him nobody's ever said to him before. She calls their affair 'our exceedingly, achingly sweet and strange thing.' She tells him, 'It keeps dissolving me.' She tells him, 'In the middle of a conversation with someone, I'm suddenly not there.' She calls him '*mon prince*.' She quotes Emily Dickinson. For Ira Ringold, Emily Dickinson. 'With thee, in the Desert / With thee in the thirst / With thee in the Tamarind wood / Leopard breathes—at last!'

"Well, it feels to Ira like the love of his life. And with the love of your life you don't think about the particulars. If you find such a thing, you don't throw it away. They decide to get married, and that's what Eve tells Sylphid when she gets back from France. Mommy's getting married again but this time to a wonderful man. Sylphid's supposed to buy that. Sylphid, from the *old* script.

"Eve Frame was the big world to Ira. And why shouldn't she have been? He was no baby, he'd been in a lot of rough places and knew how to be rough himself. But Broadway? Hollywood? Greenwich Village? All brand-new to him. Ira wasn't the brightest guy around when it came to personal affairs. He'd taught himself a lot. He and O'Day had brought him a long, long way from Factory Street. But that was all political stuff. And that was not sharp thinking either. It wasn't 'thinking' at all. The pseudoscientific Marxist lexicon, the utopian cant that went with it—dish that stuff out to someone as unschooled and ill educated as Ira, indoctrinate an adult who is not too skilled in brainwork with the intellectual glamour of Big Sweeping Ideas, inculcate a man of limited intelligence, an excitable type who is as angry as Ira . . . But that's a subject all its own, the connection between embitterment and not thinking.

"You're asking me about how he wound up in Newark that day you two met. Ira wasn't prone to going at life in ways that were conducive to solving the problems of a marriage. And it was early days, it was only a matter of months since the wedding to the star of stage, screen, and radio and his moving into that townhouse of hers. How could I tell him it was a mistake? The guy wasn't without vanity, after all. He was not without conceit, my brother. Wasn't without *scale* either. There was a theatrical instinct in Ira, an immodest attitude toward himself. Don't think he minded becoming someone of enhanced importance. That's an adaptation people seem able to implement in about seventy-two hours, and generally the effect is invigorating. Everything all at once filled with possibility, everything in motion, everything *imminent*—Ira in the drama in every sense of the word. He has pulled off a great big act of control over the story that was his life. He is all at once awash in the narcissistic illusion that he has been sprung from the realities of pain and loss, that his life is *not* futility—that it's anything *but*. No longer walking in the valley of the shadow of his limitations. No longer the excluded giant consigned to be the strange one forever. Barges in with that brash courage—and there he is. Out of the grips of obscurity. And proud of his transformation. The exhilaration of it. The naive dream—he's in it! The new Ira, the worldly Ira. A big guy with a big life. Watch out.

"Besides, I already *had* told him it was a mistake—and after that we didn't talk for six weeks, and then only because I went to New York and explained to him I was wrong and begged him not to hold it against me did I get the guy back. He would have shot me down for good if I'd tried it a second time. And a complete falling-out—

that would have been awful for both of us. I'd been taking care of Ira since he was born. I was seven years old, I used to push him down Factory Street in his baby carriage. After our mother died, when my father remarried and a stepmother came into the house, if I hadn't been around, Ira would have wound up in reform school. We had a wonderful mother. And she didn't have such a good time of it, either. She was married to our father. That was no picnic."

"What was your father like?" I asked.

"We don't want to go into that."

"That's what Ira used to say."

"That's the only thing there is to say. We had a father who . . . well, much later in life I learned what made him tick. But by then it was too late. Anyway, I was luckier than my brother. When our mother died, after those awful months in the hospital, I was already in high school. Then I got a scholarship to the University of Newark. I was on my way. But Ira was still a kid. A tough kid. A crude kid. Full of mistrust.

"Do you know about the canary funeral in the old First Ward, when one of the local shoemakers buried his pet canary? This'll show you how tough Ira was—and how tough he wasn't. It was in 1920. I was thirteen and Ira was seven, and on Boyden Street, a couple streets away from our tenement, there was a cobbler, Russomanno, Emidio Russomanno, a poor-looking old guy, small, with big ears and a gaunt face and a white chin beard and, on his back, a threadbare suit a hundred years old. For company in his shop Russomanno kept a pet canary. The canary was named Jimmy and Jimmy lived a long time and then Jimmy ate something he shouldn't have and died.

"Russomanno was devastated, so he hired a parade band, rented a hearse and two coaches drawn by horses, and after the canary was laid out for viewing on a bench in the cobbler shop—beautifully exhibited with flowers, candles, and a crucifix—there was a funeral procession through the streets of the whole district, past Del Guercio's grocery store, where they had clams outside in bushel baskets and an American flag in the window, past Melillo's fruit and vegetable stand, past Giordano's bakery, past Mascellino's bakery, past Arre's Italian Tasty Crust Bakery. It went past Biondi's butcher shop and De Lucca's harness shop and De Carlo's garage and D'Innocenzio's coffee store and Parisi's shoe store and Nole's bicycle shop and Celentano's *latteria* and Grande's pool hall and Basso's barbershop and Esposito's barbershop and the bootblack stand with the two scarred old dining chairs that the customers had to step up high, onto a platform, to get to.

"Gone now for forty years. City knocked down that whole Italian neighborhood in '53 to make way for low-rent high-rise housing. In '94, they blew the high-rises up on national TV. By then nobody'd been living in them for about twenty years. Uninhabitable. Now there's nothing there at all. St. Lucy's and that's it. That's all that's standing. The parish church, but no parish and no parishioners.

"Nicodemi's Café on Seventh Avenue and Café Roma on Seventh Avenue and D'Auria's bank on Seventh Avenue. That was the bank where, before the second war broke out, they extended credit to Mussolini. When Mussolini took Ethiopia, the priest rang the church bells for half an hour. Here in America, in Newark's First Ward.

"The macaroni factory and the decoration factory and the monument shop and the marionette playhouse and the movie theater and the bocce alleys and the icehouse and the print shop and the clubhouses and the restaurants. Past the mobster Ritchie Boiardo's hangout, the Victory Café. In the thirties, when Boiardo got out of jail, he built the Vittorio Castle on the corner of Eighth and Summer. Show-business people used to travel from New York to dine at the Castle. The Castle is where Joe DiMaggio ate when he came to Newark. The Castle is where DiMaggio and his girlfriend held their engagement party. It's from the Castle that Boiardo lorded it over the First Ward. Ritchie Boiardo ruled the Italians in the First Ward and Longy Zwillman ruled the Jews in the Third Ward, and these two gangsters were always at war.

"Past the dozens of neighborhood saloons the procession wound from east to west, north up one street and south down the next, all the way to the Clifton Avenue Municipal Bathhouse—the First Ward's most extravagant lump of architecture after the church and the cathedral, the massive old public bathhouse where my mother used to take us for our baths as babies. My father went there too. Shower free and a penny for the towel.

"The canary was placed in a small white coffin with four pallbearers to carry it. A huge crowd assembled, maybe as many as ten thousand people stretched out along the procession route. People were squeezed together on the fire escapes and up on the roofs. Whole families were hanging out of their tenement windows to watch.

"Russomanno rode in the carriage behind the coffin, Emidio Russomanno weeping while everybody else in the First Ward was laughing. Some people were laughing so hard they wound up hurling themselves to the ground. They couldn't stand up from laughing so hard. Even the pallbearers were laughing. It was infectious. The guy driving the hearse was laughing. Out of respect for the mourner, people on the sidewalk tried to hold it in until Russomanno's carriage had passed by, but it was just too hilarious for most of them, particularly for the kids.

"Ours was a tiny neighborhood swarming with kids: kids in the alleys, kids crowding the stoops, kids pouring out of the tenements and stampeding from Clifton Avenue down to Broad Street. All day long and, during the summertime, through half the night you could hear these kids shouting to one another, 'Guahl-yo! Guahl-yo!' Everywhere you looked, bands of kids, battalions of kids—pitching pennies, playing cards, rolling dice, shooting pool, licking ices, playing ball, making bonfires, frightening girls. Only the nuns with rulers could control these kids. Thousands and thousands of boys there were, all under ten years old. Ira was one of them. Thousands and thousands of scrappy little Italian kids, the children of the Italians who laid the railroad tracks and paved the streets and dug the sewers, the children of peddlers and factory workers and rag pickers and saloon keepers. Kids called Giuseppe and Rodolfo and Raffaele and Gaetano, and the one Jewish kid called Ira.

"Well, the Italians were having the time of their lives. They'd never seen anything like that canary's funeral. They never saw anything like it again. Sure, there were funeral processions before that, and there were bands playing funeral dirges and mourners surging through the streets. There were the feast days all year round with processions for all those saints they brought over with them from Italy, hundreds and hundreds of people venerating their society's special saint by dressing up and bearing the saint's embroidered flag and carrying candles the size of tire irons. And there was St. Lucy's *presepio* for Christmas, a replica of a Neapolitan village depicting the birth of Jesus, a hundred Italian figurines planted in it along with Mary, Joseph, and the Bambino. There were the Italian bagpipes parading with a plaster Bambino and, behind the Bambino, the people in the procession singing Italian Christmas carols. And the vendors out along the streets selling eel for Christmas Eve dinner. People turned out in droves for the religious stuff, and they stuck dollar bills all over the robe of the plaster statue of whatever saint it was and threw flower petals out their windows like ticker tape. They even released birds from cages, doves that flew crazily above the crowd from one telephone pole to the next. On a saint's day the doves must have been wishing they'd never seen the outside of a birdcage.

"On the feast of Saint Michael, the Italians would dress up a couple of little girls as angels. From the fire escapes on either side of the street, they'd swing them over the crowd from ropes the girls were harnessed to. Little skinny girls in white gowns with haloes and wings attached, and the crowd would go silent with awe when they appeared in the air, chanting some prayer, and when the girls had finished being angels, the crowd went nuts. That's when they would set the doves free and that's when the fireworks would explode and somebody would wind up in the hospital with a couple of fingers blown off.

"So, lively spectacle was nothing new to the Italians in the First

Ward. Funny characters, old-country carrying on, noise and fights, colorful stunts—nothing new. Funerals certainly weren't new. During the flu epidemic, so many people died that the coffins had to be lined up on the street. Nineteen eighteen. The funeral parlors couldn't handle the business. Behind the coffins, processions from St. Lucy's wended the couple miles to Holy Sepulcher Cemetery all day long. There were tiny coffins for the babies. You had to wait your turn to bury your baby—you had to wait for your neighbors to bury theirs first. Unforgettable terror for a kid. And yet two years after the flu epidemic, that funeral for Jimmy the canary . . . well, that topped 'em all.

"Everybody there that day was in stitches. Except for one person. Ira was the only one in Newark who wasn't in on the joke. I couldn't explain it to him. I tried, but he couldn't understand. Why? Maybe because he was stupid, or maybe because he wasn't stupid. Maybe he simply was not born with the mentality of the carnival— maybe utopianists aren't. Or maybe it was because our mother had died a few months earlier and we'd had our own funeral that Ira had wanted no part of. He wanted to be out on the street instead, kicking a ball around. He begged me not to make him change out of his overalls and go to the cemetery. He tried hiding in a closet. But he came along with us anyway. My father saw to that. At the cemetery he stood there watching us bury her, but he refused to take my hand or let me put my arm around him. He just scowled at the rabbi. Glowered at him. Refused to be touched or comforted by anyone. Didn't cry either, not a tear. He was too angry for tears.

"But when the canary died, everybody at the funeral was laughing away except Ira. Ira knew Jimmy only from walking by the cobbler's shop on the way to school and looking in the window at his cage. I don't believe he'd ever stepped inside the shop, and yet, aside from Russomanno, he was the only one around who was in tears.

"When *I* started to laugh—because it *was* funny, Nathan, *very* funny—Ira lost control completely. That was the first time I saw that happen to Ira. He started swinging his fists and screaming at me. He was a big kid even then, and I couldn't rein him in, and suddenly he was swinging at a couple of kids next to us who were also laughing themselves sick, and when I reached down to try to pluck him up and save him from being slaughtered by a whole slew of kids, one of his fists caught me on the nose. He broke my nose at the bridge, a seven-year-old. I was bleeding, the damn thing was obviously broken, and so Ira ran away.

"We didn't find him till the next day. He'd slept back of the brewery on Clifton Avenue. It wasn't the first time. In the yard, under the loading dock. My father found him there in the morning. He dragged him by the scruff of the neck all the way to school and into the room where Ira's class was already in session. When the kids saw Ira, wearing those filthy overalls he'd slept in all night and being flung into the room by his old man, they began to go 'Boo-hoo,' and that was Ira's nickname for months afterward. Boo-hoo Ringold. The Jewboy who cried at the canary funeral.

"Luckily, Ira was always bigger than the others his age, and he was strong, and he could play ball. Ira would have been a star athlete if it hadn't been for his eyes. What respect he got in that neighborhood he got from playing ball. But the fights? From then on he was in fights all the time. That's when his extremism began.

"It was a blessing, you know, that we didn't grow up in the Third Ward with the poor Jews. Growing up in the First Ward, Ira was always a loudmouth kike outsider to the Italians, and so, however big and strong and belligerent he was, Boiardo could never perceive him as local talent auditioning for the Mob. But in the Third Ward, among the Jews, it might have been different. There Ira wouldn't have been the official outcast among the kids. If only because of his size, he would probably have come to Longy Zwillman's attention. From what I understand, Longy, who was ten years older than Ira, was a lot like Ira growing up: furious, a big, menacing boy who also quit school, who was fearless in a street fight, and who had the commanding looks along with something of a brain. In bootleg-ging, in gambling, in vending machines, on the docks, in the labor movement, in the building trades—Longy eventually made it big. But even at the top, when he was teamed up with Bugsy Siegel and

Lansky and Lucky Luciano, his closest intimates were the friends he'd grown up with in the streets, Third Ward Jewish boys like himself, whom it took little to provoke. Niggy Rutkin, his hit man. Sam Katz, his bodyguard. George Goldstein, his accountant. Billy Tiplitz, his numbers man. Doc Stacher, his adding machine. Abe Lew, Longy's cousin, ran the retail clerks' union for Longy. Christ, Meyer Ellenstein, another street kid from the Third Ward ghetto— when he was mayor of Newark, Ellenstein all but ran the city for Longy.

"Ira could have wound up one of Longy's henchmen, loyally doing one of their jobs. He was ripe for recruitment. There would have been nothing aberrant in it: crime was what those boys were bred for. It was the next logical step. Had that violence in them that you need as a business tactic in the rackets to inspire fear and gain the competitive edge. Ira could have started off down at Port Newark, unloading the bootleg whiskey from Canada out of the speedboats and into Longy's trucks, and he could have ended up, like Longy, with a millionaire's mansion in West Orange and a rope around his neck.

"It's so fickle, isn't it, who you wind up, how you wind up? It's only because of a tiny accident of geography that the opportunity to string along with Longy never came Ira's way. The opportunity to launch a successful career by using a blackjack on Longy's competitors, by putting the squeeze on Longy's customers, by supervising the gaming tables at Longy's casinos. The opportunity to conclude it by testifying for two hours in front of the Kefauver committee before going home to hang himself. When Ira met someone tougher and smarter than him who was going to be the big influence, he was already in the army, and so it wasn't a Newark gangster but a Communist steelworker who worked the transformation on him. Ira's Longy Zwillman was Johnny O'Day."

"Why didn't I tell him, that first time he stayed over with us, to can the marriage and get out? Because that marriage, that woman, that beautiful house, all those books, records, the paintings on the wall, that life she had full of accomplished people, polished, interesting, educated people—it was everything he'd never known. Forget that he was now somebody himself. The guy had a *home*. He never had that before, and he was by then thirty-five. Thirty-five and he wasn't living in a room anymore, wasn't eating in cafeterias anymore, wasn't sleeping with waitresses and barmaids and worse—women, some of them, who couldn't write their names.

"After his discharge, when he first got to Calumet City to live with O'Day, Ira had an affair with a nineteen-year-old stripper. Girl named Donna Jones. Ira met her in the laundromat. Thought at first she was a local high school kid, and for a while she didn't bother to set him straight. Petite, scrappy, brassy, tough. At least the surface was tough. And she's a little pleasure factory. The kid has her hand on her pussy all the time.

"Donna's from Michigan, a resort town on the lake called Benton Harbor. In Benton Harbor, Donna used to work summers at a hotel on the lakefront. Sixteen, a chambermaid, and she gets knocked up by one of the customers over from Chicago. Which one she doesn't know. Carries the baby to term, gives it up for adoption, leaves town in disgrace, and winds up stripping in one of those Cal City joints.

"When he wasn't out being Abe Lincoln for the union on Sundays, Ira used to borrow O'Day's car to take Donna over to Benton Harbor to visit her mother. The mother worked in a little factory that manufactured candy and fudge, stuff they sold to the vacationers on Benton Harbor's main street. Resort sweets. The fudge was famous, shipped fudge all over the Middle West. Ira starts talking to the guy who runs the candy factory, he sees how they make the stuff, and pretty soon he's writing to me about marrying Donna and moving back with her to her hometown, living in a bungalow on the lake and using what's left of his separation pay to buy into this guy's business. There was also the thousand bucks he'd won shooting craps on the troopship coming home—all of it could go into the candy business. That Christmas he mailed Lorraine a gift box of fudge. Sixteen different flavors: chocolate coconut, peanut butter, pistachio, mint chocolate chip, rocky road . . . all fresh and creamy, direct from the Fudge Kitchen in Benton Harbor, Michigan. Tell me, what could be further from being a raving Red hellbent on overthrowing the American system than being a guy in Michigan who gift-wraps fudge to mail out to your old auntie for the holiday season? 'Goodies Made by the Lake'—that's the slogan on the box. Not 'Workers of the World Unite' but 'Goodies Made by the Lake.' If only Ira had married Donna Jones, *that* would have been the slogan he lived by.

"It was O'Day, not me, who talked him out of Donna. Not because a nineteen-year-old featured at the Cal City Kit Kat Klub as 'Miss Shalimar, Recommended for Good Eating by Duncan Hines' might in any way be a bad risk as a wife and mother; not because the missing Mr. Jones, Donna's father, was a drunk who used to beat his wife and kids; not because the Benton Harbor Joneses were ignorant rednecks and not a family somebody back from four years in the service should be wanting to take on as a lasting responsibility—which is what I politely tried to tell him. But to Ira everything that was a guaranteed recipe for domestic disaster constituted the argument *for* Donna. The lure of the underdog. The struggle of the disinherited up from the bottom was an *irresistible* lure. You drink deep, you drink dregs: humanity to Ira was synonymous with hardship and calamity. Toward hardship, even its disreputable forms, the kinship was unbreakable. It took O'Day to undo the all-around aphrodisiac that was Donna Jones and the sixteen flavors of fudge. It was O'Day who tore into him for personalizing his politics, and O'Day didn't do it with my 'bourgeois' reasoning. O'Day didn't apologize for presuming to criticize Ira's shortcomings. O'Day never apologized for anything. O'Day set people straight.

"O'Day gave Ira what he called 'a refresher course in matrimony as it pertains to the world revolution,' based on his own encounter with marriage before the war. 'Is this what you came out with me to the Calumet for? To prepare to run a candy factory or to run a revolution? This is no time for ridiculous aberrations! This is it, boy! This is life or death for working conditions as we've known them for the past ten years! All the factions and groups are coming together right here in Lake County. *You* see that. If we can hold this pitch, if nobody jumps ship, then damn it, Iron Man, in a year, two at most, the mills will be ours!'

"So, some eight months on, Ira told Donna it was all off, and she swallowed some pills and tried to kill herself a little. About a month later—Donna's by then back at the Kit Kat and got herself a new guy—her long-lost drunken father turns up with one of Donna's brothers at Ira's door saying he's going to teach Ira a lesson for what he did to his daughter. Ira's in the doorway fighting the two of them off, and the father pulls a knife and O'Day takes one swing and breaks the bastard's jaw and grabs the knife . . . That was the *first* family Ira was going to marry into.

"From such a farce it's not always a short way back, but by '48 the putative savior of little Donna has become Iron Rinn of *The Free and the Brave* and is up and ready for his next big mistake. You should have heard him when he learned Eve was pregnant. A child. A family of his own. And not with an ex-stripper whom his brother had disapproved of but with a renowned actress whom American radioland adored. It was the greatest thing ever to come his way. That solid foothold he'd never had before. He could hardly believe it. Two years—and this! The man wasn't impermanent anymore."

"She was pregnant? When was that?"

"After they were married. It didn't last but ten weeks. That's why he'd stayed with me and how you two met. She'd decided to abort."

We were sitting out back, on the deck, looking toward the pond and, in the distance, to the mountain range in the west. I live here by myself and the house is small, a room where I write and eat my meals—a workroom with a bathroom and a kitchen alcove off at one end, a stone fireplace at right angles to a wall of books, and a row of five twelve-over-twelve sash windows looking onto the broad hay field and a protective squadron of old maples that separates me from the dirt road. The other room is where I sleep, a nice-sized rustic-looking room with a single bed, a dresser, a wood-burning stove, exposed old beams upright in the four corners, more bookshelves, an easy chair where I do my reading, a small writing desk, and, in the west wall, a sliding glass door that opens onto the deck where Murray and I were each drinking a martini before dinner. I'd bought the house, winterized it—it had been somebody's summer cottage—and come here when I was sixty to live alone, by and large apart from people. That was four years ago. Though it isn't always desirable living as austerely as this, without the varied activities that ordinarily go to make up a human existence, I believe I made the least harmful choice. But my seclusion is not the story here. It is not a story in any way. I came here because I don't want a story any longer. I've had my story.

I wondered if Murray had as yet recognized my house as an upgraded replica of the two-room shack on the Jersey side of the Delaware Water Gap that was Ira's beloved retreat and the spot where I happened to have got my first taste of rural America when I went up, in the summers of '49 and '50, to spend a week with him. I'd loved my first time living alone with Ira in that shack, and I thought of his place immediately when I was shown this house. Though I had been looking for something larger and more conventionally a house, I bought it right off. The rooms were about the same size as Ira's and similarly situated. The long oval pond was about the same dimensions as his and about the same distance from the back door. And though my place was much brighter— over time, his stained pine-board walls had gone almost black, the beamed ceilings were low (ridiculously low for him), and the windows were small and not that plentiful—mine was tucked away on a dirt road as his was, and, if from the outside it didn't have that dark, drooping ramshackle look that proclaimed, "Hermit here— back off," the owner's state of mind was discernible in the absence of anything like a path across the hay field that led to the bolted front door. There was a narrow dirt drive that swung up and around to the workroom side of the house, to an open shed where, in the winter, I parked my car; a tumbledown wooden structure that predated the cottage, the shed could have been lifted right off Ira's overgrown eight acres.

How did the idea of Ira's shack maintain its hold so long? Well, it's the earliest images—of independence and freedom, particularly—that do live obstinately on, despite the blessing and the bludgeoning of life's fullness. And the idea of the shack, after all, isn't Ira's. It has a history. It was Rousseau's. It was Thoreau's. The palliative of the primitive hut. The place where you are stripped back to essentials, to which you return—even if it happens not to be where you came from—to decontaminate and absolve yourself of the striving. The place where you disrobe, molt it all, the uniforms you've worn and the costumes you've gotten into, where you shed your batteredness and your resentment, your appeasement of the world and your defiance of the world, your manipulation of the world and its manhandling of you. The aging man leaves and goes into the woods—Eastern philosophical thought abounds with that motif, Taoist thought, Hindu thought, Chinese thought. The "forest dweller," the last stage on life's way. Think of those Chinese paintings of the old man under the mountain, the old Chinese man all alone under the mountain, receding from the agitation of the autobiographical. He has entered vigorously into competition with life; now, becalmed, he enters into competition with death, drawn down into austerity, the final business.

The martinis were Murray's idea. A good though not a great idea, since a drink at the end of a summer's day with somebody I enjoyed, talk with a person like Murray, made me remember the pleasures of companionship. I'd enjoyed a lot of people, had not been an indifferent participant in life, had not backed away from it . . .

But the story is Ira's. Why it was impossible for *him*.

"He'd wanted a boy," Murray said. "Was dying to name it after his friend. Johnny O'Day Ringold. Doris and I had Lorraine, our daughter, and whenever he stayed over on the couch, Lorraine could always lift his spirits. Lorraine used to like to watch Ira sleep. Liked standing in the doorway watching Lemuel Gulliver sleep. He got attached to that little girl with those black bangs of hers. And she to him. When he came to the house, she'd get him to play with her Russian nested dolls. He'd given them to her for a birthday. You know, a traditional Russian woman in a babushka, the one replica nestles inside the other, till you get down to the nut-sized doll at the core. They'd make up stories about each of the dolls and how hard these little people worked in Russia. Then he'd nestle the whole thing in one of those hands of his so that you couldn't even see it. Just disappear whole inside those spatulate fingers—such long, peculiar fingers, the fingers Paganini must have had. Lorraine loved it when he did that: the biggest nesting doll of them all was this enormous uncle.

"For Lorraine's next birthday he bought her the album of the Soviet Army Chorus and Band performing Russian songs. More than a hundred men in that chorus, another hundred in the band. The basses' portentous rumblings—terrific sound. She and Ira would have a great time with those records. The singing was in Russian, and they'd listen together, and Ira would pretend to be the bass soloist, mouthing the incomprehensible words and making dramatic 'Russian' gestures, and, when the refrain came, Lorraine would mouth the incomprehensible words of the chorus. My kid knew how to be a comedian.

"There was one song she especially loved. It was beautiful too, a stirring, mournful, hymnlike folksong called 'Dubinushka,' a simple song sung with a balalaika in the background. The words to 'Dubinushka' were printed in English on the inside of the album cover, and she learned them by heart and went around the house singing them for months.

> Many songs have I heard in my native land—
> Songs of joy and sorrow.
> But one of them was deeply engraved in my memory:
> It's the song of the common worker.

That was the solo part. But what she liked best to sing was the choral refrain. Because it had 'heave-ho' in it.

> Ekh, lift up the cudgel,
> Heave-ho!
> Pull harder together,
> Heave-ho!

When Lorraine was by herself in her room, she'd line up all the hollow dolls and put on the 'Dubinushka' record, and she'd sing tragically 'Heave-ho! Heave-ho!' while pushing the dolls this way and that way all over the floor."

"Stop a minute. Murray, wait," I said, and I got up and went from the deck into the house, into my bedroom, where I had my CD player and my old phonograph. Most of my records were boxed and stored in a closet, but I knew in which box to find what I was looking for. I took out the album Ira had given to *me* back in 1948, and removed the record on which "Dubinushka" was performed by the Soviet Army Chorus and Band. I pushed the rpm switch to 78, dusted the record, and put it on the turntable. I placed the needle into the margin just before the record's last band, turned the volume up loud enough so that Murray could hear the music through the open doors separating my bedroom from the deck, and went out to rejoin him.

In the dark we listened, though now neither I to him nor he to me but both of us to "Dubinushka." It was just as Murray had described it: beautiful, a stirring, mournful, hymnlike folksong. Except for the crackle off the worn surface of the old record—a cyclical sound not unlike some familiar, natural night noise of the summer countryside—the song seemed to be traveling to us from a remote historical past. It wasn't at all like lying on my deck listening on the radio to the Saturday night concerts live from Tanglewood. "Heave-ho! Heave-ho!" was out of a distant place and time, a spectral residue of those rapturous revolutionary days when everyone craving for change programmatically, naively—madly, unforgivably—underestimates how mankind mangles its noblest ideas and turns them into tragic farce. Heave-ho! Heave-ho! As though human wiliness, weakness, stupidity, and corruption didn't stand a chance against the collective, against the might of the people pulling together to renew their lives and abolish injustice. Heave-ho.

When "Dubinushka" was over, Murray was silent and I began to hear once again everything I had filtered out while listening to him talk: the snores, twangs, and trills of the frogs, the rails in Blue Swamp, the reedy marsh just east of my house, kuck-ing and kek-ing and ki-tic-ing away, and the wrens there chattering their accompaniment. And the loons, the crying and the laughing of the manic-depressive loons. Every few minutes there was the whinny of a distant screech owl, and, continuously throughout, the western New England string ensemble of crickets sawed away at cricket Bartók. A raccoon twittered in the nearby woods, and, as time wore on, I even thought I was hearing the beavers gnawing on a tree back where the woodland tributaries feed my pond. Some deer, fooled by the silence, must have prowled too close to the house, for all at once—the deer having sensed our presence—their Morse code of flight is swiftly sounded: the snorting, the in-place thud, the stamping, hooves pounding, the bounding away. Their bodies barge gracefully into the thicket of scrub, and then, subaudibly, they race for their lives. Only Murray's murmurous breathing is heard, the eloquence of an old man evenly expirating.

Close to half an hour must have passed before he spoke. The arm of the phonograph hadn't returned to the starting position, and now I could hear the needle, too, whirring atop the label. I didn't go in to fix it and interrupt whatever it was that had quieted my storyteller and created the intensity of his silence. I wondered how long it would be before he said something, if perhaps he wouldn't speak at all but just get up and ask to be driven back to the dormitory—if whatever thoughts had been set loose in him would require a full night's sleep to subdue.

But, softly laughing, Murray said at last, "That hit me."

"Did it? Why?"

"I miss my girl."

"Where is she?"

"Lorraine is dead."

"When did that happen?"

"Lorraine died twenty-six years ago. Nineteen seventy-one. Died at thirty, leaving two kids and a husband. Meningitis, and overnight she was dead."

"And Doris is dead."

"Doris? Sure."

I went into the bedroom to lift the needle and return it to its rest. "Want to hear more?" I called to Murray.

He laughed heartily this time and said, "Trying to see how much I can take? Your idea of my strength, Nathan, is just a little too grand. I've met my match in 'Dubinushka.'"

"I doubt that," I said, going back outside and sitting in my chair. "You were telling me—?"

"I was telling you . . . I was telling you . . . Yes. That when Ira got booted off the air, Lorraine was desolate. She was only nine or ten, but she was up in arms. After Ira got fired for being a Communist, she wouldn't salute the flag."

"The American flag? Where?"

"At school," Murray said. "Where else do you salute the flag? The teacher tried to protect her, took her to one side and said you have to salute the flag. But this child wouldn't do it. A lot of anger. The real Ringold anger. She loved her uncle. She took after him."

"What happened?"

"I had a long talk with her and she got back to saluting the flag."

"What did you tell her?"

"I told her I loved my brother, too. I didn't think it was right either. I told her I thought as she did, that it was dead wrong to fire a person for his political beliefs. I believed in freedom of thought. *Absolute* freedom of thought. But I told her you don't go looking for that kind of fight. It's not an important issue. What are you achieving? What are you winning? I told her, Don't pick a fight you know you can't win, one that isn't even worth winning. I told her what I used to try to tell my brother about the problem of impassioned speech—tried from the time he was a little kid, for all the good it did him. It's not being angry that's important, it's being angry about the right things. I told her, Look at it from the Darwinian perspective. Anger is to make you effective. That's its survival function. That's why it's given to you. If it makes you ineffective, drop it like a hot potato."

As my teacher some fifty years earlier, Murray Ringold used to play things up, make a show out of the lesson, dozens of tricks to get us to stay alert. Teaching was a passionate occupation for him, and he was an exciting guy. But now, though by no means an old man who'd run out of juice, he no longer found it necessary to tear himself apart to make clear his meaning, but had brought himself close to being totally dispassionate. His tone was more or less unvaried, mild—no attempt to lead you (or mislead you) by being overtly expressive with his voice or his face or his hands, not even when singing "Heave-ho. Heave-ho."

His skull looked so fragile and small now. Yet within it were cradled ninety years of the past. There was a great deal in there. All the dead were there, for one thing, their deeds and their misdeeds converging with all the unanswerable questions, those things about which you can never be sure . . . to produce for him an exacting task: to reckon fairly, to tell this story without too much error.

Time, we know, goes very fast near the end, but Murray had been near the end so long that, when he spoke as he did, patiently, to the point, with a certain blandness—only intermittently pausing to wholeheartedly sip that martini—I had the feeling that time had dissolved for him, that it ran neither quickly nor slowly, that he was no longer living in time but exclusively within his own skin. As though that active, effortful, outgoing life as a conscientious teacher and citizen and family man had been a long battle to reach a state of ardorlessness. Aging into decrepitude was not unendurable and neither was the unfathomability of oblivion; neither was everything's coming down to nothing. It had *all* been endurable, even despising, without remission, the despicable.

In Murray Ringold, I thought, human dissatisfaction has met its match. He has outlived dissatisfaction. This is what remains after the passing of everything, the disciplined sadness of stoicism. This is the cooling. For so long it's so hot, everything in life is so intense, and then little by little it goes away, and then comes the cooling, and then come the ashes. The man who first taught me how you box with a book is back now to demonstrate how you box with old age.

And an amazing, noble skill it is, for nothing teaches you less about old age than having lived a robust life.

3

"THE REASON Ira came to see me," Murray continued, "and to stay overnight with us the day before you two met was because of what he'd heard that morning."

"She'd told him about wanting the abortion."

"No, she'd already told him that the night before, told him that she was going to Camden for an abortion. There was a doctor in Camden whom a lot of rich people went to back when abortion was a dodgy business. Her decision didn't come as a total surprise. For weeks she'd been back and forth, uncertain what to do. She was forty-one years old—she was older than Ira. Her face didn't show it, but Eve Frame wasn't a kid. She was concerned to be having a baby at her age. Ira understood that, but he couldn't accept it and refused to believe that her being forty-one was something to stand in their way. He wasn't that cautious, you know. He had that all-out steam-rolling side, and so he tried and tried to convince her that they had nothing to worry about.

"He thought he *had* convinced her. But a new issue emerged—work. It had been hard enough to tend a career and a child the first time around, with Sylphid, the daughter. Eve was only eighteen when Sylphid was born—she was a starlet then out in Hollywood. She was married to that actor, Pennington. Big name when I was young. Carlton Pennington, the silent-film hero with a profile molded precisely to classical specifications. Tall, slender, graceful man with hair as dark and sleek as a raven and a dark mustache. Elegant to the marrow of his bones. Member in good standing of both the social aristocracy and the aristocracy of eros—his acting capitalizes on the interplay of both. A fairy-tale prince—and a carnal powerhouse—in one, guaranteed to drive you to ecstasy in a silver-plated Pierce-Arrow.

"Studio arranged the wedding. She and Pennington had made such a hit together, and she was so enamored of him, that the studio decided they ought to get married. And once they were married, that they ought to have a child. All this was to squelch the rumors that Pennington was gay. Which, of course, he was.

"In order to marry Pennington there was a first husband to be gotten rid of. Pennington was the second husband. The first was a fellow named Mueller, whom she'd run away with when she was sixteen. An uneducated roughneck just back from five years in the navy, a big, burly German-American boy who'd grown up the son of a bartender in Kearny, near Newark. Crude background. Crude guy. A sort of Ira without the idealism. She met him at a neighborhood theater group. He wanted to be an actor and she wanted to be an actress. He was living in a boarding house and she was in high school and still living at home, and they ran off together to Hollywood. That's how Eve wound up in California, eloped as a kid with the bartender's boy. Within the year she was a star, and, so as to get rid of Mueller, who was nothing, her studio paid him off. Mueller did appear in a few silent films—as part of the payoff—and he even had a couple of roles as a tough in the first talkies, but his connection to Eve was all but erased from the record books. Until much later on, that is. We'll get back to Mueller. The point is that she marries Pennington, a coup for everyone: there's the studio wedding, there's the little baby, and then the twelve years with Pennington living the life of a nun.

"She used to take Sylphid to see Pennington in Europe even after she married Ira. Pennington's dead now, but he lived on the French Riviera after the war. He had a villa up in the hills back of St.

Tropez. Drunk every night, on the prowl, a bitter ex-somebody ranting and raving about the Jews who run Hollywood who ruined his career. She'd take Sylphid over to France to see Pennington, and they'd all go out for dinner in St. Tropez and he'd drink a couple bottles of wine and be staring all through dinner at some waiter, and then he'd send Sylphid and Eve back to their hotel. The next morning they'd go to Pennington's for breakfast and the waiter would be at the table in a bathrobe and they'd all have fresh figs together. Eve would return to Ira in tears, saying the man was fat and drunk and there was always some eighteen-year-old sleeping there, a waiter, or a beach bum, or a street cleaner, and she could never go to France again. But back she went—for good or bad, she took Sylphid to St. Tropez two or three times a year to see her father. It couldn't have been easy on the kid.

"After Pennington, Eve marries a real estate speculator, this guy Freedman, who she claimed spent everything she had and all but got her to sign over the house. So when Ira shows up on the radio scene in New York, naturally she falls for him. The noble rail-splitter, outgoing, unpolluted, a great big walking conscience yapping away about justice and equality for all. Ira and his ideals had attracted all sorts, from Donna Jones to Eve Frame, and everything problematic in between. Women in distress were crazy about him. The vitality. The energy. The Samson-like revolutionary giant. The luggish sort of chivalry he had. And Ira smelled good. Do you remember that? A natural smell of his. Lorraine used to say, 'Uncle Ira smells like maple syrup.' He did. He smelled like sap.

"In the beginning, the fact that Eve would deliver up her daughter to Pennington used to drive Ira nuts. I think he felt that it wasn't only to give Sylphid a chance to see Pennington—that there was still something about Pennington that Eve found attractive. And maybe she did. Maybe it was Pennington's queerness. Maybe it was that wellborn background. Pennington was old California money. That's the money he lived on in France. Some of the jewelry that Sylphid wore was Spanish jewelry collected by her father's family. Ira would say to me, 'His daughter is in the house with him, in one room, and he's in another room with a sailor. She should *protect* her daughter from this stuff. She shouldn't drag her over to France to have her witness stuff like that. Why doesn't she protect her daughter?'

"I know my brother—I know what he wants to say. He wants to say, I forbid you to go ever again. I told him, 'You're not the girl's father. You can't forbid her kid to do anything.' I said, 'If you want to leave the marriage because of this, leave it because of this. Otherwise, stay and live with it.'

"It was the first shot I'd had at even hinting at what I'd been wanting to say all along. Having a fling with her was one thing. A movie star—why not? But marriage? Glaringly wrong in every way. This woman has no contact with politics and especially not with Communism. Knows her way around the complicated plots of the Victorian novelists, can rattle off the names of the people in Trollope, but completely unknowing about society and the workaday doings of anything. The woman is dressed by Dior. Fabulous clothes. Owns a thousand little hats with little veils. Shoes and handbags made out of reptiles. Spends lots of money on clothes. While Ira is a guy who spends four ninety-nine for a pair of shoes. He finds one of her bills for an eight-hundred-dollar dress. Doesn't even know what this means. He goes to her closet and looks at the dress and tries to figure out how it can cost so much. As a Communist, he should be irritated by her from the first second. So what explains this marriage with her and not with a comrade? In the party, couldn't he have found somebody who supported him, who was together with him in the fight?

"Doris always excused him and made allowances for him, came to Ira's defense every time I started in. 'Yes,' Doris said, 'here is a Communist, a big revolutionary, a party member with his kind of zeal, and he suddenly falls in love with an unthinking actress in this year's ladylike waspy-waist jackets and long skirts, who is famous and beautiful, who is steeped like a teabag in aristocratic pretensions, and it contradicts his entire moral standard—but this is love.' 'Is it?' I would ask her. 'Looks like credulity and confusion to me.

Ira has no intuition about emotional questions. The lack of emotional intuition goes along with his being the kind of flat-footed radical he is. Those people are not very psychologically attuned.' But Doris's rebuttal is to justify him by nothing less than the annihilating power of love. 'Love,' says Doris, 'love is not something that is logical. Vanity is not something that is logical. *Ira* is not something that is logical. Each of us in this world has his own vanity, and therefore his own tailor-made blindness. Eve Frame is Ira's.'

"Even at his funeral, where there weren't twenty people, Doris stood up and made a speech on this very subject, a woman who dreaded speaking in public. She said he was a Communist with a weakness for life; he was an impassioned Communist who was not, however, made to live in the closed enclave of the party, and that was what subverted and destroyed him. He was not perfect from the Communist point of view—thank God. The personal he could not renounce. The personal kept bursting out of Ira, militant and single-minded though he would try to be. It's one thing to have your party allegiance and it's also one thing to be who you are and not able to restrain yourself. There was no side of himself that he could suppress. Ira lived everything personally, Doris said, to the hilt, including his contradictions.

"Well, maybe yes, maybe no. The contradictions were indisputable. The personal openness and the Communist secrecy. The home life and the party. The need for a child, the desire for a family—should a party member with his aspirations care about having a child like that? Even to one's contradictions one might impose a limit. A guy from the streets marries an *artiste*? A guy in his thirties marries a woman in her forties with a big adult baby who is still living at home? The incompatibilities were endless. But then, that was the challenge. With Ira, the more that's wrong, the more to correct.

"I told him, 'Ira, the situation with Pennington is *un*correctable. The only way to correct it is by not being there.' I told him more or less what O'Day had been telling him back with Donna. 'This is not politics—this is private life. You can't bring to private life the ideology that you bring to the great world. You cannot change her. What you've got, you've got; if it is insufferable, then leave. This is a woman who married a homosexual, lived twelve years untouched by a homosexual husband, and who continues her involvement with him even though he behaves in front of their daughter in a way that she considers detrimental to her daughter's well-being. She must consider it even more detrimental for Sylphid not to see her father at all. She's caught in a dilemma, probably there *is* no right thing for her to do—so let it be, don't bother her about it, let it go.'

"Then I asked, 'Tell me, are other things insufferable? Other things you want to go in and change? Because if there are, forget it. You cannot change *anything*.'

"But change was what Ira lived for. *Why* he lived. Why he lived *strenuously*. It is the essence of the man that he treats everything as a challenge to his will. He must always make the effort. He must change everything. For him that was the purpose of being in the world. Everything he wanted to change was here.

"But as soon as you want passionately what is beyond your control, you are primed to be thwarted—you are preparing to be brought to your knees.

"'Tell me,' I said to Ira, 'if you were to put all the insufferable things in a column and draw a line under them and add them up, do they add up to "Totally Insufferable"? Because if they do, then even if you only got there the day before yesterday, even if this marriage is still brand-new, you must go. Because your tendency, when you make a mistake, is not to go. Your tendency is to correct things in that vehement way that the people in this family like to correct things. That's a worry to me right now.'

"He had already told me about Eve's third marriage, the marriage after Pennington, to Freedman, and so I said to him, 'Sounds like one disaster after another. And you are going to do what, exactly—undo the disasters? The Great Emancipator off the stage as well as on? Is that why you seek her out in the first place? You're going to show her that you're a bigger and better man than the great Hollywood star? You're going to show her that a Jew isn't a rapacious capitalist like Freedman but a justice-making machine like you?'

"Doris and I had been to dinner there already. I had seen the Pennington-Frame family in action, and so I unloaded about that too. I unloaded everything. 'That daughter is a time bomb, Ira. Resentful, sullen, baleful—a person narrowly focused on exhibiting herself who otherwise is not there. She is a strong-willed person used to getting what she wants, and you, Ira Ringold, are in her way. Sure, you are strong-willed too, and bigger and older and a man. But you will not be able to make your will known. Where the daughter is concerned, you can have no moral authority *because* you are bigger and older and a man. That is going to be a source of frustration to a tycoon in the moral-authority racket like you. In you, the daughter is going to discover the meaning of a word that she could never have begun to learn from her mother: resistance. You are a six-foot six-inch hindrance, a hazard to her tyranny over the star who is mom.'

"I used strong language. I was an intense fellow myself in those days. I would get unsettled by the irrational, particularly when it emanated from my brother. I was more vehement than I should have been, but I didn't really overstate the case. I saw it right off, out of the gate, the night we went there for dinner. I would have thought you couldn't miss it, but Ira gets indignant. 'How do you know all this? How do you know all these things? Because you're so smart,' he says, 'or because I'm so dumb?' 'Ira,' I told him, 'there is a family of two living in that house, not a family of three, a family of two that has no concrete human relationships except each with the other. There is a family living in that house that can't find the right scale for *anything*. The mother in that house is being emotionally blackmailed by the daughter. You will not live happily as the protector of someone who is being emotionally blackmailed. Nothing is clearer in that household than the reversal of authority. Sylphid is the one wielding the whip. Nothing is clearer than that the daughter bears a rankling grudge against the mother. Nothing is clearer than that the daughter has got it in for the mother for some unpardonable crime. Nothing is clearer than how uncurbed the two of them are with their overwrought emotions. There is certainly no pleasure between those two. There will never be anything resembling a decent, modest state of accord between so frightened a mother and this overweening, unweaned child.

"'Ira, the relationship between a mother and a daughter or a mother and a son isn't all that complicated. I have a daughter,' I told him, 'I know about daughters. It's one thing to be with your daughter because you're infatuated with her, because you're in love; it's another to be with her because you're terrified of her. Ira, the daughter's rage at her mother's remarrying will doom your household from the start. "Every unhappy family is unhappy in its own way." I am simply describing to you the way that family is unhappy.'

"That's when he lit into me. 'Look, I don't live on Lehigh Avenue,' he told me. 'I love your Doris, she's a wonderful wife and a wonderful mother, but I'm not myself interested in the bourgeois Jewish marriage with the two sets of dishes. I never lived inside the bourgeois conventions and I have no intention of starting now. You actually propose that I give up a woman I love, a talented, wonderful human being—whose life, by the way, hasn't been a bed of roses either—give her up and run away because of this kid who plays the harp? That to you is the great problem in my life? The problem in my life is that union I belong to, Murray, moving that goddamn actors' union from where it is stuck to where it belongs. The problem in my life is the writer for my show. My problem isn't being a hindrance to Eve's kid—I'm a hindrance to Artie Sokolow, *that's* the problem. I sit down with this guy before he turns in the script, and I go over it with him, and if I don't like my lines, Murray, I tell him so. I won't *do* the goddamn lines if I don't like 'em. I sit down and I fight with him till he gives me something to say that gets across a message that is socially useful—'

"Leave it to Ira to aggressively miss the point. His mind moved, all right, but not with clarity. It moved only with force. 'I don't care,'

I told him, 'if you're strutting the stage and telling people how to write their scripts. I'm talking about something else. I'm not talking about conventional or unconventional or bourgeois or bohemian. I'm talking about a household where the mother is a pathetic carpet for the daughter to stomp on. It's crazy that you, the son of our father, who grew up in our house, won't recognize how explosive domestic arrangements can be, how ruinous to people. The enervating bickering. The daily desperation. The hour-by-hour negotiation. This is a household that is completely out of whack—'

"Well, it wasn't hard for Ira to say 'Fuck off' and never see you again. He didn't modulate. There's first gear and then suddenly there's fifth gear, and he's gone. I couldn't stop, I wouldn't stop, and so he tells me to go fuck myself and he leaves. Six weeks later I wrote him a letter he didn't answer. Then I made phone calls he wouldn't answer. In the end I went to New York and I corralled the guy and I apologized. 'You were right, I was wrong. It's none of my business. We miss you. We want you to come over. You want to bring Eve, bring her—you don't want to, don't. Lorraine misses you. She loves you and she doesn't know what happened. Doris misses you . . .' Et cetera. I wanted to say, 'You've got your eye on the wrong menace. The menace to you is not imperialist capitalism. The menace to you isn't your public actions, the menace to you is your private life. It always was and it always will be.'

"There were nights I couldn't sleep. I'd say to Doris, 'Why doesn't he *leave*? Why can't he *leave*?' And do you know what Doris would answer? 'Because he's like everybody—you only realize things when they're over. Why don't you leave *me*? All the human stuff that makes it hard for anybody to be with anybody else—don't we have it? We have arguments. We have disagreements. We have what everybody has—the little this and the little that, the little insults that pile up, the little temptations that pile up. Don't you think I know that there are women who are attracted to you? Teachers at school, women in the union, powerfully attracted to my husband? Don't you think I know you had a year, after you got back from the war, when you didn't know why you were still with me, when you asked yourself every day, "Why don't I leave her?" But you didn't. Because by and large people don't. Everyone's dissatisfied, but by and large *not* leaving is what people do. Especially people who've been left themselves, like you and your brother. Come through what you two came through and you value stability very highly. Probably overvalue it. The hardest thing in the world is to cut the knot of your life and leave. People make ten thousand adjustments to even the most pathological behavior. Why, emotionally, is a man of his type reciprocally connected to a woman of her type? The usual reason: their flaws fit. Ira cannot leave that marriage any more than he can leave the Communist Party.'

"Anyway, the baby. Johnny O'Day Ringold. Eve told Ira that when she had Sylphid out in Hollywood, it was different for her than it was for Pennington. When Pennington went off every day to work in a movie, everybody accepted it; when *she* went off every day to work in a movie, the baby was left with a governess, and so Eve was a bad mother, a neglectful mother, a selfish mother, and everybody was unhappy, including her. She told him she couldn't go through that again. It had been too hard on her and too hard on Sylphid. She told Ira that in many ways that strain was what had ruined *her* Hollywood career.

"But Ira said she wasn't in movies anymore, she was in radio. She was at the top of radio. She didn't go off every day to a studio—she went off two days a week. It wasn't the same at all. And Ira Ringold wasn't Carlton Pennington. He wouldn't leave her in the lurch with the kid. They wouldn't need any governess. The hell with that. He'd raise their Johnny O'Day himself if he had to. Once Ira got something between his teeth, he wasn't about to let go. And Eve wasn't somebody who could take the barrage. People went after her and she collapsed. And so he believed he'd convinced her on this score, too. Finally she said to him he was right, it wasn't at all the same, and she said okay, they'd have the baby, and he was euphoric, in seventh heaven—you should have heard him.

"But then that night before he came over to Newark, the night before you two met, she broke down and said she couldn't go through with it. She told him how wretched she felt denying him something he wanted so much, but she couldn't live through it all again. This went on for hours, and what could he do? What good was it going to do anybody—her, or him, or little Johnny—for this to be the backdrop to their family life? He was miserable, and they were up till three or four that night, but it was over as far as he was concerned. He was a persistent guy, but he couldn't tie her to her bed and keep her there for seven more months in order to have a child. If she didn't want it, she didn't want it. And so he told her he'd go with her down to Camden to the abortion doctor. She wouldn't be alone."

Listening to Murray, I couldn't help but be overtaken by memories of being with Ira, memories I didn't even know I continued to have, memories of how I used to gorge myself on his words and on his adult convictions, solid memories of the two of us walking in Weequahic Park and his telling me about the impoverished kids he'd seen in Iran—pronounced by Ira "Eye-ran."

"When I got to Iran," Ira told me, "the natives there suffered from every type of illness you can think of. Being Moslem, they used to wash their hands before and after defecating—but they did it in the river, the river that was in front of us, so to speak. They washed their hands in the same water they urinated in. Their living conditions were terrible, Nathan. The place was run by sheiks. And not romantic sheiks. These guys were like the dictator of the tribe. Y'understand? The army gave them money so the natives would work for us, and we gave the natives rations of rice and tea. That was it. Rice and tea. Those living conditions—I had never seen anything like it. I'd grubbed for work in the Depression, I hadn't been brought up at the Ritz—but this was something else. When we had to defecate, for instance, we defecated into GI pails—iron buckets, that's what they were. And somebody had to empty them out, and so we emptied them out in the garbage dump. And who do you think was there?"

All at once Ira couldn't go on, couldn't speak. He couldn't walk.

It would always alarm me when this happened to him. And because he knew that, he'd tap the air with his hand, signaling me to be still, to wait him out, he'd be all right.

Things that were not to his liking he could not discuss with equilibrium. His whole manly bearing could be altered almost beyond recognition by anything that involved human degradation, and, perhaps because of his own shattered development as a boy, that involved particularly the suffering and degradation of children. When he said to me, "And who do you think was there?" I knew who was there because of the way he began to breathe: "Ahhh . . . ahhh . . . ahhh." Gasping like someone about to die. When he was emotionally intact enough to resume the walk, I asked as though I didn't know, "Who, Ira? Who was there?"

"The kids. They lived there. And they would pick through the garbage dump for food—"

This time when he stopped speaking my alarm got the better of me; fearful that he might get stuck, be so overwhelmed—not only by his emotions but by an immense loneliness that seemed suddenly to strip him of his strength—that he'd never find the way back to being the brave, angry hero I adored, I knew I had to do something, anything I could, and so I tried at least to complete his thought for him. I said, "And it was awful."

He patted my back and we started walking again.

"To me it was," he finally replied. "To my army buddies it mattered not. I never heard anybody comment on it. I never saw anybody—from my own America—deploring the situation. I was really pissed. But there was nothing I could do about it. In the army there's no democracy. Y'understand? You don't go telling anybody higher up. And this had been going on for God knows how long. This is what world history *is*. That's how people live." Then he erupted, "This is how people *make* them live!"

We took trips around Newark together so that Ira could show me the non-Jewish neighborhoods I didn't really know—the First Ward, where he'd been brought up and where the poor Italians lived; Down Neck, where the poor Irish and the poor Poles lived—

and Ira all the while explaining to me that, contrary to what I might have heard growing up, these were not simply goyim but "working people like working people all over this country, diligent, poor, powerless, struggling every goddamn day to live a decent and dignified life."

We went into Newark's Third Ward, where the Negroes had come to occupy the streets and houses of the old Jewish immigrant slum. Ira spoke to everyone he saw, men and women, boys and girls, asked what they did and how they lived and what they thought about maybe changing "the crappy system and the whole damn pattern of ignorant cruelty" that deprived them of their equality. He'd sit down on a bench outside a Negro barbershop on shabby Spruce Street, around the corner from where my father had been raised in a Belmont Avenue tenement, say to the men congregated on the sidewalk, "I'm ever a guy to butt into other people's conversations," and begin talking to them about their equality, and to me he never looked more like the elongated Abraham Lincoln who is cast in bronze at the foot of the broad stairway leading up to Newark's Essex County Courthouse, Gutzon Borglum's locally famous Lincoln, seated and waiting welcomingly on a marble bench before the courthouse, in his sociable posture and by his gaunt bearded face revealing that he is wise and grave and fatherly and judicious and good. Out in front of that Spruce Street barbershop—with Ira declaiming, when someone asked his opinion, that "a Negro has the right to eat any damn place he feels like paying the check!"—I realized that I'd never before imagined, let alone seen, a white person being so easygoing and at home with Negroes.

"What most people mistake for Negro sullenness and stupidity—you know what that is, Nathan? It's a protective shell. But when they meet somebody who is free of race prejudice—you see what happens, they don't *need* that shell. They got their share of psychos, sure, but you tell me who doesn't."

When Ira one day discovered outside the barbershop a very old, bitter black man who liked nothing better than to vent his spleen in vehement discussion about the beastliness of humanity—"Everything we know of has developed not out of the tyranny of tyrants but out of the tyranny of mankind's greed, ignorance, brutality, and hatred. The tyrant of evil is *Everyman!*"—we went back several times more, and people gathered round to hear Ira going at it with this impressive malcontent who was always neatly dressed in a dark suit and a tie and who all the other men respectfully called "Mr. Prescott": Ira proselytizing one on one, one Negro at a time, the Lincoln-Douglas debates in a strange new form.

"Are you still convinced," Ira asked him, graciously, "that the working class will go along for the crumbs from the imperialist's table?" "I am, sir! The mass of men of *whatever* color is and always will be mindless, torpid, wicked, and stupid. If ever they should become less impoverished, they will be even *more* mindless, torpid, wicked, and stupid!" "Well, I've been thinking about that, Mr. Prescott, and I'm convinced that you are in error. The simple fact that there aren't enough crumbs to keep the working class fed and docile refutes that theory. All you gentlemen here are underestimating the proximity of industrial collapse. It's true that most of our working people would stick with Truman and the Marshall Plan if they were sure it would keep them employed. But the contradiction is this: the channeling of the bulk of production to war materiel, both for the American forces and for those of the puppet governments, *is impoverishing American workers.*"

Even in the face of Mr. Prescott's seemingly hard-won misanthropy, Ira tried to insert some reason and hope into the discussion, plant if not in Mr. Prescott then in the sidewalk audience an awareness of the transformations that could be effected in men's lives through concerted political action. For me it was, as Wordsworth describes the days of the French Revolution, "very Heaven": "Bliss was it in that dawn to be alive, / But to be young was very Heaven!" The two of us, white and surrounded by some ten or twelve black men, and there was nothing for us to worry about and nothing for any of them to fear: it was not we who were their oppressors or they who were our enemies—the oppressor-enemy by which we were all appalled was the way the society was organized and run.

It was after the first visit to Spruce Street that he treated me to cheesecake at the Weequahic Diner and, while we ate, told me about the Negroes he'd worked with in Chicago.

"This plant was in the heart of Chicago's black belt," he said. "About ninety-five percent of the employees were colored, and there is where the esprit I was telling you about enters in. It's the only place I've ever been where a Negro is on an absolutely equal footing with everybody else. So the whites don't feel guilty and the Negroes don't feel mad all the time. Y'understand? Promotions based solely on seniority—no finagling about it."

"What are Negroes like when you work with them?"

"As far as I can determine, there was no suspicion of us whites. First off, the colored people knew that any white the UE sent to this plant was either a Communist or a pretty faithful fellow traveler. So they weren't inhibited. They knew that we were as free from race prejudice as an adult in this time and society can be. When you saw a paper being read, about two to one it was the *Daily Worker*. The *Chicago Defender* and the *Racing Form* were about neck and neck for second place. Hearst and McCormick strictly ruled off the track."

"But what are Negroes actually like? Personally."

"Well, buddy, there are some ugly types, if that's what you're asking me. That has a basis in actuality. But that's a small minority, and an El ride through the Negro ghettos is enough to indicate to anyone with an open mind what warps people into these shapes. The characteristic I was most aware of among the Negro people is their warm friendliness. And, at our record factory, the love of music. At our factory, there were speakers all over the place, amplifiers, and anybody who wanted a special tune played—and this is all on working time—just had to request it. The guys would sing, jive—not uncommon for a guy to grab a girl and dance. About a third of the employees were Negro girls. Nice girls. We'd smoke, read, brew coffee, argue at the top of our voices, and the work went right along without a hitch or a break."

"Did you have Negro friends?"

"Sure. Sure I did. There was a big guy named Earl Something-or-Other who I took a liking to right away because he looked like Paul Robeson. It didn't take me long to discover that he was about the same kind of tramp working stiff as me. Earl would ride the streetcar and El as far as I did, and we made a point to take the same ones, the way guys do, to have somebody to chew the fat with. Right up to the plant gates, Earl and me would talk and laugh the same as we did on the job. But once inside, where there were whites he doesn't know, Earl clams right up and just says 'So long' when I get off the El. That's it. Y'understand?"

In the pages of the small brown notebooks that Ira had brought back from the war, interspersed among his observations and the statements of belief, were the names and stateside addresses of about every politically like-minded soldier he had met in the service. He had begun to track these men down, sending letters all over the country and visiting the guys who lived in New York and Jersey. One day we took a ride up to suburban Maplewood, just west of Newark, to visit former sergeant Erwin Goldstine, who in Iran had been as far to the left as Johnny O'Day—"a very well developed Marxist," Ira called him—but who, back home, we discovered, had married into a family that owned a Newark mattress factory and now, a father of three, had become an adherent of everything he had once opposed. About Taft-Hartley, about race relations, about price controls, he did not even argue with Ira. He just laughed.

Goldstine's wife and his kids were away with the in-laws for the afternoon, and we sat together in his kitchen drinking soda while Goldstine, a wiry little guy with the haughty, knowing air of a street-corner sharpie, laughed and sneered at everything Ira said. His explanation for his turnabout? "Didn't know shit from shinola. Didn't know what I was talking about." To me Goldstine said, "Kid, don't listen to him. You live in America. It's the greatest country in the world and it's the greatest system in the world. Sure, people get shit on. You think they don't get shit on in the Soviet Union? He tells you capitalism is a dog-eat-dog system. What is life if not a dog-eat-dog system? This is a system that is in tune with life. And because it is, it works. Look, everything the Communists say about capitalism is true, and everything the capitalists say about Communism is true. The difference is, our system works because it's based on the truth about people's selfishness, and theirs doesn't because it's based on a fairy tale about people's *brotherhood*. It's such a crazy fairy tale they've got to take people and put them in Siberia in order to get them to believe it. In order to get them to believe in their brotherhood, they've got to control people's every thought or shoot 'em. And meanwhile in America, in Europe, the Communists go on with this fairy tale even when they know what is really there. Sure, for a while you don't know. But what don't you know? You know human beings. So you know everything. You know that this fairy tale cannot be possible. If you are a very young man I suppose it's okay. Twenty, twenty-one, twenty-two, okay. But after that? No reason that a person with an average intelligence can take this story, this fairy tale of Communism, and swallow it. 'We will do something that will be wonderful . . .' But we know what our brother is, don't we? He's a shit. And we know what our friend is, don't we? He's a semi-shit. And *we* are semi-shits. So how can it be wonderful? Not even cynicism, not even skepticism, just ordinary powers of human observation tell us *that is not possible.*

"You want to come down to my capitalist factory and watch a mattress being made the way a capitalist makes a mattress? You come down and you'll talk to real working guys. This guy's a radio star. You're not talking to a workingman, you're talking to a radio star. Come on, Ira, you're a star like Jack Benny—what the hell do you know about work? The kid comes to my factory and he'll see how we manufacture a mattress, he'll see the care we take, he'll see how I have to stand over the whole operation every step of the way to see they don't fuck up my mattress. He'll see what it is to be the evil owner of the means of production. It's to work your ass off twenty-four hours a day. The workers go home at five o'clock—I don't. I'm there till midnight every night. I come home and I don't sleep 'cause I'm doing the books in my head and then I'm there again at six in the morning to open the place up. Don't let him fill you full of Communist ideas, kid. They're all lies. Make money. Money's not a lie. Money's the democratic way to keep score. Make your money—then, if you still have to, *then* make your points about the brotherhood of man."

Ira leaned back in his chair, raised his arms so that his huge hands were interlaced behind his neck, and, his contempt undisguised, said—though not to our host but, so as to gall him to the utmost, pointedly to me—"You know one of life's best feelings? Maybe *the* best? Not being afraid. The mercenary schmuck whose house we are in—you know what his story is? He is afraid. That's the simple fact of it. In World War II Erwin Goldstine was not afraid. But now the war is over, and Erwin Goldstine is afraid of his wife, afraid of his father-in-law, afraid of the bill collector—he is afraid of everything. You look with your big eyes into the capitalist shop window, you want and you want, you grab and you grab, you take and you take, you acquire and you own and you accumulate, and there is the end of your convictions and the beginning of your fear. There is nothing that I have that I can't give up. Y'understand? Nothing has come my way that I'm tied and bound to like a mercenary is. How I ever got from my father's miserable house on Factory Street to being this character Iron Rinn, how Ira Ringold, with one and a half years of high school behind him, got to meeting the people I meet and knowing the people I know and having the comforts I have now as a card-carrying member of the privileged class—that is all so unbelievable that losing everything overnight would not seem so strange to me. Y'understand? Y'understand me? I can go back to the Midwest. I can work in the mills. And if I have to, I will. Anything but to become a rabbit like this guy. That's what you now are politically," he said, looking at last at Goldstine—"not a man, a rabbit, a rabbit of no consequence."

"Full of shit in Iran and full of shit still, Iron Man." Then, again to me—I was the sounding board, the straight man, the fuse on the bomb—Goldstine said, "Nobody could ever listen to anything he says. Nobody could ever take him seriously. The guy's a joke. He can't think. Never could. Doesn't know anything, doesn't see anything, doesn't learn anything. The Communists get a dummy like Ira and they use him. Mankind at its stupidest doesn't come any stupider." Then, turning to Ira, he said, "Get out of my house, you dumb Communist prick."

My heart was already wildly thumping before I even saw the pistol that Goldstine had drawn out of a kitchen cabinet drawer, out of the drawer right behind him where the silverware was stored. Up close, I'd never seen a pistol before, except tucked safely away in the hip holster of a Newark cop. It wasn't because Goldstine was small that the pistol looked big. It *was* big, improbably big, black, and well made, molded, machined—eloquent with possibility.

Though Goldstine was standing and pointing the pistol at Ira's forehead, even up on his feet he wasn't much taller than Ira was seated.

"I'm scared of you, Ira," Goldstine said to him. "I've always been scared of you. You're a wild man, Ira. I'm not going to wait for you to do to me what you did to Butts. Remember Butts? Remember little Butts? Get up and get out, Iron Man. Take Kid Asslick with you. Asslick, didn't the Iron Man ever tell you about Butts?" Goldstine said to me. "He tried to kill Butts. He tried to drown Butts. He dragged Butts out of the mess hall—didn't you tell the kid, Ira, about you in Iran, about the rages and the tantrums in Iran? Guy weighing a hundred and twenty pounds comes at the Iron Man here with a mess kit knife, a very dangerous weapon, you see, and the Iron Man picks him up and carries him out of the mess hall and drags him down to the docks, and he holds him upside down over the water, holds him by his feet, and he says, 'Swim, hillbilly.' Butts is crying, 'No, no, I can't,' and the Iron Man says, 'Can't you?' and drops him in. Headfirst over the side of the dock into the Shatt-al-Arab. River's thirty feet deep. Butts goes straight down. Then Ira turns and he is screaming at *us*. 'Leave the redneck bastard alone! Get out of here! Nobody go near that water!' 'He's drowning,

Iron Man.' 'Let him,' Ira says, 'stay back! I know what I'm doing! Let him go down!' Somebody jumps in the water to try and get at Butts, and so Ira jumps in after him, lands on him, starts pummeling this guy's head and gouging his eyes and holding *him* under. You didn't tell the kid about Butts? How come? Didn't you tell him about Garwych, either? About Solak? About Becker? Get up. Get up and get out, you crazy fucking homicidal nut."

But Ira didn't move. Except for his eyes. His eyes were like birds that wanted to fly out of his face. They were twitching and blinking in a way I'd never before seen, while along the entire length of him he looked as though he'd ossified, assumed a tautness as terrifying as the flapping of his eyes.

"No, Erwin," he said, "not with a sidearm in my face. Only ways to get me out are pull the trigger or call the cops."

I couldn't have said which of them was more frightening. Why didn't Ira do what Goldstine wanted—why didn't the *two* of us get up and go? Who was crazier, the mattress manufacturer with the loaded pistol or the giant daring him to fire it? What was happening here? We were in a sunny kitchen in Maplewood, New Jersey, drinking Royal Crown from the bottle. We were all three of us Jews. Ira had come by to say hello to an old army buddy. What was *wrong* with these guys?

It was when I began to tremble that Ira ceased to look deformed by whatever antirational thought he was thinking. Across the table from him he saw my teeth chattering all on their own, my hands uncontrollably shaking all on their own, and he came to his senses and slowly rose from his chair. He raised his arms over his head the way they do when the bank robbers in the movies shout "It's a stickup!"

"All over, Nathan. Quarrel called on account of darkness." But despite the easygoing way he managed to say that, despite the surrender that was implicit in his mockingly raised arms, as we left the house through the kitchen door and made our way down the driveway to Murray's car, Goldstine continued after us, his pistol only inches from Ira's skull.

In a sort of trance state Ira drove us through the quiet Maplewood streets, past all the pleasant one-family houses where there lived the ex-Newark Jews who'd lately acquired their first homes and their first lawns and their first country club affiliations. Not the sort of people or the sort of neighborhood where you would expect to find a pistol in with the dinnerware.

Only when we crossed the Irvington line and were heading into Newark did Ira come around and ask, "You okay?"

I was miserable, though less frightened now than humiliated and ashamed. Clearing my throat so as to be sure to speak in an unbroken voice, I said, "I pissed in my pants."

"Did you?"

"I thought he was going to kill you."

"You were brave. You were very brave. You were fine."

"Walking down the driveway, I pissed in my pants!" I said angrily. "Goddamit! Shit!"

"It's *my* fault. The whole thing. Exposing you to that putz. Pulling a gun! A *gun!*"

"Why did he *do* that?"

"Butts didn't drown," Ira suddenly said. "*Nobody* drowned. Nobody was *going* to drown."

"Did you throw him in?"

"Sure. Sure I threw him in. This was the hillbilly who called me a kike. I told you that story."

"I remember." But what he'd told me was only a part of that story. "That's the night they waylaid you. They beat you up."

"Yeah. They beat me, all right. After they fished the son of a bitch out."

He let me off at my house, where no one was at home and I was able to drop my damp clothing into the hamper and take a shower and calm down. I had the shakes again in the shower, not so much because I was remembering sitting at the kitchen table with Goldstine pointing his pistol at Ira's forehead or remembering Ira's eyes looking like they wanted to fly out of his head, but because I was thinking, A loaded pistol in with the forks and the knives? In

Maplewood, New Jersey? Why? Because of Garwych, that's why! Because of Solak! Because of Becker!

All the questions I hadn't dared to ask him in the car, I started asking aloud alone in the shower. "What did you do to them, Ira?"

My father, unlike my mother, didn't see Ira as a means of social advancement for me and was always perplexed and bothered by his calling me: what is this grown man's interest in this kid? He thought something complicated, if not downright sinister, was going on. "Where do you go with him?" my father asked me.

His suspiciousness erupted vehemently one night when he found me at my desk reading a copy of the *Daily Worker*. "I don't want the Hearst papers in my house," my father told me, "and I don't want *that* paper in my house. One is the mirror image of the other. If this man is giving you the *Daily Worker*—" "What 'man'?" "Your actor friend. *Rinn*, as he calls himself." "He doesn't give me the *Daily Worker*. I bought it downtown. I bought it myself. Is there a law against that?" "Who told you to buy it? Did he tell you go out and buy it?" "He doesn't tell me to do anything." "I hope that's true." "I don't lie! It is!"

It was. I'd remembered Ira saying that there was a column in the *Worker* by Howard Fast, but it was on my own that I had bought the paper, across from Proctor's movie theater at a Market Street newsstand, ostensibly to read Howard Fast but also out of simple, dogged curiosity. "Are you going to confiscate it?" I asked my father. "No—you're out of luck. I'm not going to make you a martyr to the First Amendment. I only hope that after you've read it and studied and thought about it, you have the good sense to know that it's a sheet of lies and to confiscate it yourself."

Toward the end of the school year, when Ira invited me to spend a week up at the shack with him that summer, my father said I wasn't going unless Ira had a talk with him first.

"Why?" I demanded to know.

"I want to ask him some questions."

"What are you, the House Un-American Activities Committee? Why are you making such a big thing out of this?"

"Because in my eyes *you* are a big thing. What's his telephone number in New York?"

"You *can't* ask him questions. About what?"

"You have your right as an American to buy and read the *Daily Worker*? I have a right as an American to ask anybody anything I want. If he doesn't want to answer me, that's *his* right."

"And if he doesn't want to answer, what's he supposed to do, take the Fifth Amendment?"

"No. He can tell me to go jump in the lake. I just explained it to you: that's how we do it in the USA. I don't say that's going to work for you in the Soviet Union with the secret police, but here that's all it ordinarily takes for a fellow citizen to leave you alone about your political ideas."

"*Do* they leave you alone?" I asked bitterly. "Does Congressman Dies leave you alone? Does Congressman Rankin leave you alone? Maybe you better explain it to *them*."

I had to sit there—he told me I had to—and listen to him while he asked Ira, on the phone, to come over to his office for a talk. Iron Rinn and Eve Frame were the biggest things ever to enter the Zuckerman household from the outside world, yet it was clear from my father's tone that this didn't throw him at all.

"He said *yes?*" I asked when my father hung up.

"He said he'd be there if Nathan would be there. You're going to be there."

"Oh, no I'm not."

"Yep," my father said, "you are. You are if you want me even to begin to consider your going up there to visit. What are you afraid of, an open discussion of ideas? It's going to be democracy in action, next Wednesday, after school, at three-thirty in my office. You be on time, son."

What was I afraid of? My father's anger. Ira's temper. What if because of how my father attacked him Ira picked him up bodily the way he picked up Butts and carried him down to the lake at

Weequahic Park and threw him in? If a fight broke out, if Ira threw a lethal punch . . .

My father's chiropody office was on the ground floor of a three-family house at the bottom of Hawthorne Avenue, a modest dwelling in need of a face-lift near the rundown edge of our otherwise plainly pedestrian neighborhood. I was there early, feeling sick to my stomach. Ira, looking serious and not at all enraged (as yet), arrived promptly at three-thirty. My father asked him to be seated.

"Mr. Ringold, my son Nathan is not a run-of-the-mill boy. He is an older son who is an excellent student and who, I believe, is advanced and mature beyond his years. We are very proud of him. I want to give him all the latitude I can. I try not to stand in his way in life, as some fathers do. But because I honestly happen to think that for him the sky is the limit, I don't want anything to happen to him. If anything should happen to this boy . . ."

My father's voice grew husky and he abruptly stopped talking. I was terrified that Ira was going to laugh at him, to mock him the way he'd mocked Goldstine. I knew that my father was choked up not merely because of me and my promise but because his two youngest brothers, the first members of that large, poor family of his who were targeted to go to a real college and become real doctors, had both died of illnesses in their late teens. Studio portrait photos of them rested next to each other in twin frames on our dining room sideboard. I should have explained to Ira about Sam and Sidney, I thought.

"I have to ask you a question, Mr. Ringold, that I don't want to ask you. I don't consider another person's beliefs—religious, political, or otherwise—my business. I respect your privacy. I can assure you that whatever you say here will not go beyond this room. But I want to know whether you are a Communist, and I want my son to know whether you are a Communist. I'm not asking if you ever have been a Communist. I don't care about the past. I care about right now. I have to tell you that back before Roosevelt I was so disgusted with the way things were going in this country, and with the anti-Semitism and anti-Negro prejudice in this country, and with how the Republicans scorned the unfortunate in this country, and with how the greed of big business was milking the people of this country to death, that one day, right here in Newark—and this will come as a shock to my son, who thinks his father, a lifelong Democrat, is to the right of Franco—but one day . . . Well, Nathan," he said, looking now at me, "they had their headquarters—you know where the Robert Treat Hotel is? Right down the street. Upstairs. Thirty-eight Park Place. They had offices up there. One was the office of the Communist Party. I never even told this to your mother. She would have killed me. She was my girlfriend then—this must be 1930. Well, one time, one day, I was angry. Something had happened, I don't even remember what it was any longer, but I read something in the papers and I remember that I went up there, and nobody was there. The door was locked. They had gone to lunch. I rattled the door handle. That's as close as I got to the Communist Party. I rattled the door and said, 'Let me in.' You didn't know that, did you, son?"

"No," I said.

"Well, now you do. Luckily, that door was locked. And in the next election Franklin Roosevelt became the president, and the kind of capitalism that sent me down to the Communist Party office began to get an overhaul the likes of which this country had never seen. A great man saved this country's capitalism from the capitalists and saved patriotic people like me from Communism. Saved all of us from the dictatorial regime that *results* from Communism. Let me tell you something that shook me—the death of Masaryk. Did that bother you, Mr. Ringold, as much as it bothered me? I always admired Masaryk in Czechoslovakia, ever since I first heard his name and what he was doing for his people. I always thought of him as the Czech Roosevelt. I don't know how to account for his murder. Do you, Mr. Ringold? I was troubled by it. I couldn't believe the Communists could kill a man like that. But they did . . . Sir, I don't want to get started having a political argument. I'm going to ask you one single question, and I'd like you to answer so that my son and I know where we stand. Are you a member of the Communist Party?"

"No, Doctor, I'm not."

"Now I want my son to ask you. Nathan, I want you to ask Mr. Ringold if he is now a member of the Communist Party."

To put such a question to somebody went against my every political principle. But because my father wanted me to and because my father had asked Ira already to no ill effect and because of Sam and Sidney, my father's dead younger brothers, I did it.

"Are you, Ira?" I asked him.

"Nope. No, sir."

"You don't go to meetings of the Communist Party?" my father asked.

"I do not."

"You don't plan, up where you want Nathan to visit you—what's the name of the place?"

"Zinc Town. Zinc Town, New Jersey."

"You don't plan up there to take him to any such meetings?"

"No, Doctor, I don't. I plan on taking him swimming and hiking and fishing."

"I'm glad to hear that," said my father. "I believe you, sir."

"May I now ask *you* a question, Dr. Zuckerman?" Ira asked, smiling at my father in that droll sidewise way he smiled when he was playing Abraham Lincoln. "Why do you have me down for a Red in the first place?"

"The Progressive Party, Mr. Ringold."

"Do you have Henry Wallace down for a Red? The former vice president to Mr. Roosevelt? Do you think Mr. Roosevelt would choose a Red for vice president of the United States of America?"

"It's not as simple as that," my father replied. "I wish it were. But what's going on in the world is not simple at all."

"Dr. Zuckerman," said Ira, changing tactics, "you wonder what I'm doing with Nathan? I envy him—that's what I'm doing with him. I envy that he has a father like you. I envy that he has a teacher like my brother. I envy that he has good eyes and can read without glasses a foot thick and isn't an idiot who's going to quit school so as to go out and dig ditches. I've got nothing hidden and nothing to hide, Doctor. Except that I wouldn't mind a son like him myself someday. Maybe the world today isn't simple, but this sure is: I get a kick out of talking to your boy. Not every kid in Newark takes as his hero Tom Paine."

Here my father stood up and extended his hand to Ira. "I *am* a father, Mr. Ringold—to *two* boys, to Nathan and to Henry, his younger brother, who is also somebody to crow about. And my responsibilities as a father . . . well, that's all that this has been about."

Ira took my father's ordinary-sized hand in his huge one and pumped it once very hard, so hard—with such sincerity and warmth—that oil, or at least water, a pure geyser of something, might as a result have come gushing from my father's mouth. "Dr. Zuckerman," Ira said, "you don't want your son stolen from you, and nobody here is going to steal him."

Whereupon I had to make a superhuman effort not to start to bawl. I had to pretend to myself that my whole aim in life was not to cry, never to cry, at the sight of two men affectionately shaking hands—and I barely managed to succeed. They'd done it! Without shouting! Without bloodshed! Without the motivating, distorting rage! Magnificently they had pulled it off—though largely because Ira was not telling us the truth.

I'll insert this here and not return to the subject of the wound inflicted on my father's face. I count on the reader to remember it when that seems appropriate.

Ira and I left my father's office together, and to celebrate—purportedly to celebrate my upcoming summer visit to Zinc Town but also, complicitously, to celebrate our victory over my dad—we went to Stosh's, a few blocks away, to have one of Stosh's overstuffed ham sandwiches. I ate so much with Ira at four-fifteen that when I got home, at five of six, I had no appetite and sat at my place at the table while everybody else ate my mother's dinner—and it was then that I observed in my father's face the wound. I had planted it there earlier by going out the door of his office with Ira and not staying behind to talk a little to him until the next patient showed up.

At first I tried to think that maybe I was guiltily imagining that wound because of having felt, not necessarily contemptuous of him, but certainly superior leaving, virtually arm in arm, with Iron Rinn of *The Free and the Brave*. My father didn't want his son stolen from him, and though, strictly speaking, nobody had stolen anybody, the man was no fool and knew that he had lost and, Communist or no Communist, the six-foot six-inch intruder had won. I saw in my father's face a look of resigned disappointment, his kind gray eyes softened by—distressfully subdued by—something midway between melancholy and futility. It was a look that would never be entirely forgotten by me when I was alone with Ira, or, later, with Leo Glucksman, Johnny O'Day, or whomever. Just by taking instruction from these men, I seemed to myself somehow to be selling my father short. His face with that look on it was always looming up, superimposed on the face of the man who was then educating me in life's possibilities. His face bearing the wound of betrayal.

The moment when you first recognize that your father is vulnerable to others is bad enough, but when you understand that he's vulnerable to *you*, still needs you more than you any longer think you need him, when you realize that you might actually be able to frighten him, even to *quash* him if you wanted to—well, the idea is at such cross-purposes with routine filial inclinations that it does not even begin to make sense. All the laboring he had gone through to get to be a chiropodist, a provider, a protector, and I was now running off with another man. It is, morally as well as emotionally, a more dangerous game than one knows at the time, getting all those extra fathers like a pretty girl gets beaux. But that was what I was doing. Always making myself eminently adoptable, I discovered the sense of betrayal that comes of trying to find a surrogate father even though you love your own. It isn't that I ever denounced my father to Ira or anyone else for a cheap advantage—it was enough just, by exercising my freedom, to dump the man I loved for somebody else. If only I had hated him, it would have been easy.

In my third year at Chicago, I brought a girl home with me at Thanksgiving break. She was a gentle girl, mannerly and clever, and I remember the pleasure my parents took in talking to her. One evening, while my mother stayed in the living room entertaining my aunt, who had eaten dinner with us, my father came out to the corner drugstore with the girl and me, and sitting in a booth together we all three ate ice cream sundaes. At one point I went over to buy something like a tube of shaving cream at the pharmacy counter, and when I got back to the table, I saw my father leaning toward the girl. He was holding her hand, and I overheard him telling her, "We lost Nathan when he was sixteen. Sixteen and he left us." By which he meant that I had left *him*. Years later he would use the same words with my wives. "Sixteen and he left us." By which he meant that all my mistakes in life had flowed from that precipitate departure of mine.

He was right, too. If it weren't for my mistakes I'd still be at home sitting on the front stoop.

It was about two weeks later that Ira went as far as he could toward telling the truth. He was in Newark one Saturday to see his brother, and he and I met downtown for lunch, at a bar and grill near City Hall where, for seventy-five cents—"six bits" to Ira—they served charcoal-broiled steak sandwiches with grilled onions, pickles, home fries, cole slaw, and ketchup. For dessert we each ordered apple pie with a rubbery slice of American cheese, a combination that Ira had introduced me to and that I assumed to be the manly way you ate a piece of pie in a "bar and grill."

Then Ira opened a package he was carrying and presented me with a record album called *The Soviet Army Chorus and Band in a Program of Favorites*. Conducted by Boris Alexandrov. Featuring Artur Eisen and Alexei Sergeyev, basses, and Nikolai Abramov, tenor. On the cover of the album was a picture ("Photograph courtesy SOVFOTO") of the conductor, the band, and the chorus, some two hundred men, all wearing Russian military dress uniforms and performing in the great marble Hall of the People. The hall of the Russian working people.

"Ever hear them?"

"Never," I said.

"Take it home and listen. It's yours."

"Thanks, Ira. This is great."

But it was awful. How could I take this album home, and, at home, how could I *listen*?

Instead of driving back to the neighborhood with Ira after lunch, I told him I had to go over to the public library, the main branch on Washington Street, to work on a history paper. Outside the bar and grill I thanked him again for lunch and the present, and he got into his station wagon and drove back to Murray's on Lehigh Avenue while I proceeded down Broad Street in the direction of Military Park and the big main library. I walked past Market Street and all the way to the park, as if my destination were indeed the library, but then, instead of turning left at Rector Street, I ducked off to the right and took a back way along the river to reach Pennsylvania Station.

I asked a newsdealer in the station to change a dollar for me. I took the four quarters over to the storage area and I put one of them into the coin slot of the smallest of the lockers, and into the locker I shoved the record album. After slamming the door shut, I nonchalantly deposited the locker key in my trouser pocket, and proceeded *then* to the library, where I had nothing to do except to sit for several hours in the reference room worrying about where I was going to hide the key.

My father was around the house all weekend, but on Monday he went back to his office, and on Monday afternoons my mother went up to Irvington to visit her sister, and so after my last class I jumped on a 14 bus across the street from school, took it to the end of the line, to Penn Station, removed the record album from the locker, put it in the Bamberger's shopping bag I had folded up inside my notebook that morning and taken with me to school. At home I hid the record album in a small windowless bin in the basement where my mother stored our set of glass Passover dishes in grocery cartons. Come the spring and Passover, when she removed the dishes for us to use that week, I'd have to find another hiding place, but for the time being the album's explosive potential was defused.

Not until I got to college was I able to play the records on a phonograph, and by then Ira and I were already drifting apart. Which didn't mean that when I heard the Soviet Army Chorus singing "Wait for Your Soldier" and "To an Army Man" and "A Soldier's Farewell"—and, yes, "Dubinushka"—the vision of equality and justice for working people all over the world wasn't reawakened in me. In my dormitory room, I felt proud for having had the guts not to ditch that album—even if I still hadn't guts enough to understand that, with the album, Ira had been trying to tell me: "Yes, I'm a Communist. Of course I'm a Communist. But not a bad Communist, not a Communist who would kill Masaryk or anyone else. I am a beautiful, heartfelt Communist who loves the people and who loves these songs!"

"What happened that next morning?" I asked Murray. "Why did Ira come to Newark that day?"

"Well, Ira slept late that morning. He'd been up with Eve about the abortion till four, and around ten A.M. he was still asleep when he was awakened by someone shouting downstairs. He was in the master bedroom on the second floor on West Eleventh Street, and the voice was coming from the foot of the staircase. It was Sylphid . . .

"Did I mention that the first thing to drive Ira wild was Sylphid telling Eve that she wasn't coming to their wedding? Eve told Ira that Sylphid was doing some kind of program with a flutist and that the Sunday of the wedding was the only day the other girl could rehearse. He himself doesn't particularly care if Sylphid's coming to the wedding but Eve does, and she's crying about it and she's very distraught, and this upsets him. Constantly she gives the daughter the instruments and the power to hurt her—and then she's hurt, but this is the first time he sees it, and he's infuriated. 'Her mother's *wedding*,' Ira said. 'How can she not come to her mother's wedding if that's what her mother wants? *Tell* her she's coming. Don't ask her—*tell* her!' 'I *can't* tell her,' Eve says, 'this is her professional life, this is her music—' 'Okay, *I'll* tell her,' Ira says.

"The upshot was that Eve talked to the girl, and God knows what she said, or promised, or how she begged, but Sylphid showed up at the wedding, in those clothes of hers. A scarf in her hair. She had kinky hair, so she wears these Greek scarves, rakishly as she thought, and they drive her mother crazy. Wears peasant blouses that make her look enormous. Sheer blouses with Greek embroidery on them. Hoop earrings. Lots of bracelets. When she walks, she clinks. You hear her coming. Embroidered schmattas and lots of jewelry. Wore the Greek sandals that you could buy in Greenwich Village. The thongs that tie up to her knees and that dig in and leave marks, and this also makes Eve miserable. But at least the daughter was there, however she looked, and Eve was happy, and so Ira was happy.

"At the end of August, when both their shows were off the air, they married and went up to Cape Cod for a long weekend, and then they got back to Eve's place and Sylphid has disappeared. No note, nothing. They call her friends, they call her father in France, thinking maybe she decided to go back to him. They call the police. On the fourth day Sylphid finally checks in. She's on the Upper West Side with some old teacher she'd had at Juilliard. She'd been staying with her; Sylphid acts as though she didn't know when they were getting back, and that explains why she didn't bother to call from Ninety-sixth Street.

"That evening they all eat dinner together and the silence is awful. It doesn't help the mother any to watch the daughter eat. Sylphid's weight makes Eve frantic on a good night—and this night is not good.

"When she finished each course, Sylphid always cleaned her plate the same way. Ira'd been around army mess halls, crummy diners—lapses of etiquette didn't bother him all that much. But Eve was refinement itself, and watching Sylphid cleaning up was, as Sylphid well knew, a torment for her mother.

"Sylphid would take the side of her index finger, you see, and she'd run it around the edge of the empty plate so as to get all the gravy and the leavings. She'd lick everything off the finger and then she'd do it again and again until her finger squeaked against the plate. Well, on the night that Sylphid decided to come home after her disappearance, she started cleaning her plate that way of hers at dinner, and Eve, who was screwed pretty tight on an ordinary evening, came undone. Could not keep that smile of the ideal mother plastered serenely across her face one second more. 'Stop it!' she screams. 'Stop it! You are twenty-three years old! Stop it, please!'

"Suddenly Sylphid is up on her feet and clubbing at her mother's head—going after her with her fists. Ira leaps up, and that's when Sylphid screams at Eve, 'You kike bitch!' and Ira sinks back into his chair. 'No,' he says. 'No. That won't do. I live here now. I am your mother's husband, and you cannot strike her in my presence. You cannot strike her, period. I forbid it. And you cannot use that word, not in my hearing. Never. *Never in my hearing.* Never use that filthy word *again!*'

"Ira gets up and he leaves the house and he takes one of his calming-down hikes—from the Village walks all the way up to Harlem and back. Tries everything so as not to outright explode. Tells himself all the reasons why the daughter is upset. Our stepmother and our father. Remembers how they treated him. Remembers everything he hated about them. Everything awful that he swore he would never be in life. But what's he to do? The kid takes a swing at her mother, calls her a kike, a kike bitch—what is Ira going to do?

"He gets home around midnight and he does *nothing*. He goes to bed, gets in bed with the brand-new wife, and, amazingly, that's it.

In the morning he sits down at breakfast with the brand-new wife and with the brand-new stepdaughter and he explains that they are all going to live together in peace and harmony, and that to do this they must have respect for one another. He tries to explain everything reasonably, the way nothing was ever explained to him when he was a kid. He's still appalled by what he saw and heard, furious about it, yet he is trying his damnedest to believe that Sylphid isn't really an anti-Semite in the true Anti-Defamation League sense of the word. Which more than likely was the case: Sylphid's insistence upon ego-justice for Sylphid was so extensive, so exclusive, so *automatic,* that a grand historical hostility of even the simplest, most undemanding sort, like hating Jews, could never have taken root in her—there was no room in her. Anti-Semitism was too theoretical for her anyway. The people Sylphid could not endure she could not endure for a good, tangible reason. There was nothing impersonal about it: they stood in her way and blocked her view; they affronted the regal sense of dominance, her *droit de fille.* The whole incident, Ira rightly surmises, hasn't to do with hating Jews. About Jews, about Negroes, about any group that presents a knotty social problem—as opposed to somebody posing an immediate private problem—she does not care one way or the other. She is concerned at that moment only with him. Consequently, she allows to break out into the open a malicious epithet that she instinctively gauges to be so repugnant, so foul and disgusting and out of bounds, as to cause him to walk out the door and never again set foot in her house. 'Kike bitch' is her protest not against the existence of Jews—or even against the existence of her Jewish mother—but against the existence of *him.*

"But having figured all this out overnight, Ira goes ahead—cagily he thinks—not to ask Sylphid for an apology due him, let alone to take the hint and disappear, but to offer *her* an apology. This is how the shrewdie is going to tame her, by offering an apology for his being an interloper. For his being a stranger, an outsider, for his being not her own father but an unknown quantity whom she doesn't have any reason in the world to like or to trust. He tells her that since he's another human being, and human beings don't have a great record going for them, there's probably every reason to *dislike* him and *distrust* him. He says, 'I know the last guy wasn't so hot. But why don't you try me out? My name isn't Jumbo Freedman. I'm a different person from a different outfit with a different serial number. Why not give me a chance, Sylphid? How about giving me ninety days?'

"Then he explains to Sylphid Jumbo Freedman's rapacity—how it stems from *America's* corruption. 'It's a dirty game, American business. It's an insider's game,' he tells her, 'and Jumbo was the classic insider. Jumbo isn't even a speculator in real estate, which would be bad enough. He is a stalking horse for the speculator. He gets a piece of the deal and he doesn't even put down a dime. Now, basically, in America big money is made through secrets. Y'understand? Transactions that are deep underground. Sure, everybody's supposed to play by the same rules. Sure, there is the pretense to virtue, the pretense that everybody is playing fair. Look, Sylphid— do you know the difference between a speculator and an investor? An investor holds the real estate and has the risk involved; he rides the gains or suffers the loss. A speculator trades. Trades land like sardines. Fortunes are made this way. Now, before the Crash occurred, people had speculated with money they had got through taking out the value of the property, extracting from the banks the amortized value in terms of cash. What happened was that when all of these loans were called, they lost their land. The land went back to the banks. Enter the Jumbo Freedmans of the world. For the banks to raise some cash on this worthless paper they were holding, they had to sell it at an enormous discount, a penny on a dollar . . .'

"Ira the educator, the Marxist economist, Ira the star pupil of Johnny O'Day. Well, Eve is elated, a new woman, everything is wonderful again. A real man for herself, a real father for her daughter. At last a father who does what a father is supposed to do!

"'Now, the illegal part of this, Sylphid, the way it is a fixed deal,' Ira explains, 'the collusion involved . . .'

"When the lecture is finally over, Eve gets up and goes over and takes Sylphid's hand and she says, 'I love you.' But not once. Uh-uh. It's 'I love you I love you I love you I love you I love you—' She keeps holding tight to the kid's hand and saying 'I love you.' Each repetition is more heartfelt than the last. She's a performer—she can convince herself when something is heartfelt. 'I love you I love you I love you'—and does Ira think to himself, Go? Does Ira think to himself, This woman is under assault, this woman is up against something I know a little something about: this is a family at war and *nothing* I do is going to work.

"No. He thinks that the Iron Man who has beaten back every disadvantage to get to where he's gotten is not going to be defeated by a twenty-three-year-old. The guy is tenderized by sentiment: he's madly in love with Eve Frame, he's never known a woman like her, he wants to have a child by her. He wants to have a home and a family and a future. He wants to eat dinner the way people do—not alone at some counter somewhere, pouring sugar into his coffee out of a grimy canister, but around a nice table with a family of his own. Just because a twenty-three-year-old throws a temper tantrum, is he going to deny himself everything he has ever dreamed of? Fight the bastards. *Educate* the bastards. *Change* them. If anybody can make things work and straighten people out, it's Ira and his persistence.

"And things do calm down. No fisticuffs. No explosions. Sylphid appears to be getting the message. Sometimes at the dinner table she even tries for two minutes to listen to what Ira is saying. And he thinks, It was the shock of my arrival. That's all it was. Because he's Ira, because he doesn't give in, because he doesn't quit, because he explains everything to everybody sixty-two times, he believes he's got it licked. Ira demands respect from Sylphid for her mother and he believes he's going to get it. But that is just the demand that Sylphid cannot forgive. As long as she can boss her mother around she can have everything she wants, which makes Ira an obstacle right off. Ira shouted, Ira yelled, but he was the first man in Eve's life who ever treated her decently. And that's what Sylphid couldn't take.

"Sylphid was beginning to play professionally, and she was sub-bing as second harpist in the orchestra at Radio City Music Hall. She was called pretty regularly, once or twice a week, and she'd also got a job playing at a fancy restaurant in the East Sixties on Friday night. Ira would drive her from the Village up to the restaurant with her harp and then go and pick her and the harp up when she finished. He had the station wagon, and he'd pull up in front of the house and go inside and have to carry it down the stairs. The harp is in its felt cover, and Ira puts one hand on the column and one hand in the sound hole at the back and he lifts it up, lays the harp on a mattress they keep in the station wagon, and drives Sylphid and the harp uptown to the restaurant. At the restaurant he takes the harp out of the car and, big radio star that he is, he carries it inside. At ten-thirty, when the restaurant is finished serving dinner and Sylphid's ready to come back to the Village, he goes around to pick her up and the whole operation is repeated. Every Friday. He hated the physical imposition that it was—those things weigh about eighty pounds—but he did it. I remember that in the hospi-tal, when he had cracked up, he said to me, 'She married me to carry her daughter's harp! That's why the woman married me! To haul that fucking harp!'

"On those Friday night trips, Ira found he could talk to Sylphid in ways he couldn't when Eve was around. He'd ask her about being a movie star's child. He'd say to her, 'When you were a little girl, when did it dawn on you that something was up, that this wasn't the way everyone grew up?' She told him it was when the tour buses went up and down their street in Beverly Hills. She said she never saw her parents' movies until she was a teenager. Her parents were trying to keep her normal and so they downplayed those movies around the house. Even the rich kid's life in Beverly Hills with the other movie stars' kids seemed normal enough until the tour buses stopped in front of her house and she could hear the tour guide saying, 'This is Carlton Pennington's house, where he lives with his wife, Eve Frame.'

"She told him about the production that birthday parties were for the movie stars' kids—clowns, magicians, ponies, puppet shows, and every child attended by a nanny in a white nurse's uniform. At the dining table, behind every child would be a nanny. The Penningtons had their own screening room and they ran movies. Kids would come over. Fifteen, twenty kids. And the nannies came for that too and they all sat at the back. At the movies Sylphid had to be dressed to the nines.

"She told him about her *mother's* clothes, how alarming her mother's clothes were to a little kid like her. She told him about all the girdles and the bras and the corsets and the waist cinchers and the stockings and the impossible shoes—all that stuff they wore in those days. Sylphid thought how could she possibly ever pull it off. Not in a million years. The hairdos. The slips. The heavy perfume. She remembered wondering how this was all going to happen to her.

"She even told him about her father, just a few things, but enough for Ira to realize how adoring of him she'd been as a child. He had a boat, a boat called the *Sylphid,* docked off the coast of Santa Monica. On Sundays, they sailed to Catalina, her father at the helm. The two of them rode horses together. In those days there was a bridle path that went up Rodeo Drive and down to Sunset Boulevard. Her father used to play polo behind the Beverly Hills Hotel and then go riding alone with Sylphid along the bridle path. One Christmas her father had presents for her dropped from a Piper Cub by one of the stuntmen from the studio. Swooped low over the back lawn and dropped them. Her father, she told him, had his shirts made in London. His suits and his shoes were made in London. Back then, no one in Beverly Hills walked around without ties and suits, but he was the best dressed of them all. To Sylphid, there had been no father more handsome, more delightful, more charming in all of Hollywood. And then, when she was twelve, her mother divorced him, and Sylphid found out about his escapades.

"She told Ira all this stuff on those Friday nights, and in Newark he told it to me, and I was supposed to come away thinking that I had been dead wrong, that Ira would make this kid his pal yet. It was still the beginning of all of them living together, and all the conversations were to try to make some contact with Sylphid, to make peace with her and so on. And it seemed to work—something like intimacy began to develop. He even started going in at night when Sylphid was practicing. He'd ask her, 'How the hell do you play that thing? I gotta tell you, every time I see anybody playing a harp—' And Sylphid would say, 'You think of Harpo Marx,' and they'd both laugh because that was true. 'Where does the sound come from?' he asked her. 'Why are the strings different colors? How can you remember which pedal is which? Don't your fingers hurt?' He asked a hundred questions to show he was interested, and she answered them and explained how the harp worked and showed him her calluses, and things were looking up, things were definitely beginning to look good.

"But then that morning after Eve said that she could not have the baby, and she wept and she wept, and he thought, Okay, that's it, and agreed to take her to the doctor in Camden—that morning he hears Sylphid at the bottom of the stairs. She is giving it to her mother, really laying into her, and Ira jumps out of bed to open the bedroom door, and that's when he hears what Sylphid is saying. This time she's not calling Eve a kike bitch. It's worse than that. Bad enough to send my brother straight back to Newark. And that's how you came to meet him. It puts him on our couch for two nights.

"That morning, that moment, was when Ira realized that it wasn't true that Eve felt she was too old to have a child with him. The alarm sounds and he realizes that it wasn't true that Eve was worried about the effect of a new baby on her career. He realizes that Eve had wanted the baby too, no less than he did, that it had been no easy thing to decide to abort the child of a man she loved, *especially* at the age of forty-one. This is a woman whose deepest sense is her sense of incapacity, and to experience the incapacity of not being generous enough to do this, of not being big enough to do this, of not being *free* enough to do this—*that* was why she had been crying so hard.

"That morning he realizes that the abortion wasn't Eve's decision—it was Sylphid's. That morning he realizes that it wasn't his baby to decide what to do with—it was Sylphid's baby to decide what to do with. The abortion was Eve evading the wrath of her daughter. Yes, the alarm sounds, but still not loud enough for Ira to clear out.

"Yes, all kinds of elemental things percolated up from Sylphid that had nothing to do with playing the harp. What he hears Sylphid saying to her mother is, 'If you ever, ever try that again, I'll strangle the little idiot in its crib!'"

4

THE TOWNHOUSE on West Eleventh Street where Ira lived with Eve Frame and Sylphid, its urbanity, its beauty, its comfort, its low-key aura of luxurious intimacy, the quiet aesthetic harmony of its thousand details—the warm habitation as a rich work of art—altered my conception of life as much as the University of Chicago would when I enrolled there a year and a half later. I had only to walk through the door to feel ten years older and freed from family conventions that, admittedly, I'd grown up adhering to mostly with pleasure and without much effort. Because of Ira's presence, because of the lumbering, easygoing way he strode around the place in baggy corduroy pants and old loafers and checked flannel shirts too short in the sleeves, I didn't feel intimidated by an atmosphere, unknown to me, of wealth and privilege; because of those folksy powers of appropriation that contributed so much to Ira's appeal—at home both on Newark's black Spruce Street and in Eve's salon—I quickly got the idea of how cozily comfortable, how *domesticized,* high living could be. High culture as well. It was like penetrating a foreign language and discovering that, despite the alienating exoticism of its sounds, the foreigners fluently speaking it are saying no more than what you've been hearing in English all your life.

Those hundreds and hundreds of serious books lining the library shelves—poetry, novels, plays, volumes of history, books about archeology, antiquity, music, costume, dance, art, mythology—the classical records filed six feet high in cabinets to either side of the record player, those paintings and drawings and engravings on the walls, the artifacts arranged along the fireplace mantel and crowding the tabletops—statuettes, enamel boxes, bits of precious stone, ornate little dishes, antique astronomical devices, unusual objects sculpted of glass and silver and gold, some recognizably representational, others odd and abstract—were not decoration, not ornamental bric-a-brac, but possessions bound up with pleasurable living and, at the same time, with *morality,* with mankind's aspiration to achieve significance through connoisseurship and thought. In such an environment, roaming from room to room looking for the evening paper, sitting and eating an apple in front of the fire could in themselves be part of a great enterprise. Or so it seemed to a kid whose own house, though clean, orderly, and comfortable enough, had never awakened in him or in anybody else ruminations on the ideal human condition. My house—with its library of the *Information Please Almanac* and nine or ten other books that had come into our possession as gifts for convalescing family members—seemed by comparison shabby and bleak, a colorless hovel. I could not have believed back then that there was anything on West Eleventh Street that anyone would ever want to flee. It looked to me like the luxury liner of havens, the *last* place where you would have to worry about having your equilibrium disturbed. At its heart, upright and massively elegant on the library's oriental rug, utterly graceful in its substantiality and visible the instant you turned from the entryway into the living room, was that symbol, reaching back to civilization's enlightened beginnings, of the spiritually rarefied realm of existence, the gorgeous instrument whose shape alone embodies an admonishment to every defect of coarseness and crudeness in man's mundane nature . . . that stately instrument of transcendence, Sylphid's gold-leafed Lyon and Healy harp.

*

"That library was to the rear of the living room and up a step," Murray was remembering. "There were sliding oak doors that closed the one room off from the other, but when Sylphid practiced Eve liked to listen, and so the doors were left open and the sound of that instrument carried through the house. Eve, who'd started Sylphid on the harp out in Beverly Hills when she was seven, couldn't get enough of it, but Ira could make no sense of classical music— never listened to anything, as far as I know, except the popular stuff on the radio and the Soviet Army Chorus—and so at night, when he preferred to be sitting around downstairs in the living room with Eve, talking, reading the paper, a husband at home and so forth, he kept retreating to his study. Sylphid would be plucking away and Eve would be doing her needlepoint in front of the fire, and when she'd look up, he'd be gone, upstairs writing letters to O'Day.

"But after what she'd been through in that third marriage, the fourth, when it got going, was still pretty wonderful. When she met Ira, she was coming out of a bad divorce and recovering from a nervous breakdown. The third husband, Jumbo Freedman, was a sex clown from the sound of it, expert at entertaining them in the bedroom. Had a high old time of it altogether till she came home early from a rehearsal one day and found him in his upstairs office with a couple of tootsies. But he was everything Pennington wasn't. She has an affair with him out in California, obviously very passionate, certainly for a woman twelve years with Carlton Pennington, and in the end Freedman leaves his wife and she leaves Pennington, and she, Freedman, and Sylphid decamp for the East. She buys that house on West Eleventh Street and Freedman moves in, sets up his office in what became Ira's study, and starts trading property in New York as well as in L.A. and Chicago. For a while he is buying and selling Times Square property, and so he meets the big theatrical producers, and they all start to socialize together, and soon enough Eve Frame is on Broadway. Drawing room comedies, thrillers, all starring the one-time silent-screen beauty. One after another is a hit. Eve is making money hand over fist, and Jumbo sees that it's well spent.

"Being Eve, she goes along with this guy's extravagance, acquiescing to his wild ways, is even caught up in the wild ways. Sometimes when Eve would start to cry out of nowhere and Ira would ask her why, she would tell him, 'The things he made me do—what I had to do . . .' After she wrote that book and her marriage to Ira was all over the papers, Ira got a letter from some woman in Cincinnati. Said that if he was interested in a little book of his own, he might want to come out to Ohio for a talk. She'd been a nightclub entertainer back in the thirties, a singer, a girlfriend of Jumbo's. She said Ira might like to see some photographs Jumbo had taken. Maybe she and Ira could collaborate on a memoir of their own—he'd supply the words, she, for a price, would fork over the pictures. At the time Ira was so hell-bent on getting his revenge that he wrote the woman back, sent her a check for a hundred dollars. She claimed to have two dozen, and so he sent her the hundred bucks she was asking for just in order to see one."

"Did he get it?"

"She was true to her word. She sent him one, all right, by return mail. But because I wasn't going to allow my brother to further distort people's idea of what his life had meant, I took it from him and destroyed it. Stupid. Sentimental, priggish, stupid, and not very farsighted of me, either. Circulating the picture would have been benevolent compared to what happened."

"He wanted to disgrace Eve with the picture."

"Look, once upon a time all Ira thought about was how to alleviate the effects of human cruelty. Everything was funneled through that. But after that book of hers came out, all he thought about was how to inflict it. They stripped him of his job, his domestic life, his name, his reputation, and when he realized he'd lost all of that, lost the status and no longer had to live up to it, he shed Iron Rinn, he shed *The Free and the Brave,* he shed the Communist Party. He even stopped talking so much. All that endless outraged rhetoric. Going on and on when what this huge man really wanted to do was to lash out. The talk was the way to blunt those desires.

"What do you think the Abe Lincoln act was about? Putting on that stovepipe hat. Mouthing Lincoln's words. But everything that ever tamed him, all the civilizing accommodations, he shed, and he was stripped right back to the Ira who'd dug ditches in Newark. Back to the Ira who'd mined zinc up in the Jersey hills. He reclaimed his earliest experience, when his tutor was the shovel. He made contact with the Ira before all the moral correction took place, before he'd been to Miss Frame's Finishing School and taken all those etiquette lessons. Before he went to finishing school with *you*, Nathan, acting out the drive to father and showing you what a good, nonviolent man he could be. Before he went to finishing school with *me*. Before he went to finishing school with *O'Day*, the finishing school of Marx and Engels. The finishing school of political action. Because O'Day was the first Eve, really, and Eve just another version of O'Day, dragging him up out of the Newark ditch and into the world of light.

"Ira knew his own nature. He knew that he was physically way out of scale and that this made him a dangerous man. He had the rage in him, and the violence, and standing six and a half feet tall, he had the means. He knew he needed his Ira-tamers—knew he needed all his teachers, knew he needed a kid like you, knew that he hungered for a kid like you, who'd got all he'd never got and was the admiring son. But after *I Married a Communist* appeared, he shed the finishing school education, and he reclaimed the Ira you never saw, who beat the shit out of guys in the army, the Ira who, as a boy starting out on his own, used the shovel he dug with to protect himself against those Italian guys. Wielded his work tool as a weapon. His whole life was a struggle not to pick up that shovel. But after her book, Ira set out to become his own uncorrected first self."

"And did he?"

"Ira never shirked a man-sized job, however onerous. The ditch-digger made his impact on her. He put her in touch with what she had done. 'Okay, I'll educate her,' he told me, 'without the dirty picture.'"

"And he did it."

"He did it, all right. Enlightenment through the shovel."

Early in 1949, some ten weeks after Henry Wallace was so badly defeated—and, I now know, after her abortion—Eve Frame threw a big party (preceded by a smaller dinner party) to try to cheer Ira up, and he called our house to invite me to come. I had seen him only once again in Newark after the Wallace rally at the Mosque, and until I got the astonishing phone call ("Ira Ringold, buddy. How's my boy?") I'd begun to believe that I'd never see him again. After the second time that we'd met—and gone off for our first walk ever in Weequahic Park, where I learned about "Eye-ran"—I'd mailed to him in New York a carbon copy of my radio play *The Stooge of Torquemada*. As the weeks went by and there was no response from him, I realized the mistake I'd made in giving to a professional radio actor a play of mine, even one that I considered my best. I was sure that now that he'd seen how little talent I had, I'd killed any interest he might have had in me. Then, while I was doing my homework one night, the phone rang and my mother came running into my room. "Nathan—dear, it's Mr. Iron Rinn!"

He and Eve Frame were having people to dinner, and among them would be Arthur Sokolow, whom he'd given my script to read. Ira thought I might like to meet him. My mother made me go to Bergen Street the next afternoon to buy a pair of black dress shoes, and I took my one suit to the tailor shop on Chancellor Avenue to have Schapiro lengthen the sleeves and the trousers. And then early one Saturday evening, I popped a Sen-Sen in my mouth and, my heart beating as though I were intent on crossing the state line to commit murder, I went out to Chancellor Avenue and boarded a bus to New York.

My companion at the dinner table was Sylphid. All the traps laid for me—the eight pieces of cutlery, the four differently shaped drinking glasses, the large appetizer called an artichoke, the serving dishes presented from behind my back and over my shoulder by a solemn black woman in a maid's uniform, the finger bowl, the enigma of the finger bowl—everything that made me feel like a very small boy instead of a large one, Sylphid all but nullified with a sardonic wisecrack, a cynical explanation, even just with a smirk or with a roll of her eyes, helping me gradually to understand that there wasn't as much at stake as all the pomp suggested. I thought she was splendid, in her satire particularly.

"My mother," Sylphid said, "likes to make everything a strain the way it was when she grew up in Buckingham Palace. She makes the most of every opportunity to turn everyday life into a joke." Sylphid kept it up throughout the meal, dropped into my ear remarks rife with the worldliness of someone who'd grown up in Beverly Hills—next door to Jimmy Durante—and then in Greenwich Village, America's Paris. Even when she teased me I felt relieved, as if my mishap might not lie but one course away. "Don't worry too much about doing the right thing, Nathan. You'll look a lot less comical doing the wrong thing."

I also took heart from watching Ira. He ate the same way here as he did at the hot dog stand across from Weequahic Park; he talked the same way too. He alone among the men at the table was without a tie and a dress shirt and a jacket, and though he didn't lack for ordinary table manners, it was clear from watching him spear and swallow his food that the subtleties of Eve's kitchen were not overscrupulously assessed by his palate. He did not seem to draw any line between conduct permissible at a hot dog stand and in a splendid Manhattan dining room, neither conduct nor conversation. Even here, where the silver candelabra were lit with ten tall candles and bowls of white flowers illuminated the sideboard, everything made him hot under the collar—on this night, only a couple of months after the crushing Wallace defeat (the Progressive Party had received little more than a million votes nationwide, about a sixth of what it had anticipated), even something seemingly as uncontroversial as Election Day.

"I'll tell you one thing," he announced to the table, and everyone else's voice faded while his, strong and natural, charged with protest and barbed with contempt for the stupidity of his fellow Americans, promptly commanded, *You just listen to me.* "I think this darling country of ours doesn't understand politics. Where else in the world, in a democratic nation, do people go to work on Election Day? Where else are the schools still open? If you're young and you're growing up and you say, 'Hey, it's Election Day, don't we have a day off?' your father and mother say, 'No, it's Election Day, that's all,' and what are you left to think? How important can Election Day be if I have to go to school? How can it be important if the stores and everything else are open? Where the hell are your values, you son of a bitch?"

By "son of a bitch" he was alluding to nobody present at the table. He was addressing everyone in his life he had ever had to fight.

Here Eve Frame put her finger to her lips to get him to rein himself in. "Darling," she said in a voice so soft it was barely audible. "Well, what's more important," he loudly replied, "to stay home on Columbus Day? You close the schools up because of a shitty holiday, but you don't close them up because of Election Day?" "But nobody's arguing the point," Eve said with a smile, "so why be angry?" "Look, I get angry," he said to her, "I always got angry, I hope to my dying day I *stay* angry. I get in trouble because I get angry. I get in trouble because I won't shut up. I get very angry with my darling country when Mr. Truman tells people, and they believe him, that Communism is the big problem in this country. Not the racism. Not the inequities. That's not the problem. The Communists are the problem. The forty thousand or sixty thousand or a hundred thousand Communists. They're going to overthrow the government of a country of a hundred and fifty million people. Don't insult my intelligence. I'll tell you what's going to overthrow the whole goddamn place—the way we treat the colored people. The way we treat the working people. It's not going to be the Communists who overthrow this country. This country is going to overthrow itself by treating people like animals!"

Seated across from me was Arthur Sokolow, the radio writer, another of those assertive, self-educated Jewish boys whose old neighborhood allegiances (and illiterate immigrant fathers) strongly determined their brusque, emotional style as men, young guys only recently back from a war in which they'd discovered Europe and politics, in which they'd first really discovered America through the soldiers they had to live alongside, in which they'd begun, without formal assistance but with a gigantic naive faith in the transforming power of art, to read the fifty or sixty opening pages of the novels of Dostoyevsky. Until the blacklist destroyed his career, Arthur Sokolow, though not as eminent a writer as Corwin, was certainly in the ranks of the other radio writers I most admired: Arch Oboler, who wrote *Lights Out,* Himan Brown, who wrote *Inner Sanctum,* Paul Rhymer, who wrote *Vic and Sade,* Carlton E. Morse, who wrote *I Love a Mystery,* and William N. Robson, who'd done a lot of war radio from which I also drew for my own plays. Arthur Sokolow's prizewinning radio dramas (as well as two Broadway plays) were marked by their intense hatred of corrupt authority as represented by a grossly hypocritical father. I kept fearing throughout dinner that Sokolow, a short, wide tank of a man, a defiant pile driver who'd once been a Detroit high school fullback, was going to point at me and denounce me to everyone at the table as a plagiarist because of all I had stolen from Norman Corwin.

Following dinner, the men were invited up to Ira's second-floor study for cigars while the women went to Eve's room to freshen up before the after-dinner guests began to arrive. Ira's study overlooked the floodlit statuary in the rear garden, and on the three walls of bookshelves he kept all his Lincoln books, the political library he'd carried home in three duffel bags from the war, and the library he'd since accumulated browsing in the secondhand bookshops on Fourth Avenue. After passing around the cigars and advising his guests to take whatever they liked from the whiskey cart, Ira got his copy of my radio play out of the top drawer of the massive mahogany desk—the one where I imagined he kept up his correspondence with O'Day—and began to read aloud the play's opening speech. And to read it not to denounce me for plagiarism. Rather, he began by telling his friends, including Arthur Sokolow, "You know what gives me hope for this country?" and he pointed at me, all aglow and tremulously waiting to be seen through. "I got more faith in a kid like this than in all those so-called mature people in our darling country who went into the voting booth prepared to vote for Henry Wallace, and all of a sudden they saw a big picture of Dewey in front of their eyes—and I'm talking about people in my own *family*—so they pulled down Harry Truman's lever. Harry Truman, who is going to lead this country into World War III, and that's their enlightened choice! The Marshall Plan, that is their choice. All they can think is to bypass the United Nations and to hem in the Soviet Union and to destroy the Soviet Union while siphoning off into their Marshall Plan hundreds and hundreds of millions of dollars that could go to raising the standard of living for the poor in this country. But tell me, who is going to hem in Mr. Truman when he drops his atomic bombs on the streets of Moscow and Leningrad? You think they won't drop atomic bombs on innocent Russian children? To preserve our wonderful democracy they won't do that? Tell me another one. Listen to this kid here. Still in high school and he knows more about what's wrong with this country than every one of our darling countrymen in the voting booth."

Nobody laughed or even smiled. Arthur Sokolow was backed against the bookcases, quietly paging through a book he'd taken down from Ira's Lincoln collection, and the rest of the men stood smoking their cigars and sipping their whiskey and acting as though my view of America were what they'd gone out with their wives to hear that night. Only much later did I realize that the collective seriousness with which my introduction was received signified nothing more than how accustomed they were to the agitations of their overbearing host.

"Listen," said Ira, "just listen to this. Play about a Catholic family in a small town and the local bigots." Whereupon Iron Rinn launched into my lines: Iron Rinn inside the skin, inside the *voice-*

box, of an ordinary, good-natured, Christian American of the kind I'd had in mind and knew absolutely nothing about.

"'I'm Bill Smith,'" Ira began, plunking down into his high-backed leather chair and throwing his legs up onto his desktop. "'I'm Bob Jones. I'm Harry Campbell. My name doesn't matter. It's not a name that bothers anyone. I'm white and Protestant, and so you don't have to worry about me. I get along with you, I don't bother you, I don't annoy you. I don't even hate you. I quietly earn my living in a nice little town. Centerville. Middletown. Okay Falls. Forget the name of the town. Could be anywhere. Let's *call* it Anywhere. Many people here in Anywhere give lip service to the fight against discrimination. They talk about the need to wreck the fences that keep minorities in social concentration camps. But too many carry on their fight in abstract terms. They think and speak of justice and decency and right, about Americanism, the Brotherhood of Man, and the Constitution and the Declaration of Independence. All this is fine, but it shows they are really unaware of the what and why of racial, religious, and national discrimination. Take this town, take Anywhere, take what happened here last year when a Catholic family right around the corner from me found that zealous Protestantism can be just as cruel as Torquemada was. You remember Torquemada. The hatchet man for Ferdinand and Isabella. Ran the Inquisition for the king and queen of Spain. Guy who expelled the Jews from Spain for Ferdinand and Isabella back in 1492. Yeah, you heard right, pal—1492. There was Columbus, sure, there was the *Niña,* the *Pinta,* and the *Santa María*—and then there was Torquemada. There's always Torquemada. Maybe there always will be . . . Well, here's what happened right here in Anywhere, USA, under the Stars and Stripes, where all men are created equal, and not in 1492 . . .'"

Ira flipped through the pages. "And it goes on like that . . . and here, the ending. This is the end. The narrator again. A fifteen-year-old kid has the courage to write this, y'understand? Tell me the network that would have the courage to put it on. Tell me the sponsor who in the year 1949 would stand up to Commandant

Wood and his committee, who would stand up to Commandant Hoover and his storm-trooper brutes, who would stand up to the American Legion and the Catholic War Veterans and the VFW and the DAR and all our darling patriots, who wouldn't give a shit if they called him a goddamn Red bastard and threatened to boycott his precious product. Tell me who would have the courage to do that because it is the right thing to do. Nobody! Because they don't give any more of a shit about freedom of speech than the guys I was with in the army gave a shit about it. They didn't talk to me. Did I ever tell you that? I walked into the mess hall, y'understand, two hundred and some-odd men, nobody said hello, nobody said anything because of the stuff I was saying and the letters I was writing to *Stars and Stripes*. Those guys gave you the distinct impression that World War II was being fought to spite them. Contrary to what some people may think about our darling boys, they didn't have the slightest notion, didn't know what the hell they were there for, didn't give a shit about fascism, about Hitler—what did they care? Get them to understand the social problems of Negroes? Get them to understand the devious ways capitalism endeavors to weaken labor? Get them to understand why when we bomb Frankfurt the I. G. Farben plants are not touched? Maybe I am myself handicapped by my lack of education, but the picayune minds of 'our boys' make me violently sick! 'It all comes to this,'" he suddenly read from my script. "'If you want a moral, here it is: The man who swallows the guff about racial, religious, and national groups is a sap. He hurts himself, his family, his union, his community, his state, and his country. He's the stooge of Torquemada.' Written," Ira said, angrily tossing the script down on his desk, "by a fifteen-year-old kid!"

There must have been another fifty people who showed up after dinner. Despite the extraordinary stature Ira had imposed on me up in his study, I would never have had the courage to stay and mingle with everybody pressed into the living room had it not been for Sylphid's again coming to my rescue. There were actors and actresses, directors, writers, poets, there were lawyers and literary agents and theatrical producers, there was Arthur Sokolow, and there was Sylphid, who not only called all the guests by their given names but knew in caricatured detail their every flaw. She was a reckless, entertaining talker, a great hater with the talent of a chef for filleting, rolling, and roasting a hunk of meat, and I, whose aim was to be radio's bold, uncompromising teller of the truth, was in awe of how she did nothing to rationalize, let alone to hide, her amused contempt. That one is the vainest man in New York . . . that one's need to be superior . . . that one's insincerity . . . that one hasn't the faintest idea . . . that one got so drunk . . . that one's talent is so minute, so infinitesimal . . . that one is so embittered . . . that one is so depraved . . . what's most laughable about that lunatic is her grandiosity . . .

How delicious to belittle people—and to watch them being belittled. Especially for a boy whose every impulse at that party was to revere. Worried as I was about getting home late, I couldn't deprive myself of this first-class education in the pleasures of spite. I'd never met anyone like Sylphid: so young and yet so richly antagonistic, so worldly-wise and yet, costumed in something long and gaudy as if she were a fortuneteller, so patently oddballish. So happy-go-lucky about being repelled by *everything*. I'd had no idea how very tame and inhibited I was, how eager to please, until I saw how eager Sylphid was to antagonize, no idea how much freedom there was to enjoy once egoism unleashed itself from the restraint of social fear. There was the fascination: her formidability. I saw that Sylphid was fearless, unafraid to cultivate within herself the threat that she could be to others.

The two people she announced herself least able to endure were a couple whose Saturday morning radio show happened to be a favorite of my mother's. The program, called *Van Tassel and Grant*, emanated from the Hudson River farmhouse, up in Dutchess County, New York, of the popular novelist Katrina Van Tassel Grant and her husband, the *Journal-American* columnist and entertainment critic Bryden Grant. Katrina was an alarmingly thin six-footer with long dark ringlets that once must have been thought alluring and a bearing that suggested that she did not lack for a sense of the influence she brought to bear on America through her novels. The little I knew about her up until that night—that dinnertime in the Grant house was reserved for discussion with her four handsome children of their obligations to society, that her friends in traditional old Staatsburg (where her ancestors, the Van Tassels, first settled, reportedly as local aristocracy, in the seventeenth century, long before the arrival of the English) had impeccable ethical and educational credentials—I had happened to overhear when my mother was tuned in to *Van Tassel and Grant*.

"Impeccable" was a word much favored in Katrina's weekly monologue on her rich and varied record-breaking existence in the bustling city and the bucolic countryside. Not only were *her* sentences infested with "impeccable," but so were my mother's after an hour of listening to Katrina Van Tassel Grant—whom my mother thought "cultivated"—lauding the superiority of whoever was so fortunate as to be brought within the Grants' social purview, whether it was the man who fixed her teeth or the man who fixed her toilet. "An impeccable plumber, Bryden, im*pec*cable," she said, while my mother, like millions of others, listened enraptured to a discussion of the drainage difficulties that afflict the households of even the most wellborn of Americans, and my father, who was solidly in Sylphid's camp, said, "Oh, turn that woman off, will you, please?"

It was Katrina Grant about whom Sylphid had muttered to me, "What's most laughable about that lunatic is her grandiosity"; it was about the husband, Bryden Grant, that she had said, "That one is the vainest man in New York."

"My mother goes to lunch with Katrina and she comes home white with rage. 'That woman is impossible. She tells me about the theater and she tells me about the latest novels and she thinks she knows everything and she knows *nothing*.' And it's true: when they go to lunch, Katrina invariably lectures Mother on the one thing Mother happens to know all about. Mother can't stand Katrina's books. She can't even read them. She bursts out laughing when she tries, and then she tells Katrina how wonderful they are. Mother has a nickname for everyone who frightens her—Katrina's is 'Loony.' 'You should have heard Loony on the O'Neill play,' she tells me. 'She outdid herself.' Then Loony calls at nine the next morning and Mother spends an hour with her on the phone. My mother goes through vehement indignation the way a spendthrift goes through a bankroll, then she turns right around and sucks up to her because of the 'Van' in her name. And because when Bryden drops Mother's name in his column, he calls her 'the Sarah Bernhardt of the Airwaves.' Poor Mother and her social ambitions. Katrina is *the* most pretentious of all the rich, pretentious river folk up in Staatsburg, and *he's* supposed to be a descendant of Ulysses S. Grant. Here," she said, and in the midst of the party, with guests everywhere so closely huddled together that they looked as though they had all they could do to keep their muzzles out of one another's drinks, Sylphid turned to search the wall of bookcases behind us for a novel by Katrina Van Tassel Grant. To either side of the living room fireplace, bookcases extended from floor to ceiling, rising so high that a library ladder had to be mounted to get to the topmost shelves.

"Here," she said. "*Eloise and Abelard.*" "My mother read that," I said. "Your mother's a shameless hussy," Sylphid replied, rendering me weak in the knees until I realized she was joking. Not just my mother, but nearly half a million Americans had bought it and read it. "Here—open to a page, any page, put a finger down anywhere, and then prepare to be ravished, Nathan of Newark."

I did as she told me, and when Sylphid saw where my finger was pointing she smiled and said, "Oh, you don't have to look very far to find V.T.G. at the top of her talent." Aloud to me Sylphid read, "'His hands clasped about her waist, drawing her to him, and she felt the powerful muscles of his legs. Her head fell back. Her mouth parted to receive his kiss. One day he would suffer castration as a brutal and vengeful punishment for this passion for Eloise, but for now he was far from mutilated. The harder he grasped, the harder was the pressure on her sensitive areas. How aroused he was, this man whose genius would revamp and revitalize the traditional teaching of Christian theology. Her nipples were drawn hard and sharp, and her gut tightened as she thought, "I am kissing the greatest writer and thinker of the twelfth century!" "Your figure is magnificent," he whispered in her ear, "swelling breasts, small waist! And not even the full satin skirts of your gown can conceal from view your loveliness of hip and thigh." Best known for his solution of the problem of universals and for his original use of dialectics, he knew no less well, even now, at the height of his intellectual fame, how to melt a woman's heart. . . . By morning they were sated. At last it was her chance to say to the canon and master of Notre Dame, "Now teach me, please. Teach me, Pierre! Explain to me your dialectical analysis of the mystery of God and the Trinity." This he did, patiently going into the ins and outs of his rationalistic interpretation of the Trinitarian dogma, and then he took her as a woman for the eleventh time.'

"Eleven times," said Sylphid, hugging herself from the sheer delight of what she'd heard. "That husband of hers doesn't know what *two* is. That little fairy doesn't know what *one* is." And it was a while before she was able to stop laughing—before either of us could. "'Oh, teach me, *please,* Pierre,'" cried Sylphid, and for no reason in the world—other than her happiness—she kissed me loudly on the tip of my nose.

After Sylphid had returned *Eloise and Abelard* to the shelves and we were both more or less sober again, I felt emboldened enough to ask her a question I'd been wanting to ask all evening. One of the questions I'd been wanting to ask. Not "What was it like to grow up in Beverly Hills?"; not "What was it like to live next door to Jimmy Durante?"; not "What was it like having movie star parents?" Because I was afraid of her ridiculing me, I asked only what I considered to be my most serious question.

"What's it like," I said, "to play at Radio City Music Hall?"

"It's a horror. The *conductor's* a horror. 'My dear lady, I know it's *so* difficult to count to four in that bar, but if you *wouldn't* mind, that would be *so* nice.' The more polite he is, the nastier you know he's feeling. If he's really angry, he says, 'My dear *dear* lady.' The 'dear' dripping with venom. 'That's not quite right, dear, that should be done arpeggiated.' And you have your part printed *non*-arpeggiated. You can't go back, without seeming argumentative and wasting time, and say, 'Excuse me, maestro, actually it's printed the other way.' So everybody looks at you, thinking, Don't you know how it's supposed to be done, idiot—he has to tell you? He's the world's worst conductor. All he's conducting is music from the standard repertoire, and still you have to think, Has he never *heard* this piece before? Then there's the band car. At the Music Hall. You know, this platform that moves the band into view. It moves up and backward and forward and down, and every time it moves, it jerks—it's on a hydraulic lift—and you sit and hold on to your harp for dear life even as it's going out of tune. Harpists spend half their time tuning and the other half playing out of tune. I hate all harps."

"Do you really?" I said, laughing away, in part because she was being funny and in part because, imitating the conductor, she'd been laughing too.

"They're impossibly difficult to play. They break down all the time. You *breathe* on a harp," she said, "and it's out of tune. Trying to have a harp in perfect condition makes me *crazy*. Moving it around—it's like moving an aircraft carrier."

"Then why do you play the harp?"

"Because the conductor's right—I *am* stupid. Oboists are smart. Fiddle players are smart. But not harpists. Harpists are dummies, moronic dummies. How smart can you be to pick an instrument that's going to ruin and run your life the way the harp does? There's no way, had I not been seven years old and too stupid to know better, that I would have begun playing the harp, let alone be playing it still. I don't even have conscious memories of life before harp."

"Why did you start so young?"

"Most little girls who start the harp start the harp because Mommy thinks it's such a *lovely* thing for them to do. It looks so pretty and all the music is so damned sweet, and it's played politely in small rooms for polite people who aren't the least bit interested. The column painted in gold leaf—you need sunglasses to look at it. Really refined. It sits there and reminds you of itself all the time. And it's so monstrously big, you can never put it away. *Where* are you going to put it? It's always there, sitting there and mocking you. You can never get away from it. Like my mother."

A young woman still in her coat and carrying a small black case in her hand appeared suddenly beside Sylphid, apologizing in an English accent for arriving late. With her were a stout, dark-haired young man—elegantly turned out and, as though corseted in all his privilege, holding his youthful chubbiness militarily erect—and a virginally sensuous young woman, ripish-looking, just verging on fullness, with a cascade of curling reddish gold hair to offset her fair complexion. Eve Frame rushed up to meet all the newcomers. She embraced the girl carrying the small black case, whose name was Pamela, and was then introduced by Pamela to the glamorous couple, affianced and soon to be married, who were Rosalind Halladay and Ramón Noguera.

Within only minutes Sylphid was in the library, the harp against her knees and cradled on her shoulder while she tuned it, Pamela was out of her coat and was alongside Sylphid fingering the keys of her flute, and, seated beside the two of them, Rosalind tuned a stringed instrument that I assumed was a violin but that I shortly discovered was something slightly larger called a viola. Gradually everybody in the living room turned toward the library, where Eve Frame stood waiting for silence, Eve Frame wearing an outfit I later described to my mother as well as I could and that my mother then told me was a white pleated chiffon gown and capelet with an emerald green chiffon sash. When I described her hairdo as I remembered it, my mother told me it was called a feather cut, with long curls all around and a smooth crown. Even while Eve Frame patiently waited, a faint smile intensifying her loveliness (and her fascination to me), a joyful excitement was evidently mounting within her. When she spoke, when she said, "Something beautiful is about to happen," all her elegant reserve seemed on the brink of being swept away.

It was quite a performance, particularly to an adolescent who in half an hour was going to have to get back on the number 107 Newark bus and return to a household whose intensities no longer left him anything other than frustrated. Eve Frame came and went in less than a minute, but in just the grand way she strode down the step and back into the living room in her white pleated chiffon gown and capelet, she gave the whole evening a new meaning: the adventure for which life is lived was about to unfold.

I don't want to make it seem as though Eve Frame appeared to be playing a role. Far from it: this was her *freedom* being revealed, Eve Frame unimpeded, rapturously unintimidated, in a state of serene exaltation. If anything, it was as if *we* had been assigned by *her* nothing less than the role of our lives—the role of privileged souls whose fondest dream had been made to come true. Reality had fallen victim to artistic wizardry; some store of hidden magic had purified the evening of its mundane social function, purged that glittering half-drunk assemblage of all vile instincts and low-down schemes. And this illusion had been created out of practically nothing: a few perfectly enunciated syllables from the edge of the library step, and all the nonsensical self-seeking of a Manhattan soirée dissolved into a romantic endeavor to flee into aesthetic bliss.

"Sylphid Pennington and the young London flutist Pamela Solomon will play two duets for flute and harp. The first is by Fauré and is called 'Berceuse.' The second is by Franz Doppler, his 'Casilda Fantasie.' The third and final selection will be the lively second movement, the Interlude, from the Sonata for Flute, Viola, and Harp by Debussy. The violist is Rosalind Halladay, who is visiting New York from London. Rosalind is a native of Cornwall, England, and a graduate of London's Guildhall School of Music and Drama. In London, Rosalind Halladay now plays with the orchestra of the Royal Opera House."

The flutist was a mournful-looking girl, long-faced, dark-eyed, and slender, and the more I looked at her and the more enamored

I became of her—and the more I looked at Rosalind and the more enamored I became of *her*—the more trenchantly I saw how deficient my friend Sylphid was in anything designed to promote a man's desire. With her square trunk and stout legs and that odd excess of flesh that thickened her a bit like a bison across the upper back, Sylphid looked to me, while playing the harp—and even despite the classical elegance of her hands moving along the strings—like a wrestler wrestling the harp, one of those Japanese sumo wrestlers. Because this was a thought that I was ashamed to be having, it only gathered substance the longer the performance continued.

I couldn't make head or tail of the music. Like Ira, I was deaf to the sound of anything other than the familiar (in my case, to what I heard Saturday mornings on *Make-Believe Ballroom* and Saturday nights on *Your Hit Parade*), but the sight of Sylphid gravely under the spell of the music she was disentangling from those strings and, too, the *passion* of her playing, a concentrated passion that you could see in her eyes—a passion liberated from everything in her that was sardonic and negative—made me wonder what powers might have been hers if, in addition to her musicianship, her face were as alluringly angular as her delicate mother's.

Not until decades later, after Murray Ringold's visit, did I understand that the only way Sylphid could begin to feel at ease in her skin was by hating her mother and playing the harp. Hating her mother's infuriating weakness and producing ethereally enchanting sounds, making with Fauré and Doppler and Debussy all the amorous contact the world would allow.

When I looked at Eve Frame, in the front rank of the spectators, I saw that she was looking at Sylphid with a gaze so needy that you would think that in Sylphid was the genesis of Eve Frame rather than the other way around.

Then everything that had stopped was starting up again. There was the applause, the bravos, the bows, and Sylphid, Pamela, and Rosalind came down from the stage that the library had become and Eve Frame was there to embrace each of them in turn. I was close enough to hear her say to Pamela, "You know what you looked like, my darling? A Hebrew princess!" And to Rosalind, "And you were lovely, absolutely lovely!" And finally to her daughter, "Sylphid, Sylphid," she said, "Sylphid Juliet, never, never have you played more beautifully! Never, darling! The Doppler was especially lovely."

"The Doppler, Mother, is salon garbage," Sylphid said.

"Oh, I love you!" cried Eve. "Your mother loves you so!"

Others started coming up to congratulate the trio of musicians, and the next I knew, Sylphid slipped an arm around my waist and was good-naturedly introducing me to Pamela, to Rosalind, and to Rosalind's fiancé. "This is Nathan of Newark," Sylphid said. "Nathan is a political protégé of the Beast's." Since she said it with a smile, I smiled too, trying to believe that the epithet was harmlessly meant, no more than a family joke about Ira's height.

I looked all around the room for Ira and saw that he wasn't there, but rather than asking to be excused to go and find him, I allowed myself to remain appropriated within Sylphid's grip—and engulfed by the sophistication of her friends. I had never seen anyone as young as Ramón Noguera so well dressed or so smoothly decorous and urbane. As for the dark Pamela and the fair Rosalind, each seemed so pretty to me that I couldn't look openly at either of them for more than a split second at a time, though simultaneously I was unable to forgo the opportunity to stand casually within only inches of their flesh.

Rosalind and Ramón were to be married in three weeks at the Nogueras' estate just outside Havana. The Nogueras were tobacco growers, Ramón's father having inherited from Ramón's grandfather thousands of farm acres in a region called the Partido, land that would be inherited by Ramón, and in time by the children of Ramón and Rosalind. Ramón was formidably silent—grave with his sense of self-destiny, diligently resolved to act out the position of authority bestowed upon him by the cigar smokers of the world, while Rosalind—who only a few years back had been a poor London music student from a remote corner of rural England but who was now as close to the end of all her fears as she was to the beginning of all that spending—grew more and more vivacious. And loquacious. She told us about Ramón's grandfather, the most renowned and revered of the Nogueras, for some thirty years a provincial governor as well as a vast landowner until he entered the cabinet of President Mendiata (whose chief of staff, I happened to know, was the infamous Fulgencio Batista); she told us about the beauty of the tobacco plantations where, under cloth, they grew the wrapper leaf for the Cuban cigars; and then she told us about the grand Spanish-style wedding that the Nogueras had planned for them. Pamela, a childhood friend, was being flown from New York to Havana, at the expense of the Noguera family, and would be put up at a guesthouse on the estate; and if Sylphid could find the time, said the overbrimming Rosalind, she was welcome to come along with Pamela.

Rosalind spoke with eager innocence, with a joyful blend of pride and accomplishment, about the enormous wealth of the Nogueras while I kept thinking, But what about the Cuban peasants who are the tobacco workers—who flies *them* back and forth from New York to Havana for a family wedding? In what sort of "guesthouses" do *they* live on the beautiful tobacco plantations? What about disease and malnutrition and ignorance among your tobacco workers, Miss Halladay? Instead of obscenely squandering all that money on your Spanish-style wedding, why not begin to compensate the Cuban masses whose land your fiancé's family illegitimately holds?

But I was as close-mouthed as Ramón Noguera, though, internally, nowhere near as emotionally composed as he looked to be, unflinchingly staring straight ahead as if reviewing the troops. Everything Rosalind said appalled me, and yet I could not be socially incorrect enough to tell her so. Nor could I summon up the strength to confront Ramón Noguera with the Progressive Party's assessment of his riches and their source. Nor could I move voluntarily away from Rosalind's English radiance, a young woman both physically lovely and musically gifted who seemed not to understand that by abandoning her ideals for Ramón's allurements—or, if not her ideals, by abandoning mine—by marrying into Cuba's oligarchical, landholding upper class, she was not only fatally compromising the values of an artist but, in my political estimation, trivializing herself with someone far less worthy of her talent—and her reddish gold hair and eminently caressable skin—than, for instance, me.

As it turned out, Ramón had reserved a table at the Stork Club for Pamela, Rosalind, and himself, and when he asked Sylphid to join them, he also, with a certain vacant aplomb, a kind of upper-class analogue to courtesy, turned to extend an invitation to me. "Please, sir," he said, "come as my guest."

"I can't, no—" I said, but then, without explaining—as I knew that I should, that I had to, that I must . . . as I knew *Ira* would—"I don't approve of you or your kind!" but adding instead, "Thanks. Thanks just the same," I turned and, as though I were escaping the plague rather than a marvelous opportunity for a budding writer to see Sherman Billingsley's famous Stork Club and the table where Walter Winchell sat, I rushed away from the temptations being dangled by the first plutocrat I had ever laid eyes on.

Alone I went up to a second-floor guest bedroom, where I was able to find my coat at the bottom of the dozens piled on the twin beds, and there I ran into Arthur Sokolow, who was said by Ira to have read my play. I'd been too shy to say anything to him up in Ira's study after Ira's brief reading, and, occupying himself with browsing through that Lincoln book, he hadn't appeared to have anything to say to me. Several times during the party, however, I'd overheard something he was aggressively telling someone in the living room. "That got me so goddamn mad," I heard him say. "I sat down in a white heat and wrote the piece overnight"; I heard him say, "The possibilities were unlimited. There was an atmosphere of freedom, of willingness to establish new frontiers"; then I heard him laugh and say, "Well, they fed me against the ranking number-one program in radio . . . ," and the impact on me was as though I had encountered the indispensable truth.

I got my strongest picture ever of what I wanted my life to be like when, by deliberately roaming within earshot of him, I listened to Sokolow describing to a couple of women a play he was planning to write for Ira, a one-man show based not on the speeches but on the entire life of Abraham Lincoln, from his birth to his death. "The First Inaugural, the Gettysburg Address, the Second Inaugural— that's not the story. That's the rhetoric. I want Ira up there telling the *story*. Telling how goddamn *difficult* it was: no schooling, the stupid father, the terrific stepmother, the law partners, running against Douglas, losing, that hysterical shopper his wife, the brutal loss of the son—the death of Willie—the condemnation from every side, the daily political assault from the moment the man took office. The savagery of the war, the incompetence of the generals, the Emancipation Proclamation, the victory, the Union preserved and the Negro freed—*then* the assassination that changed this country forever. Wonderful stuff there for an actor. Three hours. No intermission. Leave them speechless in their seats. Leave them grieving for what America might be like today, for the Negro *and* the white man, if he'd served his second term and overseen Reconstruction. I've thought a lot about that man. Killed by an actor. Who else?" He laughed. "Who else would be so vain and so stupid as to kill Abraham Lincoln? Can Ira do three hours up there alone? The oratorical stuff—that we know he can do. Otherwise, together we'll work on it, and he'll get it: a mightily harassed leader full of wit and cunning and intellectual power, a huge creature alternately high-spirited and savagely depressed, and," said Sokolow, laughing again, "not yet apprised of the fact that he is 'Lincoln' of the Memorial."

Now Sokolow merely smiled, and in a voice that surprised me by its gentleness, he said, "Young Mr. Zuckerman. This must be some night for you." I nodded but again found myself tongue-tied, unable to ask if he had any advice for me or any criticism of my play. A well-developed sense of reality (for a fifteen-year-old) told me that Arthur Sokolow hadn't read the play.

As I was stepping out of the bedroom with my coat, I saw

Katrina Van Tassel Grant coming toward me from the bathroom. I was a tall boy for my age but, in high-heeled shoes, she towered above me, though perhaps I would have fallen under the spell of her imposingness, felt that she considered herself to be the loftiest example of something or other, even had I been a foot taller. It all happened so spontaneously that I couldn't begin to understand how this person I was supposed to hate—and to hate so effortlessly—could be so impressive up close. A trashy writer as well as a supporter of Franco's and a foe of the USSR, yet where, when I needed it, was my antipathy? When I heard myself saying, "Mrs. Grant? Would you sign your name—for my mother?" I had to wonder who I suddenly was or what sort of hallucination I was having. This was worse than I'd behaved with the Cuban tobacco tycoon.

Smiling at me, Mrs. Grant came up with a suggestion as to who I might indeed be to explain my presence in this grand house. "Aren't you Sylphid's young man?"

I hadn't even to think to lie. "Yes," I said. I didn't know that I looked old enough, but perhaps teenage boys were a specialty of Sylphid's. Or perhaps Mrs. Grant still thought of Sylphid as just a kid. Or maybe she'd seen Sylphid kiss me on the nose, and assumed that kiss had to do with the two of us rather than with Abelard taking Eloise for the eleventh time.

"Are you a musician too?"

"Yes," I said.

"What instrument do you play?"

"The same. The harp."

"Isn't that unusual for a boy?"

"No."

"What shall I write on?" she asked.

"I think in my wallet there's a piece of paper—" But then I remembered that pinned inside my wallet was the Wallace-for-President button that I'd worn to school on my shirt pocket every day for two months and that, after the disastrous election, I had refused to part with. I now flashed it like a police badge whenever I went to get money to pay for something. "I forgot my wallet," I said.

From the beaded bag that she carried in one hand, she extracted a notepad and a silver pen. "What's your mother's name?"

She had asked kindly enough, but I couldn't tell her.

"Don't you remember?" she said with a harmless smile.

"Just *your* name. That's enough. Please."

As she was writing, she said to me, "What is your background, young man?"

I didn't at first understand that she was asking to what subspecies of humanity I belonged. The word "background" was impenetrable—and then it wasn't. I had no intention of being humorous when I replied, "I don't have one."

Now, why had she seemed a greater star to me, a more *frightening* star, than Eve Frame? Especially after Sylphid's dissection of her and her husband, how could I be so overwhelmed by the cravenness of fandom and address her in the tones of a nincompoop?

It was her power, of course, the power of celebrity; it was the power of one who partook of her husband's power as well, for with a few words spoken over the radio or with a remark in his column—with an *ellipsis* in his column—Bryden Grant was able to make and break show-business careers. Hers was the chilling power of someone whom people are always smiling at and thanking and hugging and hating.

But why did *I* kiss her ass? I didn't have a show-business career. What did I have to gain—or to lose? It had taken under a minute for me to abandon every principle and belief and allegiance I had. And I would have continued to if she had not mercifully signed her name and returned to the party. Nothing was required of me except to ignore her, as she was having no trouble ignoring me until I asked for the autograph for my mother. But my mother wasn't somebody who collected autographs, nor had anyone forced me to fawn and lie. It was just the easiest thing to do. It was worse than easy. It was automatic.

"Don't lose your courage," Paul Robeson had warned me backstage at the Mosque. Proudly I shook his hand, and I had lost it, first time out. Pointlessly lost it. I wasn't pulled into police head-quarters and beaten with a truncheon. I walked out into the hall-way with my coat. That was all it took for little Tom Paine to go off the rails.

I headed down the stairs seething with the self-disgust of some-one young enough to think that you had to mean everything you said. I would have given anything to have had the wherewithal to go back and somehow put her in her place—just because of how pathetically I had behaved instead. Soon enough my hero would do that for me, however, and with none of my egregious politeness diluting the rich recklessness of his antagonism. Ira would more than make up for all that I had omitted to say.

I found Ira in the basement kitchen, drying the dishes that were being washed in the double sink by Wondrous, the maid who'd served our dinner, and a girl about my age who turned out to be her daughter, Marva. When I walked in, Wondrous was saying to Ira, "I did not want to waste my vote, Mr. Ringold. I did not want to waste my precious vote."

"Tell her," Ira said to me. "The woman won't believe me. I don't know why. You tell her about the Democratic Party. I don't know how a Negro woman can get it into her head that the Democratic Party is going to stop breaking its promises to the Negro race. I don't know who told her that or why she would believe him. Who told you, Wondrous? I didn't. Damn it, I told you six months ago—they are not going to bring an end to Jim Crow, your weak-kneed liberals of the Democratic Party. They are not and never have been the partners of the Negro people! There was only one party in the election that a Negro could vote for, one party that fights for the underdog, one party dedicated to making the Negro in this country a first-class citizen. And it was not the Democratic Party of Harry Truman!"

"I could not throw away my vote, Mr. Ringold. That's all I would be doing. Throwing it down the drain."

"The Progressive Party nominated more Negro candidates for office than any party in American history—fifty Negro candidates for important national offices on Progressive Party tickets! For offices no Negro has ever been nominated for, let alone held! That's throwing a vote down the drain? Damn it, don't insult your intelligence, and don't insult mine. I get damn angry with the Negro community when I think that you were not alone in not thinking what you were doing."

"I'm sorry, but a man who loses like that man lost cannot do nothing for us. We got to live somehow, too."

"Well, what you *did* was nothing. Worse than nothing. What you did with your vote was to put back in power the people who are going to give you segregation and injustice and lynching and the poll tax for as long as you live. As long as Marva lives. As long as Marva's *children* live. Tell her, Nathan. You met Paul Robeson. He met Paul Robeson, Wondrous. To my mind, the greatest Negro in American history. Paul Robeson shook his hand, and what did he tell you, Nathan? Tell Wondrous what he said to you."

"He said, 'Don't lose your courage.'"

"And that's what you lost, Wondrous. You lost your courage in the voting booth. I am surprised at you."

"Well," she said, "you all can wait if you want, but we got to live somehow."

"You let me down. What's worse, you let Marva down. You let Marva's *children* down. I don't understand it and I never will. No, I do not understand the working people of this country! What I hate with a passion is listening to people who do not know how to vote in their own goddamn interest! I would like to throw this dish, Wondrous!"

"Do what you want, Mr. Ringold. Ain't *my* dish."

"I get so goddamn angry about the Negro community and what they did and did not do for Henry Wallace, what they did not do for *themselves*, that I would really like to break this dish!"

"Good night, Ira," I said, while Ira stood there threatening to break the dinner dish that he was finishing drying. "I have to go home."

Just then, Eve Frame's voice came from the top of the landing: "Come say good night to the Grants, dear."

Ira pretended not to hear and turned again to Wondrous. "Many are the fine words, Wondrous, bantered by men everywhere of a new world—"

"Ira? The Grants are leaving. Come upstairs to say good night."

Suddenly he did throw the dish, just let it fly. Marva cried "Momma!" when it struck the wall, but Wondrous shrugged—the irrationality of even white people *opposed* to Jim Crow did not surprise her—and she set about picking up the broken pieces as Ira, dishtowel in hand, streaked for the stairs, bounding up them three at a time, and shouting so as to be heard at the top of the landing. "I can't understand, when you have freedom of choice and you live in a country like ours, where supposedly nobody compels you to do anything, how anybody can sit down to dinner with that Nazi son-of-a-bitch killer. How do they do that? Who compels them to sit down with a man whose life's work is to perfect something new to kill people better than what they killed them with before?"

I was right behind him. I didn't know what he was talking about until I saw that he was headed for Bryden Grant, standing in the doorway wearing a Chesterfield overcoat and a silk scarf and holding his hat in one hand. Grant was a square-faced man with a prominent jaw and a head enviably thick with soft silver hair, a solidly constructed fifty-year-old about whom there was, nonetheless—and just because he was so attractive—something a little porous-looking.

Ira hurtled toward Bryden Grant and didn't stop himself until their faces were only inches apart.

"Grant," he said to him. "Grant, right? Isn't that your name? You're a college graduate, Grant. A Harvard man, Grant. A Harvard man and a Hearst newspaperman, and you're a Grant—of the

Grants! You are supposed to know something better than the ABCs. I know from the shit you write that your stock-in-trade is to be devoid of convictions, but are you devoid of any convictions about anything?"

"Ira! Stop this!" Eve Frame had her hands to her face, which was drained of color, and then her hands were clutching at Ira's arms. "Bryden," she cried, looking helplessly back over her shoulder while trying to force Ira into the living room, "I'm terribly, terribly—I don't know—"

But Ira easily swept her away and said, "I repeat: are you devoid, Grant, of *any* convictions?"

"This is not your best side, Ira. You are not presenting your best side." Grant spoke with the superiority of one who had learned very young not to stoop to defend himself verbally against a social inferior. "Good night, all," he said to those dozen or so guests still in the house who had gathered in the hallway to see what the commotion was about. "Good night, dear Eve," Grant said, throwing her a kiss, and then, turning to open the door to the street, took his wife by the arm to leave.

"Wernher von Braun!" Ira shouted at him. "A Nazi son-of-a-bitch engineer. A filthy fascist son of a bitch. You sit down with him and you have dinner with him. True or false?"

Grant smiled and, with perfect self-control—his calm tone divulging just the hint of a warning—said to Ira, "This is extremely rash of you, sir."

"You have this Nazi at your house for dinner. True or false? People who work and make things that kill people are bad enough, but this friend of yours was a friend of Hitler's, Grant. Worked for Adolf Hitler. Maybe you never heard about all this because the people he wanted to kill weren't Grants, Grant—they were people like me!"

All this time, Katrina had been glaring at Ira from her husband's side, and it was she who now replied on his behalf. Anyone listening for one morning to *Van Tassel and Grant* might have surmised that Katrina often replied on his behalf. That way he maintained an ominous autocratic demeanor and she got to feed a hunger for supremacy that she did nothing to conceal. While Bryden clearly considered himself more intimidating if he said little and let the authority flow from the inside outward, Katrina's frightening-ness—not unlike Ira's—came from her saying it all.

"Nothing you are shouting makes one bit of sense." Katrina Grant's mouth was full-sized and yet—I now noticed—a tiny hole was all that she employed to speak, a hole at the center of her lips the circumference of a cough drop. Through this she extruded the hot little needles that constituted her husband's defense. The spell of the encounter was upon her—this was war—and she did look impressively statuesque, even up against a lug six foot six. "You are an ignorant man, and a naive man, and a rude man, a bullying, simple-minded, arrogant man, you are a boor, and you don't know the facts, you don't know the reality, you don't know what you are talking about, now or ever! You know only what you parrot from the *Daily Worker*!"

"Your dinner guest von Braun," Ira shouted back, "didn't kill enough Americans? Now he wants to work for Americans to kill Russians? Great! Let's kill Commies for Mr. Hearst and Mr. Dies and the National Association of Manufacturers. This Nazi doesn't care who he kills, as long as he gets his paycheck and the veneration of—"

Eve screamed. It was not a scream that seemed theatrical or calculated, but in that hallway full of well-turned-out partygoers—where one man in tights was not, after all, running a rapier through another man in tights—she did seem to have arrived awfully fast at a scream whose pitch was as horrifying as any human note I had ever heard sounded, on or off a stage. Emotionally, Eve Frame did not seem to have to go far to get where she wanted to be.

"Darling," said Katrina, who had stepped forward to take Eve by the shoulders and protectively to embrace her.

"Ah, cut the crap," said Ira, as he started back down the stairs to the kitchen. "Darling's fine."

"She is *not* fine," said Katrina, "nor *should* she be. This house is not a political meeting hall," Katrina called after him, "for political thugs! Must you raise the roof every time you open your rabble-rousing mouth, must you drag into a beautiful, civilized home your Communist—"

He was instantly up out of the stairwell, and shouting, "This is a democracy, Mrs. Grant! My beliefs are my beliefs. If you want to know Ira Ringold's beliefs, all you have to do is ask him. I don't give a damn if you don't like them *or* me. These are my beliefs, and I don't give a damn if *nobody* likes them! But no, your husband draws his salary from a fascist, so anyone comes along daring to say what the fascists don't like to hear, it's 'Communist, Communist, there's a Communist in our civilized home.' But if you had enough flexibility in your thinking to know that in a democracy the Communist philosophy, *any* philosophy—"

This time when Eve Frame screamed it was a scream with neither a bottom to it nor a top, a scream that signaled a life-threatening state of emergency and that ended effectively all political discourse and, with it, my first big evening out on the town.

5

"THE JEW HATRED, this contempt for Jews," I said to Murray. "Yet she married Ira, married Freedman before him . . ."

It was our second session. Before dinner, we had sat out on the deck overlooking the pond, and while we drank our martinis, Murray had told me about the day's lectures down at the college. I shouldn't have been surprised by his mental energy, even by his enthusiasm for the three-hundred-word writing assignment—discuss, from the perspective of a lifetime, any one line in Hamlet's most famous soliloquy—that the professor had given his elderly students. Yet that a man so close to oblivion should be preparing homework for the next day, educating himself for a life that had all but run out—that the puzzle continued to puzzle him, that clarification remained a vital need—more than surprised me: a sense of error settled over me, bordering on shame, for living to myself and keeping everything at such a distance. But then the sense of error vanished. There were no more difficulties I wished to create.

I grilled chicken on the barbecue and we ate dinner outside on the deck. It was well after eight when we finished our meal, but we were only into the second week of July and, though that morning when I went for my mail the postmistress had informed me that we were going to lose forty-nine minutes of sun that month—and that if we didn't have rain soon, we would all have to go to the store for blackberry and raspberry preserves; and that the local roadkill was running four times greater than this time last year; and that there had been another sighting, near somebody's bird feeder at the edge of the woods, of our resident six-foot-tall black bear—there was as yet no end in sight for this day. Night was tucked away behind a straightforward sky proclaiming nothing but permanence. Life without end and without upheaval.

"Was she a Jew? She was," said Murray, "a pathologically embarrassed Jew. Nothing superficial about that embarrassment. Embarrassed that she looked like a Jew—and the cast of Eve Frame's face was subtly quite Jewish, all the physiognomic nuances Rebecca-like, right out of Scott's *Ivanhoe*—embarrassed that her daughter looked like a Jew. When she learned that I spoke Spanish, she told me, 'Everybody thinks Sylphid is Spanish. When we went to Spain, everybody took her for a native.' It was too pathetic even to dispute. Who cared anyway? Ira didn't. Ira had no use for it. Politically opposed. Couldn't stand religion of any kind. At Passover, Doris used to prepare a family seder and Ira wouldn't come near it. Tribal superstition.

"I think when he first met Eve Frame he was so bowled over by her, by everything—fresh to New York, fresh to *The Free and the Brave*, squiring around on his arm *The American Radio Theater*—I think that her being or not being a Jew never came up. What difference did it make to him? But anti-Semitism? That made *all* the difference. Years later he told me how whenever he said the word 'Jew' in public she would try to quiet him down. They'd take the elevator in an apartment building after visiting somebody somewhere and there'd be a woman with a baby in her arms or a baby in a carriage, and Ira wouldn't even notice them, but when they got into the street, Eve would say, 'What a perfectly hideous child.' Ira couldn't figure what was eating her until he realized that the hideous child was always the child of a woman who looked to her grossly Jewish.

"How could he stand five minutes of that crap? Well, he couldn't. But it wasn't the army, Eve Frame was no southern hillbilly, and he wasn't about to take a swing at her. Pummeled her instead with adult education. Ira tried to be an O'Day to Eve, but she was no Ira. The Social and Economic Origins of Anti-Semitism. That was the course. Sat her down in his study and read aloud to her from his books. Read aloud to her from the notepads he'd carried around with him during the war, where he'd put down his observations and thoughts. 'There is nothing superior in being Jewish—and there is nothing inferior or degrading. You are Jewish, and that's it. That's the story.'

"He bought her what was one of his favorite novels back then, a book by Arthur Miller. Ira must have given away dozens of copies of it. Called *Focus*. He gave Eve a copy, then marked it all up for her, so she wouldn't miss the important passages. He explained it to her the way O'Day used to explain books at the base library in Iran. Remember *Focus*, Miller's novel?"

I remembered it well. Ira had given me a copy too, for my sixteenth birthday, and, like O'Day, explained it to *me*. During my last years of high school, *Focus* took its place, alongside *On a Note of Triumph* and the novels of Howard Fast (and two war novels that he gave me, *The Naked and the Dead* and *The Young Lions*), as a book that affirmed my own political sympathies as well as furnishing a venerated source from which I could take lines for my radio plays.

Focus was published in 1945, the year Ira returned from overseas with his duffel bags full of books and the thousand bucks he'd won on the troopship shooting craps, and three years before the Broadway production of *Death of a Salesman* made Arthur Miller a famous playwright. The book tells of the harshly ironic fate of a Mr. Newman, a personnel officer for a big New York corporation, a cautious, anxiety-ridden conformist in his forties—too cautious to become actively the racial and religious bigot he is secretly in his heart. After Mr. Newman is fitted for his first pair of glasses, he discovers that they set off "the Semitic prominence of his nose" and make him dangerously resemble a Jew. And not just to himself. When his crippled old mother sees her son in his new glasses, she laughs and says, "Why, you almost look like a Jew." When he turns up at work in the glasses, the response to his transformation is not so benign: he is abruptly demoted from his visible position in personnel to a lowly job as a clerk, a job from which Mr. Newman resigns in humiliation. From that moment on, he who himself despises Jews for their looks, their odors, their meanness, their avarice, their bad manners, even for "their sensuous lust for women," is marked as a Jew everywhere he goes. So socially wide-ranging is the animosity he incites that it feels to the reader—or did to me as an adolescent—that it cannot be Newman's face alone that is responsible but that the source of his persecution is a mammoth, spectral incarnation of the extensive anti-Semitism that he was himself too meek to enact. "He had gone all his life bearing this revulsion toward Jews" and now that revulsion, materialized on his Queens street and throughout New York as in a terror-filled nightmare, ostracizes him brutally—in the end, violently—from the neighbors whose acceptance he had courted with his obedient conformism to their ugliest hatreds.

I went into the house and came back with the copy of *Focus* I probably hadn't opened since I got it from Ira and read it through in one night, then through again twice more, before setting it between the bookends on the bedroom desk where I kept my stash of sacred texts. On the title page Ira had inscribed a message to me. When I gave the book to Murray, he handled it a moment (a relic of his brother) before turning to the inscription to read it aloud:

> Nathan—There are so few times I find anybody to hold an intelligent conversation with. I read lots and believe that what good I get from that must be stimulated and take form in discussion with other people. You are one of those few people. I feel slightly less pessimistic as regards the future because of knowing a young person like you.
>
> Ira, April 1949

My former teacher flipped through *Focus* to see what I had underlined in 1949. He stopped a quarter of the way in and again read aloud to me, this time from one of the printed pages. "'His face,'" Murray read. "'*He* was not this face. Nobody had a right to dismiss him like that because of his face. Nobody! He was *him*, a human being with a certain definite history and he was not this face which looked like it had grown out of another alien and dirty history.'

"She reads this book at Ira's request. She reads what he underlines for her. She listens to his lecture. And what is the subject of the lecture? The subject is the subject of the book—the *subject* is the Jewish face. Well, as Ira used to say: It's hard to know how much she hears. This was a prejudice that, no matter what she heard, no matter how much she heard, she could not let go of."

"*Focus* didn't help," I said when Murray handed back the book to me.

"Look, they met Arthur Miller at a friend's house. Maybe it was at a party for Wallace, I don't remember. After Eve was introduced to him, she volunteered to Arthur Miller how *gripping* she had found his book. Probably wasn't lying, either. Eve read many books, and with a far wider understanding and appreciation than Ira, who if he didn't find political and social implications in the book, the whole thing was no good. But whatever she learned from reading or from music or art or acting—or from personal experience, from all the tremulous living she'd done—remained apart from where the hatred did its work. She couldn't escape it. Not that she was a person who couldn't make a change. She changed her name, changed husbands, changed from movies to the stage to radio when her professional fortunes altered and a change had to be made, but this was fixed in her.

"I don't mean that things didn't get better the longer Ira hammered away—or didn't look as though they'd gotten better. To avoid those lectures of his, she probably censored herself at least a little. But a change of heart? When she *had* to—to hide the way she felt from her social set, from the prominent *Jews* in her social set, to hide the way she felt from Ira himself—she did it. Indulged him, patiently listened when he was off and running about anti-Semitism in the Catholic Church and the Polish peasantry and in France during the Dreyfus affair. But when she found a face inexcusably Jewish (like the one on my wife, like Doris's), her thoughts weren't Ira's or Arthur Miller's.

"Eve hated Doris. Why? A woman who'd worked in a hospital lab? A former lab technician? A Newark mother and housewife? What threat could she possibly pose to a famous star? How much effort would it have taken to tolerate her? Doris had scoliosis, there was pain as she aged, she had to have an operation to insert a rod and that didn't go very well, and so on and so forth. The fact is that Doris, who to me was pretty as a picture from the day I met her till the day she died, had a deformation of the spine and you noticed it. Her nose was not so straight as Lana Turner's. You noticed *that*. She grew up speaking English the way it was spoken in the Bronx when she was a kid—and Eve could not bear to be in her presence. Couldn't look at her. My wife was too upsetting for her to look at.

"During those three years they were married, we were invited for dinner exactly once. You could see it in Eve's eyes. What Doris wore, what Doris said, what Doris looked like—all repellent to her. Me, Eve was apprehensive of; she didn't care for me for other reasons. I was a schoolteacher from Jersey, a nobody in her world, but she must have seen in me a potential foe and so she was always polite. And charming. The way she was with you, I'm sure. I had to admire the pluck in her: a fragile, high-strung person, easily addled, who'd come as far as she had, a woman of the world—that requires tenacity. To keep trying, to keep surfacing after all she'd been through, after all her career setbacks, to make a success in radio, to create that house, to establish that salon, to entertain all those people . . . Sure, she was wrong for Ira. And he for her. They had no business together. Nonetheless, to take him on, to take on yet another husband, to get a big new life going again, that took *something*.

"If I separated out her marriage to my brother, if I separated out her attitude to my wife, if I tried looking at her separate from that stuff—well, she was a bright, peppy little thing. Separate out all that and she was probably the same bright, peppy little thing who'd gone out to California and taken on being a silent-movie actress at the age of seventeen. She had spirit. You saw it in those silent films. Under all that civility, she masked a lot of spirit—I venture to say, *Jewish* spirit. There was a generous side to her when she could relax, which was not often. When she was relaxed, you felt that there was something in her wanting to do the right thing. She tried to pay attention. But the woman was hog-tied—it wouldn't work. You couldn't establish any sort of independent relationship with her, and she couldn't take any independent interest in you. You couldn't count on her judgment for very long, either, not with Sylphid at her other side.

"Well, after we left that night, she said to Ira, a propos of Doris, 'I hate those wonderful wives, those doormats.' But it wasn't a doormat Eve saw in Doris. She saw a Jewish woman of the sort she could not abide.

"I knew this; it didn't take Ira to clue me in. He felt too compromised to anyway. My kid brother could tell me anything, tell *anybody* anything—had since the day he could talk—but *that* he couldn't tell me until everything was kaput. But he didn't have to for me to know that the woman had got caught in her own impersonation. The anti-Semitism was just a part of the role she was playing, a careless part of what went into playing the role. In the beginning, I would think, it was almost inadvertent. It was unthinking more than malicious. In that way went along with everything else she did. The thing that's happening to her is unobserved by her.

"You're an American who doesn't want to be your parents' child? Fine. You don't want to be associated with Jews? Fine. You don't want anybody to know you were born Jewish, you want to disguise your passage into the world? You want to drop the problem and pretend you're somebody else? Fine. You've come to the right country. But you don't have to hate Jews into the bargain. You don't have to punch your way out of something by punching somebody else in the face. The cheap pleasures of Jew hating aren't necessary.

You're convincing as a Gentile without them. That's what a good director would have told her about her performance. He would have told her that the anti-Semitism is overdoing the role. It's no less a deformity than the deformity she was trying to obliterate. He would have told her, 'You're a film star already—you don't need anti-Semitism as a part of your superior baggage.' He would have told her, 'As soon as you do that, you're gilding the lily and you're not convincing at all. It's over the top, you're doing too much. The performance is logically too complete, too airless. You're succumbing to a logic that doesn't obtain in real life like that. Drop it, you don't need it, it'll work much better without it.'

"There is, after all, the aristocracy of art, if it's aristocracy she was after—the aristocracy of the performer to which she could naturally belong. Not only can it accommodate being un-anti-Semitic, it can even accommodate being a Jew.

"But Eve's mistake was Pennington, taking him for her model. She hit California and she changed her name and she was a knockout and got into pictures and then, under the studio's pressure and prodding, with its help, she left Mueller and married this silent-screen star, this rich, polo-playing, upper-class *genuine* aristocrat, and she took her idea of a Gentile from *him. He* was her director. That's where she screwed up but good. To take for your model, for your Gentile mentor, another outsider guarantees that the impersonation will not work. Because Pennington is not just an aristocrat. He's also homosexual. He's also anti-Semitic. And she picks up his attitudes. All she's trying to do is get away from where she began, and that is no crime. To launch yourself undisturbed by the past into America—that's your choice. The crime isn't even bringing an anti-Semite close to you. That's your choice too. The crime is being unable to stand up to him, unable to defend against the assault, and taking his attitudes for yours. In America, as I see it, you can allow yourself every freedom but that one.

"In my time, as in yours, the Sandhurst of this sort of thing, the foolproof training ground—if such a thing there is—for Jews de-Jewing themselves, was usually the Ivy League. Remember Robert

Cohn in *The Sun Also Rises?* Graduates from Princeton, boxes there, never thinks about the Jewish part of himself, and is still an oddity, at least to Ernest Hemingway. Well, Eve took her degree, not at Princeton, but in Hollywood, under Pennington. She settled on Pennington for his seeming normality. That is, Pennington was such an exaggerated Gentile aristocrat that she, an innocent—that is to say, a Jew—thought of him as not exaggerated but normal. Whereas the Gentile woman would have smelled this out and understood it. The Gentile woman of Eve's intelligence would never have consented to marrying him, studio or no studio; she would have understood at the outset that he was defiant and damaging and spitefully superior to the Jewish outsider.

"The enterprise was flawed from the beginning. She did not have a natural affinity with the common model of what she was interested in, so she impersonated the wrong Gentile. And she was young and she got rigidly fixed in the role, unable to improvise. Once the performance was set, A to Z, she was fearful of pulling any part of it, fearful that the whole act would come undone. There's no self-scrutiny, and so there's no possibility for minor adjustment. She's not the master of the role. The role mastered her. On the stage she would have been able to give a more subtle performance. But then, on the stage she had a level of consciousness that she did not always exhibit in life.

"Now, if you want to be a real American Gentile aristocrat, you would, whether or not you felt it, pretend to great *sympathy* for the Jews. That would be the cunning way to do it. The point about being an intelligent, sophisticated aristocrat is that, unlike everyone else, you force yourself to overcome, or to appear to overcome, the contemptuous reaction to difference. You can still hate 'em in private if you have to. But not to be able to engage Jews easily, with good-spirited ease, would morally compromise a true aristocrat. Good-spirited and easy—that's the way Eleanor Roosevelt did it. That's the way Nelson Rockefeller did it. That's the way Averell Harriman did it. Jews aren't a problem for these people. Why should they be? But they are for Carlton Pennington. And that's whose route she takes and how she became embedded in all those attitudes she didn't need.

"For her, as Pennington's mock-aristocratic young wife, the permissible transgression, the *civilized* transgression, wasn't Judaism and couldn't be; the permissible transgression was homosexuality. Until Ira came along, she was unaware not only of how offensive all the accoutrements of anti-Semitism were but of how damaging they were to *her*. Eve thought, If I hate Jews, how can I possibly be a Jew? How can you hate the thing you are?

"She hated what she was and she hated how she looked. Eve Frame, of all people, hated her looks. Her own beauty was her own ugliness, as though that lovely woman had been born with a big purple blotch spread across her face. The indignation at having been born that way, the outrage of it, never left her. She, like Arthur Miller's Mr. Newman, was not her face either.

"You must be wondering about Freedman. An unsavory character, but Freedman, unlike Doris, wasn't a woman. He was a man, and he was rich, and he offered protection from everything that oppressed Eve as much as or even more than her being a Jew. He ran her finances for her. He was going to make *her* rich.

"Freedman, by the way, had a very large nose. You'd think Eve would flee at the sight of him—a swarthy little Jew, a real estate speculator with a big nose and bowed legs and Adler elevated shoes. The guy even has an accent. He's one of those crinkly-haired Polish Jews, with the orange-reddish hair and the old-country accent and the tough little immigrant's vigor and drive. He's all appetite, a heavyset bon vivant, but large as his belly is, his prick, by all reports, is still larger and visible beyond it. Freedman, you see, is her reaction to Pennington as Pennington was her reaction to Mueller: you marry one exaggeration one time, you marry the antithetical exaggeration the next. Third time round she marries Shylock. Why not? By the end of the twenties silent films were all but over, and despite that diction (or because of it, because it was too elocutionary back then), she never took off in talkies, and now it's 1938, and she was terrified that she would never work again, and so she went to the

Jew for what you go to a Jew for—money and business and licentious sex. I suppose for a while he sexually resuscitated her. It's not a complicated symbiosis. It was a transaction. A transaction in which she got taken to the cleaners.

"You have to remember Shylock, you have also to remember *Richard III*. You'd think Lady Anne would run a million miles from Richard, duke of Gloucester. This is the foul monster who murdered her husband. She spits in his face. 'Why dost thou spit at me?' he says. 'Would it were mortal poison,' she says. Yet the next we know, she's wooed and won. 'I'll have her,' Richard says, 'but I will not keep her long.' The erotic power of a foul monster.

"Eve had no idea in the world how to oppose or how to resist, no idea how to conduct herself in a dispute or a disagreement. But everybody every day has to oppose and resist. You don't have to be an Ira, but you have to steady yourself every day. But for Eve, since every conflict is perceived as an assault, a siren is sounded, an air-raid siren, and reason never enters the picture. One second exploding with spite and fury, the next capitulating, caving in. A woman with a superficial kind of delicacy and gentleness but confused by everything, bitter and poisoned by life, by that daughter, by herself, by her insecurity, by her total insecurity from one minute to the next—and Ira falls for her.

"Blind to women, blind to politics, head-over-heels committed to both. Seizes everything with the same overengagement. Why Eve? Why choose Eve? He wants most in this world to be worthy of Lenin and Stalin and Johnny O'Day, and so he entangles himself with her. Responds to the oppressed in all forms, and responds to their oppression in exactly the wrong way. If he weren't my brother, I wonder how seriously I would have taken his hubris. Well, that must be what brothers are for—not to stand on ceremony about the bizarre."

"Pamela," Murray erupted, having had to overcome some minor impediment—the age of his brain—to get to the name. "Sylphid's best friend was an English girl named Pamela. Played the flute. I never met her. She was only described to me. Once I saw her photograph."

"I met Pamela," I said. "I knew Pamela."

"Attractive?"

"I was fifteen. I wanted something unheard-of to happen to me. That makes every girl attractive."

"A beauty, according to Ira."

"According to Eve Frame," I said, "'a Hebrew princess.' That's what she called Pamela that night I met her."

"What else? She must romantically aggrandize everything. The exaggeration washes away the stain. You had better be a princess if you are a Hebrew woman expecting to be made welcome in the home of Eve Frame. Ira had a fling with the Hebrew princess."

"Did he?"

"Ira fell in love with Pamela and wanted her to run off with him. He used to take her out to Jersey on her day off. In Manhattan she had a small apartment by herself, near Little Italy, a ten-minute walk from West Eleventh Street, but it was dangerous for Ira to show up at her place. You couldn't miss a guy that size on the street, and in those days he was doing his Lincoln all over town, free for schools and so on, and a lot of people in Greenwich Village knew who he was. On the street he was always talking to people, finding out what they did for a living and telling them how they were getting screwed by the system. So on Mondays he took the girl to Zinc Town with him. They'd spend the day and then he'd drive like hell to get back in time for dinner."

"Eve never knew?"

"Never knew. Never found out."

"And I couldn't, as a kid, have imagined it," I said. "Never had Ira down for a lady's man. Didn't go with dressing up in Lincoln's suit. I'm so stuck in my early vision of him, even now I find it unbeliev-able."

Murray, laughing, said, "That a man has a lot of sides that are unbelievable is, I thought, the subject of your books. About a man, as your fiction tells it, *everything* is believable. Christ, yes, women.

Ira's women. A big social conscience and the wide sexual appetite to go with it. A Communist with a conscience and a Communist with a cock.

"When I'd get disgusted about the women, Doris defended that, too. Doris, who you would think, from the life she led, would be the first to condemn it. But she understood him as a sister-in-law in a gentle way. About his weakness for women, she had a surprisingly gentle point of view. Doris was not so ordinary as she looked. She wasn't as ordinary as Eve Frame thought she was. Nor was Doris a saint. Eve's contempt for Doris also had something to do with her forgiving point of view. What does Doris care? He's betraying that prima donna—fine with her. 'A man attracted to women all the time. And women attracted to him. And is this bad?' Doris asked me. 'Isn't this human? Did he kill a woman? Did he take money from a woman? No. So what's so bad?' Some needs my brother knew very well how to take care of. Others he was hopeless about."

"Which were those others?"

"The need to choose your fight. Couldn't do it. Had to fight everything. Had to fight on all fronts, all the time, everyone and everything. Back in that era, there were a lot of angry Jewish guys around like Ira. Angry Jews all over America, fighting something or other. One of the privileges of being American and Jewish was that you could be angry in the world in Ira's way, aggressive about your beliefs and leaving no insult unavenged. You didn't have to shrug and resign yourself. You didn't have to muffle anything. To be an American with your own inflection wasn't that difficult anymore. Just get out in the open and argue your point. That's one of the biggest things that America gave to the Jews—gave them their anger. Especially our generation, Ira's and mine. Especially after the war. The America we came home to offered us a place to really get pissed off, without the Jewish governor on. Angry Jewish guys in Hollywood. Angry Jewish guys in the garment business. The lawyers, the angry Jewish guys in the courtroom. Everywhere. In the bakery line. At the ballpark. On the ball field. Angry Jewish guys in the Communist Party, guys who could be belligerent and antagonistic. Guys who could throw a punch, too. America was paradise for angry Jews. The shrinking Jew still existed, but you didn't have to be one if you didn't want to.

"My union. My union wasn't the teachers' union—it was the Union of Angry Jews. They organized. Know their motto? Angrier than Thou. That should be your next book. *Angry Jews since World War II.* Sure, there are the affable Jews—the inappropriate-laughing Jews, the I-love-everyone-deeply Jews, the I-was-never-so-moved Jews, the Momma-and-Poppa-were-saints Jews, the I-do-it-all-for-my-gifted-children Jews, the I'm-sitting-here-listening-to-Itzhak-Perlman-and-I'm-crying Jews, the entertaining Jew of perpetual punning, the serial Jewish joker—but I don't think that's a book you'll write."

I was laughing aloud at Murray's taxonomy, and he was too.

But after a moment, his laughter deteriorated into a cough, and he said, "I better settle down. I'm ninety years old. I better get to the point."

"You were telling me about Pamela Solomon."

"Well," Murray said, "she eventually played flute for the Cleveland Symphony Orchestra. I know this because when that plane went down back in the sixties, or maybe it was the seventies—whichever, a dozen members of the Cleveland Symphony on board, and Pamela Solomon listed among the dead. She was a very talented musician, apparently. When she first got to America she was a bit of a bohemian as well. Daughter of a proper, stifling London Jewish family, her father a doctor more English than the English. Pamela couldn't bear her family's propriety, and so she came to America. Attended Juilliard and, fresh from restrained England, fell for unrestrainable Sylphid: the cynicism, the sophistication, the American brashness. She was impressed by Sylphid's luxurious house, impressed by Sylphid's mom, the star. Motherless in America, she wasn't unhappy being gathered under Eve's wing. Though she lived only blocks away, the nights when she was visiting Sylphid she would end up having dinner and sleeping over at the house. In the mornings, down in the kitchen, she wandered around in her nightie, making herself coffee and toast and pretending either that she didn't have genitals or that Ira didn't.

"And Eve buys it, treats delightful young Pamela like her Hebrew princess and nothing more. The English accent washes away the Semitic stigma, and all in all she's so happy Sylphid has such a talented, well-behaved friend, she's so happy Sylphid has *any* friend, that she's deficient in sizing up the implications of Pamela's tuchas moving up and down the stairs inside the little-girl nightie.

"One night Eve and Sylphid went to a concert and Pamela happened to be staying over, and she wound up at home with Ira and they sat in the living room, alone together for the first time, and he asked Pamela about where she came from. His opening gambit with everyone. Pamela gave him a charming comical account of her proper family and the insufferable schools they sent her to. He asked about her job at Radio City. She was third flute-piccolo, a combined job. She was the one who got Sylphid her job subbing there. The girls would jabber together about the orchestra all the time—the politics, and the stupid conductor, and do you believe that tux he's wearing, and why doesn't he get a haircut, and nothing he does with his hands and his stick makes any sense at all. Kid stuff.

"To Ira, that night, she said, 'The principal cellist keeps flirting with me. I'm going out of my mind.' 'How many women in the orchestra?' 'Four.' 'Out of?' 'Seventy-four.' 'And how many of the men make passes at you? Seventy?' 'Uh-huh,' she said, and she laughed. 'Well, no, they don't all have the nerve, but anyone who *has* the nerve,' she told him. 'What do they say to you?' 'Oh—"That dress looks really great." "You always look so beautiful when you come to rehearsal." "I'm playing a concert next week, and I need a flutist." Things like that.' 'And what do you do about it?' 'I can take care of myself.' 'Do you have a boyfriend?' That's when Pamela told him that she had been having an affair for two years with the principal oboist.

"'A single man?' Ira asked her. 'No,' she told him, 'he's married.' 'It never bothers you that he's married?' And Pamela said, 'It's not the formal arrangement of life that interests me.' 'What about his wife?' 'I don't know his wife. I never met her. I never intend to meet her. I don't want to know anything about her particularly. It has nothing to do with his wife, it has nothing to do with his children. He loves his wife and he loves his children.' 'What does it have to do with?' 'It has to do with our pleasure. I do what I want to do for my own pleasure. Don't tell me you still believe in the sanctity of marriage. You think you take a vow and that's it, the two of you are faithful forever?' 'Yes,' he tells her, 'I believe that.' 'You've never—' 'Nope.' 'You're faithful to Eve.' 'Sure.' 'You intend to be faithful for the rest of your life?' 'Depends.' 'On what?' 'On you,' Ira said. Pamela laughs. They both laugh. 'It depends,' she says, 'on my convincing you that it's all right? That you're free to do so? That you're not the bourgeois proprietor of your wife and she's not the bourgeois proprietress of her husband?' 'Yes. Try to convince me.' 'Are you really such a hopelessly typical American that you're enslaved by middle-class American morality?' 'Yes, that's me—the hopelessly typical enslaved American. What are you?' 'What am I? I'm a musician.' 'What does that mean?' 'I'm given a score and I play it. I play what's given to me. I'm a player.'

"Now, Ira figured that he could be being set up by Sylphid, so that first night all he did when Pamela had finished showing off and started upstairs to bed was to take her hand and say, 'You're not a kid, are you? I had you down for a kid.' 'I'm a year older than Sylphid,' she tells him. 'I'm twenty-four. I'm an expatriate. I'll never go back to that idiotic country with its stupid subterranean emotional life. I love being in America. Here I'm free of all that showing-your-feelings-is-taboo crap. You can't imagine what it's like there. Here there's *life*. Here I have my own apartment in Greenwich Village. I work hard and I earn my own way in the world. I do six shows a day, six days a week. I am not a kid. Not in any way, Iron Rinn.'

"The scene went something like that. What there was to enkindle Ira is obvious. She was fresh, young, flirtatious, naive—and not naive, shrewd too. Off on her great American adventure. He admires the way this child of the upper middle class lives outside the bourgeois conventions. The squalid walk-up she lives in. Her coming alone to America. He admires the dexterity with which she adopts all her roles. For Eve she plays the sweet little girl, it's pajama-party stuff with Sylphid, at Radio City she's a flutist, a musician, a professional, and with him it's as though she'd been raised in England by the Fabians, a free, unfettered spirit, highly intelligent and unintimidated by respectable society. In other words, she's a human being—this with this one, that with that one, something else with the other one.

"And all of this is great. Interesting. Impressive. But falling in love? With Ira everything emotional had to be superabundant. When he found his target, Ira fired. He not only fell for her. That baby he'd wanted to have with Eve? He wanted now to have it with Pamela. But he was afraid of frightening Pamela away, so about this he said nothing right off.

"They just have their antibourgeois fling. She can explain to herself everything that she's doing. 'I'm a friend to Sylphid and I'm a friend to Eve, and I'd do anything for either of them, but, as long as it does them no harm, I don't see where being a friend involves the heroic self-sacrifice of my own inclinations.' She too has an ideology. But Ira is by then thirty-six, and he *wants*. Wants the child, the family, the home. The Communist wants everything that is at the *heart* of bourgeois. Wants to get from Pamela everything he thought he was getting from Eve when he got Sylphid instead.

"Out together at the shack they used to talk a lot about Sylphid. 'What is her gripe?' Ira asks Pamela. Money. Status. Privilege. Harp lessons from birth. Twenty-three and her laundry is done for her, her meals are prepared for her, her bills are paid for her. 'You know the way I was brought up? Left home at fifteen. Dug ditches. I was *never* a kid.' But Pamela explains to him that when Sylphid was only twelve years old, Eve left Sylphid's father for the coarsest savior she could find, an immigrant dynamo with a hard-on who was going to make her rich, and her mother was so intoxicated by him that Sylphid lost her for all those years, and then they moved to New

York and Sylphid lost her California friends, and she didn't know anybody and she started to get fat.

"Psychiatric bullshit to Ira. 'Sylphid sees Eve as a movie star who abandoned her to the nannies,' Pamela tells him, 'who dumped her for men and her man craziness, who betrayed her at every turn. Sylphid sees Eve as someone who keeps throwing herself at men so as not to stand on her own two feet.' 'Is Sylphid a lesbian?' 'No. Her motto is, Sex makes you powerless. Look at her mother. She tells me never to get involved with anybody sexually. She hates her mother for giving her up for all these men. Sylphid has a notion of absolute autonomy. She's going to be beholden to no one. She's tough.' 'Tough? Yeah? So how come,' Ira asks, 'she doesn't leave her mother if she's so tough? Why doesn't she go out on her own? You're not making sense. Toughness in a vacuum. Autonomy in a vacuum. Independence in a vacuum. You want to know the answer to Sylphid? Sylphid is a sadist—*sadist* in a vacuum. Every night this Juilliard graduate rubs her finger through the leavings at the edge of her dinner plate, round and round the edge of her dinner plate till it squeaks, and then, the better to drive her mother round the bend, she puts the finger in her mouth and licks it till it's clean. Sylphid is there because her mother's afraid of her. And Eve will never *stop* being afraid of her because she doesn't want Sylphid to leave her, and that's *why* Sylphid won't leave her—until she finds a still better way to torture her. Sylphid is the one wielding the whip.'

"So, you see, Ira repeated to Pamela that stuff I'd told him at the outset about Sylphid but that he'd refused to take seriously coming from me. He repeated it to his beloved as though he'd figured it out himself. As people will. The two of them had a lot of these conversations. Pamela liked these conversations. They excited her. It made her feel strong to talk freely like that with Ira about Sylphid and Eve.

"One night something peculiar happened with Eve. She and Ira were lying in bed with the lights out, ready for sleep, when she began to weep uncontrollably. Ira said, 'What's the matter?' She wouldn't answer him. 'What are you crying about? What's happened now?' 'Sometimes I think . . . Oh, I can't,' she said. She couldn't speak, and she also couldn't stop crying. He turned the light on. Told her to go ahead and get it out of her system. To say it. 'Sometimes I feel,' she said, 'that *Pamela* should have been my child. Sometimes,' she said, 'it seems more natural.' 'Why Pamela?' 'The easy way we get along. Though maybe that's because she *isn't* my daughter.' 'Maybe it is, maybe it isn't,' he said. 'Her airiness,' Eve said, 'her lightness.' And she started weeping again. Out of guilt, more than likely, for having allowed herself that harmless fairy-tale wish, the wish to have a daughter who didn't remind her every second of her failure.

"By lightness I don't think Eve necessarily meant only physical lightness, the displacement of the fat by the thin. She was pointing to something else, to some kind of excitement in Pamela. *Inner* lightness. I thought she meant that in Pamela she could recognize, almost despite herself, the susceptibility that had once vibrated beneath her own demure surface. Recognized it however childishly Pamela behaved in her presence, however maidenly she acted. After that night, Eve never said anything like this again. It happened only that one time, just when Ira's passion for Pamela, when the illegitimacy of their reckless affair, was generating its greatest heat.

"So, each lays claim to the spirited young flutist as the pleasure-piping dream creature each had failed to obtain: the daughter denied Eve, the wife denied Ira.

"'So sad. So sad,' Eve tells him. 'So very, very sad.' She holds on to him all that night. Right through to the morning, weeping, sighing, whimpering; all the pain, the confusion, the contradiction, the longing, the delusion, all the incoherence pouring out of her. He never felt sorrier for her—what with the affair with Pamela, he never felt farther from her either. 'Everything's gone all wrong. I tried and I tried,' she says, 'and nothing comes out quite right. I tried with Sylphid's father. I tried with Jumbo. I tried to give her stability and connection and a mother she could look up to. I tried to be a good mother. And then I had to be a good father. And she's had too many fathers. All I thought about was myself.' 'You haven't thought just about yourself,' he says. 'I have. My career. My careers. My acting. I always had to take care of my acting. I tried. She had good schools and good tutors and a good nanny. But maybe I should have just been with her all the time. She's inconsolable. She eats and she eats and she eats. That's her only consolation for something I didn't give her.' 'Maybe,' he says, 'that's just the way she is.' 'But there are plenty of girls who eat too much, and then they lose some weight—they don't just eat and eat and eat. I've tried everything. I've taken her to doctors, to specialists. She just keeps eating. She keeps eating to hate me.' 'Then maybe,' he says, 'if that is true, it's time for her to go out on her own.' 'What does that have to do with anything? Why should she be on her own? She's happy here. This is her house. No matter what other disruption I brought into her life, this is her house, it's always been her house, and it will be her house for as long as she wants. There's no reason that she should leave any sooner than she's ready to.' 'Suppose,' he says, 'her leaving were a way of getting her to stop eating.' 'I don't see how eating and living where she does have anything to do with each other! You're not making any sense! This is my daughter we're talking about!' 'Okay. Okay. But you just expressed a certain amount of disappointment . . .' 'I said she was eating to console herself. If she leaves here, she'll have to console herself *twice* as much. She'll have to console herself that much more. Oh, there's something terribly wrong. I should have stayed with Carlton. He was a homosexual, but he was her father. I just should have stayed with him. I don't know what I was thinking. I would never have met Jumbo, I would have never gotten involved with you, she would have had a father, and she wouldn't always be eating so much.' 'Why didn't you stay with him?' 'I know it seems as though it was selfish, as though it was for me. So that I could find satisfaction and companionship. But really I wanted *him* to be freed. Why should he be confined by family life and with this wife that he couldn't find attractive or interesting? Every time we were together I thought he must be thinking about the next busboy or waiter. I wanted him not to have to lie so much anymore.' 'But he didn't lie about that.' 'Oh, I knew it, and he knew I knew it, and everybody in Hollywood knew it, but he was still always skulking around and planning. Phone calls and disappearing and excuses as to why he was late and why he wasn't at Sylphid's party—I couldn't take another sorry excuse. He didn't care, and yet he continued to lie anyway. I wanted to relieve him of that, I wanted to relieve me of that. It wasn't for my own personal happiness, really. It was more for his.' 'Why didn't you go off by yourself, then? Why did you go off with Jumbo?' 'Well . . . that was an easy way to do it. To not be alone. To make the decision but to not be alone. But I could have stayed. And Sylphid would have had a father, and she wouldn't have known the truth about him, and we wouldn't have had the years with Jumbo, and we wouldn't have these dreadful trips to France that are just a nightmare. I could have stayed, and she could have just had an absent father like everyone else's absent father. So what if he was queer? Yes, some of it was Jumbo, and the passion. But I couldn't take the lies anymore, the false deception. It was fake deceit. Because Carlton *didn't* care, but for some modicum of dignity, of decency, he would pretend to hide it. Oh, I love Sylphid so! I love my daughter. I'd do anything for my daughter. But if it could be lighter and easier and more natural—more *like* a daughter. She's here, and I love her, but every little decision is a struggle, and her power . . . She doesn't treat me like a mother, and it makes it hard to treat her like a daughter. Though I'd do *anything* for her, *anything*.' 'Why don't you let her go away, then?' 'You keep bringing that up! She doesn't *want* to go away. Why do you think the solution is for her to go? The solution is for her to stay. She didn't get enough of me. If she were ready to go, she would have gone by now. She's not ready. She looks mature, but she isn't. I'm her mother. I'm her supporter. I love her. She needs me. I know it doesn't look as if she needs me, but she needs me.' 'But you're so unhappy,' he says. 'You don't understand. It's not me, it's Sylphid I worry about. Me, I'll get through. I always get through.' 'What do you worry about with her?' 'I want her to find a nice man. Somebody she can love and who'll take care of her. She's not dating that much,' Eve says. 'She doesn't date at all,' Ira says. 'That's not true. There was a boy.' 'When? Nine years ago?' 'A lot of men are very interested in her. At the Music Hall. A lot of musicians. She's just taking her time.' 'I don't understand what you're talking about. You have to go to sleep. Close your eyes and try to sleep.' 'I can't. I close my eyes and I think, What is going to happen to her? What is going to happen to me? So much trying and so much trying . . . and so little peace. So little peace of mind. Each day is a new . . . I know it may look like happiness to other people. I know she looks very happy and I know we look very happy together, and we really are very happy together, but each day just gets harder.' 'You look happy together?' 'Well, she loves me. She loves me. I'm her mummy. Of course we look happy together. She's beautiful. She's beautiful.' 'Who is?' he asks her. 'Sylphid. Sylphid is beautiful.' He had thought she was going to say 'Pamela.' 'Look deep into her eyes and her face. The beauty,' Eve says, 'and the strength there. It doesn't come out at you in that superficial look-at-me way. But there's deep beauty there. Very deep. She's a beautiful girl. She's my daughter. She's remarkable. She's a brilliant musician. She's a beautiful girl. She's my daughter.'

"If ever Ira knew it was hopeless, it was that night. He couldn't have seen any more purely how impossible it was. Easier to make America go Communist, easier to bring about the proletarian revolution in New York, on Wall Street, than separate a woman and her daughter who didn't want to be separated. Yes, he should have just separated *himself.* But he didn't. Why? Finally, Nathan, I have no answer. Ask why anybody makes any tragic mistake. No answer."

"Throughout these months, Ira was becoming more and more isolated in the house. On the nights when he wasn't at a union executive meeting or wasn't at the meeting of his party unit, or they weren't out for the evening together, Eve would be in the living room doing her needlepoint and listening to Sylphid plucking away and Ira'd be upstairs writing to O'Day. And when the harp went silent and he went downstairs to find Eve, she wouldn't be there.

She'd be up in Sylphid's room, listening to the record player. The two of them in bed, under the covers, listening to *Così Fan Tutte*. When he'd go up to the top floor and hear the Mozart blaring and see them together in bed, Ira felt as though *he* were the child. An hour or so later Eve would return, still warm from Sylphid's bed, to get in bed with him, and that was more or less the end of conjugal bliss.

"When the explosion comes, Eve is astonished. Sylphid must get an apartment of her own. He says, 'Pamela lives three thousand miles from her family. Sylphid can live three blocks from hers.' But all Eve does is cry. This is unfair. This is horrible. He is trying to drive her daughter out of her life. No, around the corner, he says— she is twenty-four years old, and it's time she stopped going to bed with Mommy. 'She is my daughter! How dare you! I love my daughter! How dare you!' 'Okay,' he says, '*I'll* live around the corner,' and the next morning he finds a floor-through apartment over on Washington Square North, just four blocks away. Puts down a deposit, signs a lease, pays the first month's rent, and comes home and tells her what he's done. 'You're leaving me! You're divorcing me!' No, he says, just going to live around the corner. Now you can lie in bed with her *all* night long. Though if, for variety, you should ever want to lie in bed with me all night long, he says, put on your coat and your hat and come around the corner and I will be delighted to see you. As for dinner, he tells her, who will even notice that I am not there? Just you wait. There is going to be a considerable improvement in Sylphid's outlook on life. 'Why are you *doing* this to me? To make me choose between my daughter and you, to make a mother choose—it's inhuman!' It takes hours more to explain that he is asking her to entertain a solution that would obviate the *need* for a choice, but it's doubtful that Eve ever understood what he was talking about. Comprehension was not the bedrock on which her decisions were based—desperation was. Capitulation was.

"The next night, Eve went up as usual to Sylphid's room, but this time to present her with the proposal she and Ira had agreed to, the proposal that was going to bring peace to their lives. Eve had gone with him that day to look at the apartment he'd leased on Washington Square North. There were French doors and high ceilings and ornamental moldings and parquet floors. There was a fireplace with a carved mantel. Below the rear bedroom was a walled-in garden much like the one on West Eleventh Street. It wasn't Lehigh Avenue, Nathan. Washington Square North, in those days, was as beautiful a street as there was in Manhattan. Eve said, 'It's lovely.' 'It's for Sylphid,' Ira said. He would keep the lease in his name, pay the rent, and Eve, who always made money but was always terrified about money, always losing it to some Freedman or other, Eve wouldn't have to worry about a thing. 'This is the solution,' he said, 'and is it so terrible?' She sat down in the sunlight in one of those front parlor window seats. There was a veil on her hat, one of those veils with the dots on it that she made popular in some film, and she lifted it away from her delectable little face and she began to sob. Their struggle was over. *Her* struggle was over. She jumped to her feet, she hugged him, she kissed him, she began to run from room to room, figuring out where to put the lovely old pieces of furniture that she was going to move from West Eleventh Street for Sylphid. She couldn't have been happier. She was seventeen again. Magical. Enchanting. She was the come-hither girl in the silent films.

"That night she gathered her courage and went upstairs bearing the drawing she'd made, the floor plan of the new apartment, and a list of the pieces from the house that would have gone to Sylphid anyway and so were hers to have forever right now. It took no time at all, of course, for Sylphid to register her objection and for Ira to be racing up the stairs to Sylphid's room. He found them in bed together. But no Mozart this time. Bedlam this time. What he saw was Eve on her back screaming and crying, and Sylphid in her pajamas sitting astride her, also screaming, also crying, her strong harpist's hands pinning Eve's shoulders to the bed. There were bits of paper all over the place—the floor plan for the new apartment— and there, on top of his wife, sat Sylphid, screaming, 'Can't you stand up to *anyone?* Won't you once stand up for your own daughter against him? Won't you be a mother, *ever? Ever?*"

"What did Ira do?" I asked.

"What do you think Ira did? Out of the house, roaming the streets, up to Harlem, back down to the Village, walking for miles, and then, in the middle of the night, he headed for Pamela's on Carmine Street. He tried never to see her there if he could help it, but he rang her doorbell and zoomed up the five flights and told her it was over with Eve. He wanted her to come with him to Zinc Town. He wanted to marry her. He had wanted to marry her all along, he told her, and to have a child with her. You can imagine the impact that made.

"She lived in her one bohemian room—closets without doors, the mattress on the floor, the Modigliani prints, the chianti bottle with the candle, and sheet music all over the place. A tiny walk-up forty feet square and there is that giraffe of a man storming around her, overturning the music stand, knocking over all her 78s, kicking at the bathtub, which is in the kitchen, and telling this well-brought-up English kid with her new Greenwich Village ideology who thought that what they were doing was going to be consequence-free—a big, passionate consequence-free adventure with a famous older man—that she was the mother-to-be of his unborn heirs and the woman of his life.

"Overpowering Ira, the outsized, knocking over, crazy, giraffelike Ira, the driven man, with his all or nothing, says to her, 'Pack your clothes, you're coming with me,' and so he learns, sooner than he might have otherwise, that Pamela had been wanting to end things for months. 'End? *Why?*' She couldn't stand the strain anymore. 'Strain? *What* strain?' And so she told him: every time she was with him in Jersey, he wouldn't stop holding her and fondling her and making her sick with anxiety by telling her a thousand times how much he loved her; then he'd sleep with her and she'd come back to New York and go over to see Sylphid, and all Sylphid could talk about was the man she had nicknamed the Beast; Ira and her mother she linked together as Beauty and the Beast. And Pamela had to agree with her, had to laugh about him; she too had to make jokes about the Beast. How could he be so blind to the toll this was taking on her? She couldn't run away with him and she couldn't marry him. She had a job, she had a career, she was a musician who loved her music—and she could never see him again. If he didn't leave her alone . . . And so Ira left her. He got in the car and he drove to the shack, and that's where I went to see him the next day after school.

"He talked, I listened. He didn't let on to me about Pamela; he didn't because he damn well knew my thoughts on adultery. I'd already told him more times than he liked to hear, 'The excitement in marriage *is* the fidelity. If that idea doesn't excite you, you have no business being married.' No, he didn't tell me about Pamela—he told me about Sylphid sitting on Eve. All night, Nathan. At dawn I drove back to school, shaved in the faculty bathroom, met my homeroom class; in the afternoon, after my last class, I got in the car and drove back up again. I didn't want him out there alone at night because I didn't know what he might do next. It wasn't only his home life that he was confronting head-on. That was just a part of it. The political stuff was encroaching—the accusations, the firings, the permanent blacklisting. *That's* what was undermining him. The domestic crisis wasn't yet *the* crisis. Sure, he was at risk on both sides and eventually they'd merge, but for the time being he was able to keep them separate.

"The American Legion already had Ira in their sights for 'pro-Communist sympathies.' His name had been in some Catholic magazine, on some list, as somebody with 'Communistic associations.' His whole show was under suspicion. And there was friction with the party. That was heating up. Stalin and the Jews. The Soviet anti-Semitism was beginning to penetrate the consciousness of even the party blockheads. The rumors were starting to circulate among the Jewish party members, and Ira didn't like what he was hearing. He wanted to know more. About the claims to purity of the Communist Party and the Soviet Union, even Ira Ringold wanted to know more. The sense of betrayal by the party was faintly setting in, though the full moral shock wouldn't come until Khrushchev's revelations. Then everything collapsed for Ira and his pals, the justification for all their effort and all their suffering. Six years later, the heart of their adult biographies went right down the drain. Still, as early as 1950, Ira was causing problems for himself by wanting to know more. Though that stuff he'd never talk about with me. He didn't want me implicated, and he didn't want to hear me sounding off. He knew that if we tangled on the Communist issue, we'd wind up like a lot of other families, not talking again for the rest of our lives.

"We'd already had a lulu of an argument, back in '46, when he was first out in Calumet City rooming with O'Day. I went to visit him and it was not pleasant. Because Ira, when he argued about the things that mattered to him most, would never be finished with you. Especially in those early days after the war, Ira, in a political argument, was extremely disinclined to lose. Not least with me. Uneducated little brother educating the educated big one. He'd be staring straight at me, his finger jabbing straight at me, obstreperous, forcing the issue, overriding everything I said with 'Don't insult my intelligence,' 'That is a goddamn contradiction in terms,' 'I'm not going to stand here and take that shit.' The energy for the fight was astonishing. 'I don't give a damn if nobody knows it except me!' 'If you had any knowledge of what this world is all about . . . !' He could be particularly incendiary putting me in my place as an English teacher. 'What I hate with a passion is please define what the hell you are saying!' There was nothing that was small for Ira in those days. Everything he thought about, because he thought about it, was *big*.

"My first night visiting him out where he lived with O'Day, he told me that the teachers' union should push for the development of 'the people's culture.' That should be its official policy. Why? I knew why. Because it was the official policy of the party. You've got to elevate the cultural understanding of the poor Joe on the street, and instead of classical, old-time, traditional education, you've got to emphasize those things that contribute to a people's culture. The party line, and I thought it was unrealistic in every way. But the *willfulness* in that guy. I was no pushover, I knew how to convince people that I meant business too. But Ira's antagonism was inexhaustible. Ira wouldn't quit. When I got back from Chicago, I didn't hear from him for nearly a year.

"I'll tell you what else was closing in on him. Those muscle pains. That disease he had. They told him it was one thing and then another thing and they never figured out what the hell it was. Polymyositis. Polymyalgia rheumatica. Every doctor gave it another name. That's about all they gave him, aside from Sloan's Liniment and Ben-Gay. His clothes started stinking of every kind of goo they sold for aches and pains. One doctor that I took him to myself, across the street at the Beth Israel, a physician friend of Doris's, listened to his case history, drew blood, examined him thoroughly, and described him to us as hyperinflammatory. The guy had an elaborate theory and he drew us pictures—a failure of inhibition in the cascade that leads to inflammation. He described Ira's joints as quick to develop inflammatory reactions that rapidly escalate. Quick to inflame, slow to extinguish.

"After Ira died, some doctor suggested to me—made a persuasive case to me—that Ira suffered from the disease that they believe Lincoln had. Dressed up in the clothes and got the disease. Marfan's. Marfan's syndrome. Excessive tallness. Big hands and feet. Long, thin extremities. And lots of joint and muscle pain. Marfan's patients frequently kick off the way Ira did. The aorta explodes and they're gone. Anyway, whatever Ira had went undiagnosed, at least in terms of finding a treatment, and by '49, '50, those pains were beginning to be more or less intractable, and he was feeling under political pressure from both ends of the spectrum—from the network and from the party—and the guy had me worried.

"In the First Ward, Nathan, we were not just the only Jewish family on Factory Street. More than likely we were the only family that wasn't Italian between the Lackawanna tracks and the Belleville line. These First Warders came from the mountains, little guys mostly, with big shoulders and huge heads, from the mountains east of Naples, and when they got to Newark somebody put a shovel in their hands and they began to dig and they dug for the rest of their lives. They dug ditches. When Ira quit school, he dug ditches with them. One of those Italians tried to kill him with a shovel. My brother had a big mouth and he had to fight to live in that neighborhood. He had to fight to survive on his own from the time that he was seven years old.

"But all at once he was battling on every front, and I didn't want him to do something stupid or irreparable. I didn't drive out to tell him anything in particular. This wasn't a man you told what to do. I wasn't even there to tell him what I *thought*. What I thought was that to go on living with Eve and her daughter was insane. The night Doris and I went there for dinner, you couldn't miss the strangeness of the link between those two. I remember driving back to Newark that night with Doris and saying over and over, 'There is no room for Ira in that combination.'

"Ira called his utopian dream Communism, Eve called hers Sylphid. The parent's utopia of the perfect child, the actress's utopia of let's pretend, the Jew's utopia of not being Jewish, to name only the grandest of her projects to deodorize life and make it palatable.

"That Ira had no business in that household Sylphid had let him know right off the bat. And Sylphid was right: he *had* no business there, he *didn't* belong there. Sylphid made perfectly clear to him that *de*-utopianizing her mom—giving Mom a dose of life's dung she'd never forget—was her deepest daughterly inclination. Frankly, I didn't think he had any business on the radio, either. Ira was no actor. He had the chutzpah to get up and shoot off his mouth—that he never lacked—but an actor? He did every part the same way. That easygoing crap, as though he were sitting across from you at pinochle. The simple human approach, only it wasn't an approach. It was nothing. The absence of an approach. What did Ira know about acting? He had resolved as a kid to strike out on his own, and everything that urged him on was an accident. There was no plan. He wanted a home with Eve Frame? He wanted a home with the English girl? I realize that's a primary urge in people; in Ira particularly, the urge to have a home was the residue of a very, very old disappointment. But he picked some real beauts to have a home with. Ira asserted himself into New York City with all his intensity, with all that craving for a life of weight and meaning. From the party he got the idea that he was an instrument of history, that history had called him to the capital of the world to set society's wrongs right—and to me the whole thing looked ludicrous. Ira wasn't so much a displaced person as he was a misplaced person, always the wrong size for where he was, in both spirit and physique. But that wasn't a perspective I was about to share with him. My brother's vocation is to be stupendous? Suits me. I just didn't want him to wind up unrecognizable as anything else.

"I'd brought some sandwiches for us to eat that second night, and we ate and he talked and I listened, and it must have been about three in the morning when a New York Yellow Cab pulled up at the shack. It was Eve. Ira'd had the phone off the hook for two days, and when she couldn't stand any more phoning and getting a busy signal, she'd called a taxi and taken it sixty miles into the sticks in the middle of the night. She knocked, I got up and opened the door, and she rushed by me into the room, and there he was. What followed might have been planned by her all the way out in the taxi or might as easily have been improvised. It was right out of those silent pictures she used to act in. A completely screwy performance, pure exaggerated invention, yet so right for her that she would repeat it almost exactly only a few weeks later. A favorite role. The Suppliant.

"She threw herself onto her knees in the middle of the floor and, oblivious to me—or maybe not all that oblivious—she cried, 'I beg you! I implore you! Don't leave me!' The two arms upthrust in the mink coat. The hands trembling in the air. And tears, as though it weren't a marriage at stake but the redemption of mankind. Confirming—if confirmation was necessary—that she absolutely repudiated being a rational human being. I remember thinking, Well, she's cooked her goose this time.

"But I didn't know my brother, didn't know what he couldn't withstand. People down on their knees was what he'd been protesting all his life, but I would have thought that by then he had the wherewithal to distinguish between someone driven to her knees because of social conditions and someone just acting away. There was an emotion he could not quiet in himself when he saw her like that. Or so I thought. The sucker for suffering rushing to the fore—or so I thought—and so I stepped outside and got into the taxi and had a cigarette with the driver until harmony was restored.

"Everything permeated with stupid politics. That's what I was thinking in the taxi. The ideologies that fill people's heads and undermine their observation of life. But it was only driving back to Newark that night that I began to understand how those words applied to the predicament my brother was in with his wife. Ira wasn't *merely* a sucker for her suffering. Sure, he could be swept away by those impulses that most everybody has when somebody they are intimate with starts to cave in; sure, he could arrive at a mistaken idea of what he should do about it. But that isn't what happened. Only driving home did I realize that wasn't *at all* what had happened.

"Remember, Ira belonged to the Communist Party heart and soul. Ira obeyed every one-hundred-eighty-degree shift of policy. Ira swallowed the dialectical justification for Stalin's every villainy. Ira backed Browder when Browder was their American messiah, and when Moscow pulled the plug and expelled Browder, and overnight Browder was a class collaborator and a social imperialist, Ira bought it all—backed Foster and the Foster line that America was on the road to fascism. He managed to squelch his doubts and convince himself that his obedience to every last one of the party's twists and turns was helping to build a just and equitable society in America. His self-conception was of being virtuous. By and large I believe he was—another innocent guy co-opted into a system he didn't understand. Hard to believe that a man who put so much stock in his freedom could let that dogmatizing control his thinking. But my brother abased himself intellectually the same way they all did. Politically gullible. Morally gullible. Wouldn't face it. Shut their minds, the Iras, to the source of what they were selling and celebrating. Here was somebody whose greatest strength was his power to say no. Unafraid to say no and to say it into your face. Yet all he could ever say to the party was yes.

"He had reconciled himself to her because no sponsor or network or advertising agency was going to touch Ira as long as he was married to the Sarah Bernhardt of the Airwaves. That's what he was gambling on, that they couldn't expose him, wouldn't dispose of him, as long as at his side he had radio's royalty. She was going to protect her husband and by extension protect the clique of Communists who ran Ira's show. She threw herself on the floor, she implored him to come home, and what Ira realized was that he damn well better do what she asked, because without her he was sunk. Eve was his front. The bulwark's bulwark."

"That's when the deus ex machina appears with her gold tooth. Eve discovered her. Heard about her from some actor who'd heard about her from some dancer. A masseuse. Probably ten, twelve years older than Ira and pushing fifty by then. Had that worn, twilight look about her, the sensuous female rumbling downhill, but her work kept her in shape, kept that big, warm body firm enough. Helgi Pärn. Estonian woman married to an Estonian factory worker. A solid working-class woman who likes her vodka and is a little bit of a prostitute and a little bit of a thief. A large, healthy woman who, when she first shows up, is missing a tooth. And then she comes back and the tooth has been replaced—a gold tooth, a present from a dentist she's massaging. And then she comes back with a dress, a present from a dress manufacturer she's massaging. Over the course of the year she comes back with some costume jewelry, she has a fur coat, she has a watch, soon she's buying stocks, et cetera, et cetera. Helgi is constantly being improved. She jokes about all her improvements. It's just appreciation, she tells Ira. The first time Ira gives her money she says, 'I don't take money, I take presents.' He says, 'I can't go shopping. Here. Buy yourself what you want.'

"She and Ira have the obligatory class-consciousness discussion, he tells her how Marx urged working people like the Pärns to wrest the capital from the bourgeoisie and organize as the ruling class, in control of the means of production, and Helgi's having none of it. She's Estonian, the Russians had occupied Estonia and turned it into a Soviet republic, and so she's *instinctively* anti-Communist. There is only one country for her, the United States of America. Where else could an immigrant farm girl with no education, blah blah blah blah. The improvements are comic to Ira. Ordinarily he is a little short on humor, but not where Helgi is concerned. Maybe he should have married *her*. Maybe this big, good-natured slob who does not recoil from reality was his soulmate. His soulmate the way Donna Jones was his soulmate: because of what was untamed in her. Because of what was wayward.

"He sure did get a kick out of the acquisitive side of her. 'What is it this week, Helgi?' To her it's not whoring, it's not sinister— it's self-improvement. The fulfillment of Helgi's American dream. America is the land of opportunity, and her clients appreciate her, and a girl has to make a living, and so three times a week she came around after dinner, looking like a nurse—starched white dress, white stockings, white shoes—and carrying with her a table that folded in half, a massage table. She sets the table up in his study, in front of his desk, and though he was half a foot too tall for it, he stretched himself out on it, and for a solid hour she massaged him very professionally. Afforded him, with those massages, the only real relief Ira ever got from all that pain.

"Then, still in her white uniform, altogether professionally, she concluded with something that provided more relief. A wonderful outpouring gushed forth from his penis, and momentarily the prison dissolved. In that gush was all the freedom that Ira had left. The lifelong battle to exercise fully his political, civil, and human rights had evolved itself down to coming, for dough, onto this fifty-year-old Estonian woman's gold tooth while, below them in the living room, Eve listened to Sylphid play on her harp.

"Helgi might have been a handsome woman, but the shallowness shone right through. Her English wasn't so hot, and, as I said, there was always a thin stream of vodka gurgling through her veins, and all of this together gave her the aura of somebody pretty thick. Eve nicknamed her. The Peasant. That's what they called her around West Eleventh Street. But Helgi Pärn was no peasant. Shallow maybe, but not thick. Helgi knew that Eve considered her the equivalent of a beast of burden. Eve didn't bother to hide it, didn't think she had to with a lowly masseuse, and the lowly masseuse despised her for it. When Helgi was blowing Ira, and Eve was downstairs in the living room listening to the harp, Helgi used to have fun imitating the dainty, ladylike way that she imagined Eve deigning to suck him off. Behind the blanked-out Baltic mask, there was somebody reckless who knew when to strike out and how to strike out against her dismissive betters. And when she struck out at Eve, she brought the whole thing down. When the vodka was in there, Helgi wasn't about to impose restrictions on herself.

"Revenge," announced Murray. "Nothing so big in people and nothing so small, nothing so audaciously creative in even the most ordinary as the workings of revenge. And nothing so ruthlessly creative in even the most refined of the refined as the workings of betrayal."

I was taken back to Murray Ringold's English class by the sound of that: the teacher summing up for the class, Mr. Ringold recapitulating, intent, before the hour ended, on concisely synthesizing his theme, Mr. Ringold hinting, by his emphatic tone and his careful phrasing, that "revenge and betrayal" might well be the answer to one of his weekly "Twenty Questions."

"In the army I remember getting hold of a copy of Burton's *Anatomy of Melancholy* and reading it every night, reading it for the first time in my life when we were training in England to invade France. I loved that book, Nathan, but it left me puzzled. Do you remember what Burton says about melancholy? Every one of us, he says, has the predisposition for melancholy, but only some of us get the habit of melancholy. How do you get the habit? That's a question that Burton doesn't answer. That book of his doesn't say, and so I had to wonder about it right through the invasion, wonder until from personal experience I found out.

"You get the habit by being betrayed. What does it is betrayal. Think of the tragedies. What brings on the melancholy, the raving, the bloodshed? Othello—betrayed. Hamlet—betrayed. Lear—betrayed. You might even claim that Macbeth is betrayed—by himself—though that's not the same thing. Professionals who've spent their energy teaching masterpieces, the few of us still engrossed by literature's scrutiny of things, have no excuse for finding betrayal anywhere but at the heart of history. History from top to bottom. World history, family history, personal history. It's a very big subject, betrayal. Just think of the Bible. What's that book about? The master story situation of the Bible is betrayal. Adam— betrayed. Esau—betrayed. The Shechemites—betrayed. Judah—betrayed. Joseph—betrayed. Moses—betrayed. Samson—betrayed. Samuel—betrayed. David—betrayed. Uriah—betrayed. Job—betrayed. Job betrayed by whom? By none other than God himself. And don't forget the betrayal of God. God betrayed. Betrayed by our ancestors at every turn."

6

In mid-august of 1950, only a few days before I left home for the University of Chicago (left forever, as it developed) to enroll for my first year of college, I went up on the train to spend a week in the Sussex County countryside with Ira, as I had the previous year when Eve and Sylphid were in France visiting Sylphid's father—and when my own father had first to interview Ira before granting his permission for me to go. That second summer, I arrived late in the day at the rural station a curvy five-mile drive from Ira's shack through narrow back lanes and past the dairy herds. Ira was waiting there in the Chevy coupe.

Beside him in the front seat was a woman in a white uniform whom he introduced as Mrs. Pärn. She had come out from New York that day to help him with his neck and his shoulders and was about to return on the next eastbound train. She had a folding table with her, and I remember her going to lift it out of the trunk by herself. That's what I remember—her strength in lifting the table, and that she wore a white uniform and white stockings and that she called him "Mr. Rinn" and he called her "Mrs. Pärn." I didn't notice anything special about her except her strength. I noticed her hardly at all. And after she got out of the car and, lugging her table with her, crossed over to the track where the local would take her as far as Newark, I never saw the woman again. I was seventeen. She seemed to me old and hygienic and of no importance.

In June, a list of 151 people in radio and television with purported connections to "Communist causes" had appeared in a publication called *Red Channels,* and it had set in motion a round of firings that spread panic throughout the broadcasting industry. Ira's name had not been on the list, however, nor had that of anyone else involved with *The Free and the Brave.* I had no idea that Ira had more than likely been spared because of the insulation afforded him by being Eve Frame's husband, and because Eve Frame was herself being protected (by Bryden Grant, an informer for the people running *Red Channels*) from the suspicion that might automatically have fallen on her as the wife of somebody with Ira's reputation. Eve, after all, had attended with Ira more than one political function that, in those days, could have put in question her loyalty to the United States. It didn't require much incriminating evidence—in cases of mistaken identity, it didn't require any—even for someone as unengaged by politics as Eve Frame was, to be labeled a "fronter" and to wind up out of work.

But I wasn't to know Eve's role in shaping Ira's predicament until some fifty years later, when Murray told me about it at my house. My theory at the time for why they didn't go after Ira was that they were afraid of him, afraid of the fight he'd put up, of what looked to me back then to be his indestructibility. I thought the editors of *Red Channels* were afraid that, if provoked, Ira might singlehandedly bring them down. I even had a romantic moment, while Ira was telling me about *Red Channels* over our first meal together, of thinking of the shack on Pickax Hill Road as one of those austere training camps in the Jersey sticks where heavyweights used to go for months before the big fight, the heavyweight here being Ira.

"The standards of patriotism for my profession are about to be set by three policemen from the FBI. Three ex-FBI men, Nathan, that's who's running this *Red Channels* operation. Who should be employed on radio and who shouldn't be employed will be determined by three guys whose favored source of information is the

House Un-American Activities Committee. You'll see how courageous the bosses are in the face of this shit. Watch how the profit system holds out against the pressure. Freedom of thought, of speech, due process—screw all that. People are going to be destroyed, buddy. It's not livelihoods that are going to be lost, it's *lives*. People are going to die. They're going to get sick and die, they're going to jump off buildings and die. By the time this is over, the people with names on that list are going to wind up in concentration camps, courtesy of Mr. McCarran's darling Internal Security Act. If we go to war with the Soviet Union—and nothing the right wing in this country wants more than a war—McCarran will take a personal hand in putting us all behind barbed wire."

The list neither shut Ira up nor sent him, like any number of colleagues, running for cover. Only a week after the list was published, the Korean War suddenly broke out, and in a letter to the old *Herald Tribune,* Ira (signing himself defiantly as *The Free and the Brave*'s Iron Rinn) had publicly stated his opposition to what he described as Truman's determination to turn that remote conflict into the long-awaited postwar showdown between the capitalists and the Communists and, by doing so, "maniacally to set the stage for the atomic horror of World War III and the destruction of mankind." It was Ira's first letter to an editor since he'd written from Iran to *Stars and Stripes* about the injustice of troop segregation, and it was more than an inflamed declaration against going to war with Communist North Korea. By implication it was a blatant, calculated act of resistance against *Red Channels* and its goal not simply of purging Communists but of menacing into silent submission the airwaves' liberals and non-Communist left wingers.

Korea was virtually all Ira could talk about during that week up at the shack in August 1950. Almost every evening during my previous visit, Ira and I had stretched out back on rickety beach chairs, surrounded by citronella candles to repel the gnats and mosquitoes—the lemony fragrance of citronella oil would forever after recall Zinc Town to me—and, while I looked up at the stars, Ira had told me all sorts of stories, some new, some old, about his teenage mining days, his Depression days as a homeless hobo, his wartime adventures as a stevedore at the U.S. Army base at Abadan on the Shatt-al-Arab, the river that, down near the Persian Gulf, more or less separates Iran from Iraq. I had never before known anyone whose life was so intimately circumscribed by so much American history, who was personally familiar with so much American geography, who had confronted, face to face, so much American lowlife. I'd never known anyone so immersed in his moment or so defined by it. Or tyrannized by it, so much its avenger and its victim and its tool. To imagine Ira *outside* of his moment was impossible.

For me, on those nights up in the shack, the America that was my inheritance manifested itself in the form of Ira Ringold. What Ira was saying, the not entirely limpid (or unrepetitious) flood of loathing and love, aroused exalted patriotic cravings to know firsthand an America beyond Newark, sparked those same native-son passions that had been kindled in me as a boy by the war, that had then been fostered in early adolescence by Howard Fast and Norman Corwin, and that would be sustained a year or two down the line by the novels of Thomas Wolfe and John Dos Passos. My second year visiting Ira, it began to get deliciously cold at night up in the Sussex hills at the tail end of summer, and I would be feeding the roaring flames in the fireplace with wood that I had split in the hot sun that morning, while Ira, sipping coffee out of his chipped old mug and wearing short pants, battered basketball sneakers, and a washed-out olive T-shirt from his army days—looking like nothing so much as the Great American Scoutmaster, the big natural guy who is adored by the boys, who can live off the land and scare off the bear and make sure your kid doesn't drown in the lake—would go on about Korea in a voice of protest and disgust you were unlikely to hear around the fire at any other campsite in the country.

"I cannot believe that any American citizen who has half a brain can believe that the North Korean Communist troops will get into ships and travel six thousand miles and take over the United States. But this is what people are saying. 'You have to watch out for the Communist threat. They're going to take over this country.' Truman is showing the Republicans his muscle—*that's* what he's up to. That's what this is all about. Showing his muscle at the expense of innocent Korean people. We're going in and we're going to bomb those sons of bitches, y'understand? And all to prop up this fascist of ours Syngman Rhee. President Wonderful Truman. General Wonderful MacArthur. The Communists, the Communists. Not the racism in this country, not the inequities in this country. No, the Communists are the problem! Five thousand Negroes have been lynched in this country and not one lyncher has been convicted yet. Is that the fault of the Communists? Ninety Negroes have been lynched since Truman came to the White House full of talk about civil rights. Is that the fault of the Communists, or is it the fault of Truman's attorney general, Mr. Wonderful Clark, who resorts to the outrageous persecution in an American courtroom of twelve leaders of the Communist Party, ruthlessly destroys their lives because of their beliefs, but when it comes to the lynchers refuses to raise a finger! Let's make war on the Communists, let's send our soldiers to fight the Communists—and everywhere you go, around the world, the first ones to die in the struggle against fascism are the Communists! The first ones to struggle in behalf of the Negro, in behalf of the worker . . ."

I'd heard it all before, these exact words many times, and by the end of my vacation week I couldn't wait to get out of earshot of him and go home. This time round, staying at the shack wasn't what it had been for me the first summer. With hardly an inkling of how embattled he saw himself on every front, of how compromised he felt his defiant independence to have become—still imagining that my hero was on his way to leading and winning radio's fight against the reactionaries at *Red Channels*—I couldn't understand the fear and desperation, the growing sense of failure and isolation that were feeding Ira's indignant righteousness. "Why do I do the things I do politically? I do things because I think it is *right* to do them. I have to do something, because something has to be *done*. And I don't give a damn if nobody knows it except me. I squirm, Nathan, at the cowardice of my erstwhile associates . . ."

The summer before, even though I wasn't old enough to get a license, Ira had taught me how to drive his car. When I turned seventeen and my father got around to teaching me, I was sure that if I told him that Ira Ringold had beat him to it back in August, it would hurt his feelings, and so with my father I pretended that I didn't know what I was doing and that learning to drive was brand-new to me. Ira's '39 Chevy was black, a two-door coupe, and really good-looking. Ira was so big that he looked like something out of the circus sitting at the wheel of the car, and that second summer, when he sat beside me and let me drive, I felt as though I were driving a monument around, a monument in a mad rage about the Korean War, a battle monument commemorating the battle *against* battling.

The car had been somebody's grandmother's and had only twelve thousand miles on it when Ira bought it in '48. Floor shift, three speeds forward and the reverse on the upper left of the H. Two separate seats in front, with a space behind them just large enough for a small kid to perch uncomfortably. No radio, no heater. To open the vents, you pushed down a little handle and the flaps would come up in front of the windshield, with a screen on them to keep out the bugs. Pretty efficient. No-draft windows with their own crank. Seats upholstered in that mousy gray fuzz that all cars came through with in those days. Running boards. Big trunk. The spare, with the jack, under the floor panel of the trunk. Sort of a pointed grill, and the hood ornament had a piece of glass in it. Real fenders, big and rounded, and the headlights separate, like two torpedoes, right behind that aerodynamic grill. The windshield wipers worked on a vacuum, so that when you stepped on the gas the wipers would slow down.

I can remember the ashtray. Right in the center of the dash, between the two passengers: a nice elongated piece of plastic, hinged at the bottom, that rocked out toward you. To get at the engine, you twisted a handle on the outside. No lock—you could have vandalized that engine in two seconds. Each side of the hood opened independently. The texture of the steering wheel was not slick and shiny but fibrous, and the horn was in the center only. The starter was a little round rubber pedal with a corrugated piece of rubber around its neck. The choke that was needed for a start on a cold day was on the right, and something called the throttle on the left. The throttle had no conceivable use that I understood. On the glove compartment a recessed wind-up clock. The gas-tank cover, smack on the side, to the rear of the passenger-side door, screwed off like a lid. To lock the car, you pressed the button on the driver's window, and when you got out of the car, you pulled the rotating handle down and slammed the door. That way, if you were thinking about something else, you could manage to lock the key in the car.

I could go on and on about that car because it was the first place I ever got laid. That second summer out with Ira I met the daughter of the Zinc Town chief of police, and one night I borrowed Ira's car and took her on a date to a drive-in. Her name was Sally Spreen. She was a redhead a couple of years older than me who worked at the general store and was known locally as "easy." I took Sally Spreen out of New Jersey to a drive-in across the Delaware in Pennsylvania. The drive-in speakers in those days hung inside the car window, and it was an Abbott and Costello movie. Loud. We started necking right away. She *was* easy. The funny part (if one can speak of just a part of it being funny) was that my underpants were around my left foot. And my left foot was on the accelerator, and so while I was humping her I was flooding Ira's engine. By the time I came, my underwear had somehow wound itself around the brake pedal and my ankle. Costello is yelling, "Hey, Abbott! Hey, Abbott!," the windows are steaming, the engine is flooded, her father is the chief of the Zinc Town police, and I am tied to the floor of the car.

Driving her home, I didn't know what to say or what to feel or what punishment to expect for having taken her across state lines to have sexual intercourse, and so I found myself explaining to her how American soldiers had no business fighting in Korea. I gave it to her about General MacArthur, as though *he* were her father.

When I got back to the shack, Ira looked up from the book he was reading. "Was she good?"

I didn't know what the answer was. The idea hadn't even occurred to me. "*Anybody* would have been good," I told him, and the two of us burst into laughter.

In the morning, we discovered that in my exalted state of the previous night, I had locked the key inside the car before entering the shack no longer a virgin. Again Ira laughed out loud—but otherwise, during my week at the shack, he was impossible to amuse.

Sometimes Ira invited his nearest neighbor, Raymond Svecz, over to have dinner with us. Ray was a bachelor who lived some two miles down the road, at the edge of an abandoned quarry, a most primeval-looking excavation, an enormous, terrifying manmade chasm whose broken, bottom-of-the-world nothingness gave me the willies even when it was sunlit. Ray lived there by himself in a one-room structure that decades earlier had been a storage shed for mining equipment, as forlorn a human habitat as any I'd ever seen. He had been a POW in Germany during the war and had returned home with what Ira called "mental problems." A year later, back at his job drilling in the zinc mine—in the zinc mine where Ira had himself worked with a shovel as a boy—he'd had his skull injured in an accident. Fourteen hundred feet below the surface of the earth, an overhead rock about the size of a coffin, weighing over a thousand pounds, broke off near a wall he was drilling and, though it didn't crush him, sent him hurtling to the floor, face first. Ray survived, but he never went underground again, and doctors had been rebuilding his skull ever since. Ray was handy, and Ira gave him odd jobs to do, had him weed the vegetable garden and keep it watered when he wasn't around, paid him to repair and paint things at the shack. Most weeks he paid him to do nothing, and when Ira was in residence and saw that Ray wasn't eating properly, he brought him in and fed him. Ray hardly ever spoke. An agreeable sort of dopey fellow, always nodding his head (which was said to look little like the head he'd had before the accident), very polite . . . and even when he was eating with us, Ira's attack against our enemies never stopped.

I should have expected it. I *had* expected it. I had looked forward to it. I would have thought that I couldn't get enough of it. Yet I did. I was starting college the following week, and my education with Ira had ended. With a speed that was incredible, it was over. That innocence was over too. I had walked in the shack on Pickax Hill Road one person, and I was walking out another. Whatever the name of the driving new force that had come to the surface, it had come unbidden, all by itself, and was irreversible. The tearing away from my father, the straining of filial affection prompted by my infatuation with Ira, was now being replicated in my disillusionment with him.

Even when Ira took me to see his favorite local friend, Horace Bixton—who, with his son, Frank, ran a taxidermy business in a half-converted cow barn of two rooms next to the Bixton family farmhouse on a dirt road nearby—all Ira could talk about with Horace was what he'd been talking about nonstop with me. The year before, we'd been out there and I'd had a great time listening, not to Ira going on about Korea and Communism, but to Horace going on about taxidermy. That was *why* Ira had taken me out, to hear Horace go on about taxidermy. "You could write a radio play, Nathan, starring this guy and based on taxidermy alone." Ira's interest in taxidermy was part of a working-class fascination he still had, not so much with nature's beauty, but with man's interfering with nature, with industrialized nature and exploited nature, with nature man-touched, man-worn, man-defaced, and, as it was beginning to look out in the heart of zinc country, man-ruined.

When I walked in the Bixtons' door that first time, the bizarre clutter of the small front room staggered me: tanned skins piled up everywhere; antlers strung from the ceiling, tagged and hanging from bits of wire, back and forth the whole length of the room antlers by the dozens; enormous lacquered fish also hanging from the ceiling, shiny fish with extended sails, shiny fish with elongated swords, one shiny fish with a face like a monkey; animal heads—small, medium, large, and extralarge—mounted on every square inch of wall; a populous flock of ducks and geese and eagles and owls spread across the floor, many with their wings open as if in flight. There were pheasants and wild turkeys, there was a pelican, there was a swan, there was also, scattered furtively among the birds, a skunk, a bobcat, a coyote, and a pair of beavers. In dusty glass cases along the walls were the smaller birds, doves and pigeons, a small alligator as well as coiled snakes, lizards, turtles, rabbits, squirrels, and rodents of every kind, mice, weasels, and other ugly little things I could not name realistically nestled in wilted old natural tableaux. And the dust was everywhere, cloaking fur, feathers, pelts, everything.

Horace, a slight elderly man, himself not much taller than the span of the wings of his vulture, and wearing overalls and a khaki tractor hat, came out from the back to shake my hand, and when he saw my startled expression, he smiled apologetically. "Yeah," he said, "we don't throw much out."

"Horace," Ira said, looking way, way down to this elfin person who, Ira had told me, made his own hard cider and smoked his own meats and knew every bird by its song, "this is Nathan, a young high school writer. I told him what you told me about a good taxidermist: the test of a good taxidermist is to create the illusion of life. He says, 'That's the test of a good writer,' and so I brought him over so you two artistes could chew the fat."

"Well, we take our work seriously," Horace informed me. "We do everything. Fish, birds, mammals. Game heads. All positions, all species."

"Tell him about that beast," Ira said with a laugh, pointing to a tall bird on stalky legs that looked to me like a nightmare rooster.

"That's a cassowary," Horace said. "Big bird from New Guinea. Don't fly. This here was in a circus. A traveling circus sideshow, and it died, and back in '38 they brought it to me and I stuffed it, and the circus never came back for it. That's an oryx," he said, beginning to differentiate his handiwork for me. "That's Cooper's hawk flying. Cape buffalo skull—that's called the European mount, the top half of the skull. These are the antlers of an elk. Huge. A wildebeest—the top of the skull with the fur there . . ."

We were half an hour making the safari through the front showroom, and when we stepped into the back workroom—"the shop," as Horace called it—there was Frank, a balding man of about forty, a full-scale model of his father, sitting at a bloody table skinning a fox with a knife that, we later learned, Frank himself had made out of a hacksaw blade.

"Different animals, you know, have different smells," Horace explained to me. "You smell the fox?"

I nodded.

"Yep, there's an odor associated with the fox," Horace said. "It's not as pleasant as it might be."

Frank had nearly all of the fox's right hind leg skinned clear down to raw muscle and bone. "That one," said Horace, "is going to be mounted whole. It's going to look like a lifelike fox." The fox, freshly shot, lay there looking like a lifelike fox already, only asleep. We all sat around the table while Frank kept working neatly away. "Frank has very nimble fingers," Horace said with a father's pride. "A lot of people can do the fox and the bear and the deer and the big birds, but my son can do the songbirds, too." Frank's prize homemade tool, Horace said, was a tiny brain spoon, for the small birds, of a kind you could not begin to buy. By the time Ira and I got up to go, Frank, who was deaf and could not speak, had skinned the whole fox so it was down to an emaciated-looking red carcass about the size of a newborn human baby.

"People eat fox?" Ira asked.

"Not normally," said Horace. "But during the Depression we used to try things. Everybody was in the same fix then, you know—no meat. We ate possum, woodchuck, rabbits."

"What was good?" Ira asked.

"It was all good. We was always hungry. During the Depression you ate anything you could get. We ate crow."

"What's crow like?"

"Well, the trouble with crow is you don't know how old the darn things are. One crow, it was like shoe leather. Some of those crows were only really fit for soup. We used to eat squirrel."

"How do you cook a squirrel?"

"Black cast-iron pot. Wife used to trap squirrels. She'd skin 'em, and when she had three, she'd cook 'em in the pot. You just eat 'em like chicken legs."

"Got to bring my little woman over," Ira said, "so's you can give her the recipe."

"One time the wife tried to feed me raccoon. But I knew. She said it was black bear." Horace laughed. "She was a good cook. She died on Groundhog Day. Seven years ago."

"When did you get that in, Horace?" Ira was motioning above Horace's tractor hat to the outthrust head of a wild boar mounted on the wall; it hung between shelves loaded with the wire frames and the frames of burlap impregnated with plaster over which animal skins were stretched and adjusted and sewn back together to create the illusion of life. The boar was every inch a beast, a great beast at that, blackish with a brown throat and a whitish mask of hairs between the eyes and adorning its jowls, and a snout as big and black and hard as a wet black stone. Its jaws were set menacingly open so that you could see the rawness of the mouth's carnivorous interior and the imposing white tusklike teeth. The boar had the illusion of life, all right; so too, as yet, did Frank's fox, whose stink I could hardly stand.

"Boar looks real," Ira said.

"Oh, that's real. The tongue isn't real, though. The tongue is fake. Hunter wanted the original teeth. Usually we use fake ones, because by and by the originals crack. They kind of get brittle and fall apart. But he wanted its real teeth in there so we put its real ones in there."

"How long did that take you, from day one?"

"That would be about three days, twenty hours."

"How much you get to do that boar?"

"Seventy dollars."

"To me that seems cheap," Ira said.

"You're used to New York City prices," Horace told him.

"You get the whole boar or just the head?"

"Usually the whole skull is in there and it's cut off at the back of the neck. We do get on occasion whole bear, black bear—a tiger I did."

"A tiger? Did you? You never told me that." I could see that though Ira was leading Horace on for the benefit of my education as a writer, he also liked questioning him in order to hear him reply in his small, sharp, chirpy voice, a voice that sounded as if it had been whittled out of a piece of wood. "Where was the tiger shot?" Ira asked.

"It's a guy who owns 'em, like pets. One of them died. And they're valuable, the skins, and he wanted this one made into a rug. He called up, and he put it on a stretcher, and Frank got it right in the car and brought it in, the whole thing. Because they didn't know how to skin it or anything."

"And did you know how to do a tiger, or did you have to look it up in a book?"

"A book, Ira? No, Ira, no book. Once you been doing it for a while you can figure out just about any animal."

Ira said to me, "You got any questions you want Horace to answer? Anything you want to know for school?"

Just to be listening, I couldn't have been any happier, and so I mouthed "No."

"Was it fun to skin that tiger, Horace?" Ira asked.

"Yes. I enjoyed it. I got a fellow and I hired him to take a home movie, a movie of the whole process, and I showed it at Thanksgiving that year."

"Before or after dinner?" Ira asked.

Horace smiled. Though there was no irony that I could discern in the practice of taxidermy, the taxidermist himself had a good American sense of fun. "Well, you're eating all day long, aren't you?

Everybody remembered that Thanksgiving. In a taxidermy family they're used to things like that, but you can still always come up with a surprise, you know."

And so the talk continued, an amiable, quiet conversation with a little laughter in it that finished up with Horace making me a gift of a deer toe. Ira throughout was as gentle and untroubled as I'd ever seen him with anyone. Except for my nausea from smelling the fox, I couldn't remember ever having been so unagitated myself in Ira's company. Nor had I ever before seen him so serious about something that wasn't world affairs or American politics or the failings of the human race. Talking about cooking crows and making a tiger into a rug and the cost of stuffing a wild boar outside New York City freed him to be unexcitable, at peace, almost unrecognizable as himself.

There was something so winning about those two men's good-humored absorption in each other (particularly with a beautiful animal being relieved of its lovely looks right under their noses) that I had to wonder afterward if this person who didn't have to get all stirred up and go through all that Ira-ish emotion to have a conversation wasn't perhaps the real, if unseen, inactive Ira and the other, the furious radical, an impersonation, an imitation of something, like his Lincoln or the boar's tongue. The respect and fondness that Ira had for Horace Bixton suggested even to me, a boy, that there was a very simple world of simple people and simple satisfactions into which Ira might have drifted, where all his vibrating passions, where all that equipped him (and ill equipped him) for society's onslaught might have been remade and even pacified. Maybe with a son like Frank whose nimble fingers he could be proud of and a wife who knew how to trap and cook a squirrel, maybe by appropriating those sorts of near-at-hand things, by making his own hard cider and smoking his own meats and wearing overalls and a khaki tractor hat and by listening to the song-birds sing . . . And then again, maybe not. Maybe to be, like Horace, without a great enemy would have made life even more impossible for Ira to tolerate than it already was.

The second year we went out to see Horace, there was no laughter in the conversation and Ira did all the talking.

Frank was skinning a deer's head—"Frank," Horace said, "can do deer head with his eyes closed"—while Horace sat hunched over the other end of the worktable "preparing skulls." Laid out before him was an assortment of very small skulls he was repairing with wire and glue. Some science teachers at a school over in Easton wanted a collection of small mammal skulls, and they knew Horace might have what they wanted because, he told me, grinning at the fragile, tiny bones before him, "I don't throw nothin' out."

"Horace," Ira was saying, "can any American citizen who has half a brain believe that the North Korean Communist troops will get into ships and travel six thousand miles and take over the United States? Can you believe that?"

Without looking up from the skull of a muskrat whose loose teeth he was fixing in its jaw with glue, Horace slowly shook his head.

"But this is exactly what people are saying," Ira told him. "'You have to watch out for the Communist threat—they're going to take over this country.' This Truman is showing the Republicans his muscle—that's what he is up to. That's what this is all about. Showing his muscle at the expense of innocent Koreans. We're going in there and all to prop up this fascist bastard Syngman Rhee. We're going to bomb those sons of bitches, y'understand? President Wonderful Truman. General Wonderful MacArthur . . ."

And, unable to stop myself from being bored by the tireless harangue that was Ira's primal script, I was thinking, spitefully, "Frank doesn't know how lucky he is to be deaf. That muskrat doesn't know how lucky it is to be dead. That deer . . ." Et cetera.

Same thing happened—Syngman Rhee, President Wonderful Truman, General Wonderful MacArthur—when we went by the rock dump out on the highway one morning to say hello to Tommy Minarek, a retired miner, a burly, hearty Slovak who had been working in the mines when Ira first showed up in Zinc Town in

1929 and who had taken a fatherly interest in Ira back then. Now Tommy worked for the town, looking after the rock dump—its one tourist attraction—where, along with serious mineral collectors, families sometimes drove out with their kids to go hunting through the vast dump for chunks of rock to take home and put under an ultraviolet light. Under the light, as Tommy explained to me, the minerals "fluoresce"—glow, that is, with fluorescent red, orange, purple, mustard, blue, cream, and green; some look to be made of black velvet.

Tommy sat on a big flat rock at the entrance to the dump, hatless in all weather, a handsome old fellow with a wide, square face, white hair, hazel eyes, and all his teeth. He charged the adults a quarter to go in and, though the town told him to charge the kids a dime, he always let the kids in free. "People come from all over the world to go in there," Tommy told me. "Some through the years that come every Saturday and Sunday, even wintertime. I make fires for certain people and they give me a few bucks for that. They come every Saturday or Sunday, rain or shine."

On the hood of Tommy's jalopy, parked directly beside the large flat rock where Tommy sat, he had samples of minerals from the collection in his own cellar spread out on a towel for sale, chunky specimens selling for as much as five and six dollars, pickle jars full of smaller specimens for a dollar fifty, and small brown paper bags full of bits and pieces of rock, which went for fifty cents. He kept the fifteen-, twenty-, and twenty-five-dollar stuff in the trunk of the car.

"In the back," he told me, "I got the more valuable things. I can't put 'em out here. I go sometimes across the road to Gary's machine shop, to use the toilet or somethin', and the stuff is out here . . . I had two specimens last fall, in the back, guy put a black thing over 'em, and he's lookin' with a light, and I had two fifty-dollar specimens in the car and he got 'em both."

The year before, I had sat alone with Tommy outside the rock dump, watching him deal with the tourists and the collectors and listening to his spiel (and later I wrote a radio play about that morning called *The Old Miner*). That was the morning after he'd come to have a hot dog dinner with us at the shack. Ira was at me, educating me, all the time when I was up at the shack, and Tommy was brought in as visiting lecturer, to give me the lowdown on the plight of the miner before the union came in.

"Tell Nathan about your dad, Tom. Tell him what happened to your dad."

"My dad died from workin' in the mine. Him and another guy went in a place where two other guys worked every day, in a raise, a vertical hole. Both of them didn't show up that day. It's a ways up, over a hundred feet up. My dad and another guy the boss sent in there, a young guy, a husky guy—was he a beautiful built guy! I went to the hospital and I seen the guy and he wasn't in bed, and my dad was stretched out, didn't even move. I never seen him move. The second day I come in, this other guy was talkin' to another guy, joking, he wasn't even in bed even. My dad was in bed."

Tommy was born in 1880 and started working in the mines in 1902, "May the twenty-fourth," he told me, "1902. That's about the time Thomas Edison was up here, the famous inventor, experimentin'." Though Tommy, despite his years in the mines, was a robust, upright human specimen who hardly looked to be seventy, he had himself to confess that he was not as alert as he'd once been, and every time he got a little befuddled or got stalled in his story, Ira had to get him on the trail again. "I don't think that quick no more," Tommy told us. "I have to follow myself back, starting with the ABCs, you know, and try to hit into it. Get into it somewhere. I'm still alert, but not as good as I was."

"What was the accident?" Ira asked Tommy. "What happened to your dad? Tell Nathan what happened to him."

"The station broke. See, we put a timber in the back of this four-by-four hole at a certain degree—we put one back there, have to dig it out with a pick to make it slantlike, so I wedge this in and I cut it at an angle. One in the front and one over here. And then we put a two-inch plank on there."

Ira interrupted to try to push him ahead, to the good stuff. "So what happened? Tell him how your dad died."

"It collapsed. The vibration collapsed it. The machine and everything went down. Over a hundred feet. He never recovered. His bones were all broke. He died about a year after. We had this old-fashioned stove, and he had his feet right in there, trying to stay warm. Couldn't keep warm."

"Did they have any workmen's compensation? You ask, Nathan, ask the questions. That's what you do if you want to be a writer. Don't be shy. Ask Tommy if he had workmen's compensation."

But I *was* shy. Here, eating hot dogs with me, was a real miner, thirty years in the zinc mines. I couldn't have been any more shy if Tommy Minarek had been Albert Einstein. "Did they?" I asked.

"Give you anything? The company? He didn't get a penny," Tommy said bitterly. "The company was the trouble and the bosses was the trouble. The bosses down there didn't seem to care for their house. You know what I mean? For their territory that they worked in every day. Like me, if I was a boss down there, I would check these planks goin' over where the people walk over the holes. I don't know how deep them holes are, but certain people got killed down there, walkin' on these planks, and the plank broke. Rotten. They never took care of them to check them darn planks. They never did it."

"Didn't you have a union then?" I asked.

"We had no union. My father didn't even get a penny."

I tried to think of what else I ought to know as a writer. "Didn't you have the United Mine Workers down here?" I asked.

"We had it later. In the forties already. It was too late by then," he said, outrage again in his voice. "He was dead, I was retired—and the union didn't help that much anyway. How could they? We had one leader, our local president—he was good, but what could he do? You couldn't do nothin' with a power like that. Look, years before we had a guy tried to organize us. This person went to get water for his house from a spring down the road. Never come back. Nobody ever heard of him anymore. Tryin' to organize the union."

"Ask about the company, Nathan."

"The company store," Tommy said. "I seen people get a white slip."

"Tell him, Tom, what a white slip is."

"You didn't get no pay. The company store got all his money. A white slip. I seen that."

"Owners make a lot of money?" Ira asked.

"The president of the zinc company, the main guy, he's got a big mansion over here, up on the hill alone. Big house up there. I heard one of his friends say, when he died, that he had nine and a half million dollars. That's what he owned."

"And what'd you get to start?" Ira asked him.

"Thirty-two cents an hour. First job I worked in the boiler house. I was twenty-some years old. Then I went down in the mines. Highest I could get was ninety cents because I was like a boss. A headman like. Next to the boss. I did everything."

"Pensions?"

"Nothin'. My father-in-law got a pension. He got eight dollars. Thirty-some years he worked. Eight dollars a month, that's what he got. I didn't see no pension."

"Tell Nathan how you eat down there."

"We have to eat underground."

"Everybody?" Ira asked.

"The bosses are the only ones who come up twelve o'clock and eat in their washroom. The rest of us, underground."

The next morning, Ira drove me out to the rock dump to sit there with Tommy and learn from him on my own all I could about the evil consequences of the profit motive as it functioned in Zinc Town. "Here's my boy, Tom. Tom's a good man and a good teacher, Nathan."

"I try to be the best," Tommy said.

"He was my teacher down in the mines. Weren't you, Tom?"

"That I was, Gil."

Tommy called Ira Gil. When I had asked, at breakfast that morning, why Tommy called him Gil, Ira laughed and said, "That's what they called me down there. Gil. Never really knew why. Somebody called me that one day, and it just stuck. Mexicans, Russians, Slovaks, all called me Gil."

In 1997, I learned from Murray that Ira had not been telling me the truth. They had called him Gil because up in Zinc Town he had called himself Gil. Gil Stephens.

"I taught Gil how to set the explosives when he was a kid. By then I was a runner, I was the one that drills and sets up everything, the explosives, the timbers and everything. Taught Gil here to drill, and in every one of them you put a stick of dynamite in there, and put a circuit wire through."

"I'm going, Tom. I'll pick him up later. Tell him about the explosives. Educate this city slicker, Mr. Minarek. Tell Nathan about the smell from the explosives and what that does to a man's insides."

Ira drove off, and Tommy said, "The smell? You have to get used to that. I had it once, bad. I was mucking out a pillar, not a pillar, an entrance, a four-by-four entrance. And we drilled and fired it, and we put water on it all night, on that muck, we call it muck, and the next day it smelled like hell. I got a whiff of that good. It bothered me for a while. I was sick. Not as sick as some of the guys, but sick enough."

It was summertime, already hot at nine A.M., but even out at the ugly rock dump, with the big machine shop across the highway where they had the not-so-hygienic toilet Tommy used, it was blue overhead and beautiful, and pretty soon families started driving up in cars to visit. One guy stuck his head out the car window and asked me, "Is this the one where the kids can go in and pick rocks and stuff?"

"Yep," I said, instead of "Yes."

"You got kids here?" Tommy asked him.

He pointed to two in the back seat.

"Right here, sir," Tommy said. "Go in and look around. And

when you go out, right here, half a buck a bag here for a miner who mined 'em for thirty years, special rocks for the kids."

An elderly woman drove up in a car full of kids, her grandchildren probably, and when she got out, Tommy politely saluted her. "Lady, when you're going out, and you want a nice bag of rocks for the little ones from a miner who mined 'em for thirty years, stop here. Fifty cents a bag. Special rocks for the kids. They fluoresce beautifully."

Getting in the swing of things—getting in the swing of the *joys* of the profit motive as it functioned in Zinc Town—I told her, "He's got the good stuff, lady."

"I'm the only one," he told her, "who makes these bags. These bags are from the good mine. The other is completely different. I don't put no junk in there. There's *real* stuff in there. If you see 'em under light, you'll enjoy what's in there. There's pieces in there only comes from this mine, nowhere else in the world."

"You're in the sun without a hat," she told Tommy. "You don't get hot sitting there like that?"

"Been doing this many years," he told her. "See these ones on my car? These fluoresce different colors. They look ugly but they're nice under light, they got different things in 'em. It's got a lot of different mixtures in."

"This is a fella"—"fella," not "fellow," said I—"who really knows rocks. Thirty years in the mines," I said.

Then a couple pulled up who looked more like city people than any of the other tourists. As soon as they got out of their car, they began to examine Tommy's higher-priced specimens on the hood of the car and to consult together quietly. Tommy whispered to me, "They want my rocks in the worst way. I got a collection, nobody can touch it. This here's the most extraordinary mineral deposit on this planet—and I got the best of 'em."

Here I piped up. "This guy's got the best stuff. Thirty years in the mines. He's got beautiful rocks here. Beautiful rocks." And they bought four pieces, for a sale totaling fifty-five dollars, and I thought, I'm helpin'. I'm helpin' a real miner.

"If you want any minerals again," I said as they got back with their purchase into their car, "you come here. This here's the most extraordinary mineral deposit on this planet."

I was having a fine time of it until, close to noon, Brownie arrived and the silly gratuitousness of the role I was so enthusiastically playing was revealed even to me.

Brownie—Lloyd Brown—was a couple of years older than me, a skinny, crewcutted, sharp-nosed boy, pale and harmless-looking in the extreme, particularly in the white shopkeeper's apron that he wore over a clean white shirt and a clip-on black bow tie and a pair of fresh dungarees. Because his relation to himself was so transparently simple, his chagrin when he saw me with Tommy was plastered all over him and pitiable. Compared with Brownie, I felt like a kid with the most abundant and frenzied existence, even just sitting quietly beside Tommy Minarek; compared with Brownie, that's what I *was*.

But if something about my complexity mocked him, something about his simplicity also mocked me. I turned everything into an adventure, looking always to be altered, while Brownie lived with a sense of nothing other than hard necessity, had been so shaped and tamed by constraint as to be able to play only the role of himself. He was without any craving that wasn't brewed in Zinc Town. The only thoughts he ever wanted to think were the thoughts that everybody else in Zinc Town thought. He wanted life to repeat and repeat itself, and I wanted to break out. I felt like a freak wanting to be other than Brownie—perhaps for the very first time but not for the last. What would it be like to have that passion to break out vanish from my life? What must it be like to be Brownie? Wasn't that what the fascination with "the people" was really all about? *What is it like to be them?*

"You busy, Tom? I can come back tomorrow."

"Stay here," Tommy said to the boy. "Sit down, Brownie."

Deferentially, Brownie said to me, "I just come here every day on my lunch hour and I talk to him about rocks."

"Sit down, Brownie, my boy. So what do you got?"

Brownie laid a worn old satchel at Tommy's feet, and from it he began to extract rock specimens about the size of the ones Tommy was displaying on the hood of his car.

"Black willemite, huh?" Brownie asked.

"No, that's hematite."

"I thought it was a funny-looking willemite. And this?" he asked. "Hendricksite?"

"Yep. Little willemite. There's calcite, too, in there."

"Five bucks for that? Too much?" Brownie asked.

"Somebody may want it," Tommy said.

"You in this business too?" I asked Brownie.

"This was my dad's collection. He was in the mill. Got killed. I'm selling it to get married."

"Nice girl," Tommy told me. "And she's a sweet girl. She's a doll. A Slovak girl. The Musco girl. Nice girl, honest girl, clean girl who uses her head. There's no girls like her anymore. He's gonna live with Mary Musco all his life. I tell Brownie, 'You be good to her, she'll be good to you.' I had a wife like that. Slovak girl. Best in the world. Nobody in the world can take her place."

Brownie held up another specimen. "Bustamite there with that?"

"That's bustamite."

"Got a little willemite crystal on it."

"Yep. There's a little willemite crystal right there."

This went on for close to an hour, until Brownie started packing his specimens back in the satchel to return to the grocery store where he worked.

"He's gonna take my place in Zinc Town," Tommy told me.

"Oh, I don't know," Brownie said. "I won't know as much as you do."

"But you still have to do it." All at once Tommy's voice was fervent, almost anguished, when he spoke. "I want a Zinc Town guy to take over my place here. I want a Zinc Town guy! That's why I'm teaching you here as much as I can. So you can get somewhere. You're the one who's entitled to it. A Zinc Town person. I don't want to teach somebody else, from out of town."

"Three years ago I started coming here lunchtime, I didn't know anything. And he taught me so much. Right, Tommy? I did pretty good today. Tommy can tell you the mine," Brownie said to me. "He can tell you where in the mine it came from. What level, how deep. He says, 'You gotta hold the rocks in your hand.' Right?"

"Right. You gotta hold the rocks in your hand. You gotta handle that mineral. You gotta see the different matrixes that they come in. If you don't learn that, you're not going to learn Zinc Town minerals. He even knows now, he knows if this is from the other mine or if it's from this mine."

"He taught me that," Brownie said. "I couldn't tell what mine it came from in the beginning. I can tell now."

"So," I said, "you're going to be sitting out here someday."

"I hope so. Like this right here, this is from this mine, right, Tom? And this is from this mine too?"

Because in another year I hoped to go off on a scholarship to the University of Chicago and, after Chicago, become the Norman Corwin of my generation, because I was going everywhere and Brownie was going nowhere—but mostly because Brownie's father had been killed in the mill and my own was alive and well and worrying about me in Newark—I spoke even more fervently than Tommy had to this aproned grocer's assistant whose aspiration in life was to marry Mary Musco and fill Tommy's seat. "Hey, you're good! That's good!"

"And why?" said Tom. "Because he learned right here."

"I learned from this man," Brownie told me proudly.

"I want him to be the next one to take my place."

"Here comes some business, Tom. I gotta run," Brownie said. "Nice to meet you," he said to me.

"Nice to meet *you*," I replied, as though I were the older man and he the child. "When I come back in ten years," I said, "I'll see you out here."

"Oh," said Tom, "he'll be here, all right."

"No, no," Brownie shouted back, for the first time laughing lightheartedly as he headed on foot down the highway. "Tommy'll still be here. Won't you, Tom?"

"We'll see."

In fact, it was Ira who would be out there ten years later. Tommy had educated Ira, too, once Ira was blacklisted from radio and living alone up in the shack and needing a source of income. That was where Ira dropped dead. That's when Ira's aorta gave out, while he was sitting on Tommy's flat rock selling mineral specimens to the tourists and their kids, telling them, "Lady, half a buck a bag here for them when your boys come out, special rocks right from the mine that I mined there for thirty years."

This was how Ira had ended his days—as the overseer at the rock dump whom the local old-timers all called Gil, out there even in the wintertime, making fires for certain people for a few bucks. But I didn't learn this until the night that Murray told me Ira's story there on my deck.

The day before I left that second year, Artie Sokolow and his family drove out to Zinc Town from New York to spend the afternoon with Ira. Ella Sokolow, Artie's wife, was about seven months pregnant, a jolly, dark-haired, freckled-faced woman whose Irish immigrant father, Ira told me, had been a steamfitter up in Albany, one of those big, idealistic union men who are patriotic through and through. "The 'Marseillaise,' 'The Star-Spangled Banner,' the Russian national anthem," Ella laughingly explained that afternoon, "the old man would stand up for all of them."

The Sokolows had twin boys of six, and though the afternoon began happily enough with a game of touch football—refereed in a manner by Ira's neighbor, Ray Svecz—and was followed by a picnic lunch that Ella had brought along from the city and that all of us, including Ray, ate up the slope from the pond, it ended with Artie Sokolow and Ira down by the pond, toe to toe and barking at each other in a way that horrified me.

I had been sitting on the picnic blanket talking to Ella about *My Glorious Brothers,* a book by Howard Fast that she had just finished reading. It was a historical novel set in ancient Judea, about the Maccabees' struggle against Antiochus IV in the second century

B.C., and I, too, had read it and even reported on it in school for Ira's brother the second time he was my English teacher.

Ella had been listening to me the way she listened to everyone: taking it all in as if she were being warmed by your words. I must have gone on for close to fifteen minutes, repeating word for word the internationalist-progressive critique I'd written for Mr. Ringold, and all the time Ella gave every indication that what I was saying couldn't have been more interesting. I knew how much Ira admired her as a lifelong radical, and I wanted her to admire me as a radical too. Her background, the physical grandeur of her pregnancy, and certain gestures she made—sweeping gestures with her hands that made her seem to me strikingly uninhibited—all bestowed on Ella Sokolow a heroic authority that I wanted to impress.

"I read Fast and I respect Fast," I'd been telling her, "but I think he lays too much emphasis on the Judeans' fight to return to their past condition, to their worship of tradition and the days of post-Egyptian slavery. There's entirely too much that's merely nationalistic in the book—"

And that was when I heard Ira shout, "You're caving in! Running scared and caving in!"

"If it's not there," Sokolow shot back, "no one knows it's not there!"

"*I* know it's not there!"

The rage in Ira's voice made it impossible for me to go on. All I could think about, suddenly, was the story—which I had refused to believe—that ex-Sergeant Erwin Goldstine had told me in his Maplewood kitchen, about Butts, about the guy in Iran Ira had tried to drown in the Shatt-al-Arab.

I said to Ella, "What's the matter?"

"Just give them room," she said, "and hope they calm down. *You* calm down."

"I just want to know what they're arguing about."

"They're blaming each other for things that have gone wrong. They're arguing over things having to do with the show. Calm down, Nathan. You haven't been around enough angry people. They'll cool off."

But they didn't look it. Ira particularly. He was storming back and forth at the edge of the pond, his long arms lashing out every which way, and each time he turned back to Artie Sokolow, I thought he was going to pounce on him with his fists. "Why do you *make* these goddamn changes!" Ira shouted.

"Keep it in," Sokolow replied, "and we stand to lose more than we gain."

"Bullshit! Let the bastards know we mean business! Just put the fucking thing back in!"

I said to Ella, "Shouldn't we do something?"

"I've heard men arguing all my life," she told me. "Men having one another's carcasses for the sins of omission and commission that they don't seem able to avoid perpetrating. If they were hitting each other it would be something else. But otherwise, your responsibility is to stay away. If you enter where people are already agitated, anything you do will fuel the fire."

"If you say so."

"You've led a very protected life, haven't you?"

"Have I?" I said. "I try not to."

"Best to stay out of it," she told me, "partly out of dignity, to let the guy cool down without your intervention, and partly out of self-defense, and partly because your intervention is only going to make it worse."

Meanwhile, Ira hadn't stopped roaring. "One fucking punch a week—and now we're not even going to get *that* in? So what are we doing on the radio, Arthur? Advancing our careers? A fight is being forced upon us, and you are running! It's the showdown, Artie, and you are gutlessly running away!"

Impotent though I knew I would be if these two powder kegs were to start swinging, I nonetheless jumped up and, with Ray Svecz trailing behind me in his goofy way, ran toward the pond. Last time I'd pissed in my pants. I couldn't let that happen again. With no more idea than Ray had of what could be done to avert a disaster, I ran directly into the fray.

By the time we reached them, Ira had already backed off and was pointedly walking away from Sokolow. It was clear he was still furious with the guy, but it was also evident how hard he was trying to bring himself down. Ray and I caught up with him and then walked along beside him while, intermittently, beneath his breath, Ira carried on a rapid conversation with himself.

The admixture of his absence and his presence so disturbed me that I finally spoke. "What's wrong?" When he didn't seem to hear, I tried to think of what to say that would get his attention. "It's about a script?" All at once he flared up and said, "I'll kill him if he does it again!" And it was not an expression he was using merely for dramatic effect. It was difficult, despite my resistance, not to believe one hundred percent in the meaning of his words.

Butts, I thought. Butts. Garwych. Solak. Becker.

On his face was a look of total fury. Pristine fury. Fury, which along with terror is the primordial power. All that he was had evolved out of that look—also all that he was not. I thought, He's lucky he's not locked up, an alarmingly unexpected conclusion to occur spontaneously to a hero-worshiping kid interlinked for two years with the virtuousness of his hero, and one I dismissed once I was no longer so agitated—and one that I was then to have verified for me by Murray Ringold forty-eight years on.

Eve had made her way out of her past by impersonating Pennington; Ira had made his way out of his by force.

Ella's twin boys, who'd fled from the edge of the pond when the argument flared up, were lying in her arms on the picnic blanket when I returned with Ray. "I think daily living may be harsher than you know," Ella said to me.

"Is this daily living?" I asked.

"Wherever *I've* lived," she said. "Go on. Go on about Howard Fast."

I did my best, but it continued to unsettle me, if not Sokolow's working-class wife, to think of her husband and Ira squaring off.

Ella laughed aloud when I was through. You could hear her naturalness in her laugh as well as all the crap that she had learned

· 213 ·

to put up with. She laughed the way some people blush: all at once and completely. "Wow," she said. "I'm not sure now *what* I read. My own evaluation of *My Glorious Brothers* is simple. Maybe I don't do enough deep thinking, but I just think, Here's a bunch of rough, tough, and decent guys who believe in the dignity of all men and are willing to die for it."

Artie and Ira had by then cooled off enough to make their way up from the pond to the picnic blanket, where Ira said (trying, apparently, to say something that might ease everybody, himself included, back into the original spirit of the day), "I gotta read it. *My Glorious Brothers.* I gotta get that book."

"It'll put steel in your spine, Ira," Ella said to him, and then, opening wide the big window that was her laugh, she added, "not that I ever thought yours needed any."

Whereupon Sokolow leaned over her and bellowed, "Yes? Whose does? *Just whose does?*"

With that, the Sokolow twins burst into tears, and this in turn caused poor Ray to do the same. Angry herself now for the first time, in something like a mad rage, Ella said, "Christ Almighty, Arthur! Hold yourself together!"

What had lain beneath the afternoon's eruptions I understood more fully that evening when, alone with me in the shack, Ira started in angrily about the lists.

"Lists. Lists of names and accusations and charges. Everybody," Ira said, "has a list. *Red Channels.* Joe McCarthy. The VFW. The HUAC. The American Legion. The Catholic magazines. The Hearst newspapers. Those lists with their sacred numbers—141, 205, 62, 111. Lists of anybody in America who has ever been disgruntled about anything or criticized anything or protested anything—or associated with anybody who has ever criticized or protested anything—all of them now Communists or fronting for Communists or 'helping' Communists or contributing to Communist 'coffers,' or 'infiltrating' labor or government or education or Hollywood or the theater or radio and TV. Lists of 'fifth columnists' busily being compiled in every office and agency in Washington. All the forces of reaction swapping names and mistaking names and linking names together to prove the existence of a mammoth conspiracy *that does not exist*."

"What about you?" I asked him. "What about *The Free and the Brave*?"

"We've got a lot of progressive-thinking people on our show, sure. And the way they're going to be described to the public now is as actors 'who cunningly sell the Moscow line.' You're going to hear a lot of that—a lot worse than that. 'The dupes of Moscow.'"

"Just the actors?"

"And the director. And the composer. And the writer. Everyone."

"You worried?"

"I can go back to the record factory, buddy. If worse comes to worst, I can always come up here and grease cars at Steve's garage. I've done it before. Besides, you can fight them, you know. You can fight the bastards. Last I heard there was a Constitution in this country, a Bill of Rights *somewhere*. If you look with your big eyes into the capitalist shop window, if you want and you want, if you grab and you grab, if you take and you take, if you acquire and you own and you accumulate, then that is the end of your convictions and the beginning of your fear. But there is nothing that I have that I can't give up. Y'understand? Nothing! How I ever got from my miserable father's shit-eaten house on Factory Street to being this big character Iron Rinn, how Ira Ringold, with one and a half years of high school behind him, got to meeting the people I meet and knowing the people I know and having the comforts I have as a card-carrying member of the comfortable bourgeoisie—that is all so unbelievable that losing everything overnight would not seem so strange to me. Y'understand? Y'understand me? I can go back to Chicago. I can work in the mills. If I have to, I will. But not without standing on my rights as an American! Not without giving the bastards a fight!"

When I was alone and on the train heading back to Newark—Ira had waited at the station in the Chevy to pick up Mrs. Pärn, who, on the day I left, was traveling all the way from New York again to work on those knees of his, aching terribly after our football game of the previous day—I even began to wonder how Eve Frame could stand him, day in and day out. Being married to Ira and his anger couldn't have been much fun. I remembered hearing him deliver virtually the same speech about the capitalist shop window, about his father's miserable house, about his one and a half years of high school, on that afternoon the year before in Erwin Goldstine's kitchen. I remembered variants of that speech being delivered by Ira ten, fifteen times. How could Eve take the sheer repetition, the redundancy of that rhetoric and the attitude of the attacker, the relentless beating from the blunt instrument that was Ira's stump speech?

On that train back to Newark, as I thought of Ira blasting away with his twin apocalyptic prophecies—"The United States of America is about to make atomic war on the Soviet Union! Mark my words! The United States of America is on the road to fascism!"—I didn't know enough to understand why suddenly, so disloyally, when he and people like Artie Sokolow were being most intimidated and threatened, I was so savagely bored by him, why I felt myself to be so much smarter than he. Ready and eager to turn away from him and the irritating, oppressive side of him and to find my inspiration far from Pickax Hill Road.

If you're orphaned as early as Ira was, you fall into the situation that all men must fall into but much, much sooner, which is tricky, because you may either get no education at all or be oversusceptible to enthusiasms and beliefs and ripe for indoctrination. Ira's youthful years were a series of broken connections: a cruel family, frustration in school, headlong immersion in the Depression—an early orphaning that captured the imagination of a boy like me, himself so fixed in a family and a place and its institutions, a boy only just emerging from the emotional incubator; an early orphaning that freed Ira to connect to whatever he wanted but also left him unmoored enough to give himself to something almost right off the bat, to give himself totally and forever. For all the reasons you can think of, Ira was an easy mark for the utopian vision. But for me, who was moored, it was different. If you're *not* orphaned early, if instead you're related intensely to parents for thirteen, fourteen, fifteen years, you grow a prick, lose your innocence, seek your independence, and, if it's not a screwed-up family, are let go, ready to begin to be a man, ready, that is, to choose new allegiances and affiliations, the parents of your adulthood, the chosen parents whom, because you are not asked to acknowledge them with love, you either love or don't, as suits you.

How are they chosen? Through a series of accidents and through lots of will. How do they get to you, and how do you get to them? Who are they? What is it, this genealogy that isn't genetic? In my case they were men to whom I apprenticed myself, from Paine and Fast and Corwin to Murray and Ira and beyond—the men who schooled me, the men I came from. All were remarkable to me in their own way, personalities to contend with, mentors who embodied or espoused powerful ideas and who first taught me to navigate the world and its claims, the adopted parents who also, each in his turn, had to be cast off along with their legacy, had to disappear, thus making way for the orphanhood that is total, which is manhood. When you're out there in this thing all alone.

Leo Glucksman was also an ex-GI, but he had served *after* the war and was now only into his mid-twenties, rosy-cheeked and a little round and looking no older than his first- and second-year college students. Though Leo was still completing his dissertation for a literature Ph.D. at the university, he appeared before us at every session of the class in a three-piece black suit and a crimson bow tie, more formally attired by far than any of the older faculty members. When the weather turned cold he could be seen crossing the quadrangle draped in a black cape that, even on a campus as untypically tolerant of idiosyncrasy and eccentricity—and as understanding of originality and its oddity—as the University of Chicago's was in those days, titillated students whose bright (and amused) "Hi, Professor" Leo would acknowledge by sharply whacking the pavement with the metal tip of the cane he sported. After taking a hasty look late one afternoon at *The Stooge of Torquemada*—which, to kindle Mr. Glucksman's admiration, I'd thought to bring to him, along with the assigned essay on Aristotle's *Poetics*—Leo startled me by dropping it with disgust onto his desk.

His speech was rapid, his tone fierce and unforgiving—no sign in that delivery of the foppishly overdressed boy genius plumply perched back of his bow tie on his cushioned seat. His plumpness and his personality exemplified two very different people. The clothes registered a third person. And his polemic a fourth—not a mannerist but a real adult critic exposing to me the dangers of the tutelage I'd been under with Ira, teaching me to assume a position less rigid in confronting literature. Precisely what I was ready for in my new recruitment phase. Under Leo's guidance I began to be transformed into the descendant not just of my family but of the past, heir to a culture even grander than my neighborhood's.

"Art as a *weapon?*" he said to me, the word "weapon" rich with contempt and itself a weapon. "Art as taking the right *stand* on everything? Art as the advocate of good things? Who taught you all this? Who taught you art is slogans? Who taught you art is in the service of '*the people*'? Art is in the service of *art*—otherwise there is no art worthy of *anyone's* attention. What *is* the motive for writing serious literature, Mr. Zuckerman? To disarm the enemies of price control? The motive for writing serious literature is *to write serious literature.* You want to rebel against society? I'll tell you how to do it—write *well.* You want to embrace a lost cause? Then don't fight in behalf of the laboring class. They're going to make out fine. They're going to fill up on Plymouths to their heart's content. The workingman will conquer us all—out of his mindlessness will flow the slop that is this philistine country's cultural destiny. We'll soon have something in this country far worse than the government of the peasants and the workers—we will have the *culture* of the peasants and the workers. You want a lost cause to fight for? Then fight for the *word.* Not the high-flown word, not the inspiring word, not the pro-this and anti-that word, not the word that advertises to the respectable that you are a wonderful, admirable, compassionate person on the side of the downtrodden and the oppressed. No, for the word that tells the literate few condemned to live in America that you are on the *side* of the word! This play of yours is crap. It's awful. It's infuriating. It is crude, primitive, simple-minded, propagandistic crap. It *blurs* the world with words. And it reeks to high heaven of your virtue. Nothing has a more sinister effect on art than an artist's desire to prove that he's *good*. The terrible temptation of idealism! You must achieve *mastery* over your idealism, over your virtue as well as over your vice, aesthetic mastery over everything that drives you to write in the first place—your outrage, your politics, your grief, your love! Start preaching and taking positions, start seeing your own perspective as superior, and you're worthless as an artist, worthless and ludicrous. Why do you write these proclamations? Because you look around and you're 'shocked'? Because you look around and you're 'moved'? People give up too easily and fake their feelings. They want to have feelings right away, and so 'shocked' and 'moved' are the easiest. The stupidest. Except for the rare case, Mr. Zuckerman, *shock is always fake.* Proclamations. Art has no *use* for proclamations! Get your lovable shit out of this office, please."

Leo thought better of my Aristotle essay (or, generally, of me), for at my next conference he startled me—no less than he had with his vehemence about my play—by ordering my presence at Orchestra Hall to hear Raphael Kubelik lead the Chicago Symphony Orchestra in Beethoven on Friday night. "Have you ever heard of Raphael Kubelik?" "No." "Beethoven?" "I've heard of him, yes." I said. "Have you ever *heard* him?" "No."

I met Leo on Michigan Avenue, outside Orchestra Hall, half an hour before the performance, my teacher in the cape he'd had made in Rome before being mustered out of the army in '48 and I in the hooded mackinaw bought at Larkey's in Newark to take to college in the icy Middle West. Once we were seated, Leo removed from his briefcase the score for each of the symphonies we were to hear and, throughout the concert, looked not at the orchestra on the stage—

which you were supposed to look at, I thought, only occasionally closing your eyes when you were carried away—but rather into his lap, where, with his considerable concentration, he read along in the score while the musicians played first the *Coriolan* Overture and the Fourth Symphony, and after the intermission, the Fifth. Except for the first four notes of the Fifth, I couldn't distinguish one piece from the others.

Following the concert, we took the train back to the South Side and went to his room at International House, a Gothic residence hall on the Midway that was home to most of the university's foreign students. Leo Glucksman, himself the son of a West Side grocer, was slightly better prepared to tolerate their proximity on his hallway—exotic cooking smells and all—than he was that of his fellow Americans. The room he lived in was tinier even than his office cubicle at the college, and he made tea for us by boiling water in a kettle set on a hot plate resting on the floor and squeezed in among the clutter of printed matter piled along the walls. Leo sat at his book-laden desk, his round cheeks lit up by his gooseneck lamp, and I sat in the dark, amid more piles of his books, on the edge of the narrow unmade bed only two feet away.

I felt like a girl, or what I imagined a girl felt like when she wound up alone with an intimidating boy who too obviously liked her breasts. Leo snorted to see me turn timorous, and with that same disgusted sneer with which he had undertaken to demolish my career in radio, he said, "Don't worry, I'm not going to touch you. I just cannot bear that you should be so fucking conventional." And then and there he proceeded to initiate an introduction to Søren Kierkegaard. He wanted me to listen to him read what Kierkegaard, whose name meant no more to me than Raphael Kubelik's, had already surmised in backwater Copenhagen a hundred years ago about "the people"—whom Kierkegaard called "the public," the correct name, Leo informed me, for that abstraction, that "monstrous abstraction," that "all-embracing something which is nothing," that "monstrous nothing," as Kierkegaard wrote, that "abstract and deserted void which is everything and nothing" and which I mawkishly sentimentalized in my script. Kierkegaard hated the public, Leo hated the public, and Leo's purpose in his darkened International House room after that Friday night's concert and the concerts he took me to on the Fridays following was to save my prose from perdition by getting me to hate the public too.

"'Everyone who has read the classical authors,'" read Leo, "'knows how many things a Caesar could try out in order to kill time. In the same way the public keeps a dog to amuse it. That dog is the scum of the literary world. If there is someone superior to the rest, perhaps even a great man, the dog is set on him and the fun begins. The dog goes for him, snapping and tearing at his coat-tails, allowing itself every possible ill-mannered familiarity—until the public tires, and says it may stop. That is my example of how the public levels. Their betters and superiors in strength are mishandled—and the dog remains a dog which even the public despises. . . . The public is unrepentant—it was not really belittling anyone; it just wanted a little amusement.'"

This passage, which meant far more to Leo than it could begin to mean to me, was nonetheless Leo Glucksman's invitation to join him in being "someone superior to the rest," in being, like the Danish philosopher Kierkegaard—and like himself, as he could one day soon envision himself—"a great man." I became Leo's willing student and, through his intercession, Aristotle's willing student, Kierkegaard's willing student, Benedetto Croce's willing student, Thomas Mann's willing student, André Gide's willing student, Joseph Conrad's willing student, Fyodor Dostoyevsky's willing student . . . until soon my attachment to Ira—as to my mother, my father, my brother, even to the place where I'd grown up—was, I believed, thoroughly sundered. When someone is first being educated and his head is becoming transformed into an arsenal armed with books, when he is young and impudent and leaping with joy to discover all the intelligence tucked away on this planet, he is apt to exaggerate the importance of the churning new reality and to deprecate as unimportant everything else. Aided and abetted by the uncompromising Leo Glucksman—by his bile and manias as much as by that perpetually charged-up brain—this is what I did, with all my strength.

Every Friday night, in Leo's room, the spell was cast. All the passion in Leo that was not sexual (and a lot that was but had to be suppressed) he brought to bear on every idea that I had previously been made of, particularly on my virtuous conception of the artistic mission. Leo went at me on those Friday nights as though I were the last student left on earth. It began to seem to me that just about everybody gave me a shot. Educate Nathan. The credo of everybody I dared say hello to.

Occasionally now, looking back, I think of my life as one long speech that I've been listening to. The rhetoric is sometimes original, sometimes pleasurable, sometimes pasteboard crap (the speech of the incognito), sometimes maniacal, sometimes matter-of-fact, and sometimes like the sharp prick of a needle, and I have been hearing it for as long as I can remember: how to think, how not to think; how to behave, how not to behave; whom to loathe and whom to admire; what to embrace and when to escape; what is rapturous, what is murderous, what is laudable, what is shallow, what is sinister, what is shit, and how to remain pure in soul. Talking to me doesn't seem to present an obstacle to anyone. This is perhaps a consequence of my having gone around for years looking as if I needed talking to. But whatever the reason, the book of my life is a book of voices. When I ask myself how I arrived at where I am, the answer surprises me: "Listening."

Can that have been the unseen drama? Was all the rest a masquerade disguising the real no good that I was obstinately up to? Listening to them. Listening to them talk. The utterly wild phenomenon that is. Everyone perceiving experience as something not to have but to have so as to talk about it. Why is that? Why do they want me to hear them and their arias? Where was it decided that this was my use? Or was I from the beginning, by inclination as much as by choice, merely an ear in search of a word?

"Politics is the great generalizer," Leo told me, "and literature the great particularizer, and not only are they in an inverse relationship to each other—they are in an *antagonistic* relationship. To politics, literature is decadent, soft, irrelevant, boring, wrongheaded, dull, something that makes no sense and that really oughtn't to be. Why? Because the particularizing impulse *is* literature. How can you be an artist and renounce the nuance? But how can you be a politician and *allow* the nuance? As an artist the nuance is your *task*. Your task is *not* to simplify. Even should you choose to write in the simplest way, à la Hemingway, the task remains to impart the nuance, to elucidate the complication, to imply the contradiction. Not to erase the contradiction, not to deny the contradiction, but to see where, within the contradiction, lies the tormented human being. To allow for the chaos, to let it in. You *must* let it in. Otherwise you produce propaganda, if not for a political party, a political movement, then stupid propaganda for life itself—for life as it might itself prefer to be publicized. During the first five, six years of the Russian Revolution the revolutionaries cried, 'Free love, there will be free love!' But once they were in power, they couldn't permit it. Because what is free love? Chaos. And they didn't want chaos. That isn't why they made their glorious revolution. They wanted something carefully disciplined, organized, contained, predictable scientifically, if possible. Free love disturbs the organization, their social and political and cultural machine. Art also disturbs the organization. Literature disturbs the organization. Not because it is blatantly for or against, or even subtly for or against. It disturbs the organization because it is not general. The intrinsic nature of the particular is to be particular, and the intrinsic nature of particularity is to fail to conform. Generalizing suffering: there is Communism. Particularizing suffering: there is literature. In that polarity is the antagonism. Keeping the particular alive in a simplifying, generalizing world— that's where the battle is joined. You do not have to write to legitimize Communism, and you do not have to write to legitimize capitalism. You are out of both. If you are a writer, you are as unallied to the one as you are to the other. Yes, you see differences, and of course you see that this shit is a little better than that shit, or that that shit is a little better than this shit. Maybe much better. *But you see the shit.* You are not a government clerk. You are not a militant. You are not a believer. You are someone who deals in a very different way with the world and what happens in the world. The militant introduces a faith, a big belief that will change the world, and the artist introduces a product that has no place in that world. It's useless. The artist, the serious writer, introduces into the world something that wasn't there even at the start. When God made all this stuff in seven days, the birds, the rivers, the human beings, he didn't have ten minutes for literature. 'And then there will be literature. Some people will like it, some people will be obsessed by it, want to do it . . .' No. No. He did not say that. If you had asked God then, 'There will be plumbers?' 'Yes, there will be. Because they will have houses, they will need plumbers.' 'There will be doctors?' 'Yes. Because they will get sick, they will need doctors to give them some pills.' 'And literature?' 'Literature? What are you talking about? What use does it have? Where does it fit in? Please, I am creating a universe, not a university. *No literature.*'"

Uncompromising. Tom Paine's irresistible attribute, Ira's, Leo's, and Johnny O'Day's. Had I gone down to East Chicago to meet O'Day on my arrival in Chicago—which was what Ira had arranged for me to do—my life as a student, perhaps all life thereafter, might have fallen under different enticements and different pressures and I might have set out to abandon the secure strictures of my background under the passionate tutelage of a monolith quite different from the University of Chicago. But the burden of a Chicago education, not to mention the demands being made by Mr. Glucksman's supplemental program to deconventionalize my mind, meant that it wasn't until early December that I was able to take a Saturday morning off and travel by train to meet Ira Ringold's army mentor, the steelworker whom Ira had once described to me as "a Marxist from the belt buckle both ways."

The tracks of the South Shore Line were at Sixty-third and Stony Island, only a fifteen-minute walk from my dormitory. I boarded the orange-painted car and took a seat, the conductor sounded off the names of the dirty towns along the line—"Hegewisch . . . Hammond . . . East Chicago . . . Gary . . . Michigan City . . . *South Bend*"—and I was as stirred up again as if I were listening to *On a Note of Triumph*. Coming as I did from industrial north Jersey, I confronted a not unfamiliar landscape. Looking south to Elizabeth, Linden, and Rahway from the airport, we too had the complex superstructure of refineries off in the distance and the noxious refinery odors and the plumes of fire, up at the top of the towers, burning off the gas from the distilling of petroleum. In Newark we had the big factories and the tiny job shops, we had the grime, we had the smells, we had the crisscrossing rail lines and the lots of steel drums and the hills of scrap metal and the hideous dump sites. We had black smoke rising from high stacks, a lot of smoke coming up everywhere, and the chemical reek and the malt reek and the Secaucus pig-farm reek sweeping over our neighborhood when the wind blew hard. And we had trains like this one that ran up on embankments through the marshes, through bulrushes and swamp grass and open water. We had the dirt and we had the stink, but what we didn't have and couldn't have was Hegewisch, where they'd built the tanks for the war. We didn't have Hammond, where they built the girders for bridges. We didn't have the grain elevators along the shipping canal coming down from Chicago. We didn't have the open-hearth furnaces that lit up the sky when the mills were pouring steel, a red sky that on clear nights I could see, from as far away as my dormitory window, way down in Gary. We didn't have U.S. Steel and Inland Steel and Jones Laughlin and Standard Bridge and Union Carbide and Standard Oil of Indiana. We had what New Jersey had; concentrated here was the power of the Midwest. What they had here was a steelmaking operation, miles and miles of it stretching along the lake through two states and vaster than any other in the world, coke furnaces and oxygen furnaces transforming iron ore into steel, overhead ladles carrying tons of molten steel, hot metal pouring like lava into molds, and amid all this flash and dust and danger and noise, working in temperatures of a hundred degrees, sucking in vapors that could ruin them, men at labor around the clock, men at work that was never finished. This was an America that I was not a native of and never would be and that I possessed as an American nonetheless. While I stared from the train window—took in what looked to me to be mightily up-to-date, modern, the very emblem of the industrial twentieth century, and yet an immense archeological site—no fact of my life seemed more serious than that.

To my right I saw block after block of soot-covered bungalows, the steelworkers' houses, with gazebos and birdbaths in the backyards, and beyond the houses the streets lined with low, ignominious-looking stores where their families shopped, and so strong was the impact on me of the sight of a steelworker's everyday world, its crudity, its austerity, the obdurate world of people who were always strapped, in debt, paying things off—so inspiring was the thought *For the hardest work the barest minimum, for breaking their backs the humblest rewards*—that, needless to say, none of my feelings would have seemed strange to Ira Ringold, while all of them would have appalled Leo Glucksman.

"What about this wife the Iron Man's got?" was almost the first thing O'Day said to me. "Maybe I'd like her if I knew her, but that's an imponderable. Some people I value have intimate friends to whom I'm indifferent. The comfortable bourgeoisie, the circle he now lives in with her . . . I'm not so sure. There's a problem with wives altogether. Most guys who marry are too vulnerable—they've given hostages to reaction in the person of their wives and kids. So it's left to a little coterie of hardened characters on their own to take care of what's got to be taken care of. Sure, all this is a grind, sure, it'd be nice to have a home, to have a soft woman waiting at the end of the day, maybe to have a couple of kids. Even guys who know what it's all about get fed up once in a while. But my immediate responsibility is to the hourly paid workingman, and for him I'm not doing a tithe of the work I should be doing. Whatever the sacrifice, what you have to remember is that movements like these are always upwards, regardless of how the immediate issue turns out."

The immediate issue was that Johnny O'Day had been driven from the union and had lost his job. I met him at a rooming house where he hadn't paid rent in two months; he had a week more to come up with the money or be thrown out. His small room had a window onto some sky and was neatly kept. The mattress of the single bed rested not on a box spring but on metal webbing and was tightly, even beautifully, made up, and the dark green paint on the iron bedstead wasn't chipped or peeling—as it was on the noisy radiator—but was disheartening to look at all the same. Altogether the furnishings were no more meager than those that Leo lived among at International House, and yet the aura of desolation startled me and—until O'Day's quiet, even voice and his peculiarly sharp enunciation began very powerfully to mute the presence of everything except O'Day himself—made me think I ought to get up and go. It was as though whatever wasn't in that room had vanished from the world. The instant he came to the door and let me in and politely invited me to be seated across from him, on one of the room's two bridge chairs, at a table just large enough for his typewriter, I had a sense not so much of everything's having been torn away from O'Day except this existence but, worse, of O'Day's having, almost sinisterly, torn *himself* away from everything that was not this existence.

Now I understood what Ira was doing in the shack. Now I understood the seed of the shack and the stripping back of everything—the aesthetic of the ugly that Eve Frame was to find so insufferable, that left a man lonely and monastic but also unencumbered, free to be bold and unflinching and purposeful. What O'Day's room represented was discipline, that discipline which says that however many desires I have, I can circumscribe myself down to this room. You can risk anything if at the end you know you can tolerate the punishment, and this room was a part of the punishment. There was a firm impression to be taken from this room: the connection between freedom and discipline, the connection between freedom and loneliness, the connection between freedom and punishment. O'Day's room, his cell, was the spiritual essence of Ira's shack. And what was the spiritual essence of O'Day's room? I'd find that out some years later when, on a visit to Zurich, I located the house with the commemorative tablet bearing Lenin's name, and after bribing a janitor with a handful of Swiss marks, was allowed to see the anchorite room where the revolutionary founder of Bolshevism had lived in exile for a year and a half.

O'Day's appearance should have been no surprise. Ira had described him exactly as he still was, a man constructed like a heron: a lean, taut, blade-faced six-footer with close-cut gray hair, eyes that also appeared to have turned gray, a sharp, large knife of a nose, and skin—a *hide*—lined as though he were well beyond his forties. But what Ira hadn't described was how zealotry had bestowed the look of a body that had a man locked up inside serving the severe sentence that was his life. It was the look of a being who has no choice. His story has been made up beforehand. He has no choice about anything. To tear himself from things in behalf of his cause—that's all there is for him to do. And he is not susceptible to others. It isn't just the physique that is a filament of steel, enviably narrow; the ideology, too, is tool-like and contoured like the edgewise silhouette of the heron's fuselage.

I remembered Ira's telling me that O'Day carried a light punching bag in his gear and that in the army he was so quick and strong that, "if forced to," he could lick two or three guys together. I'd been wondering all the way down on the train if there'd be a punching bag in his room. And there was. It wasn't in a corner hanging at head height, as I'd been imagining it and as it would have been if we'd been in a gym. It was on the floor, lying on its side against a closet door, a stout tear-shaped leather bag so old and battered it looked less like leather than like the bleached-out body part of some slaughtered animal—as though to keep in fighting trim O'Day worked with the testicle off a dead hippopotamus. A notion not rational but impossible—because of my initial fear of him—to make go away.

I remembered the words that O'Day had spoken the night that he'd poured out his frustration to Ira about not being able to spend his days "building the party here in the harbor": "I ain't that good at organizing, that is true. You have to be something of a hand holder with timid Bolsheviks, and I lean more to bopping their heads." I remembered because I had gone home and entered those words into my radio play then in progress, a play about a strike in a steel plant, wherein every last drop of the argot of Johnny O'Day emerged inviolate from one Jimmy O'Shea. Once O'Day had written to Ira, "I'm getting to be the official son of a bitch of East Chicago and environs, and that means winding up in Fist City." *Fist City* became the title of my next play. I couldn't help it. I wanted to write about things that seemed important, and the things that seemed important were things I didn't know. And what with the words at my disposal then, I instantly transformed everything into agitprop anyway, thus losing within seconds whatever was important about the important and immediate about the immediate.

O'Day was broke, and the party too broke to hire him as an organizer or to help him financially in any way, and so he was filling his days writing leaflets for mill-gate distribution, using the few dollars secretly contributed by some of his old steelworker buddies to pay for the paper and to rent a mimeograph machine and a staple machine, and then, at the end of each day, himself handing out the leaflets over in Gary. The change he had left he spent on food.

"My case against Inland Steel isn't finished," he told me, going right to the point, leveling with me as though I were an equal, an ally, if not already a comrade, talking to me as though Ira had somehow caused him to think that I was twice my age, a hundred times more independent, a thousand times more courageous. "But it looks as if management and the Red-baiters in the USA-CIO have got me fired and blacklisted for good. In every walk of life, all over this country, the move is on to crush the party. They don't know that it isn't Phil Murray's CIO that decides the great historic issues. Witness China. It's the American worker who will decide the great historic issues. In my occupation there are already more than a hundred unemployed ironworkers in this local union. This is the first time since 1939 that there haven't been more jobs than men, and even the ironworkers, the most obtuse section of the whole wage-earning class, are at last beginning to question the setup. It's coming, it's coming—I assure you it's coming. Still, I got hauled before the executive board of the ironworkers' local and expelled by reason of my membership in the party. These bastards didn't want to expel me, they wanted me to repudiate my membership. The rat press, which is zeroed in on me hereabouts—here," he said, handing me a clipping from beside the typewriter, "yesterday's *Gary Post-Tribune*. The rat press would have made a big thing out of that, and although I'd have retained my working card in the ironmongers', the word would have gone out to the contractors and the gang bosses to blacklist me. It's a closed industry, so expulsion from the union means that I'm deprived of work in my trade. Well, to hell with 'em. I can fight better from the outside anyway. The rat press, the labor fakers, the phony city administrations of Gary and East Chicago regard me as dangerous? Good. They're attempting to keep me from making a living? Fine. I've got nobody dependent on me but me. And I don't depend on friends or women or jobs or any other conventional prop to existence. I get along anyway. If the *Gary Post*," he said, taking back from me and neatly folding in two the clipping that I hadn't dared to look at while he spoke, "and the *Hammond Times* and the rest of them think that they're going to run us Reds out of Lake County with these kind of tactics, they're playing the wrong number. If they'd left me alone, I would probably have one day soon left under my own power. But now I've got no money to go anywhere and so they are going to have to continue to deal with me. At the mill gates the attitude of the workers when I hand them my leaflets is, on the whole, friendly and interested. They flash me the V, and it's moments like that when the books balance for a while. We got our share of fascist workers, of course.

Monday night, the other night, while I was handing out my leaflets at the Gary Big Mill, a fat lug started calling me a traitor and a prick, and I don't know what all else he had in mind. I didn't wait to find out. I hope he likes soup and soft biscuits. Tell that to the Iron Man," he said, smiling for the first time, though in a distressing way, as if forcing a smile were among the more difficult things he had to do. "Tell him I'm still in pretty good shape. Come on, Nathan," he said, and it chagrined me to hear this unemployed steelworker utter my given name (that is, my new college obsessions, my budding superiority, my lapse from political commitment chagrined me) when I had just heard him describe, in the same quiet, even voice, with the same careful enunciation—and with an intimate familiarity that did not seem culled from books—*the great historic issues, China, 1939,* above all describe the harsh, sacrificial selflessness imposed by his mission to *the hourly paid workingman.* "Nathan" spoken in the very voice that had raised gooseflesh on my arms by saying *It's coming, it's coming—I assure you it's coming.* "Let's get something for you to eat," said O'Day.

From the beginning, the difference between O'Day's speech and Ira's was unmistakable to me. Perhaps because there was nothing contradictory in O'Day's aims, because O'Day was living the life he proselytized, because the speech was a pretext for nothing else, because it appeared to rise from the core of the brain that is *experience,* there was a tautened to-the-point quality to what he said, the thinking firmly established, the words themselves seemingly shot through with will, nothing inflated, no waste of energy, but instead, in every utterance, a wily shrewdness and, however utopian the goal, a deep practicality, a sense that he had the mission as much in his hands as in his head; a sense, unlike that communicated by Ira, that it was intelligence and not a lack of intelligence that was availing itself of—and wielding—his ideas. The tang of what I thought of as "the real" permeated his talk. It wasn't difficult to see that the something Ira's speech was a weak imitation of was O'Day's. The tang of the real . . . though also the speech of someone in whom nothing ever laughed. With the result that there was a kind of madness to his singleness of purpose, and that also distinguished him from Ira. In attracting, as Ira did, all the human contingencies that O'Day had banished from life, there was sanity, the sanity of an expansive, disorderly existence.

By the time I got back on the train that evening, the power of O'Day's unrelenting focus had so disoriented me that all I could think about was how I was to tell my parents that three and a half months was enough: I was quitting college to move down to the steel town of East Chicago, Indiana. I wasn't asking them to support me financially. I would find work to support myself, menial work, more than likely—but that was just as well, if not the whole idea. I could no longer justify continuing to accede to bourgeois expectations, theirs *or* mine, not after my visit with Johnny O'Day, who, despite all the soft-spokenness concealing the passion, came across as the most dynamic person I had ever met, more so even than Ira. The most dynamic, the most unshatterable, the most dangerous.

Dangerous because he didn't care about me the way Ira did and didn't know about me the way Ira did. Ira knew I was somebody else's kid, understood intuitively—and had been told by my father for good measure—and didn't try to take from me my freedom or take me away from where I came from. Ira never tried to indoctrinate me beyond a certain point, nor was he desperate to hold on to me, though all his life he was probably love-hungry enough and love-starved enough to be always yearning for close attachments. He just borrowed me for a while when he came to Newark, occasionally borrowed me to have somebody to talk to when he was lonely visiting Newark or by himself up at the shack, but never took me anywhere near a Communist meeting. That whole other life of his was almost entirely invisible to me. All I got was the rant and the raving and the rhetoric, the window dressing. He was not *just* unrestrained—with me there was tact in Ira. Fanatically obsessive as he was, toward me there was a great decency, a tenderness, and a consciousness of a kind of danger that he was willing to face himself but didn't wish to expose a kid to. With me there was a big-bodied good-naturedness that was the other side of the fury and the rage. Ira saw fit to educate me only to a point. I never saw the zealot whole.

But to Johnny O'Day I wasn't anybody's son he had to protect. To him I was a body to be recruited.

"Don't trifle with the Trotskyites at that university," O'Day had told me at lunch, as though Trotskyites were a problem I'd come to East Chicago to talk over with him. Huddled head to head, we ate hamburgers in the booth of a dark tavern where his credit was still good with the Polish proprietor and where a boy like me, a sucker for manly intimacy, found the situation much to his liking. The little street, not far from the mill, was all taverns except for a grocery on one corner and a church on the other and, right across the way, an open lot that was half scrap heap, half garbage dump. The wind was strong from the east and smelled of sulfur dioxide. Inside, the smell was of smoke and beer.

"I'm unorthodox enough to contend that it's all right to play with Trotskyites," O'Day said, "as long as you wash your hands afterward. There are people who handle venomous reptiles every day, going so far as to milk them of their poison in order to provide an antidote to it, and few of them are fatally bitten. Precisely because they know the reptiles *are* venomous."

"What's a Trotskyite?" I asked.

"You don't know about the fundamental divergence of Communists and Trotskyites?"

"No."

For the next few hours he told me. The story was replete with terms like "scientific socialism," "neo-fascism," "bourgeois democracy," with names unknown to me like (to begin with) Leon Trotsky, names like Eastman, Lovestone, Zinoviev, Bukharin, with events unknown to me like "the October Revolution" and "the 1937 trials," with formulations beginning "The Marxian precept that the contradictions inherent in a capitalist society . . ." and "Obedient to their fallacious reasoning, Trotskyites conspire to keep the aims from being achieved by . . ." But no matter how abstruse or complicated the story's ins and outs, coming from O'Day every word struck me as pointed and not at all remote, not a subject he was talking about to talk about it, not a subject he was talking about for me to write a term paper about it, but a struggle whose ferocity he had suffered through.

It was nearly three when he relaxed his hold on my attention. His way of having you listen was extraordinary and had much to do with a promise he silently made not to imperil you so long as you concentrated on his every word. I was exhausted, the tavern was all but empty, and yet I had the sense that everything possible was going on around me. I remembered back to that night, as a high school kid, when I'd defied my father and gone off to be Ira's guest at the Wallace rally in Newark, and once again I felt in communion with a quarrel about life that *mattered*, the glorious battle that I had been looking for since I'd turned fourteen.

"Come on," O'Day said, after glancing at his watch, "I'm going to show you the face of the future."

And there we were. There *I* was. There *it* was, the world where I had long secretly dreamed of being a man. The whistle blew, the gates opened wide, and here they came—the workers! Corwin's far-flung ordinary men, unspectacular but free. The little guy! The common man! The Poles! The Swedes! The Irish! The Croatians! The Italians! The Slovenes! The men who jeopardized their lives making steel, risked being burned or crushed or blown apart, and all for the profit of the ruling class.

I was so excited I couldn't see faces, I couldn't really see bodies. I saw only the crude mass of them heading through the gates for home. The mass of the American masses! Brushing by me, knocking into me—the face, the *force* of the future! The impulse to cry out—in sadness, anger, protest, triumph—was overwhelming, as was the urge to join that mob not quite a menace and not quite a mob, to join the chain, the rush of men in their thick-soled boots, and follow them all home. The noise of them was like the noise of a crowd in an arena before a fight. And the fight? The fight for American equality.

From a pouch slung over his hip, O'Day took a wad of leaflets and thrust them at me. And there, within sight of the mill, this smoking basilica that must have been a mile long, the two of us stood side by side giving a leaflet to any man coming off the seven-to-three shift who stuck out a hand to take one. Their fingers touched mine and my whole life was turned inside out. Everything in America that was against these men was against me too! I took the leafleteer's vow: I would be nothing but the instrument of their will. I would be nothing but rectitude.

Oh yes, you feel the pull with a man like O'Day. Johnny O'Day doesn't take you fifty percent of the way and leave you alone. He takes you all the way. The revolution is going to wipe out this and replace it with that—the un-ironic clarity of the political Casanova. When you're seventeen years old and you meet a guy who has an aggressive stance and who has it all figured out idealistically and all figured out ideologically and who has no family and no relatives and no house—who is without all that stuff that was pulling Ira in twenty different directions, without all those *emotions* pulling Ira in twenty directions, without all that upheaval a man like Ira takes on because of his nature, without the turbulence of wanting to make a revolution that will change the world while also mating with a beautiful actress and acquiring a young mistress and fiddling with an aging whore and longing for a family and struggling with a stepchild and inhabiting an imposing house in the show-business city and a proletarian shack in the backwoods, determined to assert unflaggingly one being in secret and another in public and a third in the interstices between the two, to be Abraham Lincoln and Iron Rinn and Ira Ringold all rolled up into a frenzied, overexcitable group self—who instead is claimed by nothing but his idea, who is responsible to nothing but the idea, who understands almost mathematically what he needs to live an honorable life, then you think as I did, *Here is where I belong!*

Which was probably what Ira had thought on encountering O'Day in Iran. O'Day had viscerally influenced him the same way. Takes you and ties you to the world revolution. Only Ira had wound up with all that other inadvertent, undesigned, unpremeditated stuff, bouncing all those other balls with the same enormous effort to prevail—while all that O'Day had, was, and wanted was nothing other than *the real thing*. Because he wasn't a Jew? Because he was a goy? Because, as Ira had told me, O'Day had been raised in a Catholic orphanage? Was that why he could be so thoroughly, so ruthlessly, so visibly living nothing but the bare, bare bones?

There was none of the softness in him that I knew was inside me. Did he see my softness? I would not let him. My life with its softness squeezed out, here in East Chicago with Johnny O'Day! Down here at the mill gate at seven A.M. and three P.M. and eleven P.M. distributing leaflets after each shift. He will teach me how to write them, what to say and how best to say it so as to move the workingman to action and make of America an equitable society. He will teach me everything. I am someone moving out of the comfortable prison of his human irrelevance and, here at the side of Johnny O'Day, entering the hypercharged medium that is history. A menial job, an impoverished existence, yes, but here at the side of Johnny O'Day, not a meaningless *life*. To the contrary, everything of significance, everything profound and important!

From such emotions you would not imagine that I could ever find my way back. But by midnight I still hadn't phoned my family to tell them my decision. O'Day had given me two thin pamphlets to read on the train to Chicago. One was called *Theory and Practice of the Communist Party*, the first course in a "Marxist Study Series" prepared by the National Education Department of the Communist Party, in which the nature of capitalism, of capitalist exploitation, and of the class struggle were devastatingly exposed in just under fifty pages. O'Day promised that the next time we met, we would discuss what I'd read and he would give me the second course, which "developed on a higher theoretical level," he told me, "the subjects of the first course."

The other pamphlet I took back on the train that day, *Who Owns America?* by James S. Allen, argued—predicted—that "capitalism, even in its most powerful embodiment in America, threatens to reproduce disaster on an ever widening scale." The cover was a cartoon, in blue and white, of a porky-looking fat man in top hat and tails, seated arrogantly atop a swollen moneybag labeled "Profits," his own bloated belly adorned with a dollar sign. Smoking away in the background—and representing the property expropriated unjustly by the rich ruling class from the "principal victims of capitalism," the struggling workers—were the factories of America.

I had read both pamphlets on the train; in my dormitory room I read through them again, hoping to find in their pages the strength to phone home with my news. The final pages of *Who Owns America?* were entitled "Become a Communist!" These I read aloud, as though addressing me were Johnny O'Day himself: "Yes, together we will win our strikes. We will build our unions, we will gather together to fight at every step and stage the forces of reaction, of fascism, of war-making. Together we will seek to build up a great independent political movement that will contest the national election with the parties of the trusts. Not for one moment will we give rest to the usurpers, to the oligarchy which is bringing ruin to the nation. Let no one question your patriotism, your loyalty to the nation. Join the Communist Party. As a Communist, you will be able to fulfill, in the deepest sense of the word, your responsibility as an American."

I thought, Why isn't this reachable? Do it the way you got on that bus and went downtown and attended that Wallace rally. Is your life yours or is it theirs? Have you the courage of your convictions or haven't you? Is this America the kind of America you want to live in or do you intend to go out and revolutionize it? Or are you, like every other "idealistic" college student you know, another selfish, privileged, self-involved hypocrite? What are you afraid of—the hardship, the opprobrium, the danger, or O'Day himself? What are you afraid of if *not* your softness? Don't look to your parents to get you out of this. Don't call home and ask permission to join the Communist Party. Pack your clothes and your books and get back down there and do it! If you don't, is there really any distinction to be made between your capacity for daring to change and Lloyd Brown's, between your audacity and the audacity of Brownie, the grocer's assistant who wants to inherit Tommy Minarek's seat out at the rock dump in Zinc Town? How much does Nathan's failure to renounce his family's expectations and battle his way to genuine freedom differ from Brownie's failure to oppose *his* family's expectations and battle *his* way to freedom? He stays in Zinc Town selling minerals, I stay in college studying Aristotle—and I end up being Brownie with a degree.

At one in the morning I crossed the Midway from my dormitory through a snowstorm—my first Chicago blizzard blowing in—to International House. The Burmese student on desk duty recognized me, and when he unlocked the security door and I said, "Mr. Glucksman," he nodded and, despite the hour, let me through. I went up to Leo's floor and knocked on the door. You could smell curry in the hallway hours after one of the foreign students had cooked up dinner for himself on the hot plate in his room. I was thinking, Some Indian kid comes all the way from Bombay to study in Chicago, and you're afraid to live in Indiana. Stand up and fight against injustice! Turn around, go—the opportunity is yours! Remember the mill gate!

But because I had been pitched so high for so many hours—for so many adolescent *years*, been overcome with all these new ideals and visions of truth—when Leo, in his pajamas, opened his door, I burst into tears and, by doing so, misled him badly. Out of me poured all that I hadn't dared show to Johnny O'Day. The softness, the boyness, all the unworthy un-O'Dayness that was me. Everything nonessential that was me. Why isn't this reachable? I lacked what I suppose Ira also lacked: a heart without dichotomies, a heart like the enviably narrow O'Day's, unequivocal, ready to renounce everyone and everything except the revolution.

"Oh, Nathan," Leo said tenderly. "My dear friend." It was the first time he had called me anything other than "Mr. Zuckerman." He sat me down at his desk and, standing over me just inches away, watched while, still weeping, I undid the buttons of a mackinaw already wet and heavy with snow. Maybe he thought that I was preparing to undo everything. Instead, I began to tell him about the man I had met. I told him that I wanted to move down to East Chicago and to work with O'Day. I had to, for the sake of my conscience. But could I do it without telling my parents? I asked Leo if that was honorable.

"You shit! You whore! Go! Get out of here! You two-faced little cocktease whore!" he said, and shoved me from the room and slammed the door.

I didn't understand. I didn't really understand Beethoven, I was continuing to have trouble with Kierkegaard, and what Leo was shouting and why he was shouting it was also incomprehensible to me. All I'd done was to tell him I was contemplating living alongside a forty-eight-year-old Communist steelworker who, as I described him, looked a little like an aging Montgomery Clift—and Leo, in turn, throws me out.

Not just the Indian student across the hall but nearly all the Indian students and Oriental students and African students on the corridor came out of their rooms to see what the commotion was. Most of them, at this hour, were in their underwear, and what they were looking at was a boy who had only just discovered that heroism was not as easy to come by at seventeen as was a seventeen-year-old's talent for being drawn to heroism and to the moral aspect of just about everything. What they thought they saw was something else altogether. What they thought they saw I myself still couldn't figure out until, at my next humanities class, I realized that Leo Glucksman would henceforth mark me down not merely as nobody superior, let alone nobody destined to be a great man, but as the most callow, culturally backward, comical philistine ever, scandalously, to have been admitted to the University of Chicago. And nothing I said in class or wrote for class during the remainder of the year, none of my lengthy letters explaining myself and apologizing and pointing out that I *hadn't* left the college to join up with O'Day would ever disabuse him.

*

I sold magazines door to door in Jersey that next summer—not quite the same as distributing handbills at an Indiana steel mill at dawn, dusk, and in the dark of night. Though I was on the phone with Ira a couple of times and we made a plan for me to come out to see him at the shack in August, to my relief he had to cancel at the last minute and then I was back at school. Some weeks later, in the final days of October 1951, I heard that he and Artie Sokolow, as well as the director, the composer, the program's two other leading actors, and the famous announcer Michael J. Michaels, had been fired from *The Free and the Brave*. My father gave me the news on the phone. I didn't regularly see a newspaper, and the news, he told me, had appeared the day before in both Newark papers, as well as in every one of the New York dailies. "Redhot Iron" they had called him in the headline of the *New York Journal-American*, where Bryden Grant was a columnist. The story had broken in "Grant's Grapevine."

I could tell from my father's voice that what he was most worried about was me—about the implications of my having been befriended by Ira—and so indignantly I said to him, "Because they call him a Communist, because they lie and call *everybody* a Communist—" "They can lie and call you one too," he said, "*yes.*" "Let them! Just let them!" But no matter how much I shouted at my liberal chiropodist father as though he were the radio executive who had fired Ira and his cohorts, no matter how loudly I claimed that the accusations were as inapplicable to Ira as they would be to me, I knew from having spent just that one afternoon with Johnny O'Day how mistaken I could be. Ira had served over two years with O'Day in Iran. O'Day had been his best friend. When I knew him, he was still getting long letters from O'Day and writing back to him. Then there was Goldstine and all he'd said in his kitchen. Don't let him fill you full of Communist ideas, kid. The Communists get a dummy like Ira and they use him. Get out of my house, you dumb Communist prick . . .

I had willfully refused to put all this together. This and the record album and more.

"Remember that afternoon in my office, Nathan, when he came

over from New York? I asked him and you asked him, and what did he tell us?"

"The truth! He told the truth!"

"'Are you a Communist, Mr. Ringold?' I asked him. 'Are you a Communist, Mr. Ringold?' you asked him." With something shocking in his voice I had never heard before, my father cried, "If he lied, if that man lied to my son . . . !"

What I'd heard in his voice was a willingness to kill.

"How can you be in business with somebody who lies to you about something that fundamental? *How?* It wasn't a child's lie," my father said. "It was an adult lie. It was a motivated lie. It was an *unmitigated* lie."

On he went, while I was thinking, Why did Ira bother, why didn't he tell me the truth? I would have gone up to Zinc Town anyway, or tried to. But then, he didn't just lie to me. That wasn't the point. He lied to everyone. If you lie about it to everyone, automatically and all the time, you're doing it deliberately to change your relationship to the truth. Because nobody can improvise it. You tell the truth to this person, you tell the lie to the other person—it won't work. So the lying is part of what happens when he put on that uniform. It was in the nature of his commitment to lie. Telling the truth, particularly to me, never occurred to him; it would have not only put our friendship at risk but put me at risk. There were lots of reasons why he lied, but none that I could explain to my father, even if I had understood them all at the time.

After speaking with my father (and my mother, who said, "I begged Dad not to call you, not to upset you"), I tried to telephone Ira at West Eleventh Street. The phone was busy all evening, and when I dialed again the next morning and got through, Wondrous—the black woman whom Eve used to summon to the dinner table with the little bell that Ira loathed—said to me, "He don't live here no more," and hung up. Because Ira's brother was still very much "my teacher," I restrained myself from phoning Murray Ringold, but I did write to Ira, to Newark, to Lehigh Avenue, in care of Mr. Ringold, and again to the box address up in Zinc Town. I got no answer. I read the clippings my father sent me about him from the papers, crying aloud, "Lies! Lies! Filthy lies!" but then I remembered Johnny O'Day and Erwin Goldstine and I didn't know what to think.

Less than six months later there appeared in America's bookstores—rushed into publication—*I Married a Communist* by Eve Frame, as told to Bryden Grant. The jacket, front and back, was a replica of the American flag. On the front of the jacket the flag was ripped raggedly open, and within the oval tear was a recent black-and-white photograph of Ira and Eve: Eve looking softly lovely in one of her little hats, with the dotted veil she'd made famous, wearing a fur jacket, and carrying a circular purse—Eve smiling brightly at the camera as she walked arm in arm down West Eleventh Street with her husband. But Ira didn't look at all happy; from beneath his fedora, he stared through his heavy glasses into the camera with a grave and troubled expression. Very nearly at the bull's-eye center of that book jacket proclaiming "*I Married a Communist,* by Eve Frame, as told to Bryden Grant," Ira's head was circled boldly in red.

In the book, Eve claimed that Iron Rinn, "alias Ira Ringold," was "a Communist madman" who had "assaulted and browbeaten" her with his Communist ideas, lecturing her and Sylphid every night at dinner, shouting at them and doing his best to "brainwash" both of them and make them work for the Communist cause. "I don't believe I've ever seen anything so heroic in my life as my young daughter, who loved nothing so much as to sit quietly all day playing her harp, arguing strenuously in defense of American democracy against this Communist madman and his Stalinist, totalitarian lies. I don't believe I've ever seen anything so cruel in my life as this Communist madman using every tactic out of the Soviet concentration camp to bring this brave child to her knees."

On the facing page was a photograph of Sylphid, but not the Sylphid I knew, not the large, sardonic twenty-three-year-old in the gypsy clothes who had hilariously helped me through my dinner that night at the party and who afterward had delighted me by filleting one after another of her mother's friends, but a tiny, round-faced Sylphid with big black eyes, in pigtails and a party dress, smiling at her beautiful mommy over a Beverly Hills birthday cake. Sylphid in a white cotton dress embroidered with little strawberries, its full skirt puffed out with petticoats and cinched by a full sash tied at the back in a bow. Sylphid at forty-two pounds and six years of age, in white anklets and black Mary Janes. Sylphid not as Pennington's child or even Eve's but as God's. The picture achieving what Eve intended at the outset with the misty daydream of a name: the deprofanation of Sylphid, the etherealization from solid to air. Sylphid as saint, perfectly innocent of all the vices and taking up no room in this world whatsoever. Sylphid as everything that antagonism is not.

"Momma, Momma," the brave child cries helplessly to her mother in one climactic scene, "those men up in his study are speaking Russian!"

Russian agents. Russian spies. Russian documents. Secret letters, phone calls, hand-delivered messages pouring into the house day and night from Communists all over the country. Cell meetings in the house and in "the secret Communist hideaway in the remotest wilds of New Jersey." And "in a parlor-floor apartment briefly leased by him in Greenwich Village, on Washington Square North, across from the famous statue of General George Washington—an apartment acquired by Iron Rinn chiefly for the purpose of providing a safe haven for Communists on the run from the FBI."

"Lies!" I cried. "Completely crazy lies!" But how was I to know for sure? How was anyone? What if the startling preface to her book was *true?* Could it possibly be? For years I wouldn't read Eve Frame's book, protecting as long as I could my original relationship to Ira even when I had been progressively abandoning him and his haranguing to a point where I had all but accomplished the rejection of him. But because I didn't want this book to be the awful end to our story, I skipped around and didn't read thoroughly beyond the preface. Nor was I avidly interested in what was written in the papers about the treacherous hypocrisy of the leading actor of *The*

Free and the Brave, who'd been personifying all these great American characters despite having cast himself in a more sinister role entirely. Who had, according to Eve's testimony, been personally responsible for submitting every one of Sokolow's scripts to a Russian agent for suggestions and approval. To see somebody I'd loved publicly vilified—why would I want to take part in that? There was no pleasure in it, and there was also nothing I could do about it.

Even putting aside the charge of espionage, accepting that the man who had brought me into the world of men could have lied to our family about being a Communist was no less painful for me than accepting that Alger Hiss or the Rosenbergs could have lied to the nation by denying that they were Communists. I refused to read any of it, as I had earlier refused to believe any of it.

This was how Eve's book began, the preface, the bombshell of an opening page:

> Is it right for me to do this? Is it easy for me to do this? Believe me, it is far from easy. It is the most awful and difficult task of my entire life. What is my motive? people will ask. How can I possibly consider it my moral and patriotic duty to inform on a man I loved as much as I loved Iron Rinn?
>
> Because as an American actress I have sworn myself to fight the Communist infiltration of the entertainment industry with every fiber of my being. Because as an American actress I have a solemn responsibility to an American audience that has given me so much love and recognition and happiness, a solemn and unshakable responsibility to reveal and expose the extent of the Communist grip on the broadcasting industry that I came to know through the man I was married to, a man I loved more than any man I have ever known, but a man who was determined to use the weapon of mass culture to tear down the American way of life.
>
> That man was the radio actor Iron Rinn, alias Ira Rin-

gold, card-carrying member of the Communist Party of the United States of America and American ringleader of the underground Communist espionage unit committed to controlling American radio. Iron Rinn, alias Ira Ringold, an American taking his orders from Moscow.

I know why I married this man: out of a woman's love. And why did he marry me? Because he was ordered to by the Communist Party! Iron Rinn never loved me. Iron Rinn exploited me. Iron Rinn married me the better to infiltrate his way into the world of American entertainment. Yes, I married a Machiavellian Communist, a vicious man of enormous cunning who nearly ruined my life, my career, and the life of my beloved child. And all of it to advance Stalin's plan for world domination.

7

"THE SHACK. Eve hated it. When they were first lovers, she'd tried fixing it up for him; she hung curtains, bought dishes, glasses, place settings, but there were mice, wasps, spiders got into the place, and she was terrified of them, and it was miles to the general store, and since she didn't drive, a local farmer who smelled of manure had to drive her there to shop. All in all, there was nothing much for her to do in Zinc Town except fend off all the discomforts, and so she started to campaign for them to buy a place in the south of France, where Sylphid's father had a villa, so that Sylphid could be near him in the summers. She said to Ira, 'How can you be so provincial? How will you ever learn anything that isn't screaming about Harry Truman if you won't travel, if you won't go to France to see the French countryside, if you won't go to Italy to see the great paintings, if you won't go anywhere except to New Jersey? You don't listen to music. You won't go to museums. If a book isn't about the working class, you don't read it. How can an actor—' And he would say, 'Look, I'm no actor. I'm a working stiff who earns his living in radio. You *had* a la-di-da husband. You want to go back and try him again? You want a husband like your friend Katrina has, a cultivated Harvard man like Mr. Loony, like Mr. Katrina Van Gossip Grant?'

"Whenever she'd bring up France and buying a vacation house

there, Ira got going—it never took much. It wasn't in him casually to dislike somebody like Pennington or Grant. It wasn't in him casually to dislike anything. There was no disagreement that his outrage couldn't make use of. 'I traveled,' he'd tell her. 'I worked on the docks in Iran. Saw enough human degradation in Iran . . .' and so on and so forth.

"The upshot was that Ira wouldn't give up the shack, and that was another source of contention between them. In the beginning the shack was a holdover from his old life and for her a part of his rube charm. After a while she saw the shack as a foothold apart from her, and that also filled her with terror.

"Maybe she loved him and that's what spawned the fear of losing him. Her histrionics never registered on me as love. Eve cloaked herself in the mantle of love, the fantasy of love, but was too weak and vulnerable a person not to be filled with resentment. She was too intimidated by everything to provide love that was sensible and to the point—to provide anything but a caricature of love. That's what Sylphid got. Imagine what it must have meant to be Eve Frame's daughter—*and* Carlton Pennington's daughter—and you begin to understand how Sylphid evolved. A person like that you don't make overnight.

"The whole despised part of Ira, everything disgustingly un-tamed in him, was also wrapped up for her in that shack, but Ira wouldn't get rid of it. If nothing else, as long as the shack remained a shack, it was Sylphid-proof. Nowhere for her to sleep other than on the daybed in the front room, and the few times each summer she visited for a weekend she was bored and miserable. The pond too muddy for her to swim in, the woods too buggy for her to walk in, and though Eve would endlessly try to keep her entertained, she sulked indoors for a day and a half and then headed back on the train to her harp.

"But that last spring they were together, plans began to be laid to fix the place up. Big renovation to start after Labor Day. Modern-izing the kitchen, modernizing the bathroom, large new windows, brand-new floors, new doors that fit, new lighting, blown insulation and a new oil-heating system to properly winterize the place. Paint job inside and out. And a large addition at the back, a whole new room with a huge stone fireplace and with a picture window overlooking the pond and the woods. Ira hired a carpenter, a painter, an electrician, a plumber, Eve made lists and drawings, and all of it was to be ready for Christmas. 'What the hell,' Ira said to me, 'she wants it, let her have it.'

"His coming apart had begun by then, only I didn't realize it. He didn't either. He thought he was being shrewd, you see, thought he could finesse it. But his aches and pains were killing him, and his morale was shot, and the decision wasn't made by what was strong in him but by what was breaking. He thought by making things more to her liking he could minimize the friction and ensure her protecting him against the blacklist. He was afraid now of losing her by losing his temper, and so he began to try to save his political hide by letting all that unreality of hers flow freely over him.

"The fear. The acute fear there was in those days, the disbelief, the anxiety over discovery, the suspense of having one's life and one's livelihood under threat. Was Ira convinced keeping Eve could protect him? Probably not. But what else was there for him to do?

"What happened to his cunning strategy? He hears her calling the new addition 'Sylphid's room,' and that takes care of the cunning strategy. He hears her outside with the excavator saying, 'Sylphid's room this' and 'Sylphid's room that,' and when she comes inside the house, all glowing and happy, Ira's already undergone the transformation. 'Why do you say that?' he asks her. 'Why do you call that Sylphid's room?' 'I did no such thing,' she says. 'You did. I heard you. That's not Sylphid's room.' 'Well, she *is* going to stay there.' 'I thought it was just going to be the big backroom, the new living room.' 'But the daybed. She'll be sleeping there on the new daybed.' 'Will she? When?' 'Why, when she comes here.' 'But she doesn't like it here.' 'But she will when the house is as lovely as it's going to be.' 'Then screw it,' he says. 'The house won't be lovely. The house will be shitty. Fuck the whole project.' 'Why are you doing this to me?

Why are you doing this to my daughter? What is *wrong* with you, Ira?' 'It's over. The renovation is off.' 'But *why?*' 'Because I can't stand your daughter and your daughter can't stand me—that is why.' 'How *dare* you say anything against my daughter! I'm getting out of here! I will not stay here! You are persecuting my daughter! I will not have it!' And she picked up the phone and called for the local taxi, and in five minutes she was gone.

"Four hours later he found out to where. He gets a phone call from a real estate woman over in Newton. She asks to speak to Miss Frame, and he tells her Miss Frame isn't around, and she asks if he'll give Miss Frame a message—the two darling farmhouses they saw *are* on the market, either one is perfect for her daughter, and she can show them to her the next weekend.

"What Eve had done, after she left, was to spend the afternoon looking for a summer place in Sussex County to buy for Sylphid.

"That's when Ira phoned me. He said to me, 'I don't believe it. Looking for a house for her up here—I don't *comprehend* it.' 'I do,' I said. 'To bad mothering there is no end. Ira, the time has come to move on to the next improbability.'

"I got in the car and I went up to the shack. I spent the night, and the next morning I brought him to Newark. Eve phoned our house every evening, begging him to come back, but he told her that was it, their marriage was over, and when *The Free and the Brave* returned to the air, he stayed with us and commuted to New York to work.

"I told him, 'You are in the hands of this thing like everybody else. You are going to go down or not go down like everybody else. The woman you are married to is not going to protect you from whatever is in store for you or for the show or for whomever else they decide to destroy. The Red-baiters are on the march. Nobody is going to fool them for long even by living a *quadruple* life. They're going to get you with her or they're going to get you without her, but at least without her you're not going to be encumbered by somebody useless in a crisis.'

"But, as the weeks passed, Ira became less and less convinced that I was right, and so did Doris, and maybe, Nathan, I wasn't right.

Maybe if, for his own calculated reasons, he'd gone back to Eve, her aura, her reputation, her connections would have worked together to save him and his career. That is possible. But what was going to save him from the marriage? Every night, after Lorraine had gone to her room, we'd sit in the kitchen, Doris and I going over and over the same ground while Ira listened. We'd gather at the kitchen table with our tea, and Doris would say, 'He's put up with her nonsense for three years now, when there's been no sane reason to put up with it. Why can't he put up with her nonsense for another three years, when at last there *is* a sane reason to put up with it? For whatever motive, good or bad, he has never pushed to completely end the marriage in all this time. Why should he do it now, when being her husband might possibly be helpful to him? If he can salvage some benefit, at least his ridiculous union with those two won't have been in vain.' And I would say, 'If he returns to the ridiculous union, he is going to be destroyed by the ridiculous union. It is more than ridiculous. Half the time he's so miserable, he has to come over here to sleep.' And Doris would say, 'He's going to be more miserable when he's on the blacklist.' 'Ira is going to wind up on the blacklist either way. With his big mouth and his background, Ira is not going to be spared.' And Doris would say, 'How can you be sure everyone is going to get it? The whole thing is so irrational to begin with, so without any rhyme or reason—' And I would say, 'Doris, his name has appeared in fifteen, twenty places already. It's got to happen. It's inevitable. And when it happens, we know whose side she'll stand by. Not his, Sylphid's—to protect Sylphid from what's happening to *him*. I say end the marriage and the marital misery and accept that he is going to wind up on the blacklist wherever he is. If he goes back to her, he's going to fight with her, he's going to battle the daughter, and soon enough she is going to realize why he is there, and that will make it even worse.' 'Eve? Realize anything?' Doris said. 'Reality doesn't seem to make a dent in Miss Frame. Why is reality going to rear its head now?' 'No,' I said, 'the cynical exploitation, the parasitical leeching—it's too demeaning. I don't like it in and of itself, and I don't like it because

Ira is not capable of pulling it off. He is open, he is impulsive, he is direct. He is a hothead and he is not going to be able to do it. And when she finds out why he is there, well, she will make things even *more* miserable and confused. She doesn't have to figure it out herself—somebody can do it for her. Her friends the Grants will figure it out. They probably have already. Ira, if you go back there, what are you going to do to change the way you live with her? You're going to have to become a lapdog, Ira. You can do that? *You?*' 'He'll just be shrewd and go his way,' Doris said. 'He *can't* be shrewd and go his way,' I said. 'He'll never be "shrewd" because everything there drives him crazy.' 'Well,' said Doris, 'losing everything he's worked for, being punished in America for what he believes in, his enemies getting the upper hand, that will make Ira even crazier.' 'I don't like it,' I said, and Doris said, 'But you didn't like it from the outset, Murray. Now you're using this to get him to do what you have wanted him to do all along. The hell with exploiting her. Exploit her—that's what she's there for. What is marriage without exploitation? People in marriages get exploited a million times over. One exploits the other's position, one exploits the other's money, one exploits the other's looks. I think he should go back. I think he needs all the protection he can get. Just *because* he is impulsive, *because* he is a hothead. He's in a war, Murray. He's under fire. He needs camouflage. She is his camouflage. Wasn't she Pennington's camouflage because he was a homosexual? Now let her be Ira's because he's a Red. Let her be useful for *something*. No, I don't see the objection. He schlepped the harp, didn't he? He saved her from that kid beating her brains in, didn't he? He did what he could do for her. Now let her do what she can do for him. Now, by luck, through sheer circumstance, those two people can finally do something aside from bitch and moan about Ira and war on each other. They don't even have to be conscious of it. Through no effort on their part, they can be of use to Ira. What's so wrong with that?' 'The man's honor is at stake, that's what,' I said. 'His integrity is at stake. It's all too mortifying. Ira, I argued with you about joining the Communist Party. I argued with you about Stalin and I argued with you about the Soviet Union. I argued with you and it made no difference: you were committed to the Communist Party. Well, this ordeal is part of that commitment. I don't like to think of you groveling. Perhaps the time has come to drop *all* the mortifying lies. The marriage that's a lie and the political party that's a lie. Both are making of you much less than you are.'

"The debate went on for five consecutive nights. And for five nights he was silent. I'd never known him to be so silent. So *calm.* Finally, Doris turned to him and said, 'Ira, this is all we can say. Everything has been discussed. It's your life, your career, your wife, your marriage. It's your radio show. Now it is your decision. It's up to you.' And he said, 'If I can manage to hold on to my position, if I can manage not to be swept aside and thrown into the trash can, then I am doing more for the party than if I sit around and worry about my integrity. I don't worry about being mortified, I worry about being effective. I want to be effective. I'm going back to her.' 'It won't work,' I said. 'It will work,' he told me. 'If it's clear in my mind why I'm there, I will make *sure* it works.'

"That very night, half an hour, forty-five minutes later, the downstairs doorbell rang. She'd hired a cab to drive her to Newark. Her face was drawn, ghostlike. She came racing up the stairs, and when Eve saw Doris with me at the top of the landing, she flashed that smile that an actress is able to flash on the spot—smiled as though Doris were a fan waiting outside the studio door to snap a photograph with her box camera. Then she was by us, and there was Ira, and she was on her knees. Same stunt as that night out at the shack. The Suppliant again. Repeatedly and promiscuously the Suppliant. The aristocratic pretension of stateliness and this kind of perverse, unembarrassable behavior. 'I implore you—don't leave me! I'll do anything!'

"Our little, bright, budding Lorraine had been in her room doing her homework. She had come out into the living room in her pajamas to say good night to everyone when there, in her very own house, was this famous star whom she listened to every week on *The American Radio Theater,* this exalted personage letting life run all over her. All the chaos and rawness of someone's inmost being on exhibit on our living room floor. Ira told Eve to get up, but when he tried to lift her she wrapped her arms around his legs and the howl she let loose made Lorraine's mouth fall open. We'd taken Lorraine to see the stage show at the Roxy, we'd taken her to the Hayden Planetarium, we'd gone up in the car to see Niagara Falls, but as far as spectacles went, this was the pinnacle of her childhood.

"I went and kneeled down beside Eve. Okay, I thought, if what he wants to do is to go back, if this is what he wants more of, he is about to get it, and in spades. 'That's it,' I said to her. 'Come on, let's get up now. Let's go into the kitchen, get you some coffee.' And that was when Eve looked over and saw Doris standing by herself, still holding the magazine she'd been reading. Doris, plain as can be, in her bedroom slippers and her housedress. Her face was blank, as I remember it—stunned, sure, but certainly not mocking. However, just her being there was enough of a challenge to the high drama that was Eve Frame's life for Eve to take aim and fire. 'You! What are *you* staring at, you hideous, twisted little Jew!'

"I have to tell you that I saw it coming; rather, I knew something was coming that wasn't exactly going to advance Eve's cause, and so I wasn't as flabbergasted as my little girl was. Lorraine burst into tears, and Doris said, 'Get her out of the house,' and Ira and I lifted Eve up from the floor and took her into the hallway and down the stairs, and we drove her to Penn Station. Ira sat in the front beside me, and she sat in the back as though she were oblivious to what had happened. All the way to Penn Station she had that smile on her face, the one for the cameras. Underneath the smile there was nothing at all, not her character, not her history, not even her misery. She was just what was stretched across her face. She wasn't even alone. There was no one to *be* alone. Whatever shaming origins she had spent her life escaping had resulted in this: someone from whom life itself had escaped.

"I pulled up in front of Penn Station, we all got out of the car, and stonily, very stonily, Ira said to her, 'Go back to New York.' She said, 'But aren't you coming?' 'Of course not.' 'Why did you come in the car, then? Why do you come to the train with me?' Could that have been why she'd been smiling? Because she believed she'd triumphed and Ira was returning with her to Manhattan?

"This time, the scene wasn't enacted for my little family. This time it was an audience of fifty or so people heading into Penn Station who were brought to a standstill by what they saw. Without a qualm really, this regal presence who endowed the idea of decorum with such tremendous significance threw her two hands up toward the sky and, upon all of downtown Newark, imposed the magnitude of her misery. A woman totally inhibited and under wraps—until she's totally uninhibited. Either inhibited and bound by shame, or uninhibited and shameless. Nothing ever in between. 'You tricked me! I loathe you! I despise you! Both of you! You are the worst people I have ever known!'

"I remember hearing somebody in the crowd then, some guy rushing up who was asking, 'What are they doing, making a movie? Ain't that what's-her-name? Mary Astor?' And I remember thinking that she would never be finished. The movies, the stage, the radio, and now this. The aging actress's last great career—shouting her hatred in the street.

"But after that, nothing happened. Ira returned to the show while staying on with us, and nothing more was said about going back to West Eleventh Street. Helgi came to massage him three times a week, and nothing more happened. Very early on, Eve had tried to call, but I took the phone to tell her that Ira couldn't speak to her. Would *I* speak to her? Would I at least *listen* to her? I said yes. What else could I do?

"She knows what she did wrong, she says, she knows why Ira is hiding out in Newark: because she had told him about Sylphid's recital. Ira was jealous enough of Sylphid as it was, and he could not reconcile himself to the upcoming recital. But when Eve had decided to tell him about it, she had believed that it was her duty to let him know beforehand everything that a recital entailed. Because it's not just renting a hall, she told me, it's not just showing up and playing a concert—it's a production. It's like a wedding. It's a huge event that consumes a musician's family for months before it happens. Sylphid would herself be preparing for the entire next year. For a performance to qualify as a recital, you have to play at least sixty minutes of music, which is an enormous task. Just choosing the music would be an enormous task, and not for Sylphid alone. There were going to be endless discussions about what Sylphid should begin with and what she should end with and what the chamber piece should be, and Eve had wanted Ira to be prepared so he wouldn't go berserk every time she left him alone to sit down with Sylphid to discuss the program. Eve had wanted him to know beforehand what he, as a family member, was going to have to put up with: there was going to be publicity, frustration, crises—like all other young musicians, Sylphid was going to get cold feet and want to back out. But Eve also wanted Ira to know that it would be worth it in the end, and she wanted me to tell him that. Because a recital was what Sylphid needed to break through. People are stupid, Eve said. They like to see harpists who are tall, blond, and willowy, and Sylphid happened not to be tall, blond, and willowy. But she was an extraordinary musician and the recital was going to prove that once and for all. It was going to be held at Town Hall, and Eve would underwrite it, and Sylphid was to be coached by her old Juilliard teacher, who had agreed to help her prepare, and Eve was going to get every friend she had to attend, and the Grants promised to make certain that the critics were there from all the papers, and Eve had no doubt that Sylphid was going to do wonderfully and get wonderful reviews, and then Eve herself could shop them around to Sol Hurok.

"What was I to say? What difference would it have made if I had reminded her of this, that, or the other thing? She was a selective amnesiac whose forte was to render inconvenient facts inconsequential. To live without remembering was her means of survival. She had it all figured out: the reason Ira was staying with us was because of her having believed it her duty to tell him truthfully about the Town Hall recital and everything it would entail.

"Well, the fact was that when Ira was with us he never mentioned Sylphid's recital. His head was too full of the blacklist for him to be worrying about Sylphid's recital. I doubt that when Eve was telling him about it, it had even registered on him. Following that phone call, I wondered if she had told him about it at all.

"The letter she sent next I marked 'Addressee Unknown' and, with Ira's consent, returned unopened. The second letter I handled the same way. After that, the calls and the letters stopped. It looked for a while as though the disaster were over. Eve and Sylphid were up in Staatsburg on weekends with the Grants. She must have been giving them an earful about Ira—and, perhaps, about me too—and getting an earful about the Communist conspiracy. But still nothing happened, and I began to believe that nothing would happen so long as he remained officially married and the Grants figured there was some remote danger in it for the wife if the husband was exposed in *Red Channels* and fired.

"One Saturday morning, who should turn up on *Van Tassel and Grant* but Sylphid Pennington and her harp. I would think the imprimatur awarded Sylphid by making her the guest of that program that day was a favor to Eve meant to insulate the stepdaughter against any taint of association with the stepfather. Bryden Grant interviewed Sylphid, and she told him her funny stories about being in the orchestra at the Music Hall, and then Sylphid played a few selections for the radio audience, and after that Katrina launched into her weekly monologue on the state of the arts—an extensive fantasy, that Saturday, of the music world's expectations for young Sylphid Pennington's future, of the anticipation already mounting for her debut recital at Town Hall. Katrina explained how after she had arranged for Sylphid to play for Toscanini he had said such-and-such about the young harpist, and after she had arranged for Sylphid to play for Phil Spitalny he had said so-and-so, and there was no famous musical name, high or low, she didn't make use of, and Sylphid had never played for any of them.

"It was bold and spectacular and absolutely in character. Eve could say anything if she felt cornered; Katrina could say anything at any time. Exaggeration, misrepresentation, bald fabrication—that was her talent and skill. As it was her husband's. As it was Joe McCarthy's. The Grants were just Joe McCarthy with a pedigree. With *conviction*. It was a little hard to believe that McCarthy was caught up with his lies the way those two were. 'Tailgunner Joe' could never completely smother his cynicism; McCarthy always looked to me sort of loosely covered in his human shabbiness, whereas the Grants and their shabbiness were one.

"So—nothing happened and nothing happened, and Ira began looking for an apartment of his own in New York . . . and *that's* when something happened—but with Helgi.

"Lorraine got a bang out of this big broad and her gold tooth and her dyed hair swirled up in a helter-skelter blond bun storming into our apartment with her table and speaking in that shrill voice with the Estonian accent. In Lorraine's bedroom, where she massaged Ira, Helgi was always laughing. I remember saying to him once, 'You get along with these people, don't you?' 'Why shouldn't I?' he said. 'There's nothing wrong with them.' That's when I wondered if the greatest mistake any of us ever made was not letting him alone to marry Donna Jones, not letting him alone to earn a livelihood in the American heartland, unrebelliously manufacturing fudge and raising a family with his ex-stripper.

"Well, one morning in October, Eve is by herself and desperate and frightened and she gets it into her head to have Helgi hand-deliver a letter to Ira. She phones her up in the Bronx and tells her, 'Take a taxi to me. I'll give you the money. Then you can carry the letter with you when you go to Newark.'

"Helgi arrives all dressed up, in her fur coat and her fanciest hat and her best outfit, and carrying the massage table. Eve is upstairs writing the letter and Helgi is told to wait in the living room. Helgi sets down the table that goes with her everywhere, and she waits. She waits and she waits, and there's a bar and there's the cabinet with the dainty glasses, and so she finds the key to the cabinet, and she gets a glass and she locates the vodka and she pours herself a drink. And Eve is still upstairs in the bedroom, in her peignoir, writing letter after letter and tearing each one up and starting all over again. Every letter she writes to him is wrong, and with every letter she writes, Helgi pours another drink and smokes another cigarette, and soon Helgi is wandering around the living room and the library and into the hallway and looking at the pictures of Eve when she was a gorgeous young movie star and pictures of Ira and Eve with Bill O'Dwyer, the ex-mayor of New York, and with Impellitteri, the current mayor, and she pours herself another drink, lights another cigarette, and thinks about this woman with all her money and fame and privilege. She thinks about herself and her hard life, and she gets more and more sorry for herself and more and more drunk. Big and strong as she is, she even starts to weep.

"By the time Eve comes down and gives her the letter, Helgi is stretched out on the sofa, in her fur coat and her hat, still smoking and still drinking but now she's not weeping. By now she's worked herself up into an incredible state and she's furious. The boozer's lack of control doesn't begin and end with the booze.

"Helgi says, 'Why do you keep me waiting an hour and a half?' Eve takes one look and says, 'Leave this house.' Helgi doesn't even get off the sofa. She spots the envelope in Eve's hand and she says, 'What do you say in this letter that takes an hour and a half? What do you write him? Do you apologize for what a bad wife you are? Do you apologize that he does not have any physical satisfaction from you? Do you apologize that you don't give him the things a man needs?' 'Shut your mouth, you stupid woman, and leave here immediately!' 'Do you apologize that you never give the man a blow job? Do you apologize that you don't know *how* to? Do you know who gives him a blow job? Helgi gives him a blow job!' 'I am calling the police!' 'Good. The police will arrest you. I will show the police—here, here is how she sucks him off, like the perfect lady, and they will put you in jail for fifty years!'

"When the police come, Helgi's still at it, still going strong—out on West Eleventh Street, telling the world. 'Does the wife give him the blow jobs? No. The Peasant gives him the blow jobs.'

"They take her down to the precinct station, book her—drunk and disorderly conduct, trespassing—and Eve is back in the smoke-filled living room and she's hysterical and she doesn't know what to do next, and then she sees that two of her enamel boxes are missing. She has a beautiful collection of tiny enamel boxes on a side table. Two of them are gone and she calls the police station. 'Check her,' she says, 'there are things missing.' They look in Helgi's handbag. Sure enough, there they are, the two boxes and also Eve Frame's monogrammed silver lighter. It turned out that she'd stolen one from our house too. We never knew where it had gone and I went around saying, 'Where the hell is that lighter?' and then when Helgi wound up at the precinct station, I figured it out.

"I was the one who bailed her out. The phone call she made from the station after they booked her was to our house, to Ira, but I was the one who went there and got her. I drove her up to the Bronx, and on the drive I got the drunken tirade about the rich bitch not pushing her around anymore. Back home, I told Ira the whole story. I told him he'd been waiting all his life for the class war to break out, and guess where it happened? In his living room. He'd explained to Helgi how Marx had urged the proletariat to wrest the wealth from the bourgeoisie, and that was exactly what she'd set out to do.

"The first thing Eve does, after calling the cops about the theft, is to call Katrina. Katrina speeds over from their townhouse, and before the day is out, everything inside Ira's desk finds its way into Katrina's hands and from her hands into Bryden's hands and from there into his column and from there onto the front page of every New York newspaper. In her book Eve would claim that she was the one who broke into the mahogany desk up in Ira's study and found his letters from O'Day and his diary books where he'd recorded the names and serial numbers, the names and home addresses of every Marxist whom he had met in the service. She was much celebrated for this in the patriotic press. But that break-in, I believe, was Eve boasting, performing again, pretending to be the patriots' hero-ine—Eve boasting and maybe simultaneously protecting the integrity of Katrina Van Tassel Grant, who would not have hesitated to break into anything in order to preserve American democracy but whose husband was then planning his first campaign for the House of Representatives.

"There in 'Grant's Grapevine,' in Ira's writing, are Ira's subversive thoughts, recorded in a secret diary while he was purportedly serving overseas as a loyal sergeant in the U.S. Army. 'The papers and censor and such have distorted the news of Poland, thus creating a wedge between us and Russia. Russia was and is willing to compromise but it has not been presented so by our papers. Churchill directly advocates a total reactionary Poland.' 'Russia requests independence for all colonial peoples. The rest just emphasize self-government plus trusteeships.' 'British cabinet dissolves. Good. Now Churchill's policy of anti-Russia and of status quo may never materialize.'

"That's it. There it is. Dynamite that so terrifies the sponsor and the network that by the end of the week 'Redhot Iron' is finished and so is *The Free and the Brave.* So are some thirty others whose names are down in Ira's diaries. In time, so am I.

"Now, since long before Ira's troubles began my union activities had made me public enemy number one to our superintendent of schools, maybe the school board would have found a way to get me labeled a Communist and fired without the help of Eve's heroism. It was only a matter of time, with or without her assistance, until Ira and his radio program would have gone under, and so maybe nothing that happened to any of us required that she first give that stuff to Katrina. Still, it's instructive to think about what exactly Eve did in falling prey to the Grants and delivering Ira whole to his worst enemies."

Once more, we were together in eighth-period English, with Mr. Ringold perched at the edge of his desk, wearing the tan glen-plaid suit that he'd bought on Broad Street with his army separation pay—at the American Shop's sale for returning GIs—and that, throughout my high school years, he alternated with his other American Shop suit, a gray double-breasted sharkskin. In one hand he would be hefting the blackboard eraser that he wouldn't hesitate to hurl at the head of a student whose answer to a question did not meet his minimum daily requirement for mental alertness, while with the other hand he would regularly cut the air, enumerating dramatically each of the points to be remembered for the test.

"It demonstrates," he told me, "that when you decide to contribute your personal problem to an ideology's agenda, everything that is personal is squeezed out and discarded and all that remains is what is useful to the ideology. In this case, a woman contributes her husband and their marital difficulties to the cause of zealous anti-Communism. Essentially what Eve contributes is an incompatibility that she herself couldn't resolve from day one between Sylphid and Ira. A standard difficulty between stepchild and stepparent, even if somewhat intensified in the Eve Frame household. Everything that Ira was with Eve otherwise—good husband, bad husband, kind man, harsh man, understanding man, stupid man, faithful man, unfaithful man—everything that constitutes marital effort and marital error, everything that is a consequence of marriage's having nothing in common with a dream—is squeezed out, and what is left is what the ideology can make use of.

"Afterward the wife, if she is so inclined (and maybe Eve was and maybe she wasn't), can protest, 'No, no, it wasn't like that. You don't understand. He wasn't only what you are saying he was. He wasn't, with me, at all what you are saying he was. With me he could also be this, he could also be that.' Afterward an informer like Eve may realize that it's not only what she said that's responsible for the bizarre distortion of him that she reads in the press; it's also all that she left out—that she deliberately left out. But by then it's too late. By then the ideology has no time for her because it no longer has a *use* for her. 'This? That?' replies the ideology. 'What do we care about This and That? What do we care about the daughter? She is just more of that flabby mass that is life. Get her out of our way. All we need from you is what advances the righteous cause. Another Communist dragon to be slain! Another example of their treachery!'

"As for Pamela's panicking—"

But it was after eleven, and I reminded Murray, whose course at the college had finished earlier that day—and whose evening's narration seemed to me to have reached its pedagogical crescendo—that he was due to take the bus down to New York the following morning and that perhaps it was time for me to drive him back to the Athena dormitory.

"I could listen and listen," I told him, "but maybe you should get some sleep. In the history of storytelling stamina, you've already taken the title from Scheherazade. We've been sitting out here for six nights."

"I'm fine," he said.

"You're not getting tired? Cold?"

"It's beautiful out here. No, I'm not cold. It's warm, it's lovely. The crickets are counting, the frogs are grunting, the fireflies are inspired, and I haven't had occasion to go on like this since I was running the teachers' union. Look. The moon. It's orange. The perfect setting for peeling back the skin of the years."

"That it is," I said. "You have a choice up on this mountain: either you can lose contact with history, as I sometimes choose to, or mentally you can do what you're doing—by the light of the moon, for hours on end, work to regain possession of it."

"All those antagonisms," Murray said, "and then the torrent of betrayal. Every soul its own betrayal factory. For whatever reason: survival, excitement, advancement, idealism. For the sake of the damage that can be done, the pain that can be inflicted. For the cruelty in it. For the *pleasure* in it. The pleasure of manifesting one's latent power. The pleasure of dominating others, of destroying people who are your enemies. You're surprising them. Isn't that the pleasure of betrayal? The pleasure of tricking somebody. It's a way to pay people back for a feeling of inferiority they arouse in you, of being put down by them, a feeling of frustration in your relationship with them. Their very existence may be humiliating to you, either because you aren't what they are or because they aren't what you are. And so you give them their comeuppance.

"Of course there are those who betray because they have no choice. I read a book by a Russian scientist who, in the Stalin years, betrayed his best friend to the secret police. He was under heavy interrogation, terrible physical torture for six months—at which point he said, 'Look, I cannot resist any longer, so please tell me what you want. Whatever you give me I will sign.'

"He signed whatever they wanted him to sign. He was himself sentenced to life in prison. Without parole. After fourteen years, in the sixties, when things changed, he was released and he wrote this book. He says that he betrayed his best friend for two reasons: because he was not able to resist the torture and because he knew that it didn't matter, that the result of the trial was already established. What he said or didn't say would make no difference. If he didn't say it, another tortured person would. He knew his friend, whom he loved to the end, would despise him, but under brutal torture a normal human being cannot resist. Heroism is a human exception. A person who lives a normal life, which is made up of twenty thousand little compromises every day, is untrained to suddenly not compromise at all, let alone to withstand torture.

"For some people it takes six months of torture to make them weak. And some start off with an advantage: they are already weak. They are people who know only how to give in. With a person like that, you just say, 'Do it,' and they do it. It happens so rapidly they do not even know it is a betrayal. Because they do what they are asked to do, it seems okay. And by the time it sinks in, it's too late: they have betrayed.

"There was an article in the paper not long ago about a man in East Germany who informed on his wife for twenty years. They found documents about him in the files of the East German secret police after the Berlin Wall came down. The wife had a professional position and the police wanted to follow her and the husband was the informer. She didn't know anything about it. She's found out only since they've opened the files. For twenty years it went on. They had kids, they had in-laws, they threw parties, they paid bills, they had operations, they made love, they didn't make love, they went to the seashore in the summertime and bathed in the sea, and all this time he was informing. He was a lawyer. Smart, very well read, even wrote poetry. They gave him a code name, he signed an agreement, and he had weekly meetings with an officer, not at police headquarters but at a special apartment, a private apartment. They told him, 'You are a lawyer, and we need your help,' and he was weak and he signed. He had a father he supported. His father had a terrible enfeebling disease. They told him that if he helped them out they would take good care of his father, whom he loved. It often works that way. Your father is sick, or your mother, or your sister, and they ask you to help and so, keeping uppermost in mind your ill father, you justify the betrayal and sign the agreement.

"To me it seems likely that more acts of personal betrayal were tellingly perpetrated in America in the decade after the war—say, between '46 and '56—than in any other period in our history. This nasty thing that Eve Frame did was typical of lots of nasty things people did in those years, either because they had to or because they felt they had to. Eve's behavior fell well within the routine informer practices of the era. When before had betrayal ever been so destigmatized and rewarded in this country? It was everywhere during those years, the accessible transgression, the *permissible* transgression that any American could commit. Not only does the pleasure of betrayal replace the prohibition, but you transgress without giving up your moral authority. You retain your purity at the same time as you are patriotically betraying—at the same time as you are realizing a satisfaction that verges on the sexual with its ambiguous components of pleasure and weakness, of aggression and shame: the satisfaction of undermining. Undermining sweethearts. Undermining rivals. Undermining friends. Betrayal is in this same zone of perverse and illicit and fragmented pleasure. An interesting, manipulative, underground type of pleasure in which there is much that a human being finds appealing.

"There are even those who have the brilliance of mind to practice the game of betrayal for itself alone. Without any self-interest.

Purely to entertain themselves. It's what Coleridge was probably getting at by describing Iago's betrayal of Othello as 'a motiveless malignity.' Generally, however, I would say there is a motive that provokes the vicious energies and brings *out* the malignity.

"The only hitch is that in the halcyon days of the Cold War, turning somebody in to the authorities as a Soviet spy could lead right to the chair. Eve, after all, wasn't turning Ira in to the FBI as a bad husband who fucked his masseuse. Betrayal is an inescapable component of living—who doesn't betray?—but to confuse the most heinous public act of betrayal, treason, with every other form of betrayal was not a good idea in 1951. Treason, unlike adultery, is a capital offense, so reckless exaggeration and thoughtless imprecision and false accusation, even just the seemingly genteel game of naming names—well, the results could be dire in those dark days when our Soviet allies had betrayed us by staying in Eastern Europe and exploding an atomic bomb and our Chinese allies had betrayed us by making a Communist revolution and throwing out Chiang Kai-shek. Joseph Stalin and Mao Tse-tung: there was the moral excuse for it all.

"The lying. A river of lies. Translating the truth into a lie. Translating one lie into another lie. The *competence* people display in their lying. The *skill*. Carefully sizing up the situation and then, with a calm voice and a straight face, delivering the most productive lie. Should they speak even the *partial* truth, nine times out of ten it's in *behalf* of a lie. Nathan, I've never had a chance to tell this story to anyone this way, at such length. I've never told it before and I won't again. I'd like to tell it right. To the end."

"Why?"

"I'm the only person still living who knows Ira's story, you're the only person still living who cares about it. That's why: because everyone else is dead." Laughing, he said, "My last task. To file Ira's story with Nathan Zuckerman."

"I don't know what I can do with it," I said.

"That's not my responsibility. My responsibility is to tell it to you. You and Ira meant a lot to each other."

"Then go ahead. How did it end?"

"Pamela," he said. "Pamela Solomon. Pamela panicked. When she learned from Sylphid that Eve had broken into Ira's desk. She thought what people seem generally to think when they first get wind of someone else's catastrophe: how does this affect me? So-and-So in my office has a brain tumor? That means I have to take inventory alone. So-and-So from next door went down on that plane? He died in that crash? No. It can't be. He was coming over on Saturday to fix our garbage disposal.

"There was a photograph that Ira had taken of Pamela at the shack. A photograph of her in her bathing suit, by the pond. Pamela was afraid (mistakenly) that the picture was in the desk, along with all the Communist stuff, and that Eve had seen it, or that, if it wasn't there, Ira was going to go to Eve and show it to her, stick it in her face and say, 'Look!' Then what would happen? Eve would be furious and call her a hussy and throw her out of the house. And what would *Sylphid* think of Pamela? What would Sylphid *do*? And what if Pamela was deported? That was the worst possibility of all. Pamela was a foreigner in America—what if her name got dragged into Ira's Communist mess, and it wound up in the papers and she was deported? What if Eve made *sure* she was deported, for trying to steal her husband? Goodbye, bohemia. Back to all that suffocating English propriety.

"Pamela wasn't necessarily wrong in her appraisal of the danger to her of Ira's Communist mess and of the mood of the country. The atmosphere of accusation, threat, and punishment was everywhere. To a foreigner particularly, it looked like a democratic pogrom full of terror. There was enough danger around to justify Pamela's fear. In that political climate, those were reasonable fears. And so, in response to her fears, Pamela brought to bear upon the predicament all her considerable intelligence and common-sense realism. Ira was right to have spotted her for a quick-witted and lucid young woman who knew her mind and did what she wanted.

"Pamela went to Eve and told her that one summer day two years back she'd run into Ira in the Village. He was in the station wagon, on his way to the country, and he told her Eve was already there and asked why she didn't hop in and come out to spend the day. It was so hot and awful that she didn't bother to think things through. 'Okay,' she said, 'I'll go get my bathing suit,' and he waited for her and they drove out to Zinc Town, and when they arrived she discovered that Eve *wasn't* there. She tried to be agreeable and to believe whatever excuse he made and even got into her suit and went for a swim with him. That's when he took the photograph and tried to seduce her. She burst into tears, fought him off, told him what she thought of him and what he was doing to Eve, and then she got the next train back to New York. Because she didn't want to make trouble for herself, she had kept his sexual advances secret. Her fear was that if she didn't, everybody would blame her and think she was a slut just for having got into the car with him. People would call her all kinds of names for letting him take that picture. Nobody would even listen to her side of the story. He would have crushed her with every conceivable lie had she dared expose his treachery by telling the truth. But now that she understood the *scope* of his treachery, she couldn't, in good conscience, remain silent.

"What happens next is that one afternoon, after my last class, I get to my office and there's my brother waiting for me. He's in the corridor, he's signing his autograph for a couple of teachers who've spotted him, and I unlock my door and he comes into the office, and he throws on my desk an envelope with 'Ira' written on it. The return address is the *Daily Worker*. Inside is a second envelope, this one's addressed to 'Iron Rinn.' In Eve's handwriting. It's her blue vellum stationery. The office manager at the *Worker* was a friend of Ira's, and he'd driven all the way out to Zinc Town to deliver it to him.

"It seems that the day after Pamela went to Eve with her story, Eve does the strongest thing she can think of, for the time being the strongest punch she can throw. She gets all dressed up in her lynx jacket and a million-dollar black velvet dream of a dress with white lace trim and her best open-toed black shoes, and she puts on one of her stylish black veiled felt hats, and marches over, not to '21' for lunch with Katrina, but to the *Daily Worker* office. The *Worker* was down on University Place, only a few blocks from West Eleventh Street. Eve takes the elevator to the fifth floor and demands to see the editor. She's led into his office, where she removes the letter from her lynx muff and places it on his desk. 'For the martyred hero of the Bolshevik revolution,' she says, 'for the people's artist and mankind's last best hope,' and turns and walks out. Racked and timorous as she was in the face of any opposition, she could also be impressively imperious when she was tanked up with righteous resentment and having one of her delusionary grande-dame days. She was capable of these transformations—and she didn't go in for half measures, either. At whichever end of the emotional rainbow, the excesses could be persuasive.

"The office manager was given the letter, and he got in his car and he carried it out to Ira. Ira had been living alone in Zinc Town since he'd been fired. Every week he'd drive to New York to confer with lawyers—he was going to sue the network, sue the sponsor, sue *Red Channels*. In the city he'd stop by and visit Artie Sokolow, who'd had his first heart attack and was confined to bed at home on the Upper West Side. Then he'd come to Newark to see us. But by and large Ira was out at the shack, infuriated, brooding, devastated, obsessed, making dinner for his neighbor who'd been in the mining accident, Ray Svecz, eating with him and sounding off about his case to this guy who was fifty-one percent not there.

"It was later on the day that Eve's letter was delivered to him that Ira shows up at my office, and I read it. It's in my file with the rest of Ira's papers; I can't do it justice by paraphrasing it. Three pages long. Scorchingly written. Obviously zipped off in one draft and perfect. Real bite to it, a ferocious document, and yet very competently done. Under the pressure of her rage, and on monogrammed blue note paper, Eve was quite the neo-classicist. I wouldn't have been surprised had that lambasting of him concluded in a fanfare of heroic couplets.

"Remember Hamlet cursing out Claudius? The passage in the second act, just after the player-king gives his speech about Priam's slaughter? It's in the middle of the monologue that begins 'O what a rogue and peasant slave am I!' 'Bloody, bawdy villain!' Hamlet says. 'Remorseless, treacherous, lecherous, kindless villain! / O! Vengeance!' Well, the gist of Eve's letter is more or less along those lines: You know what Pamela means to me, I confided one night to you, and to you alone, all that Pamela means to me. 'An inferiority complex.' That's what Eve described as Pamela's problem. A girl with an inferiority complex, far from home and country and family, Eve's ward, Eve's responsibility to look after and protect, and yet, just as he uglified everything he had ever laid his hands on, he cunningly undertook to turn a girl of Pamela Solomon's background into a striptease artist like Miss Donna Jones. To lure Pamela out to that isolated hellhole under false pretenses, to salivate like a pervert over her picture in her bathing suit, to fasten those gorilla paws of his on her defenseless body—for the sheer pleasure of it, to turn Pamela into a common whore, and to humiliate Sylphid and herself in the most sadistic way he could contrive.

"But this time, she told him, you went too far. I remember your telling me, she said, how, at the feet of the great O'Day, you had marveled at Machiavelli's *The Prince.* Now I understand what you learned from *The Prince.* I understand why my friends have been trying for years to convince me that in every last thing you say or do, you are, to the letter, a ruthless, depraved Machiavellian who cares not at all for right or wrong but worships only success. You try to force to have sex with you this lovely, talented young woman struggling with an inferiority complex. Why didn't you try having sex with me as a means, perhaps, of expressing love? When we met, you were living alone on the Lower East Side in the squalid arms of your beloved lumpenproletariat. I gave you a beautiful house full of books and music and art. I provided you with a handsome study of your own and helped you to build up your library. I introduced you to the most interesting, intelligent, talented people in Manhattan, offered you entrée into a social world such as you'd never dreamed of for yourself. As best I could, I tried to give you a family. Yes, I have a demanding daughter. I have a troubled daughter. I know that. Well, life is full of demands. For a responsible adult, life *is* demands . . . On and on in that vein, uphill all the way, philosophical, mature, sensible, wholeheartedly rational—until she ended with the threat:

"Since you may recall that your paragon brother wouldn't allow me to talk to you or to write to you when you were hiding in his house, I went through your comrades to reach you. The Communist Party would appear to have more access to you—and your heart, such as it is—than anyone. You *are* Machiavelli, the quintessential artist of control. Well, my dear Machiavelli, since you don't seem to have understood yet the consequences of anything you have ever done to another human being in order to have your way, it may be time you were taught.

"Nathan, remember the chair in my office, beside my desk—the hot seat? Where you kids sat and sweated while I used to go over your compositions? That's where Ira sat while I went over that letter. I asked, 'Is it true you made a pass at this girl?' 'For six months I had an affair with this girl.' 'You fucked her.' 'Many times, Murray. I thought she was in love with me. I'm astonished that she could do this.' 'Are you now?' 'I was in love with her. I wanted to marry her and have a family with her.' 'Oh, it gets better. You don't think, do you, Ira? You act. You act, and that's it. You shout, you fuck, you act. For six months you fucked her daughter's best friend. Her surrogate daughter. Her *ward*. And now something happened and you're "astonished."' 'I loved her.' 'Speak English. You loved fucking her.' 'You don't understand. She'd come to the shack. I was *mad* for her. I *am* astonished. I am absolutely astonished by what she has done!' 'By what *she* has done.' 'She betrays me to my wife—and then she lies in the process!' 'Yes? So? Where's the astonishing part? You've got a problem here. You've got a big problem with that wife.' 'Do I? What's she going to do? She did it already, with her pals the Grants. I'm fired already. I'm out on my ass. She's making it into a sexual thing, you see, and it wasn't that. Pamela knows that isn't what it was.' 'Well, that's what it is now. You're caught, and your wife is promising *new* consequences. What will those be, do you think?' 'Nothing. There's nothing left. This stupidity,' he said, waving the letter at me, 'a letter hand-delivered by her to the *Worker. This* is the consequence. Listen to me. I never did a thing Pamela didn't want. And when she didn't want me anymore, it killed me. I dreamed of a girl like this all my life. It *killed* me. But I did it. I walked down those stairs and out into the street and I left her alone. I never bothered her again.' 'Well,' I said, 'be that as it may, honorable as you were in gentlemanly taking your leave of six months of fancy fucking with your wife's surrogate daughter, you're in a bit of hot water now, my friend.' 'No, it's *Pamela* who's in hot water!' 'Yes? You going to *act* again? You going to act once *again* without thinking? No. I'm not going to let you.'

"And I didn't let him, and he didn't do anything. Now, how much impetus writing this letter gave Eve to rush into the book is hard to say. But if Eve was in search of a motive to really go all out and do the big irrational thing that she'd been born to do, the stuff she got from Pamela couldn't have hurt. You would think that having married a cipher like Mueller, followed by a homosexual like Pennington, followed by a sharpie like Freedman, followed by a Communist like Ira, she'd have fulfilled whatever obligation she had to the forces of unreason. You would think she might have worked off the worst of 'How-could-you-do-this-to-me?' just by going over to the *Worker* in her lynx jacket with the matching muff. But no, it was Eve's destiny always to take her irrationality to greater and greater heights—and this is where the Grants come in again.

"It was the Grants who wrote that book. It was *double* ghostwritten. It was Bryden's name they used on the jacket—'as told to Bryden Grant'—because that was almost as good as having Winchell's name on the jacket, but it's the talent of the pair of them that shines through. What did Eve Frame know about Communism? There were Communists at the Wallace rallies she'd gone to with Ira. There were Communists on *The Free and the Brave,* people who came to their house and had dinner and were at all the soirées. This little unit of people involved with the show was very interested in controlling as much of it as possible. There was the secrecy, the conspiratorial edge—hiring like-minded people, influencing the ideological bias of the script however they could. Ira would sit in his study with Artie Sokolow and try to force into the script every corny party cliché, every so-called progressive sentiment they could get away with, manipulating the script to stick whatever ideological junk they thought of as Communist content into any historical context whatsoever. They imagined they were going to influence public thinking. *The writer must not only observe and describe but participate in the struggle. The non-Marxist writer betrays the objective reality; the Marxist one contributes to its transformation. The party's gift to the writer is the only right and true worldview.* They believed all that. Crapola. Propaganda. But crapola is not forbidden by the Constitution. And the radio in those days was full of it. *Gangbusters. Your FBI.* Kate Smith singing 'God Bless America.' Even your hero Corwin—propagandist for an idealized American democracy. In the end it wasn't so different. They weren't espionage agents, Ira Ringold and Arthur Sokolow. They were publicity agents. There is a distinction. These guys were cheap propagandists, against which the only laws are aesthetic, laws of literary taste.

"Then there was the union, AFTRA, the battle for control of the union. A lot of shouting, terrible infighting, but that was nationwide. In my union, in virtually every union, it was right wingers and left wingers, liberals and Communists struggling for control. Ira was a member of the union executive board, he was on the phone with people, God knows he could shout. Sure, things were said in her presence. And what Ira said, he meant. The party was no debating society to Ira. It was not a discussion club. It wasn't the Civil Liberties Union. What does it mean, 'a revolution'? It means a revolution. He took the rhetoric seriously. You can't call yourself a revolutionary and not be serious in your commitment. It was not something fake. It was something genuine. He took the Soviet Union seriously. At AFTRA, Ira meant business.

"Now, I never saw Ira at most of this stuff. I'm sure *you* never saw

Ira at most of this stuff. But Eve never saw *anything* of this stuff. She was oblivious to *all* of it. Actuality wasn't something that mattered to Eve. The woman's mind was rarely on what the people around her were saying. She was a complete stranger to the business of life. It was too coarse for her. Her mind was never on Communism or anti-Communism. Her mind was never on anything present, except when Sylphid was present.

"'As told to' meant that the whole malevolent story was dreamed up by the Grants. And dreamed up not at all for Eve's sake, and not merely to destroy Ira, much as Katrina and Bryden hated his guts. The consequences for Ira were part of their fun but largely beside the point. The Grants dreamed it all up for Bryden to ride his way into the House on the issue of Communism in broadcasting.

"That writing. That *Journal-American* prose. Plus Katrina's syntax. Plus Katrina's sensibility. *Her* fingerprints are all over the thing. I knew right off that Eve hadn't written it, because Eve couldn't write that badly. Eve was too literate and too well read. Why did she allow the Grants to write her book? Because systematically she made herself the slave of just about everyone. Because what the strong are capable of is appalling, and what the weak are capable of is also appalling. It's all appalling.

"*I Married a Communist* came out in March of '52, when Grant had already announced his candidacy, and then in November, in the Eisenhower landslide, he was swept into the House as representative from New York's Twenty-ninth District. He would have been elected anyway. That radio show of theirs was a big Saturday morning favorite, and for years he had that column, and he had Ham Fish behind him, and he was a Grant, after all, the descendant of a U.S. president. Still, I doubt that Joe McCarthy himself would have traveled up to Dutchess County to appear by his side if it hadn't been for all the big-shot Reds 'Grant's Grapevine' had helped to expose and root out of the networks. Everyone was in Poughkeepsie campaigning for him. Westbrook Pegler was up there. All those Hearst columnists were his pals. All the haters of FDR who'd found in the Communist smear a way to drive the Democrats into the ground. Either Eve had no idea what she was being used for by the Grants or, more likely, she knew but didn't care, because the experience of being an attacker made her feel so strong and brave, striking back at the monsters at last.

"Yet knowing Ira as she did, how could she publish this book and not expect him to do something? This wasn't a three-page letter to Zinc Town. This was a big national best-seller that made a bang. The thing had all the ingredients to become a best-seller: Eve was famous, Grant was famous, Communism was *the* international peril. Ira was himself less famous than either of them, and though the book would guarantee that he would never work in radio again and that his accidental career was over, for the five or six months the book was at the top of the charts, for that season, Ira was conspicuous as he'd never been before. In a single stroke Eve managed to depersonalize her own life while endowing the specter of Communism with a human face—her husband's. I married a Communist, I slept with a Communist, a Communist tormented my child, unsuspectingly America listened to a Communist, disguised as a patriot, on network radio. A wicked two-faced villain, the real names of real stars, a big Cold War backdrop—of course it became a best-seller. Her indictment of Ira was of the sort that could win a large public hearing in the fifties.

"And it didn't hurt to name all the other Jewish Bolsheviks affiliated with Ira's show. The Cold War paranoia had latent anti-Semitism as one of its sources, and so, under the moral guidance of the Grants—who themselves loved the ubiquitous troublemaking left-wing Jew just about as much as Richard Nixon did—Eve could transform a personal prejudice into a political weapon by confirming for Gentile America that, in New York as in Hollywood, in radio as in movies, the Communist under every rock was, nine times out of ten, a Jew to boot.

"But did she imagine that this openly aggressive hothead was going to do nothing in response? This guy who used to have these ferocious arguments at her dinner table, who used to storm around their living room shouting at people, who, after all, *was* a Communist, who knew what it was to take political action, who'd tenaciously gained control of his union, who'd managed to rewrite Sokolow's scripts, to bully a bully like Artie Sokolow—she thought he was now going to take *no* action? Didn't she know him at all? What about the portrait in her book? If he's Machiavelli, then he's Machiavelli. Everybody run for cover.

"I'm really angry, she thinks, I'm angry about Pamela and I'm angry about Helgi and I'm furious about the renovation of the shack and all the other crimes against Sylphid, and I'm going to get the attention of this lecherous, heartless Machiavellian bastard. Well, damn right she got his attention. But surely the obvious thing about getting Ira's attention by sticking a hot poker up his ass in public is that you're going to enrage him. People don't yield to that kind of shit cheerfully. People don't like seeing exposés on the best-seller list that falsely denounce them, and you wouldn't even have to be Ira Ringold to take umbrage. And to take action. Only that never occurs to her. The righteous resentment that fuels her project, the *blamelessness* that fuels her project can't imagine anybody doing anything to her. All she has done is to settle the score. Ira did all the horrible things—she is merely coming back with her side of the story. She gets last licks, and the only consequences she imagines are consequences she deserves. It has to be that way— what did *she* do?

"That same self-blinding that led to so much pain with Pennington, with Freedman, with Sylphid, with Pamela, with the Grants, even with Helgi Pärn—in the end, that self-blinding was the worm that destroyed her. It's what the high school Shakespeare teacher calls the tragic flaw.

"A great cause had taken possession of Eve: her own. Her cause, presented in the grandiose guise of a selfless battle to save America from the Red tide. Everybody has a failed marriage—she herself has four of them. But she also has the need to be special. A star. She wants to show that she also is important, that she has a brain and that she has the power to fight. Who is this actor Iron Rinn? *I* am the actor! *I* am the one with the name, and I possess the *power* of the name! I am not this weak woman whom you can do anything you want to. I am a star, damn it! Mine isn't an ordinary failed marriage. It's a *star's* failed marriage! I didn't lose my husband because of the horrible trap I'm in with my daughter. I didn't lose my husband because of all those kneeling 'I implore you's.' I didn't lose my husband because of his drunken whore with the gold tooth. It has to be grander than that—and I must be blameless. The refusal to own up to what it is in the human dimension turns it into something melodramatic and false and sellable. I lost my husband to Communism.

"And what that book was really about, actually accomplishing, Eve hadn't the faintest idea. Why was Iron Rinn served up to the public as a dangerous Soviet espionage agent? To get another Republican elected to the House. To get Bryden Grant into the House and put Joe Martin into the speaker's chair.

"Grant was ultimately elected eleven times. A considerable personage in Congress. And Katrina became *the* Republican hostess of Washington, the sovereign of social authority throughout the Eisenhower years. For someone riddled with envy and conceit, no position in the world could have been more rewarding than deciding who sat across from Roy Cohn. In the hierarchical anxieties of the Washington dinner party, Katrina's capacity for rivalry, the sheer cannibal vigor of her taste for supremacy—for awarding and depriving the ruling class itself of their just desserts—found its . . . imperium, I think the word would be. That woman drew up an invitation list with the autocratic sadism of Caligula. *She* knew the enjoyment of humiliating the powerful. *She* sent a tremor or two through that capital. Under Eisenhower and again, later, under Bryden's mentor Nixon, Katrina straddled Washington society like fear itself.

"In '69, when there was that spurt of speculation that Nixon was going to find Grant a place in the White House, the congressman husband and the hostess-novelist wife made the cover of *Life*. No, Grant never got to be Haldeman, but at the end, he too was capsized by Watergate. Threw his lot in with Nixon and, in the face of all the evidence against his leader, defended him on the floor of the House right down to the morning of the resignation. That's what got Grant defeated in '74. But then, he'd been emulating Nixon from the start. Nixon had Alger Hiss, Grant had Iron Rinn. To catapult them into political eminence, each of them had a Soviet spy.

"I saw Katrina on C-SPAN at the Nixon funeral. Grant had died some years before and she's died since. She was my age, maybe a year or two older. But out there at the funeral at Yorba Linda, with the flag waving at half-mast among the palm trees, and Nixon's birthplace in the background, she was still our Katrina, white-haired and wizened but still very much a force for the good, chatting it up with Barbara Bush and Betty Ford and Nancy Reagan. Life seemed never to have forced her to acknowledge, let alone to surrender, a single one of her pretensions. Still wholeheartedly determined to be the national authority in rectitude, stringent in the extreme about the right thing's being done. Saw her talking there to Senator Dole, our other great moral beacon. She didn't look to me to have relinquished one bit the idea that every word she spoke was of the utmost importance. Still oblivious to the intro-spection of silence. Still the righteous watchdog over everyone else's integrity. And unrepentant. Divinely unrepentant and brandishing that preposterous self-image. For stupidity, you know, there is no cure. The woman is the very embodiment of moral ambition, and the perniciousness of it, and the folly of it.

"All that mattered to the Grants was how to make Ira serve their cause. And what *was* their cause? America? Democracy? If ever patriotism was a pretext for self-seeking, for self-devotion, for self-adoration . . . You know, we learn from Shakespeare that in telling a story you cannot relax your imaginative sympathy for any charac-ter. But I am not Shakespeare, and I still despise that hatchet man and his hatchet wife for what they did to my brother—and did so effortlessly, employing Eve the way you do a dog to fetch the paper from the front porch. Remember what Gloucester says of old Lear? 'The king is in high rage.' I came down with a bad case of high rage myself when I spotted Katrina Van Tassel at Yorba Linda. I told myself, She's nothing, nobody, a bit player. In the vast history of twentieth-century ideological malevolence, she's played a clownish walk-on role and no more. But it was still barely endurable for me to watch her.

"But the whole funeral of our thirty-seventh president was barely endurable. The Marine Band and Chorus performing all the songs designed to shut down people's thinking and produce a trance state: 'Hail to the Chief,' 'America,' 'You're a Grand Old Flag,' 'The Battle Hymn of the Republic,' and, to be sure, that most rousing of all those drugs that make everybody momentarily forget everything, the national narcotic, 'The Star-Spangled Banner.' Nothing like the elevating remarks of Billy Graham, a flag-draped casket, and a team of interracial pallbearing servicemen—and the whole thing topped off by 'The Star-Spangled Banner,' followed hard upon by a twenty-one-gun salute and 'Taps'—to induce catalepsy in the multitude.

"Then the realists take command, the connoisseurs of deal making and deal breaking, masters of the most shameless ways of undoing an opponent, those for whom moral concerns must always come last, uttering all the well-known, unreal, sham-ridden cant about everything but the dead man's real passions. Clinton exalting Nixon for his 'remarkable journey' and, under the spell of his own sincerity, expressing hushed gratitude for all the 'wise counsel' Nixon had given him. Governor Pete Wilson assuring everyone that when most people think of Richard Nixon, they think of his 'towering intellect.' Dole and his flood of lachrymose clichés. 'Doctor' Kissinger, high-minded, profound, speaking in his most puffed-up unegoistical mode—and with all the cold authority of that voice dipped in sludge—quotes no less prestigious a tribute than Hamlet's for his murdered father to describe 'our gallant friend.' 'He was a man, take him for all and all, I shall not look upon his like again.' Literature is not a primary reality but a kind of expensive upholstery to a sage himself so plumply upholstered, and so he has no idea of the equivocating context in which Hamlet speaks of the unequaled king. But then who, sitting there under the tremendous pressure of sustaining a straight face while watching the enactment of the Final Cover-up, is going to catch the court Jew in a cultural gaffe when he invokes an inappropriate masterpiece? Who is there to advise him that it's not Hamlet on his father he ought to be quoting but Hamlet on his uncle, Claudius, Hamlet on the conduct of the new king, his father's usurping murderer? Who there at Yorba Linda dares to call out, 'Hey, Doctor—quote *this*: 'Foul deeds will rise / Though all the earth o'erwhelm them, to men's eyes'?

"Who? Gerald Ford? Gerald Ford. I don't ever remember seeing Gerald Ford looking so focused before, so charged with intelligence as he clearly was on that hallowed ground. Ronald Reagan snapping the uniformed honor guard his famous salute, that salute of his that was *always* half meshugeh. Bob Hope seated next to James Baker. The Iran-Contra arms dealer Adnan Khashoggi seated next to Donald Nixon. The burglar G. Gordon Liddy there with his arrogant shaved head. The most disgraced of vice presidents, Spiro Agnew, there with his conscienceless Mob face. The most winning of vice presidents, sparkly Dan Quayle, looking as lucid as a button. The heroic effort made by that poor fellow: always staging intelligence and always failing. All of them mourning platitudinously together in the California sunshine and the lovely breeze: the indicted and the unindicted, the convicted and the unconvicted, and, his towering intellect at last at rest in a star-spangled coffin, no longer grappling and questing for no-holds-barred power, the man who turned a whole country's morale inside out, the generator of an enormous national disaster, the first and only president of the United States of America to have gained from a handpicked successor a full and unconditional pardon for all the breaking and entering he committed while in office.

"And Van Tassel Grant, adored widow of Bryden, *that* selfless public servant, reveling in her importance and jabbering away. All through the service, the mouth of reckless malice jabbering on and on in her televised grief over our great national loss. Too bad she wasn't born in China instead of the USA. Here she had to settle for being a best-selling novelist and a famous radio personality and a top-drawer Washington hostess. There she could have run Mao's Cultural Revolution.

"In my ninety years I've witnessed two sensationally hilarious funerals, Nathan. Present at the first as a thirteen-year-old, and the second I saw on TV just three years ago, at the age of eighty-seven. Two funerals that have more or less bracketed my conscious life. They aren't mysterious events. They don't require a genius to ferret out their meaning. They are just natural human events that reveal as plainly as Daumier did the unique markings of the species, the thousand and one dualities that twist its nature into the human knot. The first was Mr. Russomanno's funeral for the canary, when the cobbler got hold of a casket and pallbearers and a horse-drawn hearse and majestically buried his beloved Jimmy—and my kid brother broke my nose. The second was when they buried Richard Milhous Nixon with a twenty-one-gun salute. I only wish the Italians from the old First Ward could have been out there at Yorba Linda with Dr. Kissinger and Billy Graham. *They* would have known how to enjoy the spectacle. They would have hurled themselves on the ground with laughter when they heard what those two guys were up to, the indignities to which they descended to dignify that glaringly impure soul.

"And had Ira been alive to hear them, he would have gone nuts all over again at the world getting everything wrong."

8

"ALL HIS RANTING Ira now directed at himself. How could this farce have wrecked his life? Everything to the side of the main thing, all the peripheral stuff of existence that Comrade O'Day had warned him against. Home. Marriage. Family. Mistresses. Adultery. All the bourgeois shit! Why hadn't he lived like O'Day? Why hadn't he gone to prostitutes like O'Day? *Real* prostitutes, trustworthy professionals who understand the rules, and not blabbermouth amateurs like his Estonian masseuse.

"The recriminations started to hound him. He should never have left O'Day, have left the UE shop at the record factory, have come to New York, married Eve Frame, grandiosely conceived of himself as this Mr. Iron Rinn. In Ira's own estimation he should never have done *any* of the living he did once he left the Midwest. He shouldn't have had a human being's appetite for experience or a human being's inability to read the future or a human being's propensity for making mistakes. He shouldn't have allowed himself to pursue a single one of a virile and ambitious man's worldly goals. Being a Communist laborer dwelling alone in a room in East Chicago under a sixty-watt bulb—that was now the ascetic height from which he had fallen into hell.

"The pile-on of humiliation, that was the key to it. It wasn't as though a book had been thrown at him—the book was a bomb that had been thrown at him. McCarthy, you see, would have the two hundred or three hundred or four hundred Communists on his nonexistent lists, but allegorically one person would have to stand for them all. Alger Hiss is the biggest example. Three years after Hiss, Ira became another. What's more, Hiss to the average person was still the State Department and Yalta, stuff far, far away from the ordinary Joe, while Ira's was popular-culture Communism. To the confused popular imagination, this was the democratic Communist. This was Abe Lincoln. It was very easy to grasp: Abe Lincoln as the villainous representative of a foreign power, Abe Lincoln as America's greatest twentieth-century traitor. Ira became the personification of Communism, the personalized Communist for the nation: Iron Rinn was Everyman's Communist traitor in ways that Alger Hiss could never be.

"Here's this giant who was pretty damn strong, in many ways pretty damn insensitive, but the calumny heaped upon him he finally couldn't take. Giants get felled too. He knew he couldn't hide from it and he thought, as time passed, he could never wait it out. He began to think that now that the lid was off there would always be something coming at him from somewhere. The giant couldn't find anything effectual to deal with it, and that's when he caved in.

"I went up and got him, and he lived with us until we couldn't handle the situation anymore, and I put him in the hospital in New York. He sat in that chair for the first month, rubbing his knees and rubbing his elbows and holding his ribs where they ached, but otherwise lifeless, staring into his lap and wishing he were dead. I'd go to see him and he would barely speak. Every once in a while he'd say, 'All I wanted to do . . .' That was it. Never went any further, not out loud. That was all he said to me for weeks. A couple of times he muttered, 'To be like this . . .' 'I never intended . . .' But mostly it was 'All I wanted to do . . .'

"They didn't have much to help mental patients in those days. No pills other than a sedative. Ira wouldn't eat. He sat in that first unit—the Disturbed Unit, they called it—eight beds there and Ira in his robe and pajamas and slippers, looking more like Lincoln with each passing day. Gaunt, exhausted, wearing Abraham Lincoln's mask of sorrow. I would be visiting, sitting beside him holding his hand and thinking, If it weren't for that resemblance, none of this would have happened to him. If only he hadn't been responsible to his looks.

"It was four weeks before they moved him up to the Semi-Disturbed Unit, where the patients got dressed in their clothes, and they had recreational therapy. Some of them went off to play volleyball or to play basketball, though Ira couldn't because of his joint pain. He had been living for over a year with pain that was intractable, and maybe that undid him more than the calumny. Maybe the antagonist who destroyed Ira was physical pain, and the book would not have come close to defeating him if he hadn't been undermined by his health.

"The collapse was total. The hospital was awful. But we couldn't have kept him at the house. He would lie in Lorraine's room cursing himself and crying his heart out: O'Day told him, O'Day warned him, O'Day had known back on the docks in Iran . . . Doris sat beside Lorraine's bed and she held him in her arms and he wailed away. All of the force that was behind those tears. Awful. You don't realize how much plain old misery can be backed up inside a titanically defiant person who's been taking on the world and battling his own nature his whole life. That's what came pouring out of him: the whole damn struggle.

"Sometimes *I* felt terrified. I felt the way I felt in the war when we were under bombardment at the Bulge. Just *because* he was so big and arrogant you had the feeling that there was nothing to be done for him by anyone. I saw that long, gaunt face of his, distorted with desperation, with all that hopelessness, with *failure*, and I was myself in a panic.

"When I would get home from school I'd help him dress; every afternoon I'd force him to shave and I'd insist on his going for a walk with me down Bergen Street. Could any city street in America have been friendlier in those days? But Ira was surrounded by enemies. The marquee on the Park Theater frightened him, the salamis in Kartzman's window frightened him—Schachtman's candy store frightened him, with the newsstand out front. He was sure every paper had his story in it, weeks after the papers had finished having their fun with him. The *Journal-American* ran excerpts from Eve's book. The *Daily Mirror* had his kisser all over the front page. Even the stately *Times* couldn't resist. Ran a human-interest story about the suffering of the Sarah Bernhardt of the Airwaves, took all that crap about Russian espionage completely seriously.

"But that's what happens. Once the human tragedy has been completed, it gets turned over to the journalists to banalize into entertainment. Perhaps it's because the whole irrational frenzy burst right through our door and no newspaper's half-baked insinuating detail passed me by that I think of the McCarthy era as inaugurating the postwar triumph of gossip as the unifying credo of the world's oldest democratic republic. In Gossip We Trust. Gossip as gospel, the national faith. McCarthyism as the beginning not just of serious politics but of serious *everything* as entertainment to amuse the mass audience. McCarthyism as the first postwar flowering of the American unthinking that is now everywhere.

"McCarthy was never in the Communist business; if nobody else knew that, he did. The show-trial aspect of McCarthy's patriotic crusade was merely its theatrical form. Having cameras view it just gave it the false authenticity of real life. McCarthy understood better than any American politician before him that people whose job was to legislate could do far better for themselves by performing; McCarthy understood the entertainment value of disgrace and how to feed the pleasures of paranoia. He took us back to our origins, back to the seventeenth century and the stocks. That's how the country began: moral disgrace as public entertainment. McCarthy was an impresario, and the wilder the views, the more outrageous the charges, the greater the disorientation and the better the all-around fun. *Joe McCarthy's The Free and the Brave—that* was the show in which my brother was to play the biggest role of his life.

"When not just the New York papers but the Jersey papers, too, joined in—well, for Ira that was the killer. They dug up whomever Ira knew out in Sussex County and got them to talk. Farmers, oldsters, local nobodies the radio star had befriended, and they all had a story about Ira coming around to tell them about the evils of capitalism. He had that great geezer pal out in Zinc Town, the taxidermist, and Ira liked to go around and listen to the guy, and the papers went to the taxidermist and the taxidermist gave them an earful. Ira couldn't believe it. But this taxidermist allows how Ira had pulled the wool over his eyes until one day when Ira came in with some young kid and the two of them tried to turn him and his son against the Korean War. Spewing real venom against General Douglas MacArthur. Calling the U.S.A. every bad name in the book.

"The FBI had a field day with him. And with Ira's reputation up there. To stake you out, to ruin you in your community, to go to your neighbors and have them do you in . . . I have to tell you, Ira always suspected that it was the taxidermist who fingered *you*. You were with Ira, weren't you, at the taxidermy shop?"

"I was. Horace Bixton," I said. "Little tiny, humorous fellow. Gave me a deer toe for a present. I sat one morning watching a fox being skinned."

"Well, you paid for that deer toe. Watching 'em skin that fox cost you your Fulbright."

I started to laugh. "Did you say turning his *son* against the war too? The son was stone deaf. The son was deaf and he was dumb. He couldn't hear a goddamn thing."

"This is the McCarthy era—didn't matter. Ira had a neighbor down the road, a zinc miner who'd been in a bad mining accident and who used to work for him. Ira spent a lot of time listening to these guys complain about New Jersey Zinc and trying to turn them around about the system, and this particular guy who was his neighbor, who he used to feed all the time, was the one the taxidermist got to take down the license plate numbers of whoever stopped at Ira's shack."

"I met the guy who'd been in the accident. He ate with us," I said.

"Ray. A rock fell on him and crushed his skull. Raymond Svecz. He'd been a POW. Ray used to do odd jobs for Ira."

"I guess Ray did odd jobs for everyone," Murray said. "He'd take down the license plate numbers of Ira's visitors and the taxidermist gave them to the FBI. The plates that turned up most often were mine, and that evidence they also used against me—that I visited my Communist-spy brother so much, sometimes even overnight. Only one guy up there stayed loyal to Ira. Tommy Minarek."

"I met Tommy."

"Charming old guy. Uneducated but an intelligent man. Had backbone. Ira took Lorraine out to the rock dump one day and Tommy gave her some stuff for free and he was all she talked about when she got home. After Tommy saw the news in the papers, he drove over to the shack and he marched straight in. 'If I had the guts,' he said to Ira, 'I woulda been a Communist myself.'

"Tommy was the one who rehabilitated Ira. It was Tommy who brought him out of his brooding and got him back into the world. Tommy had him sit right beside him out at the rock dump where he ran things so that people could see Ira there. Tommy was somebody the town respected, and so over time, people up there forgave Ira for being a Communist. Not all of them, but most. The two of them sat at the rock dump talking for three, four years together, Tommy teaching Ira all he knew about minerals. Then Tommy had a stroke and died and left his cellar full of rocks to Ira, and Ira took over Tommy's job. And the town let him. Ira sat out there, hyper-inflammatory Ira rubbing his aching joints and muscles, and ran the Zinc Town rock dump till the day *he* died. In the sunshine, a summer day, selling minerals, keeled over dead."

I wondered if Ira ever bled himself of the resolve to be argumentative, contrary, defiant, to be illegitimate when necessary, or if that all still burned on in him while he sold Tommy's specimens out front of the rock dump, across the highway from the machine shop where they had the toilet. Burned on, more than likely; in Ira everything burned on. No one in this world had less talent for frustration than Ira or was worse at controlling his moods. The rage to take action—and selling kids fifty-cent bags of rocks instead. Sitting there till he died, wanting to be something entirely different, believing that by virtue of personal attributes (his size, his animus, the father he'd suffered) he had been *destined* to be something different. Furious to have no outlet for changing the world. The embitterment of that bondage. How he must have choked on it, employing now to destroy himself his inexhaustible capacity never to desist.

"Ira would come back from Bergen Street," Murray said, "from walking past Schachtman's newsstand, a worse wreck than when he'd left the house, and Lorraine couldn't take it. Seeing her great big uncle, with whom she'd sung the song of the common worker, 'Heave-ho, heave-ho'—seeing him humbled like that was too much for her, and so we had to put him into the hospital over in New York.

"He imagined he'd ruined O'Day. He was sure he had ruined everybody whose name and address were in those two little diaries Eve had turned over to Katrina, and he was right. But O'Day was still his idol, and those letters from O'Day that were quoted piecemeal in the papers after they showed up in her book—well, Ira was sure this was the end of O'Day, and the shame of it was awful.

"I tried to contact Johnny O'Day. I'd met the guy. I knew how close they'd been in the army. I remembered when Ira was his sidekick in Calumet City. I didn't like the man, I didn't like his ideas, I didn't like his blend of superiority and cunning, that moral pass he thought he'd been given as a Communist, but I couldn't believe that he was holding Ira responsible for what had happened. I believed that O'Day could take good care of himself, that he was strong and ruthless in his principled Communistic uncaringness, as Ira had turned out not to be. I wasn't wrong, either. Out of desperation, I figured that if anybody could bring Ira around, it would be O'Day.

"But I couldn't get a phone number. He wasn't listed any longer in Gary or Hammond or East Chicago or Calumet City or up in Chicago. When I wrote to the last address Ira had for him, the envelope came back marked 'No such person at this address.' I telephoned every union office in Chicago, I phoned left-wing bookstores, phoned every outfit I could think of, trying to hunt him down. Just when I'd given up, the phone at home rang one night, and it was him.

"What did I want? I told him where Ira was. I told him what Ira was like. I said that if he would be willing to come east on the weekend and go to the hospital and sit with Ira, just sit there with him, I would wire the money for the train and he could stay overnight in Newark with us. I didn't like doing it, but I was trying to entice him, and so I said, 'You mean a lot to Ira. He always wanted to be worthy of O'Day's admiration. I think you might be able to help him.'

"And then, in that quiet, explicit way of his, in the voice of one tough, unreachable son of a bitch with a single overriding relationship to life, he answered me. 'Look, Professor,' he told me, 'your brother tricked me damn good and proper. I always prided myself that I knew who is phony and who ain't. But this time I was fooled. The party, the meetings—all a cover for his personal ambition. Your brother used the party to climb to his professional position, then he betrayed it. If he was a Red with guts, he would have stayed where the fight is, which is not in New York in Greenwich Village. But all Ira ever cared about was everybody thinking what a hero he was. Always impersonating and never the real thing. Because he was tall, that made him Lincoln? Because he spouted "the masses, the masses, the masses," that made him a revolutionary? He wasn't a revolutionary, he wasn't a Lincoln, he wasn't anything. He wasn't a man—he impersonates being a man along with everything else. Impersonates being a *great* man. The guy impersonates everything. He throws off one disguise and becomes something else. No, your brother isn't as straight as he'd like people to think. Your brother is not a very committed guy, except when it comes to the commitment to himself. He's a fake and he's a dope and he's a traitor. Betrayed his revolutionary comrades and betrayed the working class. Sold out. Bought off. Totally the creature of the bourgeoisie.

Seduced by fame and money and wealth and power. And pussy, fancy Hollywood pussy. Doesn't retain a vestige of his revolutionary ideology—nothing. An opportunistic stooge. Probably an opportunistic stoolie. You're going to tell me he left that stuff in his desk by accident? A guy in the party leaves that by accident? Or was something worked out, Professor, with the FBI? Too bad he's not in the Soviet Union—they know how to handle traitors. I don't want to hear from him and I don't want to see him. Because if I ever do see him, tell him to watch out. Tell him that no matter how thick he butters it with rationalizations, there's going to be blood on the bricks.'

"That was it. Blood on the bricks. I didn't even try to answer. Who would dare to explain the failure of purity to a militant who was only and always pure? Never in his life had O'Day been this with this one, and that with that one, and a third person with somebody else. He does not share in the fickleness of all creatures. The ideologue is purer than the rest of us because he is the ideologue with everyone. I hung up.

"God knows how long Ira might have languished in the Semi-Disturbed Unit if it hadn't been for Eve. Visitors weren't encouraged and he didn't want to see anybody anyway, aside from me and Doris, but one evening Eve showed up. The doctor wasn't around, the nurse wasn't thinking, and when Eve announced herself as Ira's wife, the nurse pointed her down the corridor, and there she was. He was looking emaciated, still pretty lifeless, hardly talking at all, and so at the sight of him she started to cry. She said she'd come to say she was sorry but that just looking at him brought her to tears. She was sorry, he mustn't hate her, she couldn't live her life knowing he hated her. Terrible pressures had been exerted on her, he couldn't understand how terrible. She didn't want to do it. She did everything not to do it . . .

"With her face in her hands, she wept and she wept, until at last she told him what we all knew from reading one sentence of that book. She told Ira that the Grants had written it, every word.

"That's when Ira spoke. 'Why did you let them?' he said. 'They forced me to,' Eve told him. 'She threatened me, Ira. Loony. She's a vulgar, terrible woman. A terrible, terrible woman. I still love you. That's what I came to say. Let me say it, please. She couldn't make me stop loving you, ever. You must know that.' 'How did she threaten you?' It was the first time in weeks he was speaking consecutively in sentences. 'It isn't that she threatened only me,' Eve said. 'She did that too. She told me that I'd be finished if I didn't cooperate. She told me that Bryden would see to it that I never worked again. I'd wind up impoverished. When I still said no, told her, No, Katrina, no, I can't do it, I can't, no matter what he's done to me, I love him . . . that's when she said that if I didn't do it, Sylphid's career would be ruined at the start.'

"Well, all at once Ira became himself again. He hit the Semi-Disturbed Unit roof. It was pandemonium. Semi-disturbed is still semi-disturbed, and those guys in that room may have been playing basketball and playing volleyball but they were still a pretty fragile lot and a couple of them went haywire. Ira was shouting at the top of that voice of his, 'You did it for *Sylphid?* You did it for your daughter's *career?*' and Eve began to howl, 'Only *you* matter! Only *you!* What about my child! My child's talent!' One of the inmates is shouting, 'Beat the shit out of her! Beat the shit out of her!' and another one bursts into tears, and by the time the attendants get down the hall, Eve is facedown on the floor, hammering her fists and screaming, 'What about my daughter!'

"They put her in a straitjacket—that's what they used in those days. They didn't gag her, however, and so Eve just let it out, all of it. 'I said to Katrina, "No, you cannot squash that kind of talent." She would destroy *Sylphid*. I couldn't destroy Sylphid. I knew *you* couldn't destroy Sylphid. I was powerless. I was simply powerless! I gave her the least little bit I could. To placate her. Because Sylphid—that talent! It wouldn't be *right!* What mother in the *world* would let her child suffer? What mother would have done any differently, Ira? Answer me! To make my child suffer for the silliness of adults and their ideas and their attitudes? How can you put the blame on me? What choice did I have? You have no idea what I go through.

You have no idea what *any* mother would go through if someone says, "I am going to destroy your child's career." You never had children. You don't understand anything *about* parents and children. You had no parents and you have no children, and you don't know what the sacrifice is all about!'

"'I don't have children?' Ira screamed. They'd gotten her onto a stretcher and were already carrying her away by then, and so Ira ran after them, ran shouting down the hall, '*Why* don't I have children? Because of you! Because of you and your greedy, selfish fucking daughter!'

"They carted her away, something they'd apparently never had to do before with somebody who'd just come by for a visit. They sedated her and they put her in a bed in the Disturbed Unit, locked her up and wouldn't let her out of the hospital until the next morning, when they were able to locate Sylphid, and she turned up to take her mother home. What impulse had brought Eve to the hospital, whether there was any truth at all to what she'd come to say—that she was forced by the Grants to do this ugly thing—whether that was just the new lie, whether even her shame was real, we never knew for sure.

"Maybe it was. It certainly could have been. In those times, anything could have been. People were fighting for their lives. If it *was* true that's what happened, then Katrina was a genius, really, a genius of manipulation. Katrina knew exactly where to get her. Katrina gave Eve her choice of people to betray, and Eve, with her pretense of powerlessness, chose what she had no choice but to choose. One is consigned to be oneself, and no one more so than Eve Frame. She became the instrument of the Grants' will. She was run by those two just like an agent."

"Well, within a matter of days Ira was into the Quiet Unit, and the next week he was out, and then he really became . . .

"Well, maybe," Murray said after a moment's reflection, "he just achieved the old survival clarity he had digging ditches, before all the scaffolding of politics and home and success and fame got erected around him, before he buried the ditchdigger alive and donned Abe Lincoln's hat. Maybe he became himself again, the actor of his own way. Ira wasn't a superior artist brought down. Ira was just brought back to where he began.

"'Revenge.' He said it to me," Murray said, "as plain and calm as that. A thousand convicts, lifers, beating their bars with their spoons couldn't have put it better. 'Revenge.' Between the pleading pathos of defense and the compelling symmetry of revenge, there was no choice. I remember him slowly kneading those joints of his and telling me that he was going to ruin her. I remember him saying, 'Throwing her life into that daughterly toilet. Then throwing mine in with it. That doesn't go down with me. It's not just, Murray. It's degrading to me, Murray. I am her mortal enemy? Okay then, she is mine.'"

"*Did* he ruin her?" I asked.

"You know what happened to Eve Frame."

"I know she died. Of cancer. Didn't she? In the sixties?"

"She died, but not of cancer. Remember that picture I told you about, the photograph Ira got in the mail from one of Freedman's old girlfriends, the picture he was going to use to compromise Eve with? The picture I tore up? I should have let him use it."

"You said that before. Why?"

"Because what Ira was doing with that picture was looking for a way *not* to kill her. His whole life had been looking for a way not to kill somebody. When he got home from Iran, his whole life was an attempt to defuse the violent impulse. That picture—I didn't realize what it was a disguise for, what it meant. When I tore it up, when I prevented him from using *that* as his weapon, he said, 'Okay, you win,' and I went back to Newark stupidly thinking I'd accomplished something, and up in Zinc Town, out in the woods, he starts target shooting. He had knives up there. I drove back to see him the next week and he makes no attempt to hide anything. Too wild with his imaginings to hide anything. He's full of murder talk. 'The smell of gunfire,' he tells me, 'it's an aphrodisiac!' He's absolutely gone. I hadn't even known that he owned a gun. I didn't know what to do. At last I perceived their true affinity, the hopeless interlinking of Ira and Eve as embattled souls: each of them disastrously inclined toward that thing that knows no limits once it gets under way. His recourse to violence was the masculine correlate of her predisposition to hysteria—distinctive gender manifestations of the same waterfall.

"I told him to give me all the weapons he had. Either give them to me right away, or I'd get on the phone and call the police. 'I suffered as much as you did,' I told him. 'I suffered more than you did in that house because I had to face it first. For six years, by myself. You don't know anything. You think I don't know about wanting to pick up a gun and shoot somebody? Everything you want to do to her now I wanted to do when I was *six years old*. And then you came along. I took care of you, Ira. I stood between you and the worst of it for as long as I was at home.

"'You don't remember this. You were two, I was eight—and you know what happened? I never told you. You had enough humiliation to deal with. We had to move. We weren't living on Factory Street yet. You were a baby and we were living beneath the Lackawanna tracks. On Nassau. Eighteen Nassau Street, backing onto the tracks. Four rooms, no light, lots of noise. Sixteen-fifty a month, the landlord upped it to nineteen, we couldn't pay, and we were evicted.

"'You know what our father did after we moved out our belongings? You and Momma and I started pushing the stuff over to the two rooms on Factory Street, and he stayed behind in the empty old flat, and he squatted down and he took a crap in the middle of the kitchen. Our kitchen. A pile of his shit right in the middle of where we used to sit at the table and eat. He painted the walls with it. No brush. Didn't need one. Painted the shit on with his hands. Big strokes. Up, down, sidewise. When he finished all the rooms, he washed in the sink, and he left without even closing the door behind him. You know what the kids called me for months after that? Shitwalls. In those days everybody got a nickname. You they called Boo-hoo, me they called Shitwalls. That was our father's legacy to me, his big boy, his oldest son.

"'I protected you then, Ira, and I'm going to protect you now. I'm not going to let you do it. I found my civilizing path into life, and you found yours, and you are not going back on that now. Let me explain something that you don't appear to understand. Why you became a Communist in the first place. Has that never dawned on you? My civilizing path was books, college, teaching school, yours was O'Day and the party. I never bought your way. I *opposed* your way. But both ways were legitimate and both worked. But what's happened now, you don't understand either. They've told you that they've decided that Communism is not a way out of violence, that it is a program *for* violence. They've criminalized your politics and, in the bargain, criminalized you—and you are going to prove them right. They say you're a criminal, so you load up your gun and strap your knife to your thigh. You say, "Goddamn right I am! The smell of gunfire—it's an aphrodisiac!"' Nathan, I talked myself hoarse. But when you are with an enraged homicidal maniac, talking like this doesn't calm him down. It inflames him further. When you are with an enraged homicidal maniac, to start telling a story about childhood, complete with the floor plan of the apartment . . .

"Look," Murray said, "I haven't told you everything about Ira. Ira had already killed somebody. That's why he left Newark and headed for the sticks and worked in the mines when he was a kid. He was on the lam. I got him up to Sussex County, beyond the beyond in those days, but not so far that I couldn't check on him and help him and get him through that thing. I drove him myself and I gave him his new name and I hid him away. Gil Stephens. The first of Ira's new names.

"He worked in the mines till he thought they were after him. Not the cops, the Mob. I told you about Ritchie Boiardo, who ran the rackets in the First Ward. The gangster who owned the restaurant, the Vittorio Castle. Ira got wind that Boiardo's thugs were out looking for him. That's when he started riding the rails."

"What had he done?"

"Ira killed a guy with a shovel. Ira killed a guy when he was sixteen."

Ira killed a guy with a shovel. "Where?" I said. "How? What happened?"

"Ira was working at the Tavern as a busboy. It was a job he'd had for about six weeks when, one night, he finished up swabbing the floors at two, and he came out alone into the street and set off for the room he rented. He lived on a dinky little street way down by Dreamland Park, where they built the project after the war. He made the turn onto Meeker at Elizabeth Avenue and was headed down the dark street across from Weequahic Park, in the direction of Frelinghuysen Avenue, when a guy emerged from the shadows where Millman's hot dog stand used to be. Out of the shadows there, and he swung at him, aiming at his head, and he caught Ira on the shoulders with a shovel.

"It was one of the Italians from the ditchdigging gang where Ira had worked after he left school. Ira had quit digging ditches to bus tables at the Tavern because of all the trouble he kept having with this guy. It was 1929, the year the Tavern opened. He was going to try to get in on the ground floor and advance from busboy to waiter. That was the goal. I'd helped get him the job. The Italian was drunk and walloped him one, and Ira wrestled the shovel away from him and knocked his teeth out with it. Then he dragged him back of Millman's, back into that pitch-black parking lot. In your day, kids on dates used to park and neck back of Millman's, and that's where Ira beat this guy up.

"Guy's name was Strollo. Strollo was the big Jew hater on the ditchdigging gang. '*Mazzu' crist, giude' maledett'.*' Christ killer, nogood Jew . . . that stuff. Strollo specialized in it. Strollo was about ten years older than Ira and not small, a big guy almost Ira's size. Ira beat him on the head until he was unconscious and left him there. He threw down Strollo's shovel and walked back out into the street and started home again, but something in him wasn't finished. Something in Ira was *never* finished. He's sixteen and forceful and full of rage, he's hot and sweaty and worked up and excited—he's *aroused*—and so he turns around and goes back of Millman's and he beats Strollo over the head until the guy is dead."

Millman's was where Ira used to take me for a hot dog after our walks in Weequahic Park. The Tavern was where Ira had taken Eve to have dinner with Murray and Doris the night they all met. That was in 1948. Twenty years earlier he'd killed someone there. The shack up in Zinc Town—that shack meant something else to him that I'd never understood. That was his reformatory. His solitary confinement.

"Where does Boiardo come in?"

"Strollo's brother worked at the Castle, Boiardo's place. Worked in the kitchen. He went to Boiardo and told him what happened. At first nobody connected Ira with the murder because he had already left the ward. But a couple of years later, it's Ira they're looking for. I suspected it was the cops who put Boiardo on to Ira, but I never knew for sure. All I knew was that somebody came to our door asking for my brother. Little Pussy pays me a visit. I grew up with Little Pussy. Little Pussy used to run the dice game in Aqueduct Alley. He ran the ziconette game in the back of Grande's till the cops broke it up. I used to play pool with Little Pussy at Grande's. He got his name because he started out professionally as a cat burglar, sneaking across the rooftops and going in through the windows with his older brother, Big Pussy. In grade school they were already up all night stealing. When they even bothered to come to school, they sat sleeping at their desks and nobody dared to wake them up. Big Pussy died of natural causes, but Little Pussy was bumped off in 1979 in real gangland style: found in his ocean-front apartment in Long Branch, wearing a bathrobe, three bullets from a .32 in his head. The next day Ritchie Boiardo tells one of his cronies, 'Perhaps it was for the best—because he talked too much.'

"Little Pussy wants to know where my brother is. I told him I hadn't seen my brother in years. He tells me, 'The Boot is looking for him.' They called Boiardo 'the Boot' because he made his phone calls from what the First Ward Italians called a telephone boot'.

'Why?' I asked. 'Because the Boot protects the neighborhood. Because the Boot helps people in time of need.' This was true. Boiardo used to go around wearing a diamond-studded belt buckle and was held in higher esteem even than the saintly guy who was their parish priest. I got word to Ira about Little Pussy and it was seven years, it was 1938, before we saw him again."

"So it was not because of the Depression that he rode the rails. It was because he was a hunted man."

"Startled to learn this?" Murray asked me. "About somebody you admired the way you admired him?"

"No," I said. "No, I'm not startled. It makes sense."

"That's one reason why he cracked up. That's what he wound up crying in Lorraine's bed. 'The whole thing failed.' The life shaped to overcome it had all fallen apart. The effort had been futile. He'd been returned to the chaos where it had all begun."

"What's the 'it'?"

"After he came out of the army, Ira wanted people around him whom he couldn't explode in front of. He went looking for them. The violence in him had scared Ira. He lived in fear of it breaking back into existence. So did I. Somebody who showed that propensity for violence so early—what was going to stop him?

"That's why Ira wanted the marriage. That's why Ira wanted that child. That's why that abortion crushed him. That's why he came to stay with us the day he found out what was behind the abortion. And that very next day, he meets you. He meets this boy who was all that he had never been and who had all that he had never had. Ira wasn't recruiting *you*. Maybe your father thought so, but no, you were recruiting *him*. When he came over to Newark that day, the abortion still so raw in him, you were irresistible to Ira. He was the Newark boy with the bad eyes and the cruel household and no education. You were the nurtured Newark boy given everything. You were the guy's Prince Hal. You were Johnny O'Day Ringold— that's what you were all about. That was your job, whether you knew it or not. To help him shield himself against his nature, against all the force in that big body, all the murderous rage. That was *my* job all my life. It's the job of lots of people. Ira was no rarity. Men trying not to be violent? *That's* the 'it.' They're all around. They're everywhere."

"Ira killed the guy with a shovel. What happened after that?" I asked him. "What happened that night?"

"I wasn't teaching in Newark. It was 1929. Weequahic High hadn't been built yet. I was teaching at Irvington High. My first job. I rented a room up by Solondz's lumberyard, near the railroad tracks. It was about four in the morning when Ira turned up. I was on the first floor and he rapped on my window. I went out, took one look at his bloody shoes and his bloody pants and his bloody hands and his bloody face, and I got him into that old Ford I had and we started driving. I didn't know where the hell I was going. Somewhere far from the Newark police. I was thinking about the cops then and not Boiardo."

"He told you what he'd done."

"Yes. You know whom else he told? Eve Frame. Years later. During their courtship. During that summer they were alone together in New York. He was crazy about her and he wanted to marry her but he had to tell her the truth about who he'd been and the worst he'd done. If it frightened her off, then it frightened her off, but he wanted her to know what she would be getting—that he had been a wild man but that the wild man had been obliterated. He said it for the reason that self-reformed people make those confessions: so she could hold him to it. He didn't understand then, he never understood, that a wild man was what Eve needed most.

"Blindly, which was her way, Eve had an insight into herself. She needs the brute. She *demanded* the brute. Who better to protect her? With a brute she was safe. It explains why she can be with Pennington during all those years he was out picking up boys and spending the night with them and coming home through a special side entrance he had built onto his study. Built it at Eve's request, so she wouldn't have to hear him returning from his trysts at four A.M. It explains why she married Freedman. It explains the men she was drawn to. Her romantic life consisted of changing brutes. If a brute came along, she was first in line. She needs the brute to protect her, and she needs the brute to be blameless. Her brutes are the guarantor of her treasured innocence. To drop to her knees before them and beg is of the greatest importance to her. Beauty and submission—that was what she lived by, her key to catastrophe.

"She needs the brute to redeem her purity, while what the brute needs is to be tamed. Who better to domesticate him than the most genteel woman in the world? What better to housebreak him than the dinner parties for his friends and the paneled library for his books and a delicate actress with beautiful diction for his wife? So Ira told Eve about the Italian and the shovel, and she wept for what he had done at sixteen and how he had suffered it and how he had survived it and how he had so bravely transformed himself into a perfect and wonderful man, and they were married.

"Who knows—maybe she thought that an ex-murderer was perfect for still another reason: on a self-confessed wild man and murderer you can safely impose this unimposable presence, Sylphid. An ordinary man would run screaming from that kid. But a brute? He could take it.

"When I first read in the papers that she was writing a book, I thought the worst. You see, Ira had even told her the guy's name. What was to stop this woman who had it in her, when she believed she was cornered, to say anything to anyone—what was to stop her from shouting 'Strollo' from the rooftops? 'Strollo, Strollo—I know who murdered the ditchdigger Strollo!' But when I read the book, nothing about the murder was in there. Either she never told Katrina and Bryden about Ira and Strollo, either there was some restraint in her after all, some sense of what people like the Grants (another couple of Eve's brutes) would do to him with it, or she had forgotten it the way she could conveniently forget any unpleasant fact. I never knew which. Maybe both.

"But Ira was sure it was going to come out. The whole world was going to see him as I saw him that night when I drove him up to Sussex County. Covered with a dead man's blood. With the blood on his face of a man he'd killed. And telling me with a laugh—the cackling laugh of a crazy kid—'Strollo just took his last strollo.'

"What had begun as an act of self-defense, he had turned into an opportunity to kill someone. He'd lucked into it. Self-defense the instigating event that provides the opportunity to murder. 'Strollo just took his last strollo,' my kid brother tells me. He'd enjoyed it, Nathan.

"'And what did *you* just take, Ira?' I asked him. 'Do you know? You just took the wrong fork in the road. You just made the biggest mistake you've ever made. You just changed everything into something else. And for what? Because the guy attacked you? Well, you beat him up! You beat him silly. You *got* your victory. You spent your rage on beating him to a pulp. But to make the victory *total,* to go back and then *murder* him—for *what?* Because he said something anti-Semitic? That necessitates killing him? The whole weight of Jewish history falls on Ira Ringold's shoulders? Bullshit! You just did something ineradicable, Ira—evil and maniacal and forever rooted in your life. You've done something tonight that can never be made right. You cannot publicly apologize for murder and make everything all right, Ira. *Nothing* can make murder all right. Ever! Murder doesn't just end one life—it ends *two.* Murder ends the human life of the murderer as well! You will never get rid of this secret. You will go to the cemetery with this secret. You will have it with you forever!'

"See, someone commits a crime like murder, I figure the Dostoyevskian reality is going to kick in. A book man, an English teacher, I expect him to manifest the psychological damage that Dostoyevsky writes about. How can you commit an act of murder and not be anguished by it? That makes you a monster, doesn't it? Raskolnikov doesn't kill the old lady and then feel okay about it for the next twenty years. A cold-blooded killer with a mind like Raskolnikov's reflects all his life on his cold-bloodedness. But Ira was not very self-reflective, ever. Ira is an action machine. However that crime contorted Raskolnikov's behavior . . . well, Ira paid the toll in a different way. The penance he paid—how he tried to resurrect his life, his bending backward to stand up straight—was not at all the same.

"Look, I didn't believe he could live with it, and I never believed *I* could live with it. Live with a brother who had gone and committed a murder like that? You would have thought I would either have disowned him or forced him to confess. The idea that I could live with a brother who had murdered somebody and just sit on it, that I could think that I had discharged my obligation to humanity . . . Murder is too big for that. But that is what I did, Nathan. I sat on it.

"But despite my silence, twenty-odd years later, the root at the root of everything was about to be exposed anyway. America was going to see the cold-blooded killer that Ira really was underneath Abraham Lincoln's hat. America was going to find out that he was no fucking good.

"And Boiardo was going to get *his* revenge. Boiardo, by about then, had left Newark for a palazzo stronghold in the Jersey suburbs, but that didn't mean that the Strollos' grievance against Ira Ringold had been forgotten by the Boot's lieutenants holding down the First Ward fort. I was always afraid a goon from the pool hall was going to catch up with Ira, that the Mob would send somebody to do him in, especially after he became Iron Rinn. You know that night he took us all to the Tavern for dinner, and he introduced us to Eve, and Sam Teiger took our picture and hung it up in the foyer there? Did I not like that! What could be worse? How drunk on metamorphosis could he get, the heroic reinvention of himself he called Iron Rinn? Back virtually at the scene of the crime, and he allows his mug to go up on the wall? Maybe *he's* forgotten who he was and what he's done, but Boiardo's going to remember and gun him down.

"But a book did the job instead. In a country where a book hadn't changed a goddamn thing since the publication of *Uncle Tom's Cabin*. A banal show-biz tell-all book, written in hackese by two opportunists exploiting an easy mark named Eve Frame. Ira shakes off Ritchie Boiardo but he couldn't elude the Van Tassel

Grants. It's not a goon dispatched by the Boot who does the job on Ira—it's a gossip columnist.

"In all my years with Doris I had never told her about Ira. But the morning I came back from Zinc Town with his gun and his knives I was tempted to. It was about five in the morning when he turned everything over to me. I drove directly to school that morning with that stuff under the front seat of my car. I couldn't teach that day—I couldn't think. I couldn't sleep that night. That was when I nearly told Doris. I'd taken away his gun and his knives, but I knew that wasn't the end of it. Somehow or other, he was going to kill her.

"'And thus the whirligig of time brings in his revenges.' Line of prose. Recognize it? From the last act of *Twelfth Night*. Feste the clown, to Malvolio, just before Feste sings that lovely song, before he sings, 'A great while ago the world begun, / With hey ho, the wind and the rain,' and the play is over. I couldn't get that line out of my head. 'And thus the whirligig of time brings in his revenges.' Those cryptogrammic *g*'s, the subtlety of their deintensification— those hard *g*'s in 'whirligig' followed by the nasalized *g* of 'brings' followed by the soft *g* of 'revenges.' Those terminal *s*'s . . . 'thus brings his revenges.' The hissing surprise of the plural noun 're-veng*es*.' Guhh. Juhh. Zuhh. Consonants sticking into me like needles. And the pulsating vowels, the rising tide of their pitch— engulfed by that. The low-pitched vowels giving way to the high-pitched vowels. The bass and tenor vowels giving way to the alto vowels. The assertive lengthening of the vowel *i* just before the rhythm shifts from iambic to trochaic and the prose pounds round the turn for the stretch. Short *i*, short *i*, long *i*. Short *i*, short *i*, short *i*, boom! Revenges. Brings in his revenges. *His* revenges. Sibilated. Hizzzzzuh! Driving back to Newark with Ira's weapons in my car, those ten words, the phonetic webbing, the blanket omniscience . . . I felt I was being asphyxiated inside Shakespeare.

"I went out again that next afternoon, drove up again after school. 'Ira,' I said, 'I couldn't sleep last night, and I couldn't teach the kids all day, because I know that you will not quit until you have brought down on yourself a horror that goes far beyond being blacklisted. Someday the blacklisting is going to end. This country may even make amends to people who were handled like you, but if you go to jail for murder . . . Ira, what are you thinking now?'

"Again it took me half the night to find out, and when finally he told me I said, 'I'm calling the doctors at the hospital, Ira. I'm getting a court order. This time I'm getting you committed for good. I'm going to see that you are confined in a hospital for the mentally ill for the rest of your life.'

"He was going to garotte her. *And* the daughter. He was going to garotte the two of them with the strings off the harp. He had the wire cutter. He meant it. He was going to cut the strings and tie them around their necks and strangle the two of them to death.

"That next morning I came back to Newark with the *wire cutter*. But it was hopeless, I knew that. I went home after school and I told Doris what had happened, and that's when I told her about the murder. I told her, 'I should have let them put him away. I should have turned him over to the police and let the law do what the law does.' I told her that when I left him in the morning, I said, 'Ira, she's got that daughter to live with. There's her punishment, terrible punishment, and it's punishment she brought upon herself.' And Ira laughed. 'Sure, it's terrible punishment,' he said, 'but not terrible enough.'

"In all the years that I had been dealing with my brother, that was the first time I collapsed. Told Doris everything and collapsed. I meant what I said to her. Out of a twisted sense of loyalty, I'd done the wrong thing. I saw my kid brother covered with blood, and I got him in the car and I was twenty-two years old and I did the wrong thing. And now, because the whirligig of time brings in his revenges, Ira was going to kill Eve Frame. The only thing left to do was to go to Eve and tell her to get out of town and take Sylphid with her. But I couldn't. I couldn't go to her and that daughter of hers and say, 'My brother's on the warpath, you better go into hiding.'

"I was defeated. I'd spent a lifetime teaching myself to be reasonable in the face of the unreasonable, teaching what I liked to call vigilant matter-of-factness, teaching myself and teaching my students and teaching my daughter and trying to teach my brother. And I'd failed. Un-Iraing Ira was impossible. Being reasonable in the face of the unreasonable was impossible. I'd already proved this in 1929. Here it was 1952, and I was forty-five years old and it was as though the intervening years had been for nothing. There was my kid brother with all of his power and all of his rage bent once again on murder, and once again I was going to be accessory to the crime. After everything—everything he'd done, everything we'd *all* done—he was going to cross the line again."

"When I told this to Doris, she got in the car and drove up to Zinc Town. Doris took over. She had that kind of authority. When she got back, she said, 'He's not going to murder anybody. Don't think,' she said, 'that I didn't *want* him to murder her. But he's not going to do it.' 'What is he going to do instead?' 'We negotiated a settlement. He's going to call in his chits.' 'What does that mean?' 'He's going to call on some friends.' 'What are you talking about? You don't mean gangsters.' 'I mean journalists. His journalist friends. *They're* going to destroy her. You let Ira alone. I'm in charge of Ira.'

"Why did he listen to Doris and not to me? How did she convince him? Who the hell knows why? Doris had a way with him. Doris had her own kind of savvy, and I turned him over to her."

"Who were the journalists?" I asked.

"Fellow-traveling journalists," Murray said. "There were plenty. Guys who admired him, the culturally authentic man of the people. Ira carried great weight with these people because of his working-class credentials. Because of his battles in the union. They'd been at the house often, for those soirées."

"And they did it?"

"They tore Eve to pieces. They did it, all right. They showed how her whole book was made up. That Ira was never a Communist. That he had nothing to do with Communists. That the Communist plot to infiltrate broadcasting was a bizarre concoction of lies.

Which did not shake the confidence of Joe McCarthy or Richard Nixon or Bryden Grant, but it could and would destroy Eve in the New York entertainment world. That was an ultraliberal world. Think of the situation. Every journalist is coming to her, taking down every word she says in their notebooks and writing it up in all the papers. Big spy ring in New York radio. The ringleader her husband. The American Legion takes her up, asks her to address them. An organization called Christian Crusade takes her up, an anti-Communist religious group. They reprint chapters from the book in their monthly magazine. There's a story celebrating her in the *Saturday Evening Post*. The *Reader's Digest* abridges a section of the book, it's the stuff they love, and this, along with the *Post*, puts Ira in every doctor's and dentist's waiting room in America. Everybody wants her to talk to them. Everybody wants to talk to her, but then time passes and there are no more journalists and nobody any longer is buying the book and little by little nobody wants to talk to her.

"In the beginning nobody questions her. They don't question the stature of a well-known actress who looks so delicate and who comes on the scene with this shit in order to sell it. *L'affaire* Frame did not bring out the best thinking in people. The party ordered him to marry her? That was his Communist sacrifice? They took even *that* without questioning it. Anything to empty life of its incongruities, of its meaningless, messy contingencies, and to impose on it instead the simplification that coheres—and misapprehends everything. The party ordered him to do it. Everything is a plot of the party. As if Ira lacked the talent to make that mistake all on his own. As if Ira needed the Comintern to help plan a bad marriage.

"Communist, Communist, Communist, and nobody in America had the least idea of what the hell a Communist was. What do they do, what do they say, what do they look like? When they're together, do they talk Russian, Chinese, Yiddish, Esperanto? Do they build bombs? Nobody knew, which is why it was so easy to exploit the menace the way Eve's book did. But then Ira's journalists went to work and the pieces begin to appear, in the *Nation,* the *Reporter,* the *New Republic,* tearing her to bits. The public machine she set in motion doesn't always go in the direction one wants. It takes its own direction. The public machine she wanted to destroy Ira begins to turn against her. It has to. This is America. The moment you start this public machine, no other end is possible except a catastrophe for everybody.

"Probably what unhinged her, what weakened her most, occurred at the outset of Ira's counteroffensive, before she even had a chance to figure out what was happening or for somebody else to take her in hand and tell her what not to do in a battle like this one. Bryden Grant got hold of the *Nation* attack, the first attack, when it was still in proof. Why should Grant care what they wrote in the *Nation* any more than he cared what they wrote in *Pravda?* What else would you expect them to write in the *Nation?* But his secretary sent the proof over to Eve, and Eve evidently phoned her lawyer and told him she wanted a judge to serve an injunction on the *Nation* to prevent them from printing the piece: everything in it was malicious and false, lies designed to destroy her name and her career and her reputation. But an injunction was prior restraint, and legally a judge couldn't do that. *After* the thing appeared she could sue for libel, but that wasn't good enough, that would be too late, she would already be ruined, so she went straight to the office of the *Nation* and demanded to see the writer. That was L. J. Podell. The *Nation*'s muckraking hatchet man, Jake Podell. People were frightened of him, and they had reason to be. Podell was still to be preferred to Ira with a shovel in his hands, though not by much.

"She went into Podell's office and there followed the Big Scene, the Academy Award–winning scene. Eve said to Podell the piece was full of lies, it was all vicious lies, and you know what the most vicious lie turned out to be? In that entire piece? Podell identified her as a closet Jew. He wrote that he'd been out to Brooklyn and uncovered the true story. He said that she was Chava Fromkin, born in Brownsville, in Brooklyn, in 1907, grew up on the corner of Hopkinson and Sutter, and that her father was a poor immigrant housepainter, an uneducated Polish Jew who painted houses. He said that nobody in her family had spoken English, not her father, not her mother, not even an older brother and sister. Both of them had been born years before Eve, in the old country. Except for Chava, they all spoke Yiddish.

"Podell even dug up the first husband, Mueller, the bartender's kid from Jersey, the ex-sailor she'd run off with at sixteen. He's still out in California, living on disability, a retired cop with a bad heart, a wife, and two kids, a good old boy with nothing but good things to say about Chava. The beautiful girl she was. The *gutsy* girl she was. A little hellion, believe it or not. How she eloped with him, Mueller said, not because she could possibly love the big idiot that he was back then, but because, as he'd known all along, he was her ticket out of Brooklyn. Knowing this and feeling for her, Mueller never stood in her way, he told Podell, never came back to haunt her for money, even after she made it big. Podell's even got some old snapshots, snapshots that Mueller (for an undisclosed sum) kindly turned over to him. He shows them to her: Chava and Mueller on a wild beach at Malibu, the Pacific big and booming behind them—two handsome, healthy, exhilarated youngsters, robust in their twenties swimsuits, ready and eager to take the big plunge. Snapshots that wound up reprinted in *Confidential* magazine.

"Now, Podell was never really in the business of exposing Jews. He was an indifferent Jew himself, and God knows he was no supporter of Israel's, ever. But here was someone who'd been lying about her background all her life and now she was lying about Ira. Podell had verifying quotations from all sorts of elderly people in Brooklyn, alleged neighbors, alleged relatives, and Eve said that it was all stupid gossip and that if he reported as the truth the things that stupid people make up about someone who is famous, she would sue the magazine right out of existence and sue him personally for every penny he had.

"Somebody there had a camera and came into Podell's office and snapped a picture of the onetime movie star just as she was reminding Podell what she could do to him. Well, any drop of self-mastery still left in her vanishes, the rational outlook, such as it was, evaporates, and she runs down the hall sobbing, and there is the managing editor and he takes her into his office and he sits her down and he says, 'Aren't you Eve Frame? I am a great admirer. What's the trouble? What can I do for you?' And she tells him. 'Oh, my, my,' he says, 'that won't do,' and he calms her down and he asks her what she wants changed in the piece, and she tells him about how she was born in New Bedford, Massachusetts, to an old seafaring family, her great-grandfather and her grandfather captains of a Yankee clipper, and though her own parents had by no means been wealthy, after the death of her father, a patent lawyer, when she was still a little girl, her mother had run a very nice tearoom. The managing editor tells her how glad he is to get the truth. He assures Eve as he sees her into a cab that he will take care that it is printed in the magazine. And Podell, who has been outside the managing editor's office taking down every word Eve says, does just that: puts it in the magazine.

"After she left, Podell went back to the piece and inserted the incident whole—the visit to the office, the Big Scene, the works. Ruthless old battering ram, inordinately fond of that sort of sport, on top of which he especially liked Ira and disliked her. Scrupulously recorded every detail of the New Bedford story and put that in as the conclusion of the piece. The others who did their stories after Podell's picked up on it, and that became another motif in the anti-Eve stories, another reason she turned on Ira, who is not only not a Communist now but himself a proud, observant Jew, et cetera. What they called Ira had almost as little relation to Ira as what she had called Ira. By the time all these savage intellects, with their fidelity to the facts, were finished with the woman, to find anything anywhere of the ugly truth that *was* the story of Ira and Eve, you would have needed a microscope.

"In Manhattan, the ostracism begins. She starts losing friends. People don't come to her parties. Nobody calls her. Nobody wants to talk to her. Nobody believes her any longer. She destroys her husband with lies? What does this say about her human quality? Gradually there's no more work for her. Radio drama is on its last legs, crushed first by the blacklist and then by TV, and Eve's been putting on the weight and television isn't interested.

"I saw her perform just twice on TV. I believe those were the only two times she ever appeared on TV. The first time we watched her, Doris was astounded. Pleasantly so. Doris said, 'You know whom she looks like now that she's built like that? Mrs. Goldberg, from Tremont Avenue in the Bronx.' Remember Molly Goldberg, on *The Goldbergs*? With her husband, Jake, and her children, Rosalie and Samily? Philip Loeb. Remember Philip Loeb? You ever meet him through Ira? Ira brought him to our house. Phil played Papa Jake on *The Goldbergs* for years and years, from the thirties, when the program first started out on radio. In 1950 they fired him from the TV program because his name was on the blacklist. Couldn't get work, couldn't pay his bills, couldn't pay his debts, so in '55 Phil Loeb checked into the Taft Hotel and killed himself with sleeping pills.

"Both parts Eve played were mothers. Awful stuff. On Broadway she'd always been a quiet, tactful, intelligent actress, and now she was sobbing and throwing herself all over the place—acting, unfortunately, much like herself. But by then she must have been mostly on her own, with nobody giving her any guidance. The Grants are down in Washington and haven't the time, and so all she's got is Sylphid.

"And that didn't last either. One Friday night, she and Sylphid appeared together on a TV program that was very popular back then. Called *The Apple and the Tree*. Remember it? Half-hour weekly program about children who had inherited some sort of talent, trait, or profession from a parent. Scientists, people in the arts, in show business, athletes. Lorraine liked to watch it, and sometimes we watched with her. It was an enjoyable program, funny, warm, even interesting sometimes, but pretty light fare, pretty light entertainment. Though not when Sylphid and Eve were the guests. They had to give the public their bowdlerized take on *King Lear*, with Sylphid as Goneril and Regan.

"I remember Doris saying to me, 'She's read and understood all those books. She's read and understood all those roles she's played. Is it so hard for her to come to her senses? What makes someone so experienced so hopelessly foolish? To be in your mid-forties, to be so much in the world, and to be so unknowing.'

"What interested me was that after publishing and promoting *I Married a Communist*, she didn't, even for a second, in passing, own up to the spite. Maybe by then she'd conveniently forgotten the book and all it had done. Maybe this was the pre-Grant, pre-monster version coming out, Eve's story of Ira before it had been properly Van Tasseled. But the about-face she achieved in revisiting her story was still something to see.

"All Eve could talk about on TV was how in love she'd been with Ira, and how happy she'd been with Ira, and how the marriage was destroyed only by his treacherous Communism. She even cried for a moment over all the happiness treacherous Communism had ruined. I remember Doris getting up and walking away from the TV set, then coming back and sitting there stewing. Afterward she said to me, 'Seeing her burst into tears like that on television—it shocked me nearly as much as if she'd been incontinent. Can't she stop crying for two minutes? She's an actress, for God's sake. Can't she try acting her age?'

"So the camera watched the Communist's innocent wife weep, all of TV-land watched the Communist's innocent wife weep, and then the Communist's innocent wife wiped her eyes and, looking nervously to the daughter every two seconds for corroboration—no, for *authorization*—made it clear that everything was wonderful between Sylphid and her once again, peace established, bygones bygones, all their old trust and love restored. Now that the Communist had been rooted out, there was no closer family, no family on better terms, this side of *The Swiss Family Robinson*.

"And every time Eve tried smiling at Sylphid with that poorly pasted-on smile, tried looking at her with the most painfully tentative look in her eyes, a look all but pleading with Sylphid to say, 'Yes, Momma, I love you, that's true'—all but blatantly begging her, 'Say it, darling, if only for television'—Sylphid gave the game away by either glowering back at her or condescending to her or irritatedly subverting every word Eve had said. There came a point at which even Lorraine couldn't take any more. Suddenly this kid shouted at the TV screen, 'Show some love, the two of you!'

"Sylphid doesn't display a split second's worth of affection for this pathetic woman struggling to hang on. Not a speck of generosity, let alone understanding. Not one conciliatory line. I'm not a kid—I don't speak of love. I don't even speak of happiness, harmony, or friendship. Just of conciliation. What I realized watching that program was that this girl could *never* have loved her mother. Because if you did, even a little, you are able to think about her sometimes as something *other* than your mother. You think of her happiness and her unhappiness. You think of her health. You think of her loneliness. You think of her *craziness*. But this girl has no imagination for any of this. The daughter has no understanding whatsoever of the life of a woman. All she has is her *J'accuse*. All she wants is to put the mother on trial before the whole nation, to make her look terrible in every way. The public grinding of Momma's bones.

"I'll never forget that picture: Eve continually looking to Sylphid as though her whole idea of herself and her worth derived from this daughter who was the most ruthless judge imaginable of her mother's every failing. You should have seen the mockery in Sylphid, deriding her mother with every scornful grimace, spurning her with every smirk, getting her licks in publicly. She's finally got the forum for her anger. Giving her famous mother a ride on TV. Her power is to say, just with her sneer, 'You who were so admired are a stupid woman.' Not very generous stuff. The stuff most kids sort out by the time they're eighteen. Ferociously self-revealing stuff. You feel there's a sexual pleasure in it when it hangs on that late in a person's life. That program made you squirm: the histrionics of the mother's defenselessness no less remarkable than the relentless blackjack of the daughter's malice. But the mask of Eve's face was what was most frightening. The unhappiest mask you could imagine. I knew then that there was nothing left of her. She looked annihilated.

"Finally, the program host mentioned Sylphid's upcoming recital at Town Hall, and Sylphid sat down and played the harp. *There*, that's why Eve agreed to degrade herself like this on TV. Of course—for Sylphid's career. Could there be any better metaphor for their relationship, I thought, than this, than Eve crying in public for all that she's lost while the daughter who doesn't care plays the harp and plugs the recital?

"A couple of years later, the daughter abandons her. When her mother is sinking and needs her most, Sylphid discovers her independence. At thirty, Sylphid determines that it's not good for a daughter's emotional well-being to live at home intertwined with a middle-aged mother who tucks her in bed every night. Whereas most children leave their parents at eighteen or twenty, live independently of them for fifteen or twenty years and then, in time, reconcile with their aging parents and try to give them a hand, Sylphid prefers to pull it off the other way round. For the best of modern psychological reasons, Sylphid goes to France to live off the father.

"Pennington was already sick by then. A couple of years later he died. Cirrhosis of the liver. Sylphid inherited the villa, the cars, the cats, and the Pennington family fortune. Sylphid gets it all, including Pennington's handsome Italian chauffeur, whom she marries. Yes, Sylphid married. Even begat a son. There's the logic of reality for you. Sylphid Pennington became a mother. Big news in the tabloids here because of an interminable legal wrangle initiated by some well-known French set designer—I forget his name, a one-time long-term lover of Pennington's. He claimed that the chauffeur was a hustler, a fortune hunter, who'd only recently come on the scene, who'd himself been an on-and-off lover of Pennington's, and who'd somehow rigged or doctored the will.

"By the time Sylphid left New York to take up life in France, Eve Frame was a hopeless drunk. Had to sell the house. Died in a drunken stupor in a Manhattan hotel room in 1962, ten years after the book. Forgotten. Fifty-five years old. Two years later, Ira died. Fifty-one. But he lived to see her suffer. And don't think he didn't enjoy it. Don't think he didn't enjoy Sylphid's walking out. 'Where is the lovely daughter we all heard so much about? Where is the daughter to say, "Momma, I'll help you"? Gone!'

"Eve's dying put Ira back in touch with the primary satisfactions, unchained the ditchdigger's pleasure principle. When all the rigging of respectability, when all the social construction that civilizes, is removed from someone who has thrived most of his life on impulse, you have a geyser, don't you? It just starts gushing. Your enemy destroyed—what could be better? Sure, it took a little longer than he hoped and, sure, this time he didn't get to do it himself, to feel the blood spurt up hot in his face, but still and all, I never saw Ira enjoy anything more than her death.

"You know what he said when she died? The same thing he'd said the night he'd murdered the Italian guy and we organized his getaway. He told me, 'Strollo just took his last strollo.' First time he'd uttered that name to me in over thirty years. 'Strollo just took his last strollo,' and then he lets loose the cackling crazy-kid laugh. The just-let-'em-try-to-do-me-in laugh. That defiant laugh I still remembered from 1929."

I helped Murray down the deck's three steps and guided him in the dark along the path to where my car was parked. We were silent as we swung along the curves of the mountain road and past Lake Madamaska and into Athena. When I looked over I saw that his head was back and his eyes were shut. First I thought he was asleep, and then I wondered if he was dead, if, after his having remembered the whole of Ira's story—after his having heard himself *tell* the whole of Ira's story—the will to go on had lost its grip even on this most enduring of men. And then I was recalling him again reading to our high school English class, sitting on the corner of his desk, but without the minatory blackboard eraser, reading scenes to us from *Macbeth,* doing all the voices, not afraid to be dramatic and perform, and myself being impressed by how manly literature seemed in his enactment of it. I remembered hearing Mr. Ringold read the scene at the end of act 4 of *Macbeth* when Macduff learns from Ross that Macbeth has slain Macduff's family, my first encounter with a spiritual state that is aesthetic and overrides everything else.

As Ross he read, "Your castle is surpris'd; your wife and babes / Savagely slaughtered. . . ." Then, after a long silence in which Macduff both comprehends and fails to comprehend, he read as Macduff—quietly, hollowly, almost in his reply like a child himself— "My children too?" "Wife, children, servants," says Mr. Ringold/ Ross, "all / That could be found." Mr. Ringold/Macduff is again speechless. So is the class: as a class, the class is by now missing from the room. Everything has vanished except whatever words of disbelief are coming next. Mr. Ringold/Macduff: "My wife kill'd too?" Mr. Ringold/Ross: "I have said." The large clock is ticking toward two-thirty up on the classroom wall. Outside, a 14 bus is grinding up the Chancellor Avenue hill. It is only minutes before the end of eighth period and the long school day. But all that matters—matters more than what happens after school or even in the future—is when Mr. Ringold/Macduff will grasp the incomprehensible. "He has no children," Mr. Ringold says. Whom is he speaking of? Who has no children? Some years later I was taught the standard interpretation, that it is Macbeth to whom Macduff is referring, that Macbeth is the "he" who has no children. But as read by Mr. Ringold, the "he" to whom Macduff is referring is, horribly, Macduff himself. "All my pretty ones? / Did you say all? . . . All? / What, all my pretty chickens and their dam / At one fell swoop?" And now Malcolm speaks, Mr. Ringold/Malcolm, harshly, as though to shake Macduff: "Dispute it like a man." "I shall do so," says Mr. Ringold/Macduff.

Then the simple line that would assert itself, in Murray Ringold's voice, a hundred times, a thousand times, during the remainder of my life: "But I must also feel it as a man." "Ten syllables," Mr. Ringold tells us the next day, "that's all. Ten syllables, five beats, pentameter . . . nine words, the third iambic stress falling perfectly and naturally on the fifth and most important word . . . eight monosyllables and the one word of two syllables a word as common and ordinary and serviceable as any there is in everyday English . . . and yet, all together, and coming where it does, what power! Simple, simple—and like a hammer!

"But I must also feel it as a man," and Mr. Ringold closes the big book of Shakespeare's plays, says to us, as he does at the end of each class, "Be seein' ya," and leaves the room.

By the time we got into Athena, Murray's eyes were open and he was saying, "Here I am with an eminent ex-student and I never let the guy speak. Never asked him about himself."

"Next time."

"Why do you live up there, alone like that? Why don't you have the heart for the world?"

"I prefer it this way," I said.

"No, I watched you listening. I don't think you do. I don't think for a moment the exuberance is gone. You were like that as a kid. That's why I got such a kick out of you—you paid attention. You still do. But what is up here to pay attention to? You should get out from under whatever's the problem. To give in to the temptation to yield isn't smart. At a certain age, that can polish you off like any other disease. Do you really want to whittle it all away before your time has come? Beware the utopia of isolation. Beware the utopia of the shack in the woods, the oasis defense against rage and grief. An impregnable solitude. That's how life ended for Ira, and long before the day he dropped dead."

I parked on one of the college streets and walked with him up the path to the dormitory. It was close to three A.M. and all the rooms were dark. Murray was probably the last of the elderly students to be leaving and the only one who'd be sleeping there that night. I wished I had invited him to stay with me. But I didn't have the heart for that either. To have anyone sleeping anywhere within sound or sight or smell of me would have broken a chain of conditioning that hasn't been that easy to forge.

"I'm going to come down to Jersey and pay you a visit," I said.

"You're going to have to come to Arizona. I don't live in Jersey anymore. Been in Arizona a long time now. I belong to a church book club that the Unitarians run; otherwise it's slim pickins. Not the ideal location if you have a mind, but I also have other problems. Staying tomorrow in New York and the next day I fly to Phoenix. You're going to have to come to Arizona if you want to see me. Only don't dawdle," he said with a smile. "The earth spins very fast, Nathan. Time is not on my side."

As the years pass there is nothing I have less talent for than saying goodbye to somebody I feel a strong attachment to. I don't always realize how strong the attachment is until the moment comes to say goodbye.

"I somehow assumed you were still in Jersey." That was the least dangerous sentiment I could think to express.

"No. I left Newark after Doris got killed. Doris was murdered, Nathan. Across the street from us, back of the hospital. I wouldn't leave the city, you see. I wasn't going to move out of the city where I had lived and taught all my life just because it was now a poor black city full of problems. Even after the riots, when Newark emptied out, we stayed on Lehigh Avenue, the only white family that did stay. Doris, bad spine and all, returned to work at the hospital. I was teaching at South Side. After I was reinstated I went back to Weequahic, where already, by then, teaching was no picnic, and after a couple of years they asked me if I'd take over the English department at South Side, where it was even worse. Nobody could teach these black kids, and so they asked me to. I spent the last ten years there, until I retired. Couldn't teach anybody anything. Barely able to hold down the mayhem, let alone teach. Discipline—that was the whole job. Discipline, patrolling the corridors, bickering until some kid took a swing at you, expulsions. Worst ten years of my life. Worse than when I was fired. I wouldn't say the disenchantment was devastating. I had a feel for the reality of the situation. But the experience was devastating. Brutal. We should have moved, we didn't, and that's the story.

"But all my life, I was one of the firebrands in the Newark system, wasn't I? My old cronies told me I was nuts. They were all in the suburbs by then. But how could I run away? I was interested in respect being shown for these kids. If there's any chance for the improvement of life, where's it going to begin if not in the school? Besides, any time as a teacher I was ever asked to do something that I thought was interesting and worthwhile, I said, 'Yeah, I'd like to do that,' and I threw myself into it. We stayed on Lehigh Avenue and I went down to South Side and I told the teachers in the department, 'We've got to find ways to induce our students to commit themselves,' and so forth.

"I got mugged twice. We should have moved after the first time and we should certainly have moved after that second time. The second time I was just around the corner from the house, four in the afternoon, when three kids surrounded me and pulled a gun. But we didn't move. And one evening, Doris is leaving the hospital, and to get to our house, all she had to do, you remember, was cross the street. Well, she never made it. Somebody hit her over the head. Just about half a mile up from where Ira killed Strollo, somebody cracked her skull open with a brick. For a handbag with nothing in it. You know what I realized? I realized I'd been had. It's not an idea I like, but I've lived with it inside me ever since.

"Had by myself, in case you're wondering. Myself with all my principles. I can't betray my brother, I can't betray my teaching, I can't betray the disadvantaged of Newark. 'Not *me*—*I'm* not leaving this place. *I'm* not fleeing. My colleagues can do as they see fit—I'm not leaving these black kids.' And so who I betray is my wife. I put the responsibility for my choices onto somebody else. Doris paid the price for my civic virtue. She is the victim of my refusal to— Look, there is no way out of this thing. When you loosen yourself, as I tried to, from all the obvious delusions—religion, ideology, Communism—you're still left with the myth of your own goodness. Which is the final delusion. And the one to which I sacrificed Doris.

"That's enough. Every action produces loss," he said. "It's the entropy of the system."

"What system?" I said.

"The moral system."

Why hadn't he told me about Doris earlier? Was the reticence a kind of heroism or a kind of suffering? This too happened to him. What else is there? We could have sat on my deck for six hundred nights before I heard the entire story of how Murray Ringold, who'd chosen to be nothing more extraordinary than a high school teacher, had failed to elude the turmoil of his time and place and ended up no less a historical casualty than his brother. This was the existence that America had worked out for him—and that he'd worked out for himself by thinking, by taking *his* revenge on his father by cri-ti-cal think-ing, by being reasonable in the face of no reason. This was what thinking in America had got him. This was what adhering to his convictions had got him, resisting the tyranny of compromise. *If there's any chance for the improvement of life, where's it going to begin if not in the school?* Hopelessly entangled in the best of intentions, tangibly, over a lifetime, committed to a constructive course that is now an illusion, to formulations and solutions that will no longer wash.

You control betrayal on one side and you wind up betraying somewhere else. Because it's not a static system. Because it's alive. Because everything that lives is in movement. Because purity is petrifaction. Because purity is a lie. Because unless you're an ascetic paragon like Johnny O'Day and Jesus Christ, you're urged on by five hundred things. Because without the iron pole of righteousness with which the Grants clubbed their way to success, without the big lie of righteousness to tell you why you do what you do, you have to ask yourself, all along the way, "Why *do* I do what I do?" And you have to endure yourself without knowing.

Here, simultaneously, we succumbed to the urge to embrace the other. Holding Murray in my arms I sensed—more than merely sensed—the extent of his decrepitude. It was hard to understand where he had found the strength, for six nights, to revisit so intensely the worst events of his life.

I didn't say anything, thinking that, whatever I said, I would drive home wishing I had been silent. As though I were still his innocent student eager to do good, I was dying to say to him, "You weren't had, Murray. That isn't the proper judgment to be made of your life. You must know that it isn't." But, as I am myself an aging man who knows what unexalted conclusions can be reached when one examines one's history probingly, I didn't.

Having let me hold on to him for close to a minute, Murray suddenly slapped my back. He was laughing at me. "The emotional demands," he said, "of leaving a ninety-year-old."

"Yes. That. And everything else. What happened to Doris. Lorraine's death," I said. "Ira. Everything that happened to Ira."

"Ira and the shovel. All that he imposed on himself," Murray said, "exacted from himself, demanded from himself because of that shovel. The bad ideas and the naive dreams. All *his* romances. His passion was to be someone he didn't know how to be. He never discovered his life, Nathan. He looked for it everywhere—in the zinc mine, in the record factory, in the fudge factory, in the labor union, in radical politics, in radio acting, in rabble-rousing, in proletarian living, in bourgeois living, in marriage, in adultery, in savagery, in civilized society. He couldn't find it anywhere. Eve didn't marry a Communist; she married a man perpetually hungering after his life. That's what enraged him and confused him and that's what ruined him: he could never construct one that fit. The enormous wrongness of this guy's effort. But one's errors always rise to the surface, don't they?"

"It's all error," I said. "Isn't that what you've been telling me? There's only error. *There's* the heart of the world. Nobody finds his life. That *is* life."

"Listen. I don't want to overstep the boundary. I'm not telling you I'm for or against it. I'm asking that when you come down to Phoenix, you'll tell me what it is."

"What what is?"

"*Your* aloneness," he said. "I remember the beginning, this very intense boy so much looking forward to participating in life. Now he's in his middle sixties, a man by himself in the woods. I'm surprised to see you out of the world like this. It's pretty damn monastic, the way you live. All that's missing from your monkhood are the bells to call you to meditation. Sorry, but I *do* have to tell you: you're still a young man by my count, much too young to be up there. What are you warding off? What the hell happened?"

Now I laughed at *him*, a laugh that allowed me to feel substantial again, charged up with my independence of everything, a recluse to be conjured with. "I listened carefully to your story, that's what happened. Goodbye, Mr. Ringold!"

"Be seein' ya."

On the deck, the citronella candle was still burning in its aluminum bucket when I got back, that little pot of fire the only light by which my house was discernible, except for a dim radiance off the orange moon silhouetting the low roof. As I left the car and started toward the house, the elongated wavering of the flame reminded me of the radio dial—no bigger than a watch face and, beneath the tiny black numerals, the color of a ripening banana skin—that was all that could be seen in our dark bedroom when my kid brother and I, contrary to parental directive, stayed up past ten to listen to a favorite program. The two of us in our twin beds and, magisterial on the night table between us, the Philco Jr., the cathedral-shaped table radio we'd inherited when my father bought the Emerson console for the living room. The radio turned as low as it could go, though still with volume enough to act on our ears as the most powerful magnet.

I blew out the candle's scented flame and stretched myself across the chaise on the deck and realized that listening in the black of a summer's night to a barely visible Murray had been something like listening to the bedroom radio when I was a kid ambitious to change the world by having all my untested convictions, masquerading as stories, broadcast nationwide. Murray, the radio: voices from the void controlling everything within, the convolutions of a story floating on air and into the ear so that the drama is perceived well behind the eyes, the cup that is the cranium a cup transformed into a limitless globe of a stage, containing fellow creatures whole. How deep our hearing goes! Think of all it means to *understand* from something that you simply hear. The godlikeness of having an ear! Is it not at least a *semi*divine phenomenon to be hurled into the innermost wrongness of a human existence by virtue of nothing more than sitting in the dark, listening to what is said?

Till dawn I remained out on the deck, lying on the chaise looking up at the stars. My first year alone in this house I taught myself to identify the planets, the great stars, the star clusters, the configuration of antiquity's great constellations, and with the aid of the stargazer's map tucked up in a corner of the second section of the Sunday *New York Times*, I charted their journey's wheeling logic. Soon that was all I cared to look at in that thumping loaf of newsprint and pictures. I'd tear out the small double-columned box called "Sky Watch"—that features, above the elucidating text, a circle encompassing the celestial horizon and that pinpoints the constellations' whereabouts at ten P.M. for the coming week—and chuck out the four pounds of everything else. Soon I was chucking out the daily paper as well; soon I had chucked everything with which I no longer wish to contend, everything but what was needed to live on and to work with. I set out to receive all my fullness from what might once have seemed, even to me, not nearly enough and to inhabit passionately only the parts of speech.

If the weather isn't bad and it's a clear night, I spend fifteen or twenty minutes before bedtime out on the deck looking skyward, or, using a flashlight, I pick my way along the dirt road to the open pasture at the peak of my hill, from where I can see, from above the treeline, the whole heavenly inventory, stars unfurled in every direction, and, just this week, the planets Jupiter in the east and Mars in the west. It is beyond belief and also a fact, a plain and indisputable fact: that we are born, that this is here. I can think of worse ways to end my day.

On the night Murray left I recalled how, as a small child, I'd been told—as a small child unable to sleep because his grandfather had died and he insisted on understanding where the dead man had gone—that Grandpa had been turned into a star. My mother took me out of bed and down into the driveway beside the house and together we looked straight up at the night sky while she explained that one of those stars was my grandfather. Another was my grandmother, and so on. What happens when people die, my mother explained, is that they go up to the sky and live on forever as gleaming stars. I searched the sky and said, "Is he that one?" and she said yes, and we went back inside and I fell asleep.

That explanation made sense then and, of all things, it made sense again on the night when, wide awake from the stimulus of all that narrative engorgement, I lay out of doors till dawn, thinking that Ira was dead, that Eve was dead, that with the exception perhaps of Sylphid off in her villa on the French Riviera, a rich old woman of seventy-two, all the people with a role in Murray's account of the Iron Man's unmaking were now no longer impaled on their moment but dead and free of the traps set for them by their era. Neither the ideas of their era nor the expectations of our species were determining destiny: hydrogen alone was determining destiny. There are no longer mistakes for Eve or Ira to make. There is no betrayal. There is no idealism. There are no falsehoods. There is neither conscience nor its absence. There are no mothers and daughters, no fathers and stepfathers. There are no actors. There is no class struggle. There is no discrimination or lynching or Jim Crow, nor has there ever been. There is no injustice, nor is there justice. There are no utopias. There are no shovels. Contrary to the folklore, except for the constellation Lyra—which happened to perch high in the eastern sky a little west of the Milky Way and southeast of the two Dippers—there are no harps. There is just the furnace of Ira and the furnace of Eve burning at twenty million degrees. There is the furnace of novelist Katrina Van Tassel Grant, the furnace of Congressman Bryden Grant, the furnace of taxidermist Horace Bixton, and of miner Tommy Minarek, and of flutist Pamela Solomon, and of Estonian masseuse Helgi Pärn, and of lab technician Doris Ringold, and of Doris's uncle-loving daughter, Lorraine. There is the furnace of Karl Marx and of Joseph Stalin and of Leon Trotsky and of Paul Robeson and of Johnny O'Day. There is the furnace of Tailgunner Joe McCarthy. What you see from this silent rostrum up on my mountain on a night as splendidly clear as that night Murray left me for good—for the very best of loyal brothers, the ace of English teachers, died in Phoenix two months later—is that universe into which error does not obtrude. You see the inconceivable: the colossal spectacle of no antagonism. You see with your own eyes the vast brain of time, a galaxy of fire set by no human hand.

The stars are indispensable.